Voices from a Distant Room

Voices from a Distant Room

Marcia Gloster

The Story Plant
Studio Digital CT, LLC
P.O. Box 4331
Stamford, CT 06907

Copyright © 2020 by Marcia Gloster
Author photo by Maureen Baker

Story Plant Paperback ISBN-13: 978-1-61188-283-4
Fiction Studio Books e-book ISBN-13: 978-1-945839-44-3

Visit our website at www.TheStoryPlant.com

First Story Plant paperback printing: April 2020

Printed in the United States of America

For those who believe, no proof is necessary. For those who don't believe, no proof is possible.
—*Stuart Chase*

Prologue

Na h-Eileanan Siar
Scotland, The Western Isles
3000 BCE

The boy was confused. Only two days had passed since he'd last visited his Shaman, but when he peeked inside his hut it was empty; the only remaining evidence that the old man had ever lived was a torn, blood-spattered cloth on the dirt floor.

With an anxious glance back to make sure no one was watching, he ducked inside. Picking up the cloth, he held it to his face, inhaling the faint tang of blood.

His father had first brought the boy to his Shaman as a toddler. Since then, captivated by the stories of the ancients, he had returned every day for thirteen circuits of the sun. Through those seasons he learned of the harsh ice that had gradually receded, giving way to the return of the warmth of the sun. His Shaman had spoken of the seekers, those who trekked from the big lands to the east only to discover that once arriving at their sandy shore they could go no further, for only a vast, endless sea awaited them. He described once dense forests inhabited by huge beasts, now long gone. But what had fired the boy's imagination were the tales of mythical creatures who were said to watch over ancient spirits — spirits born at the beginning of time that still dwelled deep within the darkest reaches of the earth. He understood the significance of the histories and legends passed down by generations of Shamans, knowing one day it would be his turn to speak of them to young boys like himself.

While the boy had grown tall and strong his Shaman had become ever more frail; his back stooped, his once thick, dark beard thinning to a gauzy white. The boy had come of age when he was expected to hunt in the dwindling forests to the north. His younger brothers had been chosen as the fishermen in the family; not so difficult as their once violent sea had become placid, no longer boasting the crashing waves of past generations. He knew it was far easier to spear a fish than track the elusive deer, muskrats, possums, and hares he pursued each and every day. The change had come the year before—a day in the warm season when he and his mates had gone out to hunt in the woods. They had come across little game that morning and, becoming bored, had chased noisily after fleet-footed voles while tossing rocks into the underbrush to scare away snakes. Later, they played hide-and-seek while laughing and gossiping about girls. As late afternoon shadows lengthened into twilight, the boy lagged behind, unaware his friends had turned homeward through the darkening forest.

A sharp pain awakened him as if from a trance. While trying to pull a splinter from his foot, he looked up, surprised to find himself facing an unfamiliar rocky outcropping. Moving closer, he noticed a fissure glimmering through the jagged boulders at its base. When he looked back, he saw it was the sun, now low on the horizon, casting a narrow beam of light as though directly into it. Realizing it was the entrance to a cave, he glanced around for any evidence of bears or wolves. Seeing only fragments of desiccated bones scattered about, he sniffed the air, picking up no scent of anything living or dead.

Curious, he ventured inside, feeling his skin prickle and questioning if he wasn't quite as alone as he had imagined. Still, he moved ahead, his eyes and ears alert to danger. After only a few steps, the rocks fell away, opening to a wide, low cavern. On crudely scraped walls he noticed odd scratches. In the half-light, his fingers touched what appeared to be drawings of strange hairy and horned beasts that resembled no animal he had ever seen. With some trepidation, he recalled his Shaman's stories of mysterious cave creatures and ancient spirits.

Still vigilant, he followed a narrow, gravel-strewn corridor to where the low ceiling began to slant downward and the light became thin. It was there that he heard what sounded like soft sighs or, he thought, the trickling of water. And yet he felt no moisture; the cave was dry. Seeing the path ahead dissolve into inky darkness, he decided to turn back. Taking a misstep, he slipped on the uneven, pebble-strewn floor and reached to the wall to steady himself. As his hand encountered the rocky surface, it flashed a fiery blue light. With a yelp of alarm, he jumped back, nearly falling over a few small stones that also began to glow at his feet. Bewildered, he glanced around, seeing no light source that would cause the rocks to shine in the deepening darkness. As he reached out to touch the wall again, he stared in disbelief—the stones only sparked when he touched them.

As was customary in the tribe, the boy went naked, grateful to be freed of the odorous animal skins that were essential to cover themselves in the cold season. Like his mates, he had a small pouch tied to a strip of cloth around his waist, into which he stuffed a handful of the glittering pebbles. Leaving the cave, he ran back through the heavily shadowed woods to the safety of the village.

Later that night, while his family slept, he crept outside his hut.

As a breeze chased clouds across a full moon, he took a few of the pebbles from his pouch, once again enthralled at their brilliant blue fire. *Magic*, he thought, and something that must be brought to his Shaman.

The next morning, when the old man asked why he appeared so excited, the boy withdrew a couple of the pebbles from his pouch. Seeing them spark, the Shaman flinched in alarm. And yet, after taking a few and turning them back and forth in his palm, he nodded in recognition. "Our ancestors spoke of stones such as these. Blue pebbles that glow."

Moving to a dim corner, the boy held one up. "They shine with no sun."

Seeing them light up in the shadows, the old man stared as though entranced. "Which must mean they have gained even more power. The legends say stones such as these were formed in the fires of creation by powerful spirits who, trying to escape the curses of horned demons, embedded themselves deep within rocky caves and could only be made visible by some sort of magic. Only then would they reveal their light. Until now I never believed they truly existed. Where did you find them?"

"In a cave. When I was hunting."

"Had you seen this cave before?"

"No. Not until yesterday."

He shook his head. "You went into an unfamiliar cave?"

"I saw no sign of bears. And no horned beasts other than a few scratches on the walls. I felt no danger."

"What sort of scratches?"

"Outlines," he said, tracing the air with his finger. "What looked like odd humpbacked animals."

"Suddenly finding a cave with nothing guarding it is strange enough. But lines depicting unknown creatures? That I would like to see."

"I can take you there."

"No, my son. My legs will no longer carry me that far. Not anymore." He looked down at the stones. "Have others seen these?"

"I was alone."

The Shaman nodded. "It may be a benign spirit that drew you there. I believe you were meant to find these. Have you more?"

"A few."

With great effort, he stood up, his once powerful frame now shrunken with advancing age. When the boy reached out to help, he shook him off. Raising withered arms to beseech the gods, his eyes became luminous and his face flushed red. In a voice unexpectedly deep and commanding, he intoned, "With these stones I will divine magic. I will make the cold season brief and the season of planting come early." As though enraptured by the glittering pebbles, his usually gentle tone became a sharp command. "Go back to the cave and bring me more. Now."

The boy glanced outside. The morning had clouded over, the air thick with an impending storm. "Why today?"

"Don't question. You may keep one, and only one, stone. It will bring you luck."

"Why only one? Wouldn't two or more bring even more luck, as you say?"

"You must not question your Shaman. Only those granted authority by the Gods are allowed possession of such stones. The fact that you found them means you have been chosen—granted a special fate. You must tell no one. Bring the stones to me, only me." His eyes became glassy, his voice low and coarse. "Only you and I will know." He pointed to the doorway. "Go now. Do not return without more stones."

Despite the Shaman's divinations, his prophecies and invocations to the gods, the cold season arrived early, closely followed by frequent snowstorms that blanketed the village for months at a time, a dismal portent of what was yet to come. No longer able to venture into the woods, the boy explained he had run out of stones. Ignoring his excuses, the old man, becoming increasingly frail and anxious about his waning powers, demanded more. With fingers like withered twigs, he reached out, his rheumy eyes narrowed, his voice a feeble whine: "You are no longer welcome until you bring more." Not comprehending his Shaman's sudden greed, the boy kept his thoughts to himself.

As the growing season approached the snow began to melt, only to be replaced by cold rains driven by piercing winds. Storms raged for weeks, decimating most of the newly planted crops. The usually placid sea grew fierce with thunderous waves, making fishing impossible. Sheep and goats perished for no apparent reason and several babies died. On the verge of starvation, the Elders gathered, turning their eyes to the diminishing powers of the Shaman, as it was he who had entreated the gods and promised prosperity, all to no avail. Assuming a dark magic was at the root of these misfortunes, they went to his hut with the accusation of sorcery, of which the sentence was death.

The very next day the skies brightened and the sea resumed its tranquil lapping. Despite their affection for their Shaman, the Elders assured their frightened tribe that by his death the gods had been appeased.

It was that same afternoon the boy went to the Shaman's hut to find the fragment of bloodied cloth. Feeling a presence behind him, he looked back, seeing one of the Elders blocking the low entrance. A large man with a craggy face and long, black, knotted hair, he was covered in the deep-blue tattoos that defined his supremacy within the tribe. He was the Elder who oversaw the honing of the enormous stones that one by one would be erected in the circular ditch that had been dug many seasons before. Although several were already in place, many more still lay prone. The boy was well aware the construction had already passed two generations and might not be complete by the passing of his own.

The Elder demanded to know what he was doing inside the hut instead of hunting. When he answered that he had just returned

11

with several good-sized muskrats, the man withdrew his challenge and in a gentler tone informed him what he already knew, that the Shaman had passed the night before. Instinctively, the boy understood his death had not been natural.

Aware he was holding something in his hand, the Elder demanded, "Show me what you have brought your Shaman."

When he opened his hand, the Elder barely reacted to the sparks. With a sharp curse, he brushed the glowing pebbles to the ground before trying to crush them beneath his foot. "Damnable spirit stones. You have brought these to the Shaman before?"

The boy shrunk back. "Yes. He had a small pile of them in the corner. Along with his magic shells and bones. You must have found them."

The Elder, looking even more frightening, shook his head. "His shells and roots have been taken to safety. We found no stones after the Shaman's death."

"How could such things disappear?"

The man scowled. "I suggest you ask the spirits. The ones that are said to inhabit those stones. Stay away from the dark place where you found them. Bring no more to the village. Your Shaman knew the legends, and yet to his peril he defied them. It is said those spirits cleave to emotions and overtake one's life. If he had as many as you say, they boded ill for him. Beware of their power."

It was a couple of evenings later that the Shaman was to be interred. A rocky cairn had been prepared at the base of what would become the center and most powerful monolith in the circle. Despite his murder, he had still been allotted what was considered a place of honor. As the sun set and shadows began to shift over the stones, the entire village gathered, raising their arms to welcome the night with chants of prayer and praise for their gods. When the refrains of mourning for their Shaman ended, the boy was taken aside by yet another Elder and again warned not to bring more stones to the village.

The next morning at dawn, on his way to hunt, the boy stopped at the burial crypt. He had listened to his Shaman's tales for many suns and moons, and he missed him. When he looked down with a prayer of his own, he noticed several rocks had been disturbed. As he knelt to rearrange them, a deep rumbling moved the earth and a fetid odor arose from within the cairn. Stumbling back in fear, he ran to join his fellow hunters.

Later, after evening prayers, he returned to the grave, relieved to find it undisturbed. Nearby he noticed several Elders gathered around the next huge white stone that would be raised into place just after the midsummer rituals. At that ceremony a new Shaman would be chosen to guide the tribe.

And yet the next morning, the Shaman's grave once again appeared unsettled. Although more rocks had been added, the boy heard what sounded like agitated muttering from deep within the cairn and the stench had worsened. Making sure no one was nearby, he whispered a quick prayer before dropping a glowing pebble into a narrow crevice. He stared silently as the voices ceased and the odor dissipated.

Over the next few mornings when he returned to the grave, he again found it in disarray, along with the same rumbling and foul stench. One morning, two Elders conferring nearby turned to watch as he surreptitiously dropped another of the stones into the stinking pile. Aware the fumes and tremors had abruptly ceased, the men came over, curious as to what the boy had done. With reluctance, he held out his hand.

The man patted his shoulder. "We know you were fond of your Shaman. Since his spirit remains unsettled, it has been decided to move his body to a burial ground just beyond the hills to the south."

When the boy looked put out, he said, "It's not far. You can visit him there if you choose. But weren't you told not to bring more stones into the village?"

"Yes," he whispered, staring at his feet. "I only brought them because they seem to calm his spirit."

The other Elder scowled. "Take them far away from here. They can calm his spirit elsewhere."

Disregarding the command not to gather more stones, the boy continued to return to the cave. And every week he made the trek to visit the Shaman's cairn, now on a grassy mound shaded by large, leafy trees. And yet each week, despite his offering of stones, he was distressed to find rocks thrown about—by no human hand, he was sure. Once, when he had gathered the courage to ask one of the kindlier Elders about the agitation from deep within the earth, the man had shaken his head, explaining they were the voices of their ancestors crying out in warning, but of what he wouldn't define. He had added, however gently, that the entire tribe believed the Shaman had overreached, and it was possible that demons had not only overtaken his soul but now dominated his spirit. He predicted he would never rest but would forever seek to entice more stones to his grave. As though in confirmation, each time the boy dropped in just one, the odor dispersed, and the grave returned to silence.

A year passed. It was well into the warm season before the boy, now sporting hair on his face along with the linear tattoos of a man and hunter, returned. As he approached the silent mound, he was dismayed to see the trees had not only shed their leaves, they had shriveled to blackened husks, and the once green grass had become brown and dry. As if sensing his presence, the rumbling began, now sounding more like anguished cries from deep within the earth, and the foul stench bloomed, poisoning the breeze. After tossing several glowing pebbles into the rocks, he knelt down in prayer. "Here is your tribute, my Shaman. The roof of the cave has collapsed and there is no longer any way to enter. These are the last of the stones I have for you. Perhaps one day someone will bring you more. Until then, I pray these will keep you in peace for now and all eternity." Hearing an inhuman shriek of rage, he backed away in terror as the earth shuddered beneath his feet. Sensing an aura of pure evil, he questioned if this was his fault. Hadn't his Shaman told him he was chosen? That a special fate awaited him? And yet, by bringing the glittering pebbles out of love, had he somehow allowed a demon to overtake his Shaman's soul? Aware that neither he nor anyone else had the power to answer such questions, he knew it was time to leave and never return.

As he wound his way through the now barren mound of cairns, the sky darkened to indigo and a bright orange moon began to rise on the horizon. He patted the pouch at his side; in it were the last of the magical stones, stones that may not have boded well for the old man, but indeed had for him. Not only had he become a strong hunter, he had also attracted the attention of quite a few of the village girls—one dark-haired beauty in particular. Looking forward to what the night might bring, he made his way back to his village and the much-anticipated midsummer harvest festival.

Part I

You don't love someone for their looks, or their clothes, or for their
fancy car, but because they sing a song only you can hear.
—*Oscar Wilde*

Chapter 1

March 1973

Sarah didn't even bother to look up. "You're late. Again."

"Sorry," Cia said, dropping her bag on the desk across from hers. "I slept through the alarm, and when I got to the subway a train had just left."

"Look. I know the divorce is still on your mind, but it's time to get over it."

"Not now, Sarah. Can we talk later?"

Sarah looked up with a grin and pointed her pencil at Cia. "Sure. Over Chinese. I'm buying."

Cia nodded, thinking that your truest friends were those who saw you through difficult times and Sarah had, indeed, been there for her.

As editors at the small but vibrant publishing company, BookEnds, they had shared an office since Cia had, in her words, scratched her way up from the secretarial pool. Although Sid, the owner, had taken credit for "recognizing natural talent," it was only after Sarah secretly handed Cia a manuscript to edit and then presented it to him to approve. After proffering not only his satisfaction, but his praise as well, Sarah, already an editor for five years, informed him that it was Cia's work, not hers. A few weeks later, he moved Cia into Sarah's office—her previous officemate having recently defected to Random House—with the message that she could handle whatever Cia still needed to be taught. By then they had become close friends, and Sarah had acted as more than just a mentor; she had also been the voice of reason during Cia's divorce from the ever-charming and often-cheating Ian.

After work, they took the subway to Sarah's cluttered, book-filled apartment in a slightly crumbling brownstone on West Seventy-Eighth Street and ordered from their favorite Chinese place.

Sarah uncorked a bottle of Almaden Red while Cia opened the white cardboard cartons. "Did you ever notice that these little boxes are like origami?" she asked, emptying one of rice before unfolding it.

"You are the only person I know who would notice such a thing. More importantly, did you see that new author, Stan something, in Sid's office today?" Sarah's look was coy.

"No. And don't start with me."

"Come on. Time has passed. This city is full of men who would love to meet a tall, gorgeous girl with big brown eyes and great legs."

"Thanks," Cia said with a laugh. "But I'm sure there are enough brown-eyed girls to go around."

Sarah shook a Marlboro out of its box. "Seriously. It's time to get out there."

"I go out."

"Yeah. With guys who are more friends than anything else."

"Not all. But it's okay. At least I trust them. Are you ever going to stop smoking?"

Flicking ash into a dish on the table, Sarah grinned. "I actually stopped last week."

"I hope this isn't because of me."

She rolled her eyes. "Of course not. And by the way, have you heard from Ian? I hear things are not going well at Park Place."

Ian. *Why did her friends always ask about Ian? That had ended two years before.*

She had met him the autumn of her first year at BookEnds. Although she was tall and slender with a pretty face, dark eyes, and thick, mahogany-colored hair, she was shy and far from confident in her work. She also tended to question her ability to relate to men; never quite knowing what to talk about, especially on a first date.

That afternoon she had been in a rush, taking a shortcut across the reception area when he walked in; over six feet of slim, lanky man with dark hair falling over his forehead. As his slate-blue eyes met hers for just an instant, she was sure she saw a trace of a smile before he turned to the receptionist. Feeling a flutter of anticipation, she glanced back, not believing she could be the recipient of that smile. Instead of stopping, she had clutched her folders to her chest and hurried away. Safe in the hallway, she took a breath while berating herself for being such a mouse.

It was a few weeks later when she saw him again, this time about to leave an editor's office. Stoking up her nerve, she walked towards him. Noticing her, he asked if she could point him in the direction of the publicity office.

"Yes. Well. It's on the other side of the office. You have to go back through reception . . ."

"Why don't you show me," he interrupted. For the first time, she heard the hint of an Irish accent in his voice.

She blinked in surprise. "Are you a writer?"

He looked amused. "Not at all. I'm an architect. My firm specializes in reconstructing old buildings. Along with Herb Lewis, the famous photographer, we've put together what I guess one would call a rather glossy coffee table book."

"I haven't heard about that. But, um, I only deal with novels. Fiction, you know."

He had smiled at her obvious nervousness. "I've seen you here before, Miss . . . I'm sorry, I don't know your name."

"Oh. Cia. Cia Reynolds."

"Nice to meet you, Cia. I'm Ian O'Connor. You'll have to tell me more about dealing with, ah, fiction. Look, I have an idea. There's a launch party for the book at our office next week. Why don't you come. Maybe we can have a drink after."

She barely stopped herself from blurting out, *Really? You're asking me to come to your party?* Instead, she managed to eke out a scratchy "Yes," at the same time not believing this fabulous man had asked her out. *Well, sort of.*

The Park Place offices occupied a newly renovated warehouse far over on the West Side, just beyond a derelict rail link called the High Line. It had recently been featured, along with a prominent mention of Ian's name, in several architectural magazines as not only contemporary, but forward-thinking.

Several well-coiffed heads turned as she stepped off the elevator, quickly swiveling back when they realized she was no one important. Her first instinct was to cut and run, but, forcing herself to take a breath, she forged ahead, finally spotting Ian surrounded by admirers, many of them women. She breathed a sigh of relief when he looked back and, seeing her, waved her over. With his hand barely brushing her back, he kept her by his side until, with a subtle glance at his watch, he whispered they could leave.

The taxi stopped in front of a dilapidated building on a narrow, cobblestoned street in the West Village. Although there was a light over the door, Cia could see no name. They entered a dimly lit barroom to the haunting sounds of Ornette Coleman and redolent with decades-old whiskey mingling with smoke, not all of it tobacco. Between timeworn photographs hung on unevenly painted walls, she noticed scrawled, faded signatures from writers, many long gone.

"What is this place, Ian? Some sort of club?"

"Not at all. It's called Chumleys. It began as a speakeasy in the days of prohibition and has been a writers' and artists' hangout ever since. As an aspiring writer, I thought you might appreciate it."

She smiled. "I do."

After settling into a booth and giving their drink order to a miniskirted waitress, Ian asked, "When you do have the time, what is it that you write?"

She was immediately intrigued, actually surprised that he had asked about her, particularly since most of the men she dated spent entire evenings blathering on and on about themselves. Doing her best to overcome her reticence, she said, "Mostly short stories. Sort of romantic fantasies about the middle ages. I like history, particularly British history."

"Why British?"

"I don't really know. I've never been to England, and yet images and ideas just seem to come to me."

"How about Irish history?"

She blushed. "Sorry. I don't know much about Ireland. I do know a bit about Scotland, though. I've spent a lot of time at the library researching it. That's not the same, is it?"

"Why Scotland?"

"There's little or nothing known about the early inhabitants, and it all seems very mysterious. For some unknown reason, I'm fascinated by it."

"Maybe," he said with a grin, "you were there in a past life."

She looked surprised. "Really? Do you believe in such things?"

"Not at all. I was only teasing. I'll be glad to tell you about Ireland. There are plenty of mysteries in our past. Will you let me read one of your stories?"

"I don't think they're worth reading. Not yet, anyway. Working all day and writing at night isn't easy."

"I know what you mean."

"And you?"

A look of excitement came into his eyes. "I want to design buildings. Large, contemporary, interestingly shaped buildings."

"I thought that's what you're doing."

"Not entirely. Most of the projects at Park Place are interior reconstruction. Whatever work we do on exteriors is still not the same as building from the ground up."

It was well after midnight when he took her home. As she was about to reach for her keys, he gave her a light kiss and said he'd call. Inside, she closed her eyes and leaned against the door, all too aware that "I'll call soon" was a hollow phrase repeated far too often. She sighed, afraid she'd never hear from him again.

When there was no call for several weeks, she became convinced her worst fears had been realized and, as usual, she had expected too much. She had just about given up hope when she picked up the phone one day and heard his deep voice. Holding her breath, she tried not to sound surprised when he asked to see her that same night. For a split second she considered saying no, that she already had plans; but somehow it came out as, "Yes."

She met him at the bar at the Four Seasons where he apologized for not calling sooner.

"It's all right, Ian. There's no need to explain."

"Actually, there is," he said, taking a long drink of his scotch. "I was seeing a woman, someone I had grown close to." He explained that her name was Grace and described her as the spoiled daughter of a wealthy family; a party girl who liked to go out every night to clubs and happenings. "It was fun for a while, but after three years I began to realize that something was missing. She was becoming secretive, and I suspected she was keeping things from me. When I finally asked her, she told me I was being silly and everything was fine. But, in truth, it wasn't. Nor had it been for a long time." With a sigh, he shook his head. "We broke up a couple of months ago. I thought it best to wait before I called you. I needed space. Time to think." He paused before looking into her eyes. "There's something about you, Cia. Something honest, no bullshit, if you understand me. I'd like to see more of you."

She sat up straight, wanting nothing more than to leap in his arms and shout, *"Yes!"* Instead, she listened, not doing much more than nodding her head or asking the occasional question — questions she hoped he didn't consider intrusive.

"You must have really been in love with her."

Looking wistful, he nodded. "I guess I was. But I'm over her now."

She wasn't so sure. Either he was or he wasn't. She'd have to be careful and not allow herself to become too involved. She reminded herself that she was only out on a date with him and not to expect anything more.

It was well after two in the morning by the time he took her home. Unsure how to react, she wanted to ask him in but worried it might be too soon. She was about to say good night when he whispered, "I think I have to kiss you now." Later she would think that, just as in romance novels, she had melted into his arms. In what had been a blur of kisses they had practically ripped off one another's clothing in sudden and overwhelming desire. It was only in the soft light of morning that she began to worry it had all happened too fast.

Dropping her chopsticks, Cia stood up and paced. Sarah, looking concerned, put down her wine glass. "What is it?"

"I still can't believe how naïve I was. Ian was so beautiful. I could never imagine what he was doing with me." She shook her head. "Girls were always chasing him, even after we were married."

"Come off it, Cia. It was more than love at first sight." She rolled her eyes. "It's usually lust at first sight, anyway."

"I should have realized his affair with Grace never really ended. It was only on pause." She took a breath. "The night he asked me to marry him I should have said no; we should leave it as it is. In 1968 it was no big deal to live together. But how could I? I saw him as not only sensitive, but strong and decisive, a man I could trust." She poured more wine. "But he wasn't any of those, was he? I've come to believe that all too often we hear what we want and ignore the underlying truth. I got lost in my own desire for what I perceived to be that one special person. It was only later that I found out the night he proposed to me was barely a week after Grace had gotten married."

"Come on, Cia. You were happy. You had a great wedding."

She smirked. "It was, wasn't it?" The families had gotten on well, already whispering about the prospect of grandchildren. And yet it was only a few months later that her parents died in a car crash. It left her, even at thirty-two, still feeling like an orphan. At least they had missed the misery and embarrassment of the divorce.

It had started in February, the night Ian called to say he had to work late. She was also busy and hardly registered it. That is, until there were too many nights when he arrived home well after midnight reeking of scotch. Once, when he claimed to have yet another big presentation the next day, she called his office at eleven, getting no answer. Later, when she questioned him about it, he shrugged, saying no one had heard the phone. The next time it happened, it dawned on her that her so-called perfect marriage might be in trouble.

One morning not long after, she found a copy of *The Post* on her desk opened to the gossip pages. She wondered why someone would leave it; she never read the tabloids. Before tossing it in the trash, she glanced again at the spread open before her. It was impossible not to miss the photo of Grace, fur-clad and laughing in front of Sardi's. In the greyed-out background was an all too familiar figure; although Ian had his hand up, it wasn't enough to hide his face.

When Sarah arrived, Cia was still staring at the murky photograph, her eyes red with tears. When she asked what was wrong, Cia, unable to speak, handed her the paper.

"Ohmygod. Shit. It's Ian. I can't believe this. Did you have any inkling that he was seeing Grace again? You always seem so happy together."

She grimaced. "I guess appearances can belie the truth."

She arrived home that evening to find Ian already waiting, a half-empty tumbler of scotch in his hand. Dropping the newspaper on his prized, mid-century chrome-and-glass table, she tried to hold back her anguish and her tears, and that left her nothing to say.

Without even glancing at the paper, he looked up at her sheepishly. "I'm sorry about last night, Cia. Actually, I'm sorry about a lot of things. I never meant for you to find out this way. Please sit down. We have to talk."

"Sarah, I will never forget standing there, not believing what I was hearing from the man I loved, and until that day was sure loved me."

"Stop, Cia. Don't put yourself through this again."

She shook her head. "I still find it hard to live with the fact that one day everything seemed fine and the next my life was over."

"But it wasn't over, was it? He gave you everything."

"None of that mattered. The apartment, the furniture, the stuff we collected together, it was all meaningless." Putting her hands up, she looked at Sarah. "It's past history, isn't it? You're right. It's time to move on."

Sarah held up her glass as if in a toast. "At last. You're only thirty-two. One day you'll meet the right guy."

"I'm not so sure there is one. Or that I would recognize him if there was."

Chapter 2

More than two years had passed since that life-changing night, and Cia had moved into a newly renovated flat in an old but charming townhouse in Chelsea. Large windows in the living room faced the street and the kitchen overlooked a small garden. It wasn't as large or modern as Ian's loft, but it was hers, and she made it as warm and welcoming as she could.

A few weeks after her night at Sarah's, Sid called her into his office to tell her he had great news. After waiting for her to settle into one of the large leather armchairs facing his desk, he grinned. "There's a writer's conference in England coming up. I'd like you to go."

Her eyes flew open. "Me?"

"Why not? Your authors can survive a few days without you."

She laughed. "I'm sure they can. But I've just moved to my new apartment and I'm about to close on the cottage." *The cottage.* It was something she had always wanted: a quiet, cozy hideaway where she could escape from the city and, hopefully, write. Although she and Ian had talked about buying a country house, he'd always said he wasn't sure they could afford it, and besides, they spent all their summer weekends on Fire Island. And yet, thanks to the divorce and her smaller apartment, she could now very well afford the eighty-year-old farmhouse with a small pond bordered by weeping willow trees.

"I know. However, the conference isn't until May, so you still have plenty of time."

Cia spent her first two nights in a cramped room in an overpriced hotel in Knightsbridge and her days wandering around London, falling more in love with the city with every step. She walked through crumbling and seedy Soho to Bloomsbury to pay homage to writers and poets from centuries past. After being overwhelmed by the masterworks at the National Gallery, she bought an overpriced print blouse at Liberty House, prowled Marks and Spencer for underwear, socks, and inexpensive wool sweaters and, in contrast, browsed her way through the far-too-pricey clothing at Harrods. The only thing that made her sad was seeing two lovers huddled on a bench and kissing in Berkeley Square.

By the time she boarded the train for the quaint, picture-perfect village of Bibury in the Cotswolds, she was looking forward to what the next four days would bring.

She was gratified the workshops turned out to be more informative than expected and the discussions with other editors, more often than not, enlightening. At lunch the second day, Stefan, a British journalist and fellow attendee, asked if she'd like to take a break and go to London with him to attend a gallery opening that evening. He added that he lived in Chelsea and had met the artist several times since they frequented the same pub.

The large gallery was white and stark, particularly in contrast to the eighteenth-century Baroque building that housed it. Except for a slender Giacometti sculpture in a far corner, the space was empty of any furniture other than a bleached wooden bench in the center and a bar, already heavily populated. Cia imagined the artist required a complete absence of color to set off his subtly hued paintings. While Stefan went to get drinks, she stopped in front of a large canvas of two nudes: one about to step out of a bath while gazing placidly out at the artist, or in this case the observer, and the other in profile, holding a towel.

Handing her a glass of champagne, Stefan whispered, "Jamieson is well known for his lush, fleshy nudes. What he's most famous for, however, are his portraits of the nobility, not to mention his seductions of that very same nobility."

Cia laughed. "Are you serious?"

"Yes. Have a look at them."

As Stefan wandered over to another painting, she sensed a presence. With a slight glance to the side, she noticed an attractive man with dark hair staring at her. Experiencing a shiver of unease, she turned her attention back to the painting.

"You've looked at that painting long enough. What do you think of it?" His voice was deep, authoritative.

Thinking him rude, she faced him. As his eyes met hers, she felt a jolt of recognition, but of what she didn't know. She was certain she'd never met him before. Unexpectedly flustered, she took a breath. "There's, um, something familiar about it. Maybe it's that the poses are unusual. It recalls Degas."

"But do you like it?"

She hesitated. "Yes. I do."

He looked at her with narrowed eyes. "You're sure?"

"Yes. I do like it." She was becoming a bit exasperated.

"Good. I would be heartbroken if you didn't." He held out his hand. "Will Jamieson. You're obviously American. Do you live here in London?"

"Oh. Sorry," she murmured, feeling her face redden. "Nice to meet you. I didn't realize you were the artist. Cia Reynolds. I'm from New York." As she reached to shake his hand, she suddenly felt as though an electric current was flowing through her fingers. Startled, she stepped back.

He looked at her curiously. "Are you all right?"

"Yes. Yes, I'm fine," she murmured, wondering if he felt it as well.

He glanced at Stefan, a few canvases away. "Is that your boyfriend? He looks familiar."

"He told me he occasionally goes to the same pub as you. And, no, he's not my boyfriend. We're attending a writers' workshop, that's all."

"Then stay and have a drink with me. This will be wrapping up soon."

"I don't want to impose. You must have plans."

"I do. But I've just decided to change them."

"I really can't. I have to go back to . . ."

He interrupted. "Tomorrow, then."

Uncertain, she shook her head. "I don't know."

He wrote an address on a folded piece of paper. "Meet me at The Queen's Elm. It's only a few streets from here. At seven." It wasn't a question.

Before she could respond, he kissed her lightly on the lips and crossed to a lively crowd awaiting him at a bar.

Cia touched her lips, tingling with the same current she had felt when his hand touched hers. *What the hell was that?* She watched him accepting congratulations and adulation from an admiring crowd in which women seemed to outnumber men. She had to admit he looked the part of the successful artist in his black velvet jacket over a dark grey shirt and black pants. Although he was probably ten or even fifteen years her senior, he gave the impression of a much younger man. She usually wasn't attracted to older men, but with dark hair just touched with grey and unusual sand-colored eyes, there was a unique intensity about him. That, and the fact that she had felt his kiss to her very toes. She glanced at the paper he had handed her, seeing it was a list of each painting with the name and price next to it. The numbers were impressive and, looking around the gallery, she noticed red dots next to many of the canvases.

Stuffing it into her bag, she walked to another wall where several large portraits were hung. Two were of older men, but the rest were of women of varying ages, all obviously aristocratic: Duchess this, or Lady that. As Stefan had said, he was an accomplished, flattering portraitist. Looking closer, she noticed many of the women had small, almost secret smiles. (She was thinking Mona Lisa.) There was surely something more between the artist and his subject than just paint and canvas.

As she and Stefan left, she looked back, seeing Will still surrounded. Stefan grinned. "I noticed Jamieson took a fancy to you. Be careful of him. He eats pretty young women for lunch."

"From the look of those portraits, I'd say it's more than young women and far more than lunch."

And yet the next evening she found herself walking into The Queen's Elm at half past seven. When she entered the crowded, smoke-filled pub, he was standing at the bar talking with a couple of men.

Seeing her, he smiled and took her hand. "I was afraid I was being stood up."

She felt her face redden. "The train was a little late."

Without a word, he put his hands to her shoulders and kissed her, this time not so lightly. She pulled back in surprise. "Mr. Jamieson . . ."

"What a lovely blush. I look forward to seeing more. Since I've kissed you twice, I think it's time you address me as Will. Come meet my friends."

She followed him to a table, her head spinning.

He introduced her to three artists and two filmmakers, along with a couple of young women who regarded her with wan smiles of curiosity. A few minutes later another man, Patrick, joined them and, with a nod, sat down across from her. Tall and gaunt, he appeared to light each cigarette from the one before. Will seemed fond of him and mentioned that he owned a gallery in Yorkshire.

After Will ordered a glass of white wine for her, she sat back, listening to their banter mixed with off-color jokes and raucous stories. At some point food arrived, and they all shared various dishes, most of which she hadn't heard of and didn't look very appealing. By that time, after several glasses of wine, it no longer mattered — food had become secondary. Will had gone out of his way to bring her into the conversation, and she was laughing along with everyone else. At about ten, she glanced at her watch and touched his sleeve. "I should leave soon. I don't want to miss the last train."

With no change of expression, he nodded. Leaving some money with Patrick, he bid them all good night.

On the sidewalk, he took her hand. "Come with me, Cia."

She stared at him. "What?"

"Come to my flat. It's a few streets over."

This was unexpected. She shook her head. "I don't think that's a good idea."

"I think it is."

His flat was the top two floors of a narrow townhouse. "I'll show you my studio," he said, unlocking the front door and leading her up a steep staircase.

She followed him, thinking she'd have a quick look at his work, thank him for the evening, and exit gracefully.

He didn't give her time to look, much less think. With only a brief glance at a couple of portraits and an unfinished nude, her hand was in his and he was leading her back downstairs.

She tried but didn't seem to be able to stop or even question what she was doing. It was as though all common sense had deserted her and she had no choice but to go with him. In his bedroom, his kisses were gentle. Each time she started to say "No," she said nothing at all. Finally moving back, she put her hands against his chest. Taking a breath, she whispered, "Will . . ."

"Kiss me, Cia. Just once more. If you want me to stop, I promise I will." As if in a trance, she closed her eyes and did as he asked. From that moment her resolve was gone and all conscious thought ceased, his kisses igniting a desire she had never imagined, and his caresses a heat she had never known. She lay clasped in his arms, having no idea how they had ended up naked in his bed. When he slowly kissed her breasts and moved over her for the first time, she experienced a surge of craving so powerful she could barely breathe. Cleaving to him in orgasm, she heard him whisper, "This was inevitable."

When she could again speak, she asked why he had said that.

"What?"

"You said, 'This was inevitable.'"

He looked at her curiously, saying he didn't recall saying such a phrase. Then it no longer mattered; his mouth was on hers and she was once again swept into sensation.

In the half-light of early morning she awoke hearing sighs, or perhaps trickling water, but from where she had no idea. Listening closer, she thought the sound was more like hushed voices, as though someone in another room was speaking softly. But how could that be? They were alone in his flat. She turned over, waking Will.

"What is it?" he whispered, taking her in his arms.

"What are those voices?"

"What voices?"

"Don't you hear them?"

"Just the wind," he murmured, beginning to caress her.

Later, when she looked out the window, the trees were still.

As she was getting ready to leave, they barely spoke. Feeling awkward, she questioned if the light of day had broken the spell of what had been a magical night. Although relieved when Will asked to see her again, she told him she was returning to New York the next afternoon. Suddenly shy, she simply handed him her business card. After walking her silently to a taxi stand, he kissed her but said nothing more. She wondered if she should have been the one to say something, maybe even asked him to write. By then it was too late, and she didn't even know the address of his flat.

On the train, she replayed the night. For some reason it suddenly seemed indistinct, as though it had taken place not hours

30

before, but rather in a dream hazily recalled from a time long past. Maybe, she thought, the reality of daylight had blurred the image of the most sensual night of her life. With every kilometer, she felt she was losing a memory she desperately wanted to keep.

In Bibury she was lucky to find a taxi idling across from the train station, the driver smoking a smelly cheroot while dozing over his newspaper.

When she entered the meeting room all eyes turned to her, still in her skirt and blouse from the day before. Feeling her face redden, she sat down, apologizing for interrupting a discussion. Stefan merely glanced at her, grinned, and shook his head.

Arriving back home the next evening, she had barely dropped her suitcase before picking up the phone to call Sarah. When there was no answer at the office or her apartment, Cia hoped she was out with Mike, an ad salesman at *Newsweek*. She had met him a few months before and he'd somehow managed, either by sheer will or an extraordinary sense of humor, to bypass her overly critical tongue, not to mention her lofty expectations. Having had too many fractious relationships that ended up going nowhere, Sarah had become overly suspicious, as she put it, of the motivations of the entire "male species." Cia's unexpected and stressful divorce had only added to her distrust.

In the office the next morning, before Sarah had even a moment to ask a question, Cia began telling her about meeting Will and whatever she could remember about her night with him.

Rolling her eyes, Sarah rummaged through a desk drawer for a half-empty pack of Kents. Lighting one, she shook her head. "Really, Cia. What were you thinking?"

"That's just it. I wasn't. It was as though some strange force took me over." She sighed. "He was amazing. I don't know if I'll ever see him again. Maybe it's best that I don't."

"Why would you say that?"

"It's strange. I know the night with him was special, and yet I don't understand why I can't remember some of it. The way he touched and kissed me, it felt familiar, not at all like the first time you make love with someone. It was as though we somehow knew each other. Am I making sense?"

Sarah grinned. "I just bought that new Erica Jong book, *Fear of Flying*. It's about what she calls a 'zipless fuck.' Totally anonymous.

You don't even need to know the guy's name. No hassle, no commitment, no expectation. Maybe that's how it should be."

Cia laughed. "I think it's been pretty much that way for men forever. Maybe it's our turn now." *And yet why do I keep thinking about him and feeling his hands on my skin.* "Look, Sarah, why don't you come to the cottage this weekend. The plumber wants me to check out the work he did in the kitchen. We can go antiquing."

"I have a date with Mike on Friday, but he's going to a bachelor party Saturday night. That would be great."

"Good. It will be fun . . ." she stopped abruptly.

"What now?"

"There was something else. Odd sounds, like whispers or sighs. I heard them in the morning at dawn."

"If his house is old, which it likely is, it was probably the pipes. Or possibly," she sniggered, "ghosts of girlfriends past?"

"Very funny."

"By the way, how was the writers' conference? Or have you already forgotten?"

"That I remember all too well. I'm about to write up my notes for Sid. Easier if you just read them."

"Nothing pornographic I hope?"

"Afraid not," she said, turning to her typewriter.

Later that morning, with notes in hand, Cia was surprised to find Sid unusually animated. Before she got even a word out, he told her to sit down; he had some interesting news.

"Don't you want me to tell you about the conference?" she asked, holding out a few typewritten pages. "I made notes."

"Good," he said, dropping them haphazardly on his desk. "I'll read them later."

"Is everything all right? Is there some problem I should know about?"

"Not at all, Cia. Quite the opposite. Do you know Lanny Winters?"

"Lanny Winters? Everyone knows him. He's one of the hottest stars in Hollywood."

"Then you know he was nominated for an Academy Award for *Trouble in Tombstone*. It was sort of a take-off on the old Wyatt Earp, Doc Holliday story."

"Yes. I saw it," she said, wondering where this could possibly be going.

With an oddly expressive grin, one worthy of the cat in *Alice in Wonderland*, he explained, "Last summer, Lanny, accompanied by a well-known photographer, took a long ride on horseback through parts of Arizona. They followed some of the old trails into the hills while documenting the locations where *Trouble in Tombstone* and many of the old cowboy movies were filmed."

Still a bit mystified, she shrugged. "So?"

"Just yesterday," he said, now looking even more eager, "his agent called to ask if we'd be interested in doing a book with him."

She blinked. "A book? A book of photography?"

"Actually, it would be more of what we fondly refer to as a coffee table book. His agent said Lanny would write the text—with help, of course—and they have hundreds of photos to go along with it."

"Sounds great, Sid. But what has this got to do with me? You have an entire department that deals with picture books. I work with fiction."

"Not for this one." He grinned. "I want you and Sarah as the editors. You have a good, visual sensibility and she's got an edge. I want editors who can guide this project without going gaga over a big star." He gave her a pointed look. "You won't, will you?"

Gaga? Breathless, she shook her head. "No. I'll do my best not to, although I can't speak for Sarah. What can I say, except that I'm flattered."

"Good," he said, standing up. "We have lunch tomorrow with Lanny and Chad, his agent. Make sure you and Sarah are ready to go by twelve."

"Have you told her?"

"No. This just happened. I knew they were shopping it around, but it appears they liked us, not to mention our offer, the best. I'll leave Sarah to you."

Trying not to show her excitement, Cia thanked him again before practically racing to her office.

Hearing Cia come in and close the door, Sarah looked up with alarm. "What's wrong?"

"Nothing. Everything is great," she said, trying to catch her breath. "Actually, beyond great," she added, beginning to explain their new project.

It was only after mentioning lunch with Lanny Winters the next day that Sarah jumped up and squealed, "I can't believe it. How did this happen?"

"I don't know . . ." Cia said, suddenly hearing a staccato knock on the door. She looked back as a tall woman with a head of massive red curls stuck her head in.

"Hey. I hear you got the Lanny Winters book. How'd you manage that?"

Cia shrugged. "Don't know, Marge."

"Well. Good luck. He's gorgeous, but I bet he'll be a bear to work with." She shook her curls. "Guess Sid didn't want a romance editor," she smirked. "Still. I'm jealous."

The next day at lunch, in a private room at the 21 Club, Cia and Sarah managed to be as businesslike as possible. Not easy with a tall, dark-haired, green-eyed actor such as Lanny Winters smiling at them. Nevertheless, they found him charming and far easier to talk with than they expected. His agent, Chad, brought along an outline for the story as well as a selection of large color photographs from the trek through Arizona.

It was well after three by the time everyone stood up and shook hands. As they left, Lanny gave Sarah and Cia—who was unable avoid a deep blush—cheek kisses. After handing off the outline and photos to Sarah, Sid announced he was going to Chad's office for further discussion.

On the street, Sarah touched her cheek. "I'm never washing my face again."

"Come on, Sarah. We're supposed to be the level-headed ones."

"How does one keep their wits around such a man? He was so laid-back, even funny." She stopped and glanced at Cia. "Speaking of men, though not on par with Lanny, I have a date with Mike tonight."

Cia nodded. "Good. I'm glad it's going well."

"Why don't I ask him to bring a friend. We should all go out and celebrate."

"Thanks. But I'm not in the mood for a blind date."

"Why not? This is special."

"It's fine, Sarah. Give me the outline and photos. I'll go through them later. Maybe next time."

When she arrived home, Cia read through the outline as well as a couple of pages of rather ragged text that Lanny had written. With a sigh, she shook her head; they'd definitely have to find a writer who would be compatible with him. The photos, in contrast, were dramatic; glorious vistas combined with close-ups, not only of scenery but of Lanny, his cowboy hat tilted at just the right angle, sitting tall in the saddle. One photo, a close-up of his face, reminded her of Will. Perhaps it was the dark hair falling over his forehead and the glint in his eye.

With a sigh she put it aside, already knowing it was a photo she would look at many times and wishing it was, indeed, an artist from London rather than an actor from LA.

Chapter 3

The receptionist rang, saying a man was waiting to see her but refused to give his name. Cia sighed, thinking it was probably some aspiring author whose manuscript she had rejected. Ready to tell him that showing up at a publisher's office without an appointment was definitely not the way to go, when she entered the reception area, she stopped abruptly.

"Hello, Cia."

She blinked. "Will? What are you doing here?"

"I came to see you."

"How did you know where I worked?"

"You mentioned it that night at the pub. You also gave me this." He held up her card.

At the pub? Why don't I remember that? Aware of the receptionist's curious stare, she stammered, "Why don't we go to my office."

Will followed, closing the door and taking her in his arms. Startled, she pushed him away. "What are you doing?"

He looked put out. "Cia, are you not happy to see me? Shall I leave?"

Flustered, she shook her head. "No. No, I'm just surprised. It's been almost two months. Since I never heard a word from you, I thought it was just a one-night stand. Or, should I say, seduction."

"Not at all," he said in a soft voice. Putting his hands to her face, he kissed her lightly: a kiss that elicited the same small shocks as the first time.

Trying to maintain her composure, she backed away. "Why are you here."

"I've come for meetings with a couple of gallery owners. I know I should have called, but time tends to get away from me. This trip was last minute. Have dinner with me tonight."

She took a breath. "I don't know."

"Sorry. I should have asked if you had plans."

"No, I don't," she said too quickly, knowing she'd chide herself for it later.

"Perfect. I'll meet you downstairs in the lobby at six. We can have a drink and talk a bit first."

Finding her voice, she told him that would be fine.

He was about to kiss her again when the door opened. They stepped away from one another just as Sarah walked in. Without hesitation, he reached out his hand. "Hello. I'm Will Jamieson. Pleasure to meet you."

Sarah looked like a deer caught in headlights. "Uh, nice to meet you," she stammered, shaking his hand.

After he left, Cia and Sarah stared at one another in mutual disbelief. "Was that who I think it was?"

Cia nodded and sat down at her desk. In the last weeks she had almost, but not quite, managed to put Will out of her mind, even avoiding another look at the photo of Lanny Winters that reminded her of him. Still, the odd familiarity of that one night still haunted her, and while she still fantasized about lying in his arms again, her musings were always followed by an unaccountable unease.

"Well," Sarah said with a broad grin. "Glad I arrived when I did. Who knows what might have transpired in here."

Dinner was in the garden of a small restaurant in the East Twenties. Will introduced Cia to Steve Berings and Carl Lorenzo, entrepreneurs who, along with several investors, were in the process of transforming an abandoned warehouse on Greene Street into a contemporary gallery space.

"The time is right," Steve said, lighting a Marlboro. "It used to be that you could snap up those old industrial buildings for next to nothing. Not anymore. We were lucky; we got in before the prices began to rise. Quite a few artists have already moved into those buildings, illegally for the most part, but that will change. We're confident that Soho is the future for art galleries." With a glance at Cia, he added, "We expect Will to add an important international component to our artist mix."

"Who are you using to do the work?"

"Park Place. They're supposed to be the best, from what we understand. Do you know them?"

That had been Ian's firm. She shook her head. "Not really."

After saying good night to Steve and Carl, Will took her arm. "How do you know so much about what's going on in Soho?"

"I'm sure anyone who reads the newspapers or *New York Magazine* is aware of it." This was neither the time nor place to discuss her ex-husband.

"Shall we walk to my hotel? It's not too far."

She stopped. "Will, I'm not sure that's a good idea. I mean, maybe we should talk, get to know one another."

Taking her hand, he continued on, "We will. I promise. But I want to hold you in my arms first."

With a sigh, she asked herself what it was about this man? What made him feel so familiar, and, more importantly, why was she unable to say no to him?

The hotel was small, tucked away in a block of townhouses in the West Twenties, not far from her apartment. The entire facade was covered by massive wisteria vines as though trying to hide between the more formidable brownstones on either side. After he took the key from an ancient white-haired man at the front desk, she followed Will up two flights of stairs, wondering how a hotel in New York could exist without an elevator. The door to his surprisingly spacious room hadn't closed before she was in his arms. As he began to kiss her, all rational thought was abandoned as she gave in to her own undeniable desire. The next thing she knew, she was once again lying in his arms and pale light was seeping through the blinds. Becoming aware of muffled sounds, she sat up, certain she was hearing the same hushed whispers as in his flat in London. Feeling his hand on her back, she turned to look at him. "There's no rush, Cia. It's still early."

"I'm hearing those odd sounds again, like in your flat."

"It's nothing," he murmured. "Perhaps just the whispers of our desire."

The next time she looked up it was almost eight. No longer hearing anything more than the usual street noises, she questioned if those whispers had been part of a dream. "Will, it's late," she said, jumping out of bed before he could entice her further. "I have to go home. I can't show up at the office in the same clothes from yesterday."

With a grin, he stretched and looked at her. "You are a lovely sight in the morning, Cia. Even with your hair standing on end. I'll pick you up at six. We'll have a quiet dinner. And this time I promise we'll talk."

She ran to the mirror, trying to smooth her tangled hair. "Promise? You said that last night." Taking a breath, she turned to look at him. "I probably shouldn't say this, but for some reason you are irresistible to me."

Taking her face in his hands, he whispered, "And you to me, Cia. And you to me."

When she arrived at the office, Sarah looked her up and down. "A bit sparkly this morning, aren't we?"

She blushed. "I have no idea what I'm doing with this man or, for that matter, who he really is."

Sarah looked puzzled. "What does that mean?"

"I don't know. There's just something . . . I can't even define it."

"I hope from the look on your face that you're seeing him again."

"Yes, Sarah. We were out with other people last night. He said we'd have time to talk tonight. We have to. He's leaving in two days."

By the time Will arrived at her office that evening, Sarah was getting ready to leave. After shaking his hand and wishing them a pleasant evening, she was out the door.

"What's with Sarah? She practically ran out of here."

"I think you intimidate her."

"Do you think I'm intimidating?"

She considered the question. "Maybe. I was a little intimidated when I first met you. However," she smiled, "I'm managing to get over it."

"I certainly hope so," he said, looking serious. "Shall we go to my hotel?"

She put her hands up. "See? That's what I mean."

With a mischievous grin, he laughed. "That wasn't intimidation. That was just raw desire. Don't look at me that way. I'm teasing you. Come on. Let's go to P.J.'s. I hear it's a 'happening' place, as they say in New York."

On her way to the elevator, Sarah saw Coralie, an executive assistant for one of the vice presidents, standing wide-eyed in the doorway of her office.

"What is it, Coralie? You look like you've seen a ghost."

"The man who just went into your office. Who is he?"

"A friend of Cia's. From London."

Looking doubtful, she shook her head. "No. He's more than that. Much more."

"Come on, Coralie. You can't do your psychic thing on everyone who comes into this office."

"You have to understand that I have no choice. It's who I am. Usually, it's not a big deal. But he is. Although he appears younger than he is, his eyes are old, ancient. They belie his youthful demeanor. Tell Cia to be careful. He's very powerful."

Sarah shook her head and continued to the elevator. Coralie had always been a bit eccentric.

In the mid 1960s, Coralie dropped out of Bryn Mawr and drove her broken-down VW Bug across the country to San Francisco. She spent the "Summer of Love" in a commune in Haight-Ashbury where, attired in colorful flowing dresses, and with flowers and feathers braided into her hair, she marched in protests, dropped LSD once or twice, smoked reams of pot and hash and made a little money by stopping people on the street to offer psychic readings. After a couple of years of, in Timothy Leary's words, "Turning on, tuning in, and dropping out," she boarded a plane to return home to New Jersey to spend a few weeks with her ailing mother. In the seat next to her was a young man who told her he was an artist who, in order to pay his rent, was now working at an advertising agency in New York. After asking if he would allow her to read his palm, she cashed in her return ticket and married him three months later. Her explanation: they were soul mates who had loved before in another life and were fated to meet again in this one. She finished college and, realizing that she excelled at organizing other people far better than herself, she began working as an executive assistant at BookEnds. Although she still wore long skirts and brightly colored shawls, she was considered an invaluable asset in the office, especially after foretelling the success of several obscure authors.

Chapter 4

P.J.'s, as always, was mobbed at the end of the workday. After pushing through the crowd at the bar and settling at a table, Cia took a breath. For whatever reason, her mind had gone blank. Questions that had been swirling in her mind all day suddenly vanished in a cloud of awkwardness.

As though aware of her discomfort, Will took her hand. "So, my lovely Cia. What do you want to know? Or, perhaps you should go first. Are you originally from New York?"

With a sigh of relief, she shook her head. "I was born in New Jersey. My mother was a school teacher who wanted to be a writer. Unfortunately, with her job, my demanding father and three kids she could never get to it. She had just finished her first short story when she died. It was sad."

"And you are carrying on for her."

"That's an interesting way to put it. Maybe I am. I'd like to write more. It's just that there never seems to be enough time."

"What did your father do?"

"He worked as a sound engineer in broadcasting. First for a radio company and then television." She went on to tell him her sister, a few years older, was married to a lawyer in Indianapolis and had a couple of kids. Her younger brother, essentially the black sheep of the family, had grown up determined to become an actor and had left home, to her parents' dismay, just after high school. He now lived in LA.

"These days he supports himself by working as a waiter at the Brown Derby in between going on casting calls. He's actually had bit parts in *Bonanza* and *The Mary Tyler Moore Show*. You probably don't get those in England."

"I honestly wouldn't know. I don't own a television. Were your parents born here?"

"Yes. Why do you ask?"

"Because all Americans, excepting, of course, your Indians, came here from somewhere else. Although, in truth, they did as well. I'm curious to know where your ancestors came from. Indulge me."

She paused for a few seconds, thinking his question a bit unusual. "I don't know much about my father's side of the family. His parents died before I was born. I think they came from Austria. Funny, I never thought to ask. I do know my mother's family lived somewhere on the east coast of Italy before emigrating to England. I have a cousin who has been researching our history for a family tree. He said my great-grandfather brought his family to the States in the late 1800s. My grandmother was born in Brooklyn."

"Do you know where they lived in England?"

"I think somewhere in the north. It's where my great-grandfather met my great-grandmother. She was also a school teacher."

Will nodded. "Did your parents approve of your marriage?"

Taken aback, she stared at him. "How did you know I was married?"

His smile was enigmatic. "Just a guess. How long have you been divorced?"

A guess? "A little over two years. Maybe you should tell me about you. Were you ever married?"

He shook his head. "I was engaged once, briefly. But no. Marriage is not my fate."

Feeling an uneasy twinge in her stomach, she asked, "What does that mean?"

He sat back and took a long pull of his beer. "Cia, have you ever had moments of déjà vu? You're somewhere, or you see someone, and suddenly it seems familiar, as though you've been there or met that person before? It's just a flash. Like an obscure memory you can't quite place."

"I guess I have." She shrugged. "To be honest, I had that feeling the night I met you at the gallery."

"And I felt the same. So you see, there must be some connection we have. Do you still sense it?"

She wasn't sure where this conversation was going. Wherever it was, or why he was pursuing it, was unsettling. "I . . . I guess so.

I'm not sure I understand. I just wanted you to tell me about you. Where you grew up, you know, things like that. What has that got to do with déjà vu? Or thinking we may have met before when we obviously haven't?"

"I have no idea. It's just one of those mysterious things in life that are impossible to explain. But let's leave it for later." He picked up his glass and touched it to hers. "As for me, my dear Cia, there's not a lot to tell. I grew up in Scotland. First in the north, where for generations my family ran a sheep farm near Inverness. When I was ten, we moved to Edinburgh. I came to London on a scholarship from the Royal College of Art but left because it was too conservative. Now I paint and teach the occasional course at Central or St. Martin's."

She shook her head. "No way. There must be more."

"What else do you want to know?"

"Well. Do you have brothers or sisters?"

"One brother. He worked with my father in the whiskey distillery. After my dad passed, he took over. Now he runs it."

"Your family is in the whiskey business? How interesting."

He laughed. "Not if you've grown up around booze most of your life."

"Then tell me about your life in London."

"I'm not leaving till Thursday night. We'll have dinner tomorrow. I promise to fill you in on my so-called life."

"Why do you make it sound so simple? I understand you're something of a celebrity."

He shook his head. "Just gossip, my love. This may not be the moment to go into details."

"Why not?"

With a smile he looked at his watch. "Because I understand the Museum of Modern Art is open tonight. I suggest we have a walk through it before dinner and other things."

Despite being aware that he was avoiding any further discussion about his life, she let it be, determined to return to the conversation later. While visiting the Renoirs, Van Goghs, Cézannes, and pondering Monet's *Water Lilies* in their own special room, Will kept the discussion to art. At dinner at a small café on West Fifty-Sixth Street, instead of talking about himself, he spent most of the time telling her stories and risqué anecdotes about artists, both past and present. Realizing she was having too much fun to interrupt, she gave up trying to ask any more questions. And then, suddenly and without further discussion, they were in his hotel room, her back against the wall, his mouth on hers, his hands pushing up her dress. "Wrap your legs around me, Cia. I have to have you now." That was all she could recall, except for the soft, muffled chants that woke her as a sliver of moon shone through the window just before dawn.

The next night, Will's last before leaving, she returned to the subject of his life in London. More open, he talked about his paintings and a gallery show coming up. He said his "patrons," as he called them, frequently invited him to their country estates while requesting portraits of various family members. "I've left a couple of very wealthy ladies waiting for their portraits to be finished," he said with a wicked grin.

She laughed, hoping he was referring to his studio and not his bed.

He kissed her palm, sparking the now familiar soft current. "I'll be back in New York in a month or two. I hope you will miss me."

How can I not?

Chapter 5

The phone rang just as Cia was about to leave the office for the weekend. When the receptionist said it was Ian, she glanced at Sarah who looked up in the middle of reapplying what must have been her third coat of pink lipstick.

"Hello, Ian. What do you want?"

Hearing Ian's name, Sarah dropped the lipstick and stared at her.

"I just wanted to wish you a pleasant weekend and ask if you could find some time to talk."

"There's nothing to talk about. Everything that had to be said already has been. Over and over, in fact."

"Come on. I heard you bought a house in the Berkshires. Why don't I drive up tomorrow?"

"You're married, Ian. You must have plans with your wife on Saturdays."

"That's what I want to talk about. Things at home aren't so great."

"Then I suggest you call a shrink. Anyway, I'm busy this weekend."

"Busy with the, ah, man I saw you with last night? Are you suddenly dating older men?"

She stopped breathing. She had noticed Ian and Grace swan into La Fonda del Sol, the restaurant where she and Will were having dinner. Despite that it wasn't one of her favorites, he had persisted, explaining there was nothing even close to it in London.

Since they were seated at a table near the back, Cia didn't think Ian had seen her. "Whom I date is none of your business. He's an artist I met in London. We're friends."

He sniggered. "He wasn't looking at you like a friend." His voice changed abruptly, turning hard. "I'll call you next week. I really do want to see your house. After all, it was bought with my money."

"Stop being a prick, Ian. You know I bought it with the inheritance from my parents. They always wanted a cottage in the woods."

"Whatever you say."

She hung up and looked at Sarah. "He's having marriage problems and wants to talk. Then he gets pissed because he saw me with another man."

"What are you going to do?"

"Nothing. He has no hold on me anymore." She picked up her coat. "Are we on for the cottage tomorrow?

"Wouldn't miss it."

"I'll pick you up at nine."

"Sounds good to me."

The day was pleasantly warm, with barely a hint of the heat and humidity that would inevitably follow. On the way to the cottage, they stopped to buy some groceries from a local shop. Although Cia had passed it many times, she had never gone in. When they entered, she realized it was far more than just a country store with local produce. On one wall, between old photographs and fading posters of long-ago county fairs, was a glass-fronted refrigerator with containers of homemade soups, and, in baskets on white painted shelves, an assortment of breads, cakes, and pies, all still warm from the oven. A tall woman with short salt-and-pepper hair and smelling pleasantly of vanilla came over, introducing herself as Sonny, the owner of what she described as, "This little piece of heaven." With a welcoming smile, she asked Cia if she had just bought the old Knowles cottage.

"Yes. How did you know?"

"Well. To be honest, I saw you with Sandra, the real estate broker a couple of months ago. She's the one who told me, along with everyone else in town. Congratulations. We can use some fresh faces around here."

"Thank you. I was under the impression that people in these small towns aren't especially welcoming of newcomers."

"Not here. Although there are always the fuddy-duddies who hate change. I hope you'll like it."

"So far, I love it. But the house needs a lot of work. This is my friend Sarah. We're planning to go looking for furniture and antiques this weekend."

"There are tons of antique shops around here. Junk shops too," she said with a grin. "If you need anyone to work on the house, let me know. I know all the carpenters in town."

"Thank you."

She hesitated, as if deciding what to say. "You know that house was empty for years."

Cia looked surprised while Sarah, about to reach for a baguette, stopped with her hand in midair. "No," Cia said. "No one ever mentioned it before."

"Well," Sonny said, lowering her voice. "Maybe I shouldn't be telling you this, but some people say it's haunted. Not by evil spirits, mind you. Rather, by a young woman who died under mysterious circumstances. I think she was in her twenties."

"A ghost in my house? How, um, interesting," she said in a somewhat sardonic tone. "A nice one, I hope."

"Tell us more," Sarah chimed in.

Sonny was happy to oblige. "Apparently, as the story goes, she had just become engaged to a man from England. He was called back on some sort of business and, before he could return, she took sick and died."

"How sad. Well, I'm not sure about ghosts, but if she's there we'll try and cheer her up. By the way, how long ago was this?"

"Oh. I believe in the late 1700s."

Cia looked confused. "I thought my house was built at the end of the last century."

"That's true. The original farm house was hit by lightning, several times in fact. It burned down a little over a hundred years ago. The cottage you bought was built a few years later on exactly the same site."

"And the supposed ghost?"

"It's been said that she moved into the 'new' house that now belongs to you."

"How would anyone know?"

Sonny grinned. "Supposedly there were sightings. But that was decades ago. Also, the lady in question was considered to be a bit daft. I wouldn't be too concerned if I were you."

Sarah looked from Cia to Sonny. "Well, if we meet your ghost, we'll let you know."

Sonny laughed. "Please do."

Cia handed Sarah one of the bags, fragrant with the scent of freshly baked bread and corn muffins, and hefted the other, inhaling just-picked garden greens mixed with the pungent aroma of a couple of cheeses Sonny insisted they try.

"Just a minute, girls," Sonny said, handing her a pie. "Early strawberries. Welcome to our village."

Cia smiled. "Thank you, Sonny."

"Come in again soon. We always have my special soups and cookies. Not to mention local gossip."

They spent the rest of the day browsing antique shops, arriving back at the cottage at dusk. After placing her purchases, a small knotty pine end table and a couple of pottery lamps, around the living room, Cia collapsed onto the old velvet sofa she had saved from her parents' house. As the evening cooled, Sarah uncorked a bottle of Bordeaux. Along with a wedge of Brie, a French baguette, and a bunch of grapes from Sonny's store, they settled in front of a crackling fire that banished the evening chill. Looking out the window, Cia watched a couple of ducks take off from the pond, shimmering pink in the glow of the sunset.

As they touched glasses, Cia sighed. "I'd love to bring Will here."

Sarah frowned. "What? I'm not enough?"

"You know what I mean."

"I do. I'm also aware that you don't know him very well."

"Actually, we talked for hours the last couple of nights, particularly the night before he left."

"Talked? Is that what you call it?"

Cia blushed. "No. We really did."

"Tell me about him."

Cia took a sip from her glass. "He was born in Inverness and moved to Edinburgh as a child. Let's see, he went to college in London." She stopped, looking puzzled.

"What is it, Cia?"

"I don't know. It's strange, but I can't seem to recall much about the conversation. I know we talked about art and that he's become very successful and teaches at art schools. And yet, why is it that I can't remember anything more about his personal life. What's wrong with me?"

"That's not like you. You have a great memory. Was he ever married? Do you think he has a girlfriend over there?"

She looked back, deep concern in her eyes. "I don't know. He was engaged, I think, but never married. Maybe I'm just tired."

Finishing her wine, Sarah wondered if it was something more than just being tired. "Enough about Will. Let's make dinner."

While Cia made a salad, Sarah lit the outside grill for the steaks and tucked foil-wrapped potatoes into the hot coals. After dinner, they settled in on the couch in front of the fireplace with coffee and slices of the warmed pie.

"So, what's the story with Mike?"

Sarah rolled her eyes. "I like the guy, don't get me wrong. But is he really The One? I don't know. I think he cares for me, and yet he's obviously in no rush for more. To be honest, I'm in no hurry to settle down either. If I meet another guy I like, I can still go out with him."

Cia smiled. "Clever girl. Take your time. Don't make the same mistake I did."

"No, Cia. It wasn't a mistake. Things change."

"And they changed big time the minute Grace got divorced. Don't let yourself get carried away."

"That's unlikely to happen. Anyway, it's getting late." She yawned. "Bed time."

Cia tamped down the fire before going to her room. After climbing into the somewhat creaky bed and shivering at the cold sheets, she again asked herself why she couldn't remember her conversations with Will but was able to recall every minute of their lovemaking. She fell asleep with sweet memories of lying warm in his arms and then the sighs, not only hers.

The next morning Sarah emerged from her room wrapped in a robe. "Is there any heat in here?" she asked Cia, who was already making coffee.

"I just turned up the thermostat. How was your night?"

"I slept like a baby. No ghosts tugging at my toes."

"No. No ghosts." Just the sound of the breeze that woke her from a lovely dream about Will.

Chapter 6

Cia didn't hear from Will for several weeks, more than enough time to question if she had allowed to herself become too emotionally involved in a relationship that was unlikely to go anywhere. She knew she could, perhaps should, have written him first, but she hadn't wanted to appear too anxious.

When a letter arrived in early July, she was relieved. Seeing his beautiful, if somewhat archaic cursive script, she reminded herself that he had spent two years at the Royal Academy.

He wrote that he regretted having let so much time go by before writing, but that she was constantly in his thoughts. He said the spring had been hectic with sittings for portraits, and he was also trying to finish a couple of paintings for a group show in Kent in just a few weeks. He added that Steve might want him to come back to New York in September. Apparently, the investors were anxious to meet the artists chosen for the first openings. He ended by saying he would be in touch if such a trip would become possible, adding again that he thought about her and missed her. It was signed, *with love, Will.*

With tears rolling down her cheeks she read the letter again before tucking it under her pillow and drifting off to sleep.

One evening a couple of weeks later, after writing back about what was happening in her life at the office—including a brief update on the Lanny Winters book—the phone rang as she was unlocking the door to her apartment. Hearing Will's voice, she felt her heart pick up a beat.

"Cia, I know this is short notice, but Steve just rang to tell me he wants me for a meeting in New York next week. I'll fly in Thursday and stay till Sunday."

She was breathless. "That's wonderful, Will. It just seems so brief."

"It is. Unfortunately, I have several classes to teach the following week."

"No matter, I look forward to seeing you."

"I hope 'look forward' is an understatement, Cia."

She could feel the blush and was glad he couldn't see it. "It is," she whispered.

"Good. Since that's settled, I'll call when I arrive."

The next morning, as soon as Cia walked in, Sarah looked up. "You're looking happy today. Let me guess, you got another letter, no, a phone call from a mysterious Scotsman."

Cia laughed. "Are you clairvoyant?"

"Not at all. I can see it in your face. Still . . ."

"Come on, Sarah, it's not a big deal."

"Maybe it is . . ." a soft voice interrupted.

Startled, both Cia and Sarah looked up to see Coralie standing in the doorway.

"What is it, Coralie?" Cia asked.

"I'm sorry. I was walking by when I overheard Sarah mentioning something about a Scotsman. I assume that's the man who came to see you a couple of months ago?"

"Yes. Why?"

Coralie glanced down the hallway before stepping into the office. "I didn't mean to interrupt, but when I saw you with him, I experienced what I can only describe as a psychic rush. Not only does he radiate an unusual energy, there's also a very strong aura surrounding him."

As Sarah rolled her eyes, Coralie's eyes bored into Cia. "This is not a joke. You have to be careful around him."

"What are you saying, Coralie? What's an aura?"

"We all have auras. Essentially, they emanate from energy we give off. I can't tell you why some can see them and others don't. There are those of us who are said to have a gift, something called synesthesia, which somehow enables us to perceive auras. When I saw your friend that day his was a deep blue with gold and silver sparking at the edges. Given that he's an artist, a communicator, the blue is not unusual, but what surprised me was the silver and gold. It indicates some spiritual force may be guiding him through this life."

51

Sarah did a double take. "This life?"

"Maybe I shouldn't have said it quite that way. There's a strong energy about him, almost otherworldly."

Cia shrugged. "So how does that affect me? It actually sounds quite positive."

"I want you to be aware that unusual, ah, things could possibly occur with him."

Like hearing those odd whispers? "What sort of things? Should I be afraid?"

"That's not what I'm saying." She turned to leave. "If you experience anything strange when you are with him, please tell me."

"I will. But I really don't get to see him very often."

"No matter. Just remember what I said."

When she left, Sarah shook her head. "Do you really believe any of that?"

Cia sat a minute. "Maybe. I mean, why not? We already know Coralie has some sort of psychic ability."

"You should have asked what color your aura is."

"Not right now," she murmured, experiencing a sense of unease. "That was becoming a little too weird."

Will called the following Thursday saying the plane had arrived late and he was rushed. "I'm off to meet with the Steve and his investors for dinner. I don't know how late it will be or quite what's happening tomorrow, so what if I just plan to meet you in the lobby of your building at six?"

She was secretly hoping he would want to see her after his dinner but told him tomorrow sounded perfect. "I wish you luck tonight. I hope everything goes well with the gallery."

"Thank you, luv. See you tomorrow."

She was just getting ready to leave when Will walked into her office. Seeing him, all restraint was abandoned, and she ran into his arms. After several lingering kisses, she whispered, "I thought you were going to meet me downstairs. "

"I was, but then I realized I couldn't hold you in my arms. It's good your roommate isn't here."

She laughed. "I'm not sure I could have helped myself even if she was."

"How lovely," he murmured, pulling her into another kiss. "Whatever am I to do with you?"

She fluttered her eyelashes. "I'm sure you have something in mind."

"I do, indeed. But let's have a drink first. I've had a long day with Steve and his investors."

"I assume all went well?"

"Yes. Tomorrow I'd like to go down there and see the space. They've just begun to work on it. I hope you'll join me."

She hugged him. "I wouldn't miss it."

Thanks to the time difference between London and New York, Will awoke early. Still, it took some time for them to leave her bed.

It was late morning, bright with summer sunshine, when they walked to the subway. As Will followed Cia down the grimy stairs to the foul-smelling, graffiti-splattered platform, he grimaced. "Your underground is worse than ours."

"I know. It's all a bit horrifying, but it's the quickest way to get to Soho. We can take a taxi back if you want. Although I imagine they'll be hard to find where we're going."

As a wildly colored spray-painted train arrived, he grabbed her hand. "I hope it's safe. We hear terrible things in London about New York's subways."

"It's all right during the day, but I wouldn't want to take one in the middle of the night. In fact, I believe the police block off the last few cars. It's too bad, really. When the subways work, it's the best way to get around."

They exited at Prince Street, gratefully breathing in fresh air. Will glanced doubtfully around the empty, garbage-strewn street. "This isn't looking much better than the subway. Does anyone actually live down here?"

Taking his arm, Cia began to walk in what she hoped was the direction of Greene Street. "I think as we get closer to West Broadway, it'll be better."

After passing deeply shadowed streets with only the occasional car parked in front of what looked to be long-abandoned buildings, Will stopped. "I'm beginning to feel this is a mistake. When I was here with Steve it didn't look nearly as bad."

"You were here during the week when there was more activity. Many of these buildings house small clothing and textile factories. Sweat shops, actually. They're all closed on Saturdays. Look." She pointed to two young men, one carrying an old wooden chair and the other lugging a large easel into the darkened doorway of a decrepit building on Mercer Street. Further along, they saw more people gathered in front of a luncheonette, which appeared to be the only place open. She glanced around the sparsely populated street. "I'll bet one day this place will become very trendy."

Looking doubtful, he shook his head. "If we live long enough. The question is, will your Park Avenue crowd come down here for an art gallery?"

"For the right artist, I think they will. Going to offbeat places has become very chic, which may be what Steve is counting on. Still, it's up to him to make it happen." She grabbed his arm. "Come on. We're almost there."

When they reached the gallery, the facade was mostly boarded up. Above, they could see blacked-out windows below a badly chipped cornice. Will sighed. "The investors want it to be ready this winter, but I'm guessing this will take far more work than they expect."

"Look, Will," Cia said, pointing to the building across the street. "There's a gallery up there. I think it says Paula Cooper."

"Well. At least that makes me feel better. But it looks closed."

"As I told you, nothing is open down here on Saturdays. As more people move in to these buildings and stores begin to open, I'm sure that will change. Come on, let's walk to West Broadway."

There was more activity, not to mention considerably more light, on West Broadway, which was wider and not as shadowy as the narrow streets to the east and west of it. A few couples wandered along while others appeared to be in an animated discussion in front of another old coffee shop. Will smiled at the sight of two young men, obviously artists, struggling to navigate a large painting through a narrow doorway.

Suddenly hearing a few fractured notes of a song, he and Cia looked down the street where three musicians with a guitar, drums, and even a flute were setting up in front of yet another ground floor space under construction. As they launched into a choppy version of "Strawberry Fields Forever," several people stopped to listen.

"Come, Will," she said, taking his hand and moving in their direction. "We have to go that way. Unless you want to go back to the gallery."

"No. I've seen all I need to."

As they walked closer, the first song ended and the young man with the flute began to play a few plaintive notes that sounded vaguely like a medieval tune called "Greensleeves." Hearing it, Will stopped abruptly.

"What is it?" Cia asked.

Feeling something brush against his arm, Will looked back, seeing a young woman with tendrils of dark hair falling around her face. She gazed back at him, her luminous eyes flashing in the sunlight. "Welcome back. It's lovely to see you again," she said, her voice an almost inaudible whisper. With a seductive smile she touched his sleeve before walking away.

"Wait," he shouted.

"Will?" Cia looked confused. "What is it?"

"That young woman. She acted as though she knew me."

"What young woman?"

"She was wearing a pale lavender dress. It was long, and she had a shawl over her shoulders. She was here . . . then somehow gone."

Glancing around, Cia shook her head. "I didn't see her. Maybe she went down that alley. Do you know her?"

"No," he said, looking bewildered. "But she seemed to know me. And she was dressed like someone from a hundred years ago. Maybe more."

"There are theater groups around here. She was probably just in costume."

He retraced his steps back to a deeply shadowed, garbage-strewn alley between two buildings. It was only when he didn't see the girl that he began to realize he hadn't really expected to.

Taking a breath, he glanced back at Cia who was staring at a building under construction across the street. On the scaffolding were posters of what looked like bad pop art along with a sign: *MBT Gallery Opening Soon.*

"Look, Will. There's another one."

He smirked. "Pop art. Anything goes these days. I guess one just has to believe," he said, his eyes still sweeping the street.

She reached up to kiss him. "By the time Steve's gallery is finished, I'm sure others will be opening as well. You won't be alone. Come on, let's walk to Houston Street. We can get a taxi there."

Still rattled at seeing the strange girl, he shook his head. "No. I'd rather walk."

She shrugged. "That works for me."

When they returned to Cia's apartment later that evening, Will once again expressed his concerns about the gallery. "I'm thinking that space may not be right for my paintings. Perhaps I should make some other contacts, maybe uptown."

She tried to be optimistic. "If Steve believes your work will sell down there, why don't you just go with it. At least to begin with."

He looked unsure. "I may ask you to be my eyes and ears. Although I'll be in touch with Steve, would you mind going down there to have a look from time to time?"

"I'd be happy to. But I'd rather you come back to see for yourself."

He hugged her. "I'll try, Cia. Unfortunately, I'm not sure when I'll be back again."

Overcoming a moment of hesitation, she stroked his hand. "What about the holidays? I know it's still months till Christmas, but couldn't you come back then?"

"I'm afraid the holidays won't be possible. I've been invited by Lady Critchlowe to her home on Majorca. Although Majorca isn't very warm at that time of year, it's far better than London."

With a pang of jealousy, Cia wondered if Lord Critchlowe would also be on the premises. She didn't like to think about Will and his life attending gallery openings and museum exhibitions, much less spending holidays and partying with the aristocracy in such places as Majorca. But who was she to question his lifestyle? She knew he was favored by London's elite — a memory that had managed to stick in her mind — and she was well aware, despite his humorous stories, that he enjoyed it all. He had explained that it was at those events, parties, or even weddings where he met the women, as well as the occasional man, who wished to have their portrait painted by the famous and seductive Mr. Jamieson. She knew she had to put those thoughts behind her, to be happy he was finally here holding her hand. Until anything changed, and she couldn't envision even in her most wish-filled daydreams that it ever would, she'd have to try to enjoy their time together while avoiding unreasonable expectations.

"What is it, Cia? You look sad."

She took a breath. "You're much more sociable than me, aren't you?"

He shrugged. "Perhaps. It's essentially part of who I am, who I have to be for my work. I can't say I don't enjoy it because I do. I like being out with people."

She shrugged. "I understand, Will. But . . ."

He took her hands in his. "Look, Cia. I'm sure you know that there have been many women in my life throughout the years, and yet I want you to understand that this is the first time anyone has meant anything to me. Otherwise, I wouldn't be here with you now. What's unfortunate is that we live so far apart."

She nodded. "I know. I keep asking myself how this happened. I mean, how was it that I went to that gallery, and then, out of nowhere . . . I met you."

"I'm not so sure it was 'out of nowhere.' Although I can't explain it, I believe there's far more to it than that. All I ask is that you be patient and allow me the time to work through some things in my life."

She bit her lip. "Some things, or someone?"

With an indulgent smile, he ran his finger across her lips. "No, my love. Suddenly there's only you. The rest of it is for me to deal with. Trust me. I will never betray you, or your love."

"I'll miss you," she whispered. "Maybe I shouldn't say it, but I will."

Taking her in his arms, he kissed her lips. "I'm glad you said it. If you didn't, I would have."

Chapter 7

Although Cia was unhappy about spending the holidays without Will, not that she had really expected to, she was taken up with work. That the work had to do with Lanny Winters and his equally charismatic young writer made the days go faster. When Will asked, in one of his more frequent letters, how her project was coming along, she answered that she was actually having fun, which elicited a slightly jealous response—that he'd heard Lanny was about to become engaged to a well-known actress. She knew it was the sort of silly gossip he never would have bothered with otherwise, and yet she admitted, if only to herself, that she found it somewhat gratifying. If Will was going off to a sunny island with London's elite, at least she was on her own island, albeit less sunny, working with a handsome actor.

One dark afternoon in the middle of January as she was editing a difficult manuscript, she felt a presence. Looking up, she saw Will standing silently in the doorway, a hint of a smile playing across his lips. With her heart beating wildly, she jumped up and ran into his arms. Pulling back from a kiss, she whispered, "Why didn't you tell me you were coming?"

"I wanted to surprise you."

"You certainly did that," she laughed, her eyes misty with joy.

"I can only stay a few days. I have yet another meeting with Steve, as well as one of his investors who has asked me to do a portrait of his twin sons."

Aware that Sarah was staring, she said, "You've met before."

He shook her hand, "Nice to see you again, Sarah."

"Likewise, I'm sure." After looking from Cia to Will, she took a breath. "Well. Think I'll run to the coffee shop downstairs. Can I get anyone anything?"

"Thanks. Coffee would be nice. Will?"

"Tea. If you don't mind."

"No problem." Before getting up, she scribbled something on a slip of paper and handed it to Cia.

Cia glanced at the note, her brow furrowed. Tucking it under a pile of papers, she glared at Sarah.

"By the way," Sarah said pointedly. "Don't forget to call Doug."

As she left, Will turned to Cia. "What was that about? Tell me if I shouldn't have come. Have you become involved with someone?"

"No, Will. That was Sarah's off-the-wall way of trying to make you jealous. Do I date? Yes, of course. Mostly men I consider friends."

She saw him hesitate, as though about to ask another question. After a few seconds of what was becoming an awkward silence, she put her hand on his arm. "I'm happy you're here."

He took her hand and kissed it. "Cia. I'm aware that I am not the best communicator."

"And yet you've been much better about writing these last months. Except from Majorca, of course. I'll consider forgiving you for that lapse."

He took her in his arms again. "I'm looking forward to that."

Sarah took her time, returning fifteen minutes later to find Cia in the office alone, a suitcase parked next to her desk. "Where's Will?"

She blushed. "We decided he'll stay at my apartment. He's in the conference room canceling his hotel."

"We?" Sarah looked doubtful.

"I asked if he'd like to," she said in a small voice, not about to admit that she had practically blurted it out. "Why did you give me that note? What was 'chill' supposed to mean?"

"You were flipping out over the guy. You don't hear from him for a month and suddenly you're rushing into his arms? You can't let him think you're just waiting around. Come on, Cia. You're smarter than that."

She nodded. "You're right. And your rather crude attempts at making him jealous seem to have worked. He said we should talk. For real, this time."

"He's too complacent."

"I know, but there's something . . ."

Sarah sniffed. "Yes. I know. I get it. I saw Coralie before. She said to remind you to be careful of him."

"Why this time?"

"Who knows? Maybe she can tell you why you can't remember some of your conversations with him."

She shook her head. "Not right now. Maybe after he leaves."

As they left the office that evening, Coralie looked up from her desk. Will caught her eye, acknowledging her with an almost imperceptible nod. Cia didn't see her catch her breath or her hands fly to her face.

By Friday, with his meetings and portrait sittings successfully concluded, Will asked if they could go somewhere outside of the city for the weekend. When Cia suggested they drive to her house in the Berkshires, he was delighted. The cottage, which had been somewhat rickety in the fall, was now, thanks to Sonny, in far better condition. She had found Cia a contractor who had fixed several rattling windows, loose floorboards, and a broken railing on the front porch. He had even been so kind as to bring her a ream of wood for the fireplace.

They left early Saturday morning, stopping at Sonny's store to pick up some groceries for the weekend. To Cia's surprise, Sonny gave Will the welcoming hug of an old friend, insisting they take along a few of her homemade scones.

That afternoon, in heavy coats with wool scarves wrapped around their necks, they walked hand in hand through snow-encrusted woods.

"Tell me about the portrait you're doing. The one for the investor."

"I told him children aren't really my thing. But he insisted, saying it was a special present for his wife." He grimaced. "I had to go to the apartment while she was at a bridge game to do some sketches. They're eight years old. Try getting kids that age to sit still."

"How will you finish it?"

"While their father kept shouting at them to stop moving, I took about fifty photographs. Once I get them developed in London, I'll hopefully have enough to work with."

"Are you feeling any better about the gallery?"

He nodded. "I went down there with Steve yesterday. The good news is, there's a new restaurant under construction on the corner.

The problem with the gallery, however, is the renovation is going slower than everyone would like."

"I know. Whenever I went down there, I saw only a couple of men working on it."

Will stopped abruptly, unexpectedly pulling her into a deep kiss.

"What was that for?" she whispered.

"I just wanted to thank you."

She looked into his eyes. "In that case, Mr. Jamieson, you are welcome to thank me any time you want." As she nuzzled close to him, something tugged at her hair.

"Don't move, Cia. My ring appears to have got caught," he said, untangling it.

She took his hand. "This looks very old, Will. I keep meaning to ask if it's from your family."

"No."

Taken aback at his terse answer, she stared at him. "Oh. Is there something mysterious? Maybe a story that goes with it?"

He hesitated for a few seconds, as if deciding how to respond. "It was given to me by an old man many years ago." He twisted it on his finger. "It's an ancient Celtic design."

When they returned to the house, he built a fire while Cia poured wine and brought out a sampling of Sonny's cheeses along with a freshly baked baguette. Wrapped in soft, woolen throws and with Will's arm around her, they huddled in front of the fireplace. Although she wanted to ask him more about the ring, she had the distinct impression that he didn't want to say anything further. And yet, that night as she clung to him in deep desire, she could have sworn she saw the stone spark briefly with what looked like blue fire. Later, well into the darkest hours of the morning, she awoke to a scratching sound on the window of the bedroom. She put it down to the wind, or perhaps a stray branch too close to the house.

Sunday morning, as they were preparing to return to the city—Will having to make a flight back to London at nine that night—she suddenly realized that despite the intense romance of the weekend, he hadn't said a word about any future between them. They were about to put their bags in the car when Will unexpectedly pulled her close. "Why are you looking so gloomy, Cia?"

"I thought we would have a chance to talk. You know, about some sort of future."

He sighed. "And yet, my love, what can we know of the future?"

She moved back with a frown. "How philosophical. That's all you have to say?"

He laughed. "Hardly. Philosophy aside, I'd like you to come to London. Sooner than later."

Feeling relief surge through her entire body, she nodded. "There may be another writer's conference coming up. In March or April. I'll ask Sid if I can spend a few extra days."

He kissed her lips. "That's more than two months away. There's no way you can come before?"

"I don't see how. I'm swamped with work, not to mention the Lanny project, and I've just started taking a creative writing class at the New School."

"Creative writing?"

She nodded. "Sort of a refresher. While you're slaving away on your portraits of aristocratic ladies or, for that matter, spoiled Park Avenue children, I intend to be writing here at the cottage on weekends."

He leaned down to kiss her. "A lovely image. Then we'll just have to cope. Let me know about the conference as soon as you can."

She put her head on his shoulder. "You know I will," she whispered.

It was late February when Cia wrote Will, telling him the writer's conference would take place in the first week of April in Lewes, a town in Sussex, about an hour from London. When she didn't hear back by early March, she didn't know what to think. Despite that he was writing fairly regularly, he still remained an enigma, and she was far from secure about their relationship. She couldn't even call him; he had never given her his number. Sid was pressuring her to make airline reservations, and she needed to know if he still wanted her to stay a few days or, in her more insecure moments, at all.

A letter finally arrived the day before she'd promised an increasingly insistent Sid that, Will or no Will, she would go ahead and make her plans. He wrote that he had just returned from a trip a few days before—he didn't mention where—and was surprised he hadn't heard from her. However, after again going through his mail, he had found her letter stuck to a travel brochure on, of all things, Scotland. With his apology, he promised to meet her at the plane, adding that he was looking forward to spending the weekend together after her conference.

The night before she was to leave, she called Sarah to say she was in a rush and ask if she could cover for her the next morning.

When she walked into the office, Sarah asked why she was so frazzled.

"I don't know what's wrong with me. I forgot to stop at the dry cleaner and the drug store yesterday. I haven't packed, and my clothes are strewn everywhere. I can't even see my bed."

Sarah laughed. "I don't recall you having such problems last year." Seeing Cia's face redden, she added, "I have the feeling it won't matter much to Will. He'll be more interested in what you're not wearing."

"Very funny," she said, gathering some papers together on her desk. "I have to go see Sid to make sure everything is in order." Seeing Sarah's wicked grin, she laughed. "Don't say another word."

Chapter 8

Still clutching her passport, Cia glanced around, relieved to see Will waving from behind the raucous crowd waiting inside the International Arrivals terminal. After a warm embrace and several kisses, he stepped back. "For a woman who has traveled all night, you look beautiful."

With a small curtsy, she smiled. "Thank you, kind sir. I hardly slept on the plane."

"Then we should go straightaway to my flat. If you're hungry, I bought some scones. Otherwise, we'll play it by ear, as you Yanks say."

"Play it by ear?" Her look was coy.

He picked up her suitcase. "Nah. I'm going to ravish you in bed."

She laughed and took his arm. "I was hoping for something like that."

That evening he took her to the Dove, a small restaurant off King's Road that was owned by a friend. Taking a candle-lit table in a shadowy corner, Will glanced around. "I think we'll be safe here."

"Safe?"

"If any of my mates come by, they won't look over here. I want you to myself tonight. You'll have a chance to meet some of my friends this weekend. I'll drive you to Lewes tomorrow."

She stroked his long fingers. "Thank you. I don't mind taking the train."

"I insist. It's not far. I'd come to collect you, but I'll be teaching that day. Tell me about the gallery. How does it look?"

"I went down there last week. They wouldn't let me in, but I could see the interior walls had been demolished and the debris cleared away. Even though it's far from finished, the space looks amazing."

He nodded. "That's good, but I hear it's slow going. There's still quite a lot of structural work to be done."

"I don't think anything down there moves quickly, Will. The good news is that more and more artists are moving in and renovating lofts."

"My gallery here is making some other contacts both in New York and Canada. I'll have to see what happens. How about you, Cia? How's the, ah, Lanny book going?"

"Good," she said, noting his slight hesitation. "We're almost finished editing the text, and Sid is hiring a freelance designer."

"Have you had more time to write?"

"I have. Thanks to the writing class I'm taking," she said with some excitement. "In fact, when I turned in a short story a couple of weeks ago, the instructor told me I should probably be teaching the class rather than taking it."

He touched his glass to hers. "Congratulations. What's it about?"

She took a breath. "Well. This may sound a bit strange, but for some unknown reason I found myself writing about a mysterious woman who goes to Stonehenge to discover her past. Actually, I wanted it to be another stone circle, but I'll have to go to the library to research that."

He grinned. "Is she a Druid?"

Cia laughed. "No. I set it in the 1800s when women seldom traveled alone. It's more about the characters she meets and the stories they tell."

"And does she find what she's looking for?"

"Yes and no. She does, however, meet a man she's sure she's known before. Why that is, I have no idea. These thoughts just keep coming to me."

"Will you send it to me? In fact, I'd like you to send me all your stories." He took her hand. "That way I'll feel closer to you."

Before she could respond, the waiter came over. Watching Will order Dover sole with fresh asparagus, which he requested slightly al dente, she sat back, her eyes misty with joy. He seemed so open, so caring, and, most of all, so loving, both in and out of bed. Still, she couldn't shake off a sense of mystery about him — of things unspoken, or perhaps held back. With a sigh, she asked herself how could she not fall in love with this man?

The next morning, when they pulled up to the ivy-covered, half-tim-bered house where the conference was being held, the first person she saw was Stefan: the same Stefan who had asked her to go with him to Will's exhibition the year before. Overcoming his obvious surprise at seeing Cia alight from Will's Mini Cooper, he ran over to give her cheek kisses. After Will retrieved her suitcase from the boot, they shook hands and Stefan offered to carry it inside. Point-ing to a partially opened door, he said, "That's the registration office. I'll meet you inside."

After Will's lingering kiss that left her feeling slightly dizzy, Cia started towards the door where Stefan was waiting. When she looked back, the blue Mini was gone.

Insisting on carrying her suitcase, Stefan walked her to her room in one of the guest houses. Cia was sure it was less that he felt she couldn't manage her luggage than the opportunity to ask about Will.

"We're friends, Stefan. I've seen him when he's come to New York for meetings. When I mentioned there was another writer's conference, he invited me to stay at his flat for a couple of days."

He frowned. "Sounds to me like you're a bit more than merely friends. I must again caution you to be careful. You know his repu-tation."

Cia felt a tightening in the pit of her stomach; that was some-thing she tried to avoid thinking about. "Not to worry, Stefan. I live in New York. We have our own lives."

Still looking doubtful, he nodded as she unlocked the door to a small room smelling faintly of mothballs and cluttered with over-stuffed furniture in slightly frayed pink and baby-blue chintz florals. "You get settled. I'll see you at tea. We can talk more then."

"That would be lovely. As long as we don't talk about Will."

Instead of unpacking, she sat down on the somewhat lumpy bed and rubbed her eyes. After the sleepless night on the plane and then falling into Will's embrace the next morning, she hadn't gotten much sleep. And yet, tired as she was, she couldn't stop thinking about the afternoon before.

It was during a pause in their lovemaking that she again heard the strange murmurs. When Will went to pick up a phone call, she had gotten quietly out of bed, slipped on his shirt, and followed the sounds to the darkened staircase that led to his studio. Determined to discover what they might be and where they were coming from, she put aside a growing sense of trepidation. Hearing him still on the phone, she forced herself to tiptoe up the stairs.

The studio stretched before her, pallid afternoon light from a skylight doing little to dispel the gloom. She stood still for a few seconds, listening. The whispers, definitely stronger now, seemed to be emanating from a deeply shadowed corner behind a work table and two large easels with partially completed canvases. Holding her breath, she took a few cautious steps forward, the floorboards creaking softly beneath her bare feet. Seeing a shadow cross one of the paintings, she stifled a cry, telling herself it was just shifting light, or, more likely, her overactive imagination. Unexpectedly, the light flashed on, startling her. Unable to avoid a small yelp, she turned quickly, relieved to see Will in a loose flannel robe.

"Sorry," she stammered. "I wanted to see your new work."

"You should have put the light on."

She wasn't about to admit she'd been following the sound of voices, voices he refused to acknowledge. "Oh. I didn't see it."

"So. What do you think?"

Facing them was a large painting of two nudes, one a voluptuous young woman with her arm around a younger girl holding a massive bouquet of flowers. Painted in tones of rose, viridian, and pale ocher, their colors and positioning evoked a powerful sensuality. "I think you asked me that same question a year ago. Your work is remarkable. A bit erotic, perhaps, but you can't stop looking."

He followed her to the other easel—the one where she had seen the shadow. On it was a canvas with a sketch of a middle-aged woman, roughed in with light washes of color.

"I started this a few days ago."

"I like it just as it is."

"I agree. But the client, a duchess, wants the whole thing. Lots of paint and the right light to bring out what she perceives to be her beauty."

She turned to him. "You don't think she's beautiful?"

"I don't have to think. I paint what I see, but I try to enhance," he paused, ". . . to create a bit of glow where necessary."

She wondered how much enhancement it took to create that glow.

"Come back downstairs. I have other things to show you."

"I like it here. I never got to see much of your studio last year."

Standing close behind her, he kissed her neck, his hand gently caressing one breast. With a sigh, she moved back against him.

"You can look later," he whispered. "Right now, the artist requires inspiration."

Awaking abruptly from a light doze, Cia wasn't sure where she was. It took a few seconds to grasp that she was no longer in Will's bedroom but lying on a scratchy woolen blanket in a rather musty room in the guesthouse in Lewes. With a glance at her watch, she jumped up, aware she was due downstairs in less than ten minutes. Hoping there would be something more substantial than bland cucumber and watercress sandwiches at tea, she hurried to hang her clothes in the armoire.

The welcoming address was held in the salon of a converted eighteenth-century farmhouse choked with rickety antique furniture and large clocks—none of which, oddly enough, told the same or, for that matter, the correct time. She hoped she hadn't embarrassed herself by gobbling up several smoked salmon sandwiches and a couple of warm, delicious scones that she'd slathered with clotted cream and jam.

When afternoon tea ended and the schedules for the workshops had been handed out, she went for a walk with Stefan. After passing neat, whitewashed houses with tidy front gardens, they stopped at The Feathers, a sagging, half-timbered pub off the High Street. As Stefan reached for the door, a huge black bird flew over them and landed on a nearby tree, cawing loudly. Looking up at its hooded yellow eyes, Cia shook off a sudden sense of foreboding while Stefan simply muttered, "Bloody freakin' birds."

Taking her arm, he steered her inside where the occupants, mostly older men on their way home from work, turned to glance at them over their pints. With a nervous smile, Cia headed to a table in a corner. After Stefan brought a couple of lagers, they touched glasses. This time it was she who brought up Will, asking what more he could tell her about him.

He shrugged. "I don't know much. Only rumors, really, of peculiar happenings surrounding his life. Years ago, when he was in his twenties, there was something about an engagement. But the girl died unexpectedly and, it was rumored, under mysterious circumstances."

Cia sat back. "How strange. He mentioned he was engaged once, but nothing more." *At least I don't think so, since I can barely remember any of our conversations.*

"After she died, he locked himself in his flat and refused to see or talk to anyone. Apparently, it went on for several months. Then suddenly, almost overnight, everything changed. He began exhibiting again and receiving commissions for portraits. His next show received incredible notices, and his gallery was clamoring for more paintings. I'm sure you know he never married."

"Yes," she said, recalling their conversation in New York when Will had mentioned there were "things" he had to deal with. Somehow, he was becoming more of an enigma, one she wanted to know more about.

"I don't want to say anything bad about him, Cia. Nevertheless, you should be aware there were questions asked, albeit quietly, that have never been answered."

"What sort of questions?"

As he opened his mouth to speak, he blinked, suddenly looking puzzled. "Bloody hell. Sorry. I don't know what happened. I forgot what I was going to say."

"It was about questions that have been asked."

He looked confused. "Why is it I can't remember? It seems completely gone."

She stared back at him, barely breathing. *Not him too.* "No matter, Stefan. We have two more days. Maybe you'll recall some of it."

He looked back at her with concern. "Please be careful about becoming too involved with him. As I told you a year ago, he has a reputation for being quite seductive."

She nodded. "I understand, Stefan." *At least I think I do.*

For Cia, those next two days were taken up less with seminars on characterization and plot development and, more often than not, with questions of her own. There were moments her mind wandered so completely that on the last night she had to copy several pages of Stefan's notes.

When she arrived at Will's flat, she rang the bell. Receiving no response, she used the key he had given her. Although his street wasn't particularly heavily traveled, when she closed the door to the darkened entry, she heard not a sound, nothing but complete silence. Dropping her bag, she tossed her coat over a high-backed chair in what he called the parlor—seldom used, from the look of it. She went to the kitchen, still aware of an absence of sound, not even the expected whispers, or whatever they were.

Searching through the cupboard, she took out a tin of Will's favorite Earl Grey along with a couple of colorful pottery cups, and lit a burner on the stove. While waiting for the water to boil, she glanced out the window where a couple of birch trees swayed in a gentle breeze. Out of nowhere, two huge back birds suddenly alighted on one of the branches, their yellow eyes focused directly on her. Shaking off a stab of fear, she tapped the glass, experiencing a sense of satisfaction, even control, when they ruffled their glossy feathers and flew off. More confident, she walked to the staircase and looked up into the darkness, asking herself if she should chance going to the studio or wait for Will. Before she could make up her mind, the silence was broken by soft sighs as a cold draft eddied around her. With a shiver of apprehension, she decided it might be best to wait until Will got home.

As she turned away from the stairs, she forced herself to stop. "Screw this," she said out loud. Hearing a piercing whistle, she jumped. Realizing it was the kettle, she ran to turn off the stove. After pouring the water into a pot to steep, she once again approached the staircase. Summoning all her courage, she raced up the stairs and flipped on the light. The studio flashed into brightness, startling her. Telling herself she was being silly, she began to walk around, all too aware of the groaning floorboards and her skin prickling in a shimmer of cool air. As before, the whispers sounded much closer up here. In an attempt to calm her jangling nerves, she stopped to glance at the portrait Will had started a few days before. Seeing a flicker of light, as though the partially finished eyes were staring down at her, she quickly backed away.

Stop it, she told herself. *It's just wet paint.* Shoring up her resolve, she took a tentative step in the direction of a heavily shadowed corner. Hearing a loud, unexpected noise, she caught her breath while her heart began beating a sudden staccato. Realizing it was coming not from the darkened corner, but from below, she ran to the stairs, relieved to see Will smiling up at her.

"I hope you don't mind that I went up to your studio," she said, trying to steady her voice while walking down to greet him. By the time she reached the bottom step, she became aware that by his very presence, the usual street sounds had returned, drowning out the sighs.

"Not at all, Cia. I'm glad I gave you the key. What were you doing up there?"

She shrugged. "Just looking at some of your paintings."

"Are you all right? You're shivering."

"It was cool. Drafty, actually."

"That's strange. I never leave the windows open. Maybe I should go up and look."

I don't think it was from any window. "I'm sure it's fine."

"How was the conference?" he asked, taking off his jacket.

"It was good. I'll tell you about it later. By the way, I made tea."

"Lovely," he said, drawing her into his arms.

"If you continue doing that," she murmured, "we'll miss tea."

"Tea can wait. I don't think I can."

That night he took her to meet a few of his friends, this time at Finch's, another of his "mates" hangouts. After the first couple of artists and writers showed up, several more, including two producers from the BBC, dropped by for a pint or two until there were ten of them squeezed around a table that comfortably held six.

This time she sat next to Patrick, the only one of Will's friends she actually remembered from the year before. The night was filled with discussions and gossip, mostly about the art scene and media. Hugh, one of the producers, asked what she thought about President Nixon and the Watergate scandal.

She shook her head. "I think he'll be impeached, or will at least resign. There appears to be little doubt that he knew about it."

"Then what was the point? He was going to win the election anyway."

"That's true. Who knows why politicians do what they do? With all his big talk he turned out to be just another crook. Anyway, aren't the words 'politician' and 'crook' synonymous?" After everyone laughed and offered a toast to crooked politicians, the conversation turned to the inevitable raucous jokes and off-color stories about artists, actors, and TV producers, both current and past. Before he left, Patrick asked Cia how long she would be staying in London. When she told him two more days, he offered to take her to the National Gallery the next afternoon while Will had a sitting for a portrait. Since Will hadn't mentioned it, she was a bit taken aback. That was before reminding herself they had spent most of the afternoon in bed and had to rush to meet his friends at the pub.

"Did Will tell you he's having a show at my gallery in Yorkshire in September?"

"No, Patrick. We haven't had much time to talk."

He glanced at Will, now in an animated conversation with the BBC guys. With a knowing smile, he said, "I'm sure he'll want you to come."

"I would love that." The very thought of going on a trip with Will made her heart beat a little faster.

The next days passed in a blur. She went to the National Gallery with Patrick and to an opening at the Tate with Will, standing proudly at his side as he introduced her to many more people than she could possibly remember. She didn't miss the glances of women, both young and not-so-young, who blatantly appraised her and walked away whispering. She merely smiled, trying to stem her jealousy that it would be they, and not she, who would be in London for the next gallery opening.

Chapter 9

By the time the plane landed at JFK, Cia was exhausted. Like the flight to London, all attempts at sleep had failed. She had spent what felt like interminable hours looking down at an endless slate-colored ocean or glancing nervously at the wings, all the while replaying her days, and especially her nights, with Will. Lying in his arms, she had wished those nights would never end. And yet, despite her wishes, the next morning inevitably dawned, and with it the mystifying sighs.

Although Will had promised to write and even call more often now that direct dialing had become possible, he'd added that he didn't know when he'd be coming to New York again. She'd been disappointed when he said nothing about the show Patrick had mentioned, but then rationalized it was still five months away.

Picking up her suitcase, she sighed and glanced around for the taxi stand.

"Welcome back," Sarah said with a grin.

Cia took one look at the stacks of papers and manuscripts piled on her desk and frowned. "Thank you. What on earth is all this? I've been gone barely a week."

"What can I say? You're a popular girl."

"Very funny."

"It's just a couple of manuscripts along with my edits on the Lanny text. Oh. And a folder with background on a new author we signed while you were attending your conference and having other, ah, activities that shall remain nameless."

Cia sat down with a sigh and rubbed her eyes. "I'm so tired. I was fine earlier this morning. Now I need a nap."

Sarah lit a cigarette. "So much for the jetsetter. So, tell me. How was Will?"

Cia reached in her purse and tossed her a pack of Rothmans. "Since you insist on smoking, try these. Will smokes them."

"Aha. Then they must be good. You still haven't answered my question."

"Will," she sighed. "I adore him, but I have to be realistic. When I'm with him, it's like I'm in another world. And yet, even though we've talked a bit, I'm still finding it difficult to imagine a future together. How can there be when we only see one another every few months? Maybe the best I can do is enjoy our times together."

"Are you still hearing strange voices, or whatever, in his flat?"

She nodded. "I tried to find out where they were coming from. I have no idea what they could be."

"And here I thought it was your house that's supposed to be haunted. By the way, Ian called."

"Yes, I know. He called last night to tell me he's unhappy and wants another chance."

"After what he put you through? Would you ever trust him again?"

"No. I don't think I could."

"Nor, in truth, should you. How about Will? Do you trust him?"

"Actually, I do. I have no reason not to. Since he's in London and I'm here, it's not the usual dating scenario. I neither expect him to call every day nor wonder where he is or what he's doing when he's not with me." *Most of the time, anyway.*

"Then maybe you should date more."

"Who? Do you have someone in mind, because I don't."

Sarah shrugged. "Mike has a friend he wants you to meet. And that guy Doug from the ad agency keeps calling."

"I don't know. Right now, I'm too tired to think."

"I'll bet you're thinking of Will."

She took a breath. "It's impossible not to."

By the time Cia arrived home that night, all she wanted was to crawl into bed. Instead she wrote Will, thanking him for the weekend as well as the opportunity to meet his friends, particularly Patrick, and for showing her a bit of the London art scene. With only a brief hesitation she signed it, *with much love, Cia. P.S. I already miss you. Come to New York soon.*

The phone rang and she picked it up, not surprised to hear Ian's voice — the seductive version — saying once again that he wanted to see her.

"Look, Ian. You should be dating other women. Not me."

"Why not?" he sounded petulant. "I want you in my life again."

"You have no idea of what my life is like right now."

An edge of irritation began to creep into his voice. "What's that supposed to mean? Is this about the guy from England? He's three thousand miles away. I'm here."

"So what?"

"Are you in love with him?"

She took a breath. "I don't know."

"That sounds like a yes. You just met him."

"Actually, it's been almost a year. And, as I recall, you and I fell in love a lot faster than that. At least I did. I'm no longer sure about you."

"That was a low shot."

"I can't do this, Ian. It's time for you to accept that there's some-one else in my life."

With seduction spinning to outrage, he shouted, "Screw that. Don't come crawling to me when your Brit disappears." She jumped as he slammed down the phone.

Disappears? She stared at the receiver before slowly putting it down. Was Will the sort of man who would just vanish from her life? She hadn't been sure a year ago, but as their relationship had not only continued but deepened, she had been happy to have been proven wrong. She thought back to an evening in London when they had stopped for a drink at a pub. He had been telling her, in his humorous fashion, about how he had badgered a small gallery owner into giving him his first show. He admitted that he'd been relentless, bringing in paintings and drawings almost every day until the man finally gave in. Since he seldom discussed the past, she'd asked, although not without some trepidation, about the girl he had been engaged to. After Stefan had mentioned it, she'd become curi-ous, but wasn't sure she should be the one to bring it up.

He had moved slightly away, as though separating himself from her, a move that may have been more instinctive than purposeful. "That's something I try not to think about, much less discuss."

"That's all right, Will. If you'd rather not, I understand."

He downed his scotch and, with a sigh, began to speak softly. "It was the late fifties, a far more morally restrictive time than now. We were not only young but naïve, although I didn't think so then. I was in love for the first time, as was she. Both of us had been brought up with certain cultural beliefs and marriage was the inevitable, the right thing to do."

She nodded. "No such thing as 'free love' in those days."

"No, Cia. Although it was only a few years before the so-called 'sexual revolution' of the mid-sixties. I used to wonder if things would have been different if we had met later." He shook his head. "We had just got engaged when she took sick and died suddenly."

"I'm so sorry. I shouldn't have asked."

"It's all right. Maybe at this point it's best that you know."

"Oh, Will," she said, experiencing a surge of emotion.

"Say no more, my love," he whispered.

Chapter 10

It was a few weeks later as they were leaving a meeting in the conference room that Sarah asked if Cia had heard from Will.

"Yes, Sarah. I told you I've received several letters since I got back, mostly about him being preoccupied with work." What she didn't mention was that it had been more than two weeks since she'd last heard from him, and there had been too many nights when she had lived through an entire range of emotions, from missing him to deep anxiety. Despite knowing that he cared for her, London was still far away, and it was entirely possible that he might have found other, more convenient companionship. Recalling the seductive looks from some of the women at the Tate exhibit, she was sure he didn't lack for opportunity.

"Still, you shouldn't be waiting for him."

"I don't know, Sarah. I want to give it more time. I know it seems silly, but somehow I feel we need to be together."

"That's an odd statement, particularly for you. Why would you 'need,' as you say, to be together?"

"I can't really define it," she said, dropping a stack of folders on her desk. "There are times I feel like we've known each other before. But before what?" She took a breath. "There are small gestures that seem insignificant, and yet are more than that; a touch, for example, that feels oddly familiar. And sometimes he'll caress my lips before he kisses me. It's things that feel affectionate, even erotic; things that are at once new, and yet not." She shrugged. "I know it sounds crazy."

"Wow. Have you ever mentioned it to him?"

"I've tried. He always says we'll talk about it later. Somehow, though, we never do."

With a grimace, Sarah slouched down in her chair. "Why do men always have to be so difficult?"

"Uh oh. That sounds ominous. An argument with Mike?"

"Not really an argument. Just a difference of opinion. He wants what he wants, and I want something else."

"What does he want that you don't?"

"A chick named Melissa."

Cia put her hands to her face so Sarah wouldn't see her laugh. "And?"

"Well. I guess I can't really blame him. I ran into them when I was out Friday night."

"You were out? Alone?"

"Um. Not quite. You know Lou? That new author we signed?"

"You didn't. And you forgot to tell me?"

"It was kind of last minute."

Cia rolled her eyes. "Last minute?"

"Yes. The minute after my cousin Kitty called to tell me she saw Mike getting out of a taxi with a, um, younger woman. Anyway, it was just dinner, Cia. I wasn't in the mood to be alone." With a sigh, she grinned. "Lou is kind of cute, though."

"Come on, Sarah. Mike is allowed to be in a cab with someone else. Maybe he works with her."

"In front of the Hilton at two in the afternoon?"

"Ouch. Now what?"

"He called Saturday saying we had to talk. He insisted whatever Kitty had seen wasn't what I thought it was and he wasn't dating, much less screwing, her. I told him yes, he was, and no, there was nothing to talk about."

"Really?"

She grinned. "Absolutely. He called three times Sunday and again this morning. Let him stew for a while." She looked up, seeing Coralie in the doorway, a worried look on her face.

"I just picked up a call for Cia. It's that man from London."

Cia looked up in surprise. "London? Are you sure?"

"Yes. Please don't forget what I told you."

Sarah jumped up. "Time for coffee," she said, herding Coralie out of the office and closing the door.

Trying to calm her rapidly beating heat, Cia picked up the phone. "Will?'

"Hello, Cia. I apologize for not calling sooner. I had to make a quick trip to Spain and communications were difficult."

Too difficult to send a card? Realizing that was something her mother would have said, she shook the thought away. "I didn't know you were away."

"The trip wasn't planned. Look. I have good news. At least I hope you'll think so. I have to be in Toronto the second week of June. It's only for a few days. Would you like to join me for the weekend?"

"I would love to," she said, trying not to sound too surprised.

"Good. Can you come Friday? That way we'll have the entire weekend."

"I'm sure I can," she said, feeling anxiety slip away as tears of relief misted her eyes.

"I'm booked at the Victoria. I may have one last meeting that morning with a gallery. If you arrive before I get back, they'll have your name." She heard him hesitate. "I'm looking forward to holding you in my arms again."

Chapter 11

Aliveried doorman helped Cia out of the taxi. "Check in is straight ahead, miss. Shall I have your bag sent up?"

"No, thank you. It's not heavy," she said, scanning the lobby. Not seeing Will, she began to walk to the reception desk, a bit apprehensive about giving his name. Unexpectedly, a deep voice behind her exclaimed, "Hey, lady!" Startled, she turned directly into Will's waiting arms. In the middle of a prolonged kiss, another voice suddenly boomed. "Unhand her, sir. Or get thee to a room."

Looking up in shock, she saw a tall dark-haired man with a massive walrus mustache that didn't quite conceal a broad smile. Will laughed. "Cia. Meet Russ McCoy. An old friend from Scotland. We went to school together."

"Welcome to Toronto. I've heard quite a lot about you these last two days."

She blushed. "I'm afraid to ask what."

"Maybe I'll tell you tomorrow. You and Will are joining me for lunch at my ranch."

"Ranch?"

He nodded. "Cows, sheep. Horses too. We can go for a ride."

She cast a worried glance at Will. "Horses?"

Will laughed. "Look, Russ, we'll play it by ear. What time should we get there?"

"It's about an hour from here. Leave about eleven. You have the directions." After thumping one another on the back, Russ nodded at Cia. "Till tomorrow, then."

Looking worried, Cia turned to Will. "Are you serious? I haven't been on a horse in years."

"No matter. If nothing else, you'll enjoy the countryside."

"Now I know why you told me to bring jeans." She reached in her bag and took out an envelope. "Before I forget, I brought some pictures from the gallery."

"Thanks," he said, taking out a few. "Still looks pretty rough, doesn't it?"

"It does. There seems to be far more work than Steve anticipated. Not only the structure, but plumbing and stuff like that."

"I understand. We can talk about that later." He took her arm. "Right now, I suggest lunch or . . . ?"

Her smile was seductive.". . . or drop my bag upstairs first?"

He grinned. "I'll get the key."

She had barely put her purse down before he had her in his arms. The months apart dissolved as they peeled off one another's clothing and fell on the bed. As they lay facing one other, his kisses intensified her desire while his hands electrified every nerve.

Breathing in his scent, she began to kiss her way down his body until he gasped and moved her on top of him. Pulling her face down to his, he whispered, "I haven't stopped thinking about you since you left London." Before she could tell him the same, a powerful sensation swept away her words.

Later, as she lay in his arms, she murmured, "I only wish we didn't live so far apart."

He ran a finger gently over her lips, eliciting a shiver of desire. "Perhaps we can arrange for you to return to London in the near future."

She opened her eyes. "Really? How?"

"We'll talk later. At the moment, the artist is preoccupied with other things."

When they picked up the rental car the next morning, Cia offered to drive. Giving her a dubious look, Will asked, "Why? You don't think I can manage to drive on the wrong side of the road?"

She laughed. "No, Will. The wrong side is in England."

Although still nervous, she finally relaxed when Will appeared to have little trouble navigating the light Saturday morning traffic. Leaving the city behind, they drove through dense forests that gave way to shimmering lakes and recently planted farmland, arriving to find Russ waiting in front of a rambling stone farmhouse. Beyond the front yard, Cia saw stables and a large corral. "You were right, Will. It's beautiful here."

Russ looked at her and then at Will. "What is it about you two? You give off an amazing vibe. Sorry. I don't know how to say it any better."

Will squeezed Cia's hand. "I think what you said was correct."

He gave Will a friendly punch on the shoulder. "Somehow I never thought I'd say that about you, Jamieson." He looked at Cia as if about to say something more, but stopped. "Come on over to the porch. Lunch is ready."

After a lunch of freshly caught trout and early summer vegetables, Russ walked them over to the stable. He had brought a bunch of carrots and handed a few to Cia to feed the horses.

"They're lovely," she said, patting the soft muzzle of a brown quarter horse.

Russ grinned. "Ready to go for a ride?"

Looking uncertain, Cia glanced at Will. "I guess. I mean, if you want . . ."

"Why not? I'm game if you are."

A stable hand brought out three horses, all with western saddles. As Russ hoisted Cia into the saddle, she asked why he didn't ride English.

"We like to go for long rides here," he said, mounting a large black stallion. "Western is more our style."

As Will rode up next to her, she giggled. "The famous painter on horseback. Wish I had a camera."

"I'll bet Will never told you we used to ride in Scotland."

Will laughed. "Remember those hairy ponies? We raced them all over the moors."

"So we did. Will liked to annoy the golfers by crossing over the golf course in Inverness. They hated us there."

Cia looked at Will in surprise as Russ guffawed and trotted on ahead. Riding out beyond the fences, they followed a trail through open fields with grazing cattle on one side and woods on the other. The only sound other than the soft thump of the horse's hooves was birdsong and the buzzing of insects. After a short distance, Russ reined in. "I have to get back. If you follow this trail, it'll bring you to a stream and a great view of the valley beyond." He winked. "There's no hurry. The horses know the way back if you get lost."

Will smiled, obviously enjoying himself. "Thanks, Russ. See you in a bit." As Russ turned back, he came up alongside Cia. "Are you all right?"

"Are you kidding? This is fabulous."

"Then I'll race you to those birch trees over the next hill," he said, spurring his horse into a gallop.

With a laugh, she chased him, catching up just as they reached the trees. He pulled up as she came along side. "I win. Do I get a prize?"

She fluttered her eyelashes. "What, sir, do you have in mind?"

"I'm afraid I'll have to get you off that horse first."

"Look," she said, pointing beyond the trees. Up ahead was the stream Russ had mentioned and, beyond, a broad green valley stretched for miles with not a fence or a soul to be seen. Riding into a well-shaded grove of trees, they dismounted, and Will tied the horses where they could graze on the long grass. He walked to the stream and looked out at the view. Cia came up behind him and put her hand on his back. "It's beautiful here, isn't it?"

He took her in his arms. "As are you. I'm happy you're here with me."

"So am I," she whispered.

"Wait. I'll be right back." She watched as he went back to his horse and untied a blanket from the back of his saddle. After spreading it on the ground under a large overhanging branch, he sat down, took off his boots and patted the space next to him. "Come to me, my love."

She glanced at the stream and then at Will. "Not yet," she whispered, slowly beginning to take off her clothes. As she dropped each piece in front of him, he stared back silently, as though waiting to see what she was going to do. Tossing him her lace-trimmed panties, she laughed and ran down to the stream where, with a yelp, she splashed icy water over herself.

Will stared, mesmerized as she made her way back up the grassy bank. With her body glistening like jewels in the warm sun, she knelt silently before him and leaned in for a kiss. When he reached out to hold her, a shadow flickered between them and a queasy dizziness began to cloud his vision. Through a hazy mist, the face he saw wasn't Cia's; instead he was looking into the dark, deep-set eyes of a young girl, perhaps fifteen or sixteen with pale white skin and wild windswept hair. As Cia's lips met his, the image dissolved, leaving in its wake a surge of intense desire. Unable to contain himself, he pulled her down on his lap.

Surprised at his sudden passionate embrace, Cia gasped and threw her head back in a paroxysm of ecstasy. As they rolled over, she heard a scream, and opening her eyes realized it was her. Cleaving to one another in fathomless desire they made love until a breeze began to stir the leaves on the branches above them. Lying in his arms with her eyes closed, she tried to catch her breath. "What just happened?" she murmured.

"I have no idea," he rasped, not about to admit to a powerful flash of déjà vu of either a moment long forgotten—which he considered unlikely—or, more worrisome, a memory out of time and place. Putting aside his confusion, he leaned over to kiss her lips. "Whatever it was, I'd like to know what caused you to suddenly go from city girl to shameless wood nymph?"

"It must be you," she said, sitting up. "I had the strangest sensation, almost a hallucination, that the trees around us had become white columns, and we were making love not in the afternoon, but at night, under a huge orange moon. Wherever did that come from?"

"That's why they call it *petite mort*: little death. When we are able to lose ourselves to another we become part of the entire universe."

With a sigh, she looked up through the branches to a cloudless sky. "I wish we could stay here forever."

"A lovely thought. Unfortunately, I think we should start back. Russ will be sending out a search party soon."

She stood up and stretched, the sunlight casting dappled shadows over her sleek body. Will stared. "You are so beautiful, Cia. Were I never to see you again, I would always remember this moment."

She laughed. "Remember me naked?"

"Why not? You look like a goddess. I'd like to paint you just like that." Putting his hands to her face, he drew her into another deep kiss.

By the time they returned, Russ was pacing around the corral. "That must have been some ride," he said, looking at Will with a less than subtle grin. "Funny. The horses don't look very tired. You two, however, appear very, uh, blissful."

Cia blushed scarlet, and Will, speechless for once, could only nod.

Russ shook his head. "Something about horses, I guess. What are you doing tonight? Want to stay?"

"Thanks, Russ. There's a jazz club I'd like to try tonight. I think it's called the Blue Underground."

"I've heard of it. Why don't you stay for an early dinner? I'll bet it doesn't even get started before eleven."

Will glanced at Cia who, her face still pink, smiled and thanked him.

The doorman was about to tell Will they could walk to the jazz club but, seeing Cia in heels, suggested a taxi. She shook her head. "I live in these things. I'll be fine."

They found it on a side street so dimly lit they could barely make out the name. Two young men with instrument cases were lounging about outside smoking something other than regular cigarettes. They stopped talking as Will approached.

"Is this the Blue Underground?"

"Yeah, man. If you're into jazz, you've come to the right place. There's a couple of cool old dudes tonight. We'll be sitting in later."

Will held the door for Cia. "Thanks. Looking forward to it."

The stairs down were poorly lit and steep, and in her heels Cia took them carefully. They entered a room where blue spotlights were barely visible through a thick haze of smoke. Taking Cia's hand, Will wove his way to a tiny table not far from the stage, essentially little more than a raised platform. A waiter in a black T-shirt and jeans came over saying the first set had just ended and asked what they wanted to drink. Will looked at Cia and ordered two Labatts.

About ten minutes later four musicians began to move to the stage, the piano player running chords while the sax player added in a few staccato bleeps. A black man in dark glasses tapped his drums as the bassist began tuning up. Without the slightest glance at one another they launched into a lively rendition of Dave Brubeck's "Take Five," which segued into "Green Dolphin Street," followed by the soft sounds of "Autumn Leaves." As the session continued, Will pointed out an older, heavyset black man playing a bass guitar who seemed to have magically appeared next to the drummer.

"That's odd," Cia whispered. "I didn't notice him before. Where did he come from?"

Will shook his head while continuing to stare at the man who, with eyes half-closed, appeared totally immersed in his music. He couldn't recall if he'd ever seen him perform before, and yet there was something about him that seemed deeply familiar. At the end of the set, Will caught his eye and he peered back with a slight nod. After a couple of rounds of enthusiastic applause, he left the stage along with the other musicians. A few minutes later, he appeared at their table. Startled, Will stood up, asking if he would join them for a drink. He smiled, saying in a gravelly voice that he was sorry to decline but would be glad to sit for a few. Hearing his accent, Will asked where he was from.

"London. By way of New Orleans, where I learned my craft. I grew up with the gospel and the blues." He took a breath and let it out slowly. "That was a long, long time ago."

Cia smiled. "I don't think you're all that old. By the way, I'm Cia and he's Will."

"They call me Brother Luke."

When Will reached out to shake his hand, he put his hands up along with a slight shake of his head. Will nodded, unaware that Cia was staring at Brother Luke's right hand. Before she could say anything, he asked if either of them had any favorite tunes, other than those that had been played so far.

Will shrugged. "I think you covered most of mine, although I always like Coltrane's 'Naima.'"

"One of my favorites. Maybe later. Though a few young upstarts will be sitting in. Then they'll be jammin'."

"Where have you played in London? I'm trying to think where I may have seen you before."

He shook his head. "I'm afraid it was well before your time, young man." Getting rather heavily to his feet, he said, "Nice meeting you. Take care of your lady, Will. I believe you'll discover she's quite special."

As Will started to get up, Brother Luke put his hand up. "No need."

Watching him limp away, Will looked doubtful. "Before my time? What an odd thing to say."

Cia put her hand on his arm. "Maybe he was just confused. I thought he was sweet. Did you notice his ring?"

"What?"

"His ring. It looked similar to yours. I just wondered if you saw it. You said yours was very old and I was surprised to see another like it."

"Are you sure it looked like mine?"

"Maybe not exactly like yours, but similar. It's not something one sees every day."

"Was there a stone in it?"

"Yes. Dark blue. That's why I asked."

He got up quickly. "Would you like another beer?"

"Sure. Where are you going? They're about to start the next set."

"I'll be right back." After signaling the waiter for two more beers, he moved in the direction of back stage where a large black man with dreadlocks stopped him.

"I was just talking with Brother Luke. I'd like to ask him a question."

The man looked perplexed. "Brother Luke? You sure?"

"Yes. Why?"

"You ain't seen Brother Luke, my man. He's been gone for some twenty years."

"Gone?"

"As in dead."

Will stared at him, trying to make sense of something that made no sense at all. "What instrument did he play?"

"He was a master on the bass guitar. It was the cancer that got him. Too bad, he was good people. Whoever you saw, it wasn't Brother Luke."

Backing away, Will tried to process what he had said. Between his vision earlier that afternoon and now Brother Luke, nothing this strange had happened in years. He shook his head. *Not quite. What about the girl in Soho?* With an anxious glance at Cia across the room, he asked himself, *Why now?*

When he returned to the table, she looked baffled. "Funny. I thought Brother Luke would be playing this set. I don't see him."

Rather than tell her she was unlikely to ever see him again, he shrugged. "He did look tired. Maybe he went home."

Sunday morning, when they went downstairs for breakfast, Will could see Cia was upset. "What is it, my love?"

"I feel like we're always saying goodbye. We barely have time to talk."

With a grin, he nodded. "That's because I always want to hold you in my arms. What if I were to ask you to come to London in September?"

She silently thanked her stars, fates, and whatever gods she could think of. "September?" she managed to say without giving away that she already knew about his exhibit.

"Patrick is having a gallery show in Yorkshire. The opening is planned for the last Saturday in September, although it could change a week or two either way. I'd like you to be there with me." When she hesitated, he said, "It would be best if you arrive the day before."

"You want me to come for a weekend?"

"I'd prefer you to stay with me the week following. That is, if you want to. We'll have plenty of time for talking and whatever then."

Is he kidding? "You're asking me to stay ten days?"

"Apparently, I am."

Feeling butterflies taking off in her stomach, she said, "I'll have to check with Sid. But I'm sure it won't be a problem."

"I'll call you when I get back to London to give you the final dates."

When she leaned over to kiss him, he stroked her cheek. "So you see, my love, it won't be so terribly long until I have you in my grasp again."

Chapter 12

Cia returned home in a state of euphoria, something Sarah picked up on as soon as she entered the office. "Tell me all about the weekend. You must leave out nothing."

Cia squinted back at her. "Are you kidding?"

"Well. Not that. Unless, of course, that's all you did."

"Very funny. Actually, we visited an old friend of Will's and went horseback riding."

Sarah's eyes went wide. "You? On a horse?"

Cia giggled. "Not the entire time."

"Aha. Still. On the ground?"

"He, ah, had a blanket."

Sarah rolled her eyes. "The man was prepared." With a sigh, she shook her head. "Certainly more prepared than we were last Friday. You missed a crazy meeting with Lanny's agent and the book designer."

"What happened? I thought the art director Sid chose was one of the hottest in the city."

"So we were told. But he seems to have, um, gone cold on this one. Chad said he hated the way the first layouts looked and asked for some other concepts. When the art director refused, with just a bit of arrogance, Sid invited him to his office and fired him."

Cia shook her head. "That's not good, Sarah. We need a promotion piece finished this week to be ready for a book fair, not to mention the book has to be printed and out before the holidays."

"That's why, after everyone finished arguing and pointing fingers, I called my friend Roz. She's a freelance designer. I think you met her at last year's Christmas party. Anyway, I introduced her to Sid, who was practically in shock that I brought in a female art director." Before Cia could interrupt, she went on, "That's when I reminded him that it's the '70s and about Women's Lib, and then I told him he was dinosaur. I doubt he thought it was funny, but since Roz was already here, he gave her some galleys and a few photos and explained what we, Chad, and Lanny wanted."

Cia smirked. "A dinosaur? You didn't."

With a broad grin, she said, "I did. That was just before he told me he was calling another big art director at Time-Life to see if he wanted the job."

"Now what?"

Sarah glanced at her watch. "Roz will be here at eleven, and the other art director is sending his pages over by messenger."

"You're making me feel guilty. That I shouldn't have gone away."

"It wouldn't have mattered. You would have been just as frustrated as the rest of us. Now tell me, how was the rest of the weekend?"

"It was really good, Sarah. Except for one strange thing."

Sarah let out an exaggerated sigh. "Why do I think 'strange' and Will somehow go together?"

"Very funny. We went to a jazz club Saturday night, and one of the musicians came over to our table. He was an older man, a little peculiar, but what was interesting is that he was wearing a ring similar to Will's. When I mentioned it, though, Will sounded surprised. I think he went looking for him."

"Did he say anything?"

"No. After that he sort of brushed it off."

"So it was probably nothing. This is becoming serious, isn't it?"

She sighed. "I only wish. But he did, at last, ask me to come to England for his show in September. He wants me to stay ten days."

"Now you can stop fretting."

"I don't fret."

"Oh, yes, you certainly do. At least when it comes to Will. Just watch out for Coralie. She's worried about you."

"Honestly, I still don't get it. What's the big deal?"

"I suggest you ask her."

She hesitated, then shook her head. "I don't think so. How's everything with Mike?"

Sarah stared at her for a moment, aware she was changing the subject. "So far so good. We went to see *Godspell* Saturday night. He seemed very taken by it."

"In what way?"

She laughed. "He said he wanted to go to church on Sunday."

"And did he?"

"No," she sniggered. "By Sunday morning he wasn't feeling quite so pious. Are you going to the cottage this weekend?"

"I hadn't thought about it. Maybe. Now that the writing course is over, I'd like to get back to work on that story about Stonehenge. I don't know why, but all sorts of strange ideas seem to be popping into my mind."

Sarah smirked. "Must be the company you're keeping."

"Very funny."

"You were terrific at that last class."

"You really think so? I was really glad you came."

"I always wanted to meet Burke. His writing is so descriptive. Teaching is one thing, but having you explain about publishing was brilliant. All those aspiring writers with no concept of the process, much less the difficulties of getting published. If nothing else, you made it real."

"Thanks. After that class he called to ask me out."

She looked surprised. "And you're just telling me now?"

"I was leaving to see Will. I forgot."

"What did you say?"

"That I was leaving for a trip and I'd call when I got back."

"Well, you're back. He's not only a great writer, he's attractive. Call him."

"I'm not sure. Not after Will asked me to come to London in the fall."

"Come on, Cia. That's still a few months away. Will is in London doing his paintings and whatever. Burke is here, now."

"To be honest, it's the 'whatever' that still worries me. You're right, though. I'll think about it."

"That's my girl," she said as the phone rang. Picking it up, she glanced at Cia. "Roz is here. Sid wants us to meet him in the conference room."

A week later, Cia went to talk with Sid. Asking for time off hadn't been a problem; she'd had two weeks of vacation coming and she had given him plenty of warning. As she got up to leave, he appeared to hesitate.

"Is there something else, Sid?"

Leaning forward on his desk, he nodded. "Stay a minute, Cia. Please don't take offense for what I am about to say, but I sometimes tend to think of you as one of my daughters. Over the last few years I've watched you grow from a diffident, insecure secretary to a confident editor. I know you went through hell with your divorce, but you seemed to have emerged a far stronger woman. And yet, this relationship with your British friend concerns me."

When she looked surprised, Sid put up his hand. "Someone, I won't say who, saw you being rather, ah, affectionate with a man in your office. She, um, considered it unlikely that it would be one of our authors. You should know by now that offices are like beehives, always buzzing."

Feeling her face burning, she wanted to ask how he knew so much. *Had to be Sarah or Coralie.* "Not to worry, Sid. I'm not about to run off to England."

"It's not so much that. If you and your friend decide that's what you both want, I'll be happy to give you my blessing. What worries me is that you seem to be waiting for something that somehow seems intangible. You have a great future here, Cia. You're doing an excellent job on the Lanny book, and everyone feels very positive about Roz."

"You have to give Sarah credit for her," Cia said.

"And I have." He shook his head. "I would never have considered a woman designer, but her layouts were terrific."

Cia held back a snappy question as to why a woman book designer would be any different than a man. There were as many female editors at BookEnds as men, so why not a female art director? If nothing else, she was gratified that Sid, along with Lanny and Chad, had chosen her. Although not a feminist, she considered having Roz on board a small but significant victory.

"I want you to know that our reviews are coming up in the fall. There may be more than a raise in your future. So please, think about that."

She was suddenly breathless. "Thank you, Sid. I appreciate your being so forthright."

"Will you grant an old man a favor?"

She laughed, breaking the tension. "Some old man."

"Go to London. Take time to assess your feelings. Talk with your, ah, friend about what he wants from this relationship. I know we men tend to shy away from such discussions, but if nothing, shall we say, dramatic happens, please promise you'll rethink this. As Picasso famously said, 'There are only two types of women, goddesses and doormats.' You, Cia, are the goddess here."

"I'm flattered you think so," she said with a slight blush. "Thank you. You've given me something to think about."

"I have one thing more to ask of you. When you're in London I'd like you to see my friend Owen Phillips, the owner of Arlington-York Press. See if you can find out what books are on their roster and if there might be any opportunities for co-publishing."

"No problem, Sid. We can revisit this before I leave."

Chapter 13

Will barely slept on the flight back to London. Each time he closed his eyes, the image of Brother Luke floated through his mind. Not since his long-ago conversation with MacDonald had there been a vision so tangible. He knew he should have been aware of it sooner, at least before Luke refused his handshake and then a drink. Also, other than seeing his ring, he was relieved Cia hadn't picked up on it, although she'd have no reason to question that he was anyone, or anything other than the elderly musician sitting opposite her.

He no longer questioned the dreams populated with odd, surreal images. Nor were the momentary hallucinations, such as he'd experienced with Cia, all that unusual. It had taken some time, but he'd eventually grown accustomed to the occasional errant shadow sweeping across his canvases as if in appraisal. That's when the voices really got going. And yet, nothing so substantial as Brother Luke had presented itself in over twenty years. *Why now, and at a jazz club in Toronto of all places?* Nor did he comprehend Luke's message that he would discover that Cia was special, particularly since it was something he already knew. That Cia had not only seen but interacted with him was not only surprising, it was, in truth, more than a little worrisome. Such a thing had never happened before, and he was beginning to question if, by the very fact of that same "specialness," she had been an unwitting participant in triggering Luke's presence. While he didn't know what that presence meant, his instincts were now on alert that something far more significant could be looming, and if so, he might be forced to explain about the ring and his past, something he wasn't ready to do.

Despite his concern, he smiled, thinking that nothing even close had ever occurred with any of his other women, although there had been a few amusing moments. The most recent had been a couple of years before, when an on-and-off girlfriend insisted she had seen one of his portraits shift. When he'd asked what "shift" meant, she had shaken her head, saying she couldn't explain it, but something had definitely moved in the painting of some old dowager. Shortly thereafter, she informed him that, after hearing weird sounds in his flat, she had become afraid to go up to his studio. Despite his attempts to defuse her anxieties, she had been adamant, saying if he desired any more "dirty weekends" with her, they would have to be at her flat in Hampstead. His response had been simply that while he understood, he regretted he would have to decline her offer.

He had known since the beginning that there was more to his ring than he had been told. Now, given these most recent incidents, he considered it might be time to ask a few more questions. The only problem was, there was no one left to ask.

A couple of days later he rang James Davies, the director of his gallery, to tell him the Toronto trip had gone well, and at least one of the galleries he'd met with was interested in scheduling an exhibit. Knowing James was a long-time jazz buff, he asked if he had ever heard of a bass guitarist named Brother Luke. To his surprise, James answered with more than a hint of excitement in his voice.

"That's a name I haven't heard in years. He was a blues guy. The real deal. Got into jazz later. Died about, what? Twenty years ago? I think I have a record or two if you want to hear him. Why are you asking?"

He couldn't very well tell him he'd actually met the man. "Someone mentioned his name in a jazz club in Toronto. Thanks, James. I may take you up on that. I'd like to hear his music."

"Any time. Meanwhile, you better get back to work. I've had a few calls about portraits. Not to mention Patrick's show in September."

"I know. It's going to be a busy few months."

Chapter 14

By early summer Cia had become quite friendly with Sonny, occasionally spending evenings with her and her husband, Connor. After meeting Will, Sonny asked about him often, and Cia, happy to be receiving almost weekly letters as well as the occasional phone call, conveyed his frequently humorous stories about the aristocratic ladies whose portraits he was painting. Since Cia always sounded so smitten, Sonny had eventually given up trying to introduce her to a couple of local bachelors.

Despite Sonny's cautions about planting a vegetable garden, Cia had gone ahead and dug up a long-abandoned flower bed, putting in lettuce, cucumbers, peppers and a few tomato plants. She had, however, heeded Sonny's advice by circling it with wire fencing, and even enlisted Charlie, Sonny's son, to stop by to water the plants during the week when she was in the city.

By late July her little garden was flourishing, and when she stopped in Sonny's store she boasted that she'd have her own vegetables in another week. Sonny, looking at her with some hidden knowledge, quietly stated, "I'll believe it when I see it."

Cia hadn't understood why Sonny was so negative. Not until the following week when, after driving up with Sarah and Mike, she rushed out Saturday morning to show off what she called her "farm" and discovered that every lettuce and pepper plant had been chewed to the ground. It had only gotten worse when Sarah, reaching out to pluck a ripe tomato, suddenly screamed.

Mike, along with an already agitated Cia, ran over, astonished to see a panicked chipmunk leap off the center stalk where it had been blissfully munching the same tomato.

Cia, dejected, slumped down on the grass. "Now I have to admit to Sonny that she was right."

Sarah, getting over her shock, picked up a few small, unchewed cucumbers and plopped down next to Cia. "Well. You still have a few of these. Maybe the critters here don't like them. Next year I suggest you plant flowers."

Cia looked at her with a resigned sigh. "All my hard work."

"I have an idea," Sarah said. "Why don't you channel all that energy into meeting some new people."

"You mean men."

"Actually, yes. A splendid idea. I think you've waited for Will long enough."

"I'll second that," Mike said.

Giving in, she shook her head. "Not until after Will's show. If nothing happens then, I promise I'll consider it."

It was late August when she had an unusual dream about Will, the first since returning from Canada, and one that left her distinctly uneasy. He was standing in a field with what appeared to be whitish columns lying randomly about while talking with Brother Luke. The columns looked oddly familiar, as though she had seen them before but was unable to recall just where. When she tried to see Brother Luke's face, he turned away as though avoiding her and didn't look back. When she called out to him, a white mist began to blur the image, and she woke up in a cold sweat.

The very next morning, Will called her office. Thinking it a strange coincidence, she told him her dream from the night before.

"That's odd," he said with some hesitation. "I dreamt of Brother Luke as well."

"Is that why you're calling?"

"Not at all. I wanted to tell you that I have the dates for Patrick's show. Can you leave the night of September twenty-eighth? It's a Friday. The opening is Saturday night."

"I'll call the travel agent tomorrow. I can't wait, Will. It's been an awfully long summer."

"Yes, Cia, for me as well. Patrick is here. We're working on the catalog. He says hello and he's looking forward to seeing you."

"Tell him the same."

"Ring me as soon as you can. I'll book the reservations here and send you the tickets."

Send me the tickets? "Are you sure?"

"Just call me with the flight you'll be taking."

"Will you be there tomorrow evening?"

"For you, I will." He paused, his voice becoming seductive. "Come here to me, Cia. It's time I held you in my arms." He sounded like he was about to say something else, but stopped.

"What is it?"

"Just that I've missed you."

Breathless, she put down the receiver, a wave of unexpected emotion surging through her mind and body. When Sarah walked in, she was still staring at the phone.

"Are you all right? You're white as a ghost." She put a cup of black coffee down in front of her. "What happened?"

Cia looked up at her. "Will just called. He's sending me a plane ticket to London."

"That's fantastic. Why aren't you excited?"

"I think I'm in shock," she said, picking up the coffee. "Thanks for this. What I really need is a drink."

Sarah blinked. "Sid has a bottle stashed in his office. Want me to get it?"

Chapter 15

As before, Will was waiting well behind the eternally impatient mob in the arrival's hall. After a perfunctory kiss, he grabbed Cia's bag. "We have to go. We're driving directly to Yorkshire."

She was surprised and not a little disappointed, anticipating a far more affectionate greeting after three months. "Why? What's the rush? I want to thank you for the plane ticket. First Class? It was far too extravagant."

Dropping her suitcase, he pulled her close, gently running a finger across her lips before kissing them. "No, Cia. Not for you." With a wicked grin, he added. "However, you may, if you so wish, thank me later."

She blushed. "I'll do my best."

"I'd like to go to the flat and make love to you right now, but the lorry with the paintings left at seven, and it's already after nine. There's a five-hour drive ahead of us. I need to be there to meet Tom, the other painter. We have to hang the show."

"Doesn't Patrick do that?"

Picking up her suitcase, he took her arm and began walking toward the exit. "Usually. But Tom and I have decided to do this one ourselves. As it is, there won't be much time. The opening is tonight. I'd have asked you to meet me there, but I'd rather have you come along with me."

As he backed out of the parking space, she leaned over to kiss his cheek. "No kissing the driver while the car is in motion. Could be dangerous," he said with a grin.

By the time they arrived at the gallery, it was mid-afternoon. Patrick came out to give a slightly groggy Cia a hug before introducing her to Tom Hawkes, the tall, bearded painter sharing the exhibit.

Tom gave her cheek kisses, saying, "If you're a friend of Will's, you deserve a kiss." Will laughed as they shook hands and clapped one another on the back.

Patrick assured Will that his paintings had arrived safely, and, since they hadn't stopped for lunch, tea and sandwiches were brought into the vast white space that comprised the main section of the gallery. Patrick explained that the building had been a wool-processing plant in the 1800s but had gone out of business in the 1930s. He said he occasionally picked up the funky odor of old wool, perhaps from the ghosts of sheep long gone. Cia looked back at him with a grimace. Meanwhile, Will and Tom began walking around the gallery, debating where each painting should be hung.

After a few minutes, Patrick turned to Cia who was watching them both become agitated. "What say we get out of here and leave them to their bickering? We'll go to the pub down the road."

The pub was a typical weathered, half-timbered building, this one with a carving of a sheep hanging over the door. Inside it was dark and smoky, smelling, as expected, of old beer and whiskey. Patrick went to the bar for a couple of beers while Cia took a table.

"I'm glad to see you, Cia," he said, sitting down and lighting an ever-present cigarette.

She raised her glass. "Thank you. I'm happy to be here."

He looked like he was about to say something but appeared to hesitate.

"What is it, Patrick?"

"Cia, I know you love Will. I see it every time you look at him."

"Am I that obvious?"

"To me, you are. It's also clear that he cares for you deeply. In that regard, there may be a few things you've already realized, and more I think you should know."

"That sounds ominous. What are you talking about?"

He took a long drink of his beer. "I hate to ask, but have you heard anything like, ah, unusual sounds in his flat?"

Looking surprised, she said, "You know about that?"

He nodded, his face serious.

"I've heard whispers, or some sort of hushed garbled voices, if that's what you mean."

"But only when you're with him. When you're, ah, close?"

She felt her face redden. "Usually, yes. I've also heard them when he wasn't home. I went upstairs to his studio twice. They sounded louder up there, and I wanted see if I could find where they were coming from."

"And did you?"

She shivered. "No."

"Have you asked him about them?"

"He always says it's the wind or the pipes. Or he changes the subject."

He took a deep breath. "Cia, I'm sure he wouldn't like this, but I'm going to tell you anyway. If only for your own protection."

"For my protection? I've never felt a sense of threat from him."

"It's not that. Has he ever mentioned why he never married?"

"I asked once, but he said it wasn't his fate. When I asked what that meant, he put me off, saying we'd talk about it another time."

"And have you?"

She shrugged. "Not really. I did ask about his engagement, which he seemed reluctant to talk about. He only said that he was very young and the girl died suddenly."

Patrick sat back and lit another cigarette. "Want one? You might need it," he said, offering her the pack.

"From the sound of your voice, yes. Maybe another beer as well?"

He went to the bar, returning with two more pints. Looking towards the door, he said in a quiet voice, "We may not have much time. They'll finish up at the gallery soon, and I don't want Will to think I'm talking behind his back. It's up to you. Shall I continue?"

"You can't stop now."

"And yet it's difficult to know where to start. Maybe at the beginning. Will, as you know, was born in Scotland, in a small town near Inverness. When he was still quite young, his family sold the farm that had been in the family for generations and moved to Edinburgh, where his father joined a large distiller of mostly high-end whiskeys and single malts. Over the years, the business prospered, and as Will got older his father wanted to bring him into the company. But, you see, Will could draw, and that's what he did, and all he wanted to do. Against his father's wishes, he applied to the Royal Academy in London and was accepted. That's where he met Francis Bacon and began working under the guidance of several

101

other well-known painters. He soon found himself in the company of artists. Not only painters, but musicians, writers, and actors as well, and he knew that was where he belonged. Although styles of art were changing rapidly in the '50s and '60s, he gravitated towards the impressionists with their unique sense of light and sensuous use of paint." He stopped and took a drink. "I know this is a lot of information, and while I'm sure you know some of it, it's important that you understand his history. Where he's coming from, as it were."

"His style, then, is the same as today?"

"Not quite. He's matured and refined it, but essentially never wavered. He continues to defy trends, and somehow it works for him. You've seen his work; he loves to paint his lush nudes, but it's his portraits that are constantly in demand. Although he still teaches at a couple of art schools, he's recently become chagrined that life drawing isn't considered as important as in the past."

"I've heard his frustration on that subject. Sorry to interrupt."

"By the time Will was in his early twenties, he was anxious to get out and make a name for himself. When he was twenty-one, he convinced a gallery owner in Chelsea to take him on. A couple of years later, he had his first one-man show."

"He did tell me about that," she said with a grin. "How he badgered the gallery owner. Still, that's young for an artist, isn't it?"

"Yes, Cia. And that's where his story really begins."

"His story? Does this have to do with the voices?"

"That and more. Far more, I'm afraid. During that first exhibit, a Scottish woman of some wealth and prestige happened by the gallery and admired his portraits. They were sensual even then, and she asked the owner about him. The next thing he knew, he had been offered his first commission. In Edinburgh, no less. After meeting the lady in London, albeit briefly, he told her he would stay with his family, who lived not far from her. But she wouldn't hear of it and insisted he stay at her house, actually a reconstructed medieval castle that had been in her husband's family for centuries."

"I assume she was a member of your seemingly limitless aristocracy?"

"Indeed, she was. Married to a duke, in fact. It was only when Will arrived that she mentioned her daughter was away in college at Cambridge and, by the way, her husband had gone out of town for a few days." He stopped to exhale smoke from yet another cigarette. "Cia, you know Will. He's always had an eye for the ladies and they for him. Not surprisingly, it turned out that she wanted a bit more than her portrait painted. She actually showed up one morning in only a dressing gown, offering to pose nude for him. And yet, he refused to be seduced. From the way he tells it, he was there to paint, not shag her. I think it may also have been that he didn't find her very attractive."

Cia laughed. "He actually refused her? Will? From the look of his portraits I thought they were all half in love with him."

He sipped his beer. "That's not far from the truth. And it's likely she was as well, although I'm not sure love had much to do with it. You know Will—there's something magnetic about him—men as well as women are drawn to him. Anyway, as for the overly amorous duchess, her daughter arrived unexpectedly during a sitting. Will was supposed to leave a few days later, but the woman had been so difficult that he'd managed to only complete a few color sketches. The way I heard it, he was pleased the girl had come home, because he was sure her mother was about to devour him with misdirected passion."

"All right, Patrick, you've hooked me. What happened?"

"It seems the lady wasn't anxious for him to meet her daughter, whom, I must say, was quite beautiful. Apparently, Will took one look and fell head over heels. The mother must have sensed it because she insisted that he complete whatever he could within the next day and take the painting back to London to finish. However, he was there just long enough to talk with the girl and ask if he could call her when she returned to Cambridge." He stopped talking abruptly as he noticed Will come in. "I'm afraid we'll have to leave this till next time."

Cia was frustrated; the story was just getting interesting. Nevertheless, she smiled at Will as he picked up a pint on his way to the table. Sitting down, he gave her a light kiss. "So, Patrick. The show is hung, as it were," he said with a laugh. "What have you two been talking about?"

"Just telling Cia a bit about Yorkshire. If you have time tomorrow, you should take her for a drive through the Dales before returning to London." With a quick glance at his watch, he said, "It's almost five. You should go to the summer house so you can change and get back to the gallery by six. The opening is at seven."

Leaving the pub, they drove through countryside broken by neat stone hedgerows. Beams of sunlight broke through low-hanging clouds, illuminating emerald green fields dotted with sheep and the occasional cow. Cia was enthralled. "This is exactly how I pictured Yorkshire. Can we go to the Dales tomorrow as Patrick suggested?"

"What?"

It was obvious his mind was elsewhere; no doubt on the exhibition. She repeated the question.

"That may be possible. Just let me see if I have to meet with anyone in the morning."

She laughed. "I understand. Work first."

They had come to a barely perceptible turn-off and began driving uphill on what was no more than a narrow lane. After another sharp turn, Cia saw a massive stone house spread over the crest of the hill in front of them.

"My god. What is that?"

"The manor house. It belongs to Patrick's cousin. The wealthy side of the family, as he says. You'll meet them later."

"That can't be a summer house, can it?

He laughed. "Not quite," he said, making another turn and coming to a halt on a graveled driveway in front of a small stone cottage with an overhanging thatched roof.

"Oh," Cia said. "This is lovely. Is this where we're staying?" She looked towards a small pond surrounded by willow trees and bushes fragrant with the last of the summer's roses. Only the sound of frogs croaking on their lily pads broke the silence. "This is so romantic."

Will took their bags from the car. "Yes. Well. Come along," he said absently. "We'll have to leave the romance for later."

When she looked at him with a frown, he pulled her into a kiss. "Later, my love. Business first."

The gallery opening was far more crowded than she'd anticipated. A couple of photographers roamed through the throng, snapping photos of what she imagined were the local aristocracy and other important guests. Patrick had told her that both Will and Tom had large followings of the well-heeled gentry from the neighboring towns and cities, even as far away as Leeds and Liverpool. Not having seen any of Tom's paintings, she went from one painting to another, finding his work unique, and yet with a slight influence, particularly in his larger canvases, that recalled a softer version of the painter Nicholas de Staël's minimal landscapes. She was glad to see several of his paintings, as well as Will's, already embellished with red dots.

After being introduced to Patrick's cousin and his wife, she told them she adored the summer house and that it reminded her of her cottage in the Berkshires. The cousin's wife looked her up and down, sniffed, snagged a glass of champagne and wandered off. Cia rolled her eyes as Patrick walked by. "Don't mind Cousin Abigail. No doubt she's jealous that you're not only prettier and younger, but you're here with Will. She's had eyes for him for years. Just ignore her."

Cia laughed. "Not much choice in that. I like the show, Patrick. Especially the contrast between Will's work and Tom's."

"Yes. It's going well," he said, scanning the crowd. "We've sold quite a few pieces already."

Looking over Patrick's shoulder, she asked, "Who is that woman Will is talking to?"

He glanced back. "Lady Delacorte. From an old Norman family. They have a country house not far from here. I'm actually a little surprised to see her. She's related to Carolyn's mother; one of the few who didn't blame Will for her death."

She nodded, aware that Will suddenly seemed distracted. Instead of paying attention to the woman nattering on before him, he was staring into a corner across the room, a spot where no one was standing.

Shaking off a whisper of uneasiness, she turned her attention back to Patrick. "Do you think we'll have time to talk tomorrow?"

He shook his head. "I doubt it. I do, however, expect to be in London next week. Perhaps when Will is painting or teaching we'll have time to visit some galleries and chat some more."

Patrick had arranged a dinner for his artists and their most loyal patrons at a restaurant not far from the gallery. Will was as excited as she had ever seen him; of the twelve pieces he brought, he had sold eight and received commissions for two portraits.

It was close to two when they returned to the cottage. Despite that Will was drunk on success as well as champagne, he lit several candles—no one had bothered to mention there was no electricity in the house—and led a slightly woozy Cia to bed. They lay facing one another, talking quietly about the night until he began to kiss her. Feeling energy from his body infusing hers, she lay back with a sigh, feeling his mouth soft against her breasts, his hands parting her thighs and his fingers creating magic. She reached to hold him as he had taught her, feeling his arousal and hearing his groan of pleasure.

It was barely dawn when she awoke to what sounded like muted chants. Before she could think much about them, Will pressed against her, kissing the back of her neck until she turned to him in deep desire. As they made love, she ran her hands down his back, loving the sleek smoothness of his skin. With a soft moan she pulled him closer, cleaving to him until sensation obliterated all conscious thought. They fell asleep in one another's arms, unaware the candles had blown out and the chants had turned to sighs.

In the morning, when they stopped at the gallery to say goodbye to Patrick, a man was waiting to speak with Will about painting his wife's portrait for her birthday. By the time they finished, it was almost noon and Will, seeing Cia frown at the thought of missing the Dale's, laughed. "All right. We'll drive to Grassington so you can see more sheep, stop in Burnsall for lunch, and then go back through Bolton Abbey on the way to London. How does that sound?"

"If those places are nearly as charming as their names, it sounds wonderful."

Before they got into the car, Patrick and Will shook hands, again congratulating one another on the success of the show. When Cia asked Patrick about Tom, he told her he had already departed for his home in the Midlands.

With a pointed look, she said, "Then I'll see you in a couple of days?"

He grinned. "Not to worry. You won't be able to miss me. I'll be camping out in the loft above the studio."

As they drove through gently rolling countryside and narrow-laned villages bordered by picturesque stone cottages, Cia was enthralled. They'd hardly left the hamlet of Hetton when they were stopped by the tail ends of what looked like hundreds of sheep meandering across the road.

She watched, fascinated, as sheep dogs raced frantically back and forth, forcing stragglers into a field. Realizing Will seemed unusually quiet, she turned to him. "What is it, Will? I'm loving this. You seem distracted."

"Nothing, Cia. I'm enjoying watching you." As the last of the sheep, protesting loudly, cleared the road, he put the car in gear. "It's been a long time since I've taken the time to drive through here. And with someone I care about."

With a rush of emotion, she reached for his hand. "I'm glad it took me to coax you into it," she whispered, unaware of the distant look in his eyes.

He wasn't about to tell her of the strange half-awake dream he'd had in the early hours just before dawn. It had to do with Carolyn and the shop where he'd seen the ring. He hadn't dreamt of her for a very long time and asked himself, *why now?* Perhaps it was seeing Lady Delacorte that triggered the memory. If so, it was one he'd just as soon forget.

His thoughts were interrupted by Cia asking if he was all right.

"I'm fine. I was just thinking about the exhibit."

She smiled. "I'm glad it went so well and that I was there to see it."

He reached over to tuck a lock of hair behind her ear. "As am I. I wanted you here, by my side."

She laughed. "I wasn't exactly by your side, Will. You were constantly surrounded by some very formidable women."

"Be fair, luv. There were quite a few men as well." He offered a sardonic grin. "They were the ones with the checkbooks."

"And you got a couple of portraits as well, didn't you?"

"One, maybe two. We'll see."

"Some of those ladies were quite pretty. Should I be jealous?"

"Beauty is in the eye of the beholder. An old cliché, but true. I need look no further than the lady sitting next to me."

"Oh," she giggled, fanning her face. "You are so seductive."

He stopped the car on the verge before leaning over to kiss her. "When I look at you, how can I not be?" After a few moments of staring at one another in an emotionally charged silence, he touched her face. "We best be on our way. If we keep this up, we'll never get back to London."

"But I like kissing you."

"Behave, Cia," he said with a laugh. "At least for now. It's not far to Grassington so I suggest you keep an eye out. There are many lovely old houses along the way, not to mention more sheep as well. We'll stop for lunch in Burnsall. I think there's even a shop with locally made sweaters and such."

Seeing her misty-eyed smile, he wondered if it had been the moment to say something intimate, endearing. And yet, he wasn't quite sure he was ready. For the last twenty years, there had been a line he'd been afraid to cross, and he needed to be very sure before taking such a step.

After lunch at a quaint old inn, they walked hand in hand along the narrow, cobbled street. As they passed the store Will had mentioned, Cia pulled him inside. Seeing a rack with woolen hats and plaid tams, she insisted he try on.

"No, Cia," he said, putting his hands up. "Those aren't my style. I always think of tams as something worn by slightly daft older men."

"That's silly. Lots of men wear them. And not all old."

"Perhaps, but something about them makes me uneasy."

She made a face. "A tam makes you uneasy?"

With a shrug, he pointed to a table with heavy, knitted sweaters. "Why don't you have a look at those."

When the sales lady came over to help her, he started to go outside for a cigarette. As he began walking toward the door, he noticed a soft pink, finely woven scarf, almost a shawl. Picking it up, he wrapped it around Cia's shoulders. "This is for you, Cia. It will keep you warm when I'm not around."

Her eyes were shining as she turned to hug him. "It's beautiful, Will. Thank you."

Glancing from Will to Cia, the sales lady smiled. "Wear it well, my dear. It suits you."

As they left the store, the scarf wrapped around Cia's neck, she stopped to kiss him. "These have been the most wonderful couple of days. Your show, this lovely little town, all those sheep. Thank you."

"Don't thank me yet. You're here for another week." He gave her a wicked grin. "Who knows what can happen?"

She looked at him, her eyes sparkling. "It doesn't matter, as long as I'm with you."

Chapter 16

When Patrick arrived a couple of days later, he found Cia in the kitchen preparing afternoon tea, stacks of tins from Fortnum & Mason piled randomly on the counter next to her. Stopping in the doorway, he sniffed the air. "What are you making?"

"Cookies. What you Brits call biscuits."

"Smells delicious. Where's Will?"

"Upstairs, painting." She glanced at him. "Do you think we'll have some time to talk? I mean about what you started telling me in Yorkshire?"

He looked concerned. "Why? Has something happened?"

She shook her head. "Not at all. It's just that I'd like to hear the rest of it."

"Not to worry, Cia. We'll find time."

"Go on up," she said with a smile. "I'll bring the tea in a few."

After giving her a hug, he went upstairs to the studio where Will was touching up a portrait. Shrugging off his jacket, Patrick grinned. "It appears I've walked into a rather unusual domestic scene. At least for you. I hope I'm not interrupting anything."

"Not at all," Will said, stepping back from the canvas. "Cia has become fond of afternoon tea. Come here a minute. What do you think of this new portrait?"

"Looks good. Do I know the lady?"

"Perhaps not. She found me through the Chelsea Arts Club."

"I see," Patrick said, absently lighting a cigarette. "I don't think I've ever seen you like this. Afternoon tea? Baking? Fortnum & Mason?"

"That's because I've never been like this. I took her to the new exhibition at the Royal Academy this morning, and she noticed

Fortnum & Mason across the street. She had such a good time looking at all the teas and biscuits, I didn't want to stop her."

"You're happy with her, aren't you?"

"Yes, Patrick, I am."

"And I'm pleased for you. What, if I may ask, are you going to
do about it?"

Will looked at him, his face solemn. "I don't know yet. You, of all
people, know my concern. It hasn't mattered, not until now."

"Have you had any, ah, moments since she's been here?"

"You mean déjà vu?"

"I was thinking more like Brother Luke."

He shook his head. "No. Nothing so tangible. Although I did sense
something at your gallery the other night. A shimmer of air in a corner."

"Please." He put up his hands. "Not in my gallery." Suddenly serious, he said, "And you think Cia had something to do with that?"

"I do, Patrick. There have been a few, let's say, odd moments
recently. It has to be something generated by the two of us, but I
have no idea why. I've also been having dreams."

"Dreams?"

"Of the past," he murmured. "The rings, MacDonald . . ."

They were interrupted by Cia bringing a tray with tea and
freshly baked cookies. "You can gossip later," she said with a happy
smile. "Right now, we are having tea."

With a quick glance at Patrick, Will took the tray and placed it
on the table in front of a slightly sagging loveseat strewn with colorful throws. Patrick dragged over a chair and picked up one of the
cookies. "What are these?"

"Chocolate chip. Do you know how difficult it is finding chocolate chips here?"

He bit into one and shook his head. "These are brilliant, Cia," he
said, glancing at Will. "You are in trouble, my man."

"As if I didn't know it," he said with a laugh. "By the way, I
spoke with Drew earlier. He and a couple of other guys asked to
meet at the pub later."

"Anything specific?"

"They're having trouble finding representation and thinking of
opening their own gallery. They want some advice."

"That's nice, Will. From a guy with paintings in three galleries,
I'm sure they'll appreciate it," he said, his tone gently sardonic.

"Perhaps," he sighed. "But it makes me feel old."

With a giggle, Cia reached over to kiss him. "They should only know how young you really are."

Rolling his eyes, Patrick reached for another cookie.

As expected, the pub was smoke-filled and noisy, and despite that Will had mentioned meeting with four artists, two more joined them. Although the conversation began calmly enough with the new gallery, it quickly progressed to an animated debate on the evolution of painting from the nineteen fifties to the present, and the huge, seemingly rapid shift from abstract to Pop Art. Most of those at the table brushed it off, still eschewing it as just another passing fad, merely a reflection of the culture-clash of the sixties.

Will, however, demurred. "I'm not so sure it's just a 'passing fad.' I think Pop Art, although a strange American phenomenon driven by an equally strange artist, has dramatically altered the view of art. Putting aside esthetics, what was viewed as obtainable only by the elite has now devolved to something more prosaic and accessible to the masses."

Whether this was good or bad created another boisterous discussion. After each of them expressed their opinions over several pints, the conversation degenerated into wild gossip and off-color jokes that continued well after hours at the flat of one of Will's friends.

On the way home, Will was curious as to what Cia thought of the evening.

"It was quite an outspoken group, wasn't it? I would have to say I found it fascinating. It appears that artists are just as passionate about their work and the work of their contemporaries as writers. And equally as scathing. Perhaps even more so."

Patrick laughed. "The only problem was, they were so busy arguing about everything, they forgot about the gallery."

By then they had reached the flat and, after wishing them goodnight, Patrick proceeded upstairs to the small, almost hidden loft space above the studio.

Taking Cia in his arms, Will slowly and sensuously began unwinding the pink scarf from around her neck. "Bed time," he whispered.

Reaching up to kiss him, she murmured, "At last."

It was still dark when the dream returned. This time Will saw himself standing in a hazy fog in front of the curio shop. As the mist cleared, the door swung open with a distinct snap, waking him with a jolt. Trying to quiet his breathing, he lay still, waiting for the thumping of his heart to subside while trying to quash the surge of images suddenly churning in his mind. When they wouldn't quit, he gave up any hope of sleep and slipped quietly out of bed. Shrugging on his robe against the pre-dawn chill, he padded upstairs to his studio.

There was a bottle of scotch still sitting on the table in front of the loveseat. While Cia was getting ready the night before, he and Patrick had had a quick drink before leaving to meet his friends. Although the whiskey looked inviting, he sat back and closed his eyes, hoping against hope that he'd fall back to sleep.

It was the spring after he had first met Carolyn. He was young, and, thanks to his early success and budding recognition, he was flush with a cocky confidence. He, along with a wide circle of friends, mostly other artists and musicians, lived an anti-establishment, Bohemian lifestyle, believing in freedom in all aspects of their lives. Girls came and went, some with smiles, others tearful that he wouldn't commit to them. He never imagined that such a thing as falling in love could happen, particularly with such a conservative girl. He likely wouldn't have rushed to ask her to marry him, but she was about to return home from college for the summer and he was afraid to lose her.

He could never quite recall how he had arrived at the curio shop. Although he had no interest in such places, some instinct compelled him to enter. Inside it was dimly lit and musty with age, and despite having a vague feeling that he should be looking for something, he had no clue to what it could be. At first he didn't see anything that interested him, not until he was about to leave. As he passed a dusty display case he noticed two unusual rings set with small, dark stones. What stopped him was that even through the cloudy glass, the stones appeared to be glowing. When he asked the proprietor, a white-bearded man with a stoop, if he could see them, the man demurred, saying he had nicer ones. Fascinated by their unusual luminescence he insisted, and, although still appearing reluctant, the old man took them out.

"What are the stones?" Will asked as the man placed them on a scrap of frayed red velvet on the counter.

"Sapphires," he answered in a weak, breathy voice. "Very ancient and very rare. Stones such as these were said to be found in caves on the western islands of Scotland thousands of years ago. Usually they're a dull blue, but there are times they shine with an ungodly brightness." Picking up the rings, he said, "You can see the design is Celtic, an unusual triskele and knot design. Very unusual. In all the years, I've only seen one or two like it."

"I'm not familiar with Celtic rings. Do the symbols have some sort of meaning?"

"Indeed. Rings like this have deep significance. The intertwining of the spirals signifies the ancient trinity of earth, air, and water. As well as life never ending."

He was taken aback. "Life never ending?"

The man nodded. "That is what the design implies." He held up the larger ring. "What makes this ring even more unique are the gold strands. As you can see, they are interwoven with some sort of metal that over the years has oxidized to black. Also, the stone is set deep, so it always appears dark."

Not when it's glowing. "That ring is very dramatic. The other less so."

"That is because the smaller ring is woven of pure gold."

Looking around, Will was sure the shop was just as dim as when he'd entered. There was no reason for the stones to be glittering, even more so than when he'd first noticed them.

The old man looked uncomfortable. "Sir, I don't think you'll find these to your taste. Allow me to show you some others."

"I'm not so sure. Can you tell me anything more about them?"

With a deep sigh, he said, "Only that they were found at an ancient henge. A ditch that surrounds a stone circle. Not Stonehenge. That was looted centuries ago. The story is that a farmer plowing not far from the ruins of a stone circle on the west coast of Wales saw something shining, and, to his surprise, he picked up a handful of odd-looking dark stones. When he brushed off the dirt, the stones appeared to have an unusual radiance. After digging further, he found the rings."

"How long ago?" he asked, more curious than ever.

"Sometime early in the last century, I believe. That these were found in the ground is unusual."

"Why was it unusual?"

113

The man paused, as though suddenly distracted. "Sorry, sir. What?"

Becoming impatient, Will shook his head. "Do you have any more rings like this?"

"No, sir. There may be others, but I have only these. It's possible these sapphires were looted over a thousand years ago by Viking raiders sailing south through the islands of the Outer Hebrides. The rings, in contrast, were likely crafted only a few centuries ago from gold and silver that washed up on the coast, most likely from one of the mercantile ships that plied the coastline in the 1600s and 1700s. There are still sunken galleons off the coast of Wales that were known to have carried precious metals and gemstones. These came to me from . . ." Once again looking confused, he glanced down at the rings. "Strange, I suddenly can't seem to remember. No matter. It'll come to me, I'm sure." He looked at Will. "Really, young man, I think if you are looking for a ring for your sweetheart, these are a bit coarse. Let me show you some others. Also antiques, but much finer."

"Please. I want to see these." With obvious reluctance, the old man dropped them in his hand. He was surprised they felt so heavy, and warm. Maybe from having been in the old man's hand.

"Allow me to show you something unusual about them." He held out his hand, and Will put the rings back in his palm. "Look closely. Do you see how they fit together? They are different sizes and yet they interlock with a barely perceptible notch. I believe these were crafted for a man and a woman who would be forever entwined. Celtic rings such as these were thought to have mystical powers. But, come along. Let me show you some nicer ones."

"Mystical powers?"

"So it is told."

He was doubtful. "What sort of mystical powers?"

"I know very little," he answered, placing them back on the velvet cloth. "It's said that when these kinds of rings, with this particular sapphire, are passed from a man to a woman they create an unbreakable bond, one that is meant to last forever." He looked up, a smile creasing his solemn demeanor. "Not so great in this world of divorce, eh?"

"How much do you want for them?"

His brief smile reverted to a frown. "I don't think you should take them. You're a young man who must have many ladies in your life. You would have to be sure that whomever you choose to give

114

the other ring to will be your soulmate, your true love, not of the moment, but forever." The old man stared at Will, his eyes deep black pools, his voice a coarse whisper. "You must understand that once given, you cannot take the ring back. You are bound forever. Until death and beyond."

Feeling a chill, Will looked at the man with narrowed eyes. "What does that mean?"

"Just what I said. I can tell you nothing more than what the legends say. These rings are meant to fit two people destined to be together for all time."

With intrigue overcoming an innate sense of foreboding, Will picked up the rings. He knew he should leave, but the longer he held them the more they appeared to glow as though releasing a spark from a fire deep within. "Can I try the larger one on? If it doesn't fit, there's no more discussion."

The man hesitated. "That is so."

The ring slid easily on the third finger of his right hand. "Perfect," he said. "What if the smaller ring doesn't fit my fiancée?"

"Once you leave here these rings belong to you. You must take care, for you cannot return them. To give the other to the wrong person would be foolhardy. There may be dire consequences if you ignore my warning."

"Dire, such as death?"

The man held out his hand. "Please, sir. Listen to me. It's probably best to leave them here. You're the first to enquire about them in decades. In truth, I've never seen them glow like this. They are showing you their power. Be warned."

Will shook his head. This was 1958, not the dark ages. "All I'm asking is if the ring doesn't fit, can it be made smaller?"

"As I just told you, it will only fit the one who is fated to be bound to you through time." His voice had reverted to a strained rasp.

Fated? Through time? What the hell is that supposed to mean? Although he had listened closely to the man's stories and warnings, they still made no sense to him. It was possible he was just trying, for whatever reason, to scare him off or, more likely, convince him to look at more expensive rings. Nevertheless, he said he wanted to buy them.

The man hesitated, as if still unsure. "May I ask your name?"

"My name is Will."

The old man closed his eyes, muttering his name over and over as if waiting for some sort of sign. With a sigh and a brief nod, he retreated to a deeply shadowed corner.

Will glanced around, thinking he heard someone whispering, or perhaps it was just the old man talking to himself.

The old man returned holding a small, black lacquered box lined in faded red velvet. "These stones were likely taken from a cave in the time of the ancients, when spirits ruled the earth. Now that they have come into the light and shown themselves to you, you must respect their power." His voice was deep with concern. "Heed my words."

"We didn't discuss price."

The man handed him the box. "There is no price, Mr. Will. These rings are now yours."

Puzzled, he asked, "Are you sure? Why would you just give them to me?"

"I believe they've been waiting for you. Take them and take care."

Whatever peculiar notions the old man had about spirits and power was fine with him. "Thank you. I will," he said, sliding the ring on his finger. It still felt unnaturally warm and when he looked down at the smaller ring it appeared to glow even more brightly in its tattered velvet-lined box. As he walked to the door, he again heard the soft yet distinct sound of whispers. When he looked back, the man was gone.

A sudden noise jolted him from his half-dream. It was Cia calling up to him. Moving slowly, he walked to the top of the stairs. "Go back to bed, luv. I couldn't sleep and came up here. I'll be down soon."

"Are you sure? You sound strange."

"I'm fine. This happens sometimes. Not to worry. Go back to sleep."

"All right." He heard her yawn. "If you're sure."

This time when he sat down on the loveseat, he poured a short drink, thinking it would, perhaps, deaden the memories.

As soon as he returned home from the shop, he rang Carolyn, asking her to meet him the next evening in Hyde Park. With her hand in his, they walked along the Serpentine until he found an unoccupied bench. As the western sky became pink with the setting sun, he asked her to marry him. She was overjoyed, and with many kisses said she would.

When he took out the ring, Carolyn stared at it as though fascinated. "It's so unusual. I've never seen anything like it." Holding it up, she smiled. "I'm sure all my friends will be jealous. What's the stone?"

"A very ancient sapphire," he said, removing his ring and joining the notches as the old man had shown him. "Look how yours and mine fit together. It's said they create a bond that lasts forever."

Although she smiled, he wasn't sure she fully understood the significance of what he had said. *Neither did I, at least not then.*

As he slid the gold ring on her finger she frowned. "It's too big," she said, her eyes misty with disappointment. "And why does it feel so warm?"

"I don't know. Maybe they retain heat from our hands. No worries. I'll have it made smaller," he said, thinking if the old man wouldn't do it, he'd find a jeweler who would. Throwing her arms around him, Carolyn made him promise to bring it to Edinburgh in two weeks. In the last glow of twilight, she said they could announce their engagement then.

It was two days later when he returned to the antiques shop. The door was ajar, and inside he saw two men talking quietly with an elderly woman who appeared to be grief-stricken.

"Who're you?" one of the men asked, his tone abrupt.

"Will Jamieson. I bought two rings here a few days ago. Is the proprietor here?"

With a brief glance at the woman, the man walked Will back toward the door. In a low voice, he said, "Only in spirit, I'm afraid. He passed yesterday. Is there a problem?"

"Not really. I wanted to see if he could make one a bit smaller." He looked back at the woman who was holding a damp, stained handkerchief to red-rimmed eyes. "I'm sorry for your loss."

With a look of curiosity, she approached him. "Please. May I see the ring?" Will held out the box, which she took and opened carefully. Shaking her head, she murmured, "Where's the other?" When he held out his hand, she shuddered. "He shouldn't have sold you these. He knew better. They were meant to remain here where they could cause no harm."

"I didn't buy them. When I offered, he gave them to me."

117

"That may even be worse."

"What are you saying?"

"He didn't tell you?"

"He only said they would create an unbreakable bond between me and the girl I love."

"Then why are you here? I'm sure he explained that they cannot be returned." Her voice had become harsh.

"I don't want to return them. Only to have one made smaller."

She backed away, her hands raised as if warding off evil spirits. "No. Impossible. It cannot be done. He didn't tell you that the ring will fit one and only one person in this life?"

"Yes. He did. I want to give this ring to the girl I intend to marry."

Before he could respond, she moved back into the shadows. "Please go. Those rings have brought us to this grief. It was after my husband gave them to you that he died."

"I'm sorry. I had no idea," he said, looking at her with questions in his eyes. He saw her hesitate before taking a step closer.

"Just before dawn he said he heard voices. When he went to investigate, he tripped and fell down the stairs." After dabbing at more tears running down her cheeks, she looked at him with narrowed eyes. "It was no accident. We've lived here for fifty years and he knew every millimeter of this house." With a look of scorn, she pointed. "It's those rings that did it. Now they are yours. Take them and leave. You have been warned." Her voice was sharp, accusative.

"Warned? I'm sorry, I still don't understand."

The woman shook her head. "He didn't tell you all of it, did he? The stones in those rings have now become part of you. When they were here they were safe in their case. No one even remembered they existed." She closed her eyes and took a breath. "But they forced themselves into the light, and with their power they lured you inside where you could see them. Once you walked out that door, they took on your life. They feel your emotions, your deepest longings and fears, and they watch as though they have eyes. They are your spirits now, and it's possible they will lead you to great success as well as deep grief. It will be how you live your life that will determine your fate. Make your choices wisely and with care. And most of all, be cautious about whom you love. These are jealous spirits, and the smaller ring is meant to fit only one. She will be the one you have known before, but not in this life. She is your eternal soul mate, and in each life you must find one another again. Take care, young man. You must not displease the spirits."

Will looked at her as though she was mad. "What sort of fantasy is this? Spirits? Eternal soul mates? All I want is to make one ring smaller."

The bigger man stepped in. "Please go. We're well rid of those spirit stones."

There was no choice, and he left in confusion. On the way to his flat, he found himself on an unfamiliar street. Looking at his watch, he realized he'd been walking aimlessly for hours while replaying the strange conversation over and over. About to turn back, he noticed a jewelry store and decided to go in. Compared to the curio shop, the place looked pristine, with gold necklaces, bracelets, and rings shining through well-tended cases.

The man behind the counter, preoccupied with polishing a silver bracelet, offered what could have been taken for a smile. "Can I help you, sir?"

Feeling optimistic, Will withdrew the gold ring from its velvet bed. "I'm hoping you can. I'd like to have this ring made smaller."

The man glanced at the ring, then back at Will, his eyes widening in shock. "No. I cannot touch that. No one can. It must be left as is."

"Why?" he asked, now even more perplexed.

"Where is the matching ring?"

When he held out his hand, the man backed away. "I've seen stones like this before. They bode ill for anyone who touches them. Please, take your rings and leave."

"What's wrong with them?" Will asked, trying to elicit another response to a story that continued to sound too outrageous to be true.

"Wherever you got these, they must have told you of the danger. It may be the twentieth century, but there are some things that cannot be explained. Those sapphires are one them. They are said to be spawned by the devil himself."

With a sigh, Will put the box with the gold ring back in his pocket. "I'm sorry. To me, they're just unusual rings. That's why I bought . . ." He stopped, suddenly aware that what he was about to say wasn't true: he hadn't purchased the rings, the old man had given them to him. What had he said? And his wife, as well? That they were now his and could not be returned or altered. Why was it that he kept forgetting? He glanced back at the man. "This is just a myth. You're certain there's no one who can resize this ring?"

The man's glance wavered for a second before he shook his head. It was enough, and Will regarded him with narrowed eyes. "What is it? There is someone, isn't there?"

Stepping back, the man put his hands up as though in fear. "No. No one will touch them."

"Are you sure?"

"I am very sure."

He left in frustration, still determined to have the ring resized. It was only when he returned to his flat that he found the terse, tear-stained letter from Carolyn breaking off the engagement. With no explanation, she wrote that he wasn't the man she thought she loved, and she never wanted to see him again.

Not understanding what could have happened, he rang her immediately, but she refused to take his call. When he tried again, her mother answered, saying Carolyn didn't want to speak with him and to please not call again. Before he could say another word she hung up.

He knew he should go to her but finding himself in the middle of a project with another artist, he couldn't leave. It wasn't until four days later, with the gold ring in his pocket, that he finally took the train to Edinburgh. He was determined to find out what had happened, and hoping by his presence to win her back.

He arrived in the late afternoon, surprised to see at least a dozen cars parked on the circular drive in front of the massive house. His first thought was that they might be having a party, but the entire place seemed oddly quiet, as if shrouded in gloom. Undaunted, he rang the bell. When a housekeeper opened the door, the first thing he saw was his portrait of the mother hanging in a prominent position in the vestibule. Ignoring it, he asked for Carolyn. The maid hesitated before bursting into tears. Through deep sobs, she told him she was sorry, but the young lady had died two days before of a rare form of pneumonia.

With tears stinging his own eyes, he looked past the maid, seeing the girl's mother glaring at him, her face contorted in rage. "Leave here, now," she hissed. Although he was twenty feet away, he heard her as clearly as if she was whispering in his ear.

He stared back in despair, knowing nothing he could say would change anything; it had come down to a matter of life and death, and death had won. Before turning away, he glanced back at the portrait. No rage there, just a coquettish smile of seduction; a seduction that never happened.

As long afternoon shadows from a circular tower crept over him, he looked up just as a curtain moved in a high window. Later he would question if he had really seen, or just imagined, the face of death peering out the cracked, cloudy glass.

Suddenly a cold, harsh wind sprang up, the trees sighing as young spring leaves were ripped from their branches and swirled around him. With a stab of fear, he grasped the box in his pocket as an icy wind, or perhaps a whisper, caressed his cheek.

Since his taxi had long disappeared, he had no choice but to walk to the nearest town, about a mile away. Deep in his own grief, he wrapped his jacket around himself, hardly feeling the chill. Seeing a pub, he went in and ordered a pint of lager. He needed more than that but knew no amount of alcohol could eradicate the profound emptiness and sorrow that pervaded his entire being. Nothing that had happened that day, much less the days before, made any sense to him. Sitting at a rough-hewn table in a darkened corner, he downed three more, trying to blot out the impenetrable pain that would forever haunt his mind and his soul.

Riddled with guilt, he boarded the train back to London. Although he intended to go straight to his flat, for some unknown reason the taxi took a detour. When he looked out, he suddenly realized they were on the street with the jewelry store, the one where he had stopped to ask about resizing the ring. Since it wasn't on the way home, he didn't understand how they had ended up in front of it. Without taking time to think, he told the driver to stop.

When he entered the shop the same man was there, and with a look of alarm he stepped back from his glass case. "Why have you come back? There is nothing I can do for you."

Will stood his ground. "I believe you know someone who can. I don't care about resizing the ring any longer. The girl is dead, and I'm sure it has to do with the ring. I want a name."

The man shook his head and crossed himself. "I'm sorry, sir, but . . ."

"Please."

Will saw him take a breath. "The girl has truly died?"

"Do you think I would say it if it wasn't true?"

With a nervous glance out at the street, he whispered, "If you go 'round the corner, you'll find an alleyway, Blue Crescent Lane. Third door on the left. The name's MacDonald. That's all I can say."

"He will know to talk to me?"

He gave a quick nod. "He will. When you speak with him, you'll understand. Be cautious, young man."

Will left and found the lane, not more than a narrow medieval alley with a row of crumbling wooden buildings, most boarded up. He stopped and knocked lightly on a scuffed blue door, the paint faded and peeling. A reedy voice called out, "It's open."

A steep staircase faced him, and from the first step he was aware of warped wood creaking ominously beneath his feet. In the pale half-light of a soot-encrusted window he saw an old man slouched in a tattered club chair, the fabric torn and discolored. His face was deeply wrinkled, and white hair sprouted from all angles of his gaunt head.

"Mr. MacDonald?"

"Just MacDonald," he stated in a garrulous voice. "What is it you want of me?"

Will held out his hand. "I want to know about this . . . this ring."

The man smirked before looking up at him with a rictus of a grin. "What's yer name?"

"Will. Will Jamieson."

"The painter," he nodded, mumbling to himself. "Throw those old newspapers off that chair and sit down."

Will did as he asked and sat down facing him. "How do you know of me?"

"No matter. Where is the other?"

"The other?"

"The other ring." His tone was gruff.

Will fumbled in his pocket. "Here. Still in the box."

"And someone has, ah, already passed because of these rings?"

Startled, Will asked how he could possibly know. But MacDonald just stared back at him with a terse shake of his head.

"Two, actually. My fiancée . . ." His voice broke.

MacDonald hardly noticed. "Hand me the box."

After placing the box in his palm, Will watched as MacDonald ran his fingers over it. The top creaked, opening to his touch, and Will flinched as the sapphire sparked, briefly shattering the gloom. The man nodded as though some communication had passed between him and the stone. Removing the gold ring, he placed it carefully on the table next to him. With a yellowed fingernail, he flipped up the tattered velvet cushion, extracting a minuscule sepia-colored parchment.

"I didn't know there was anything underneath."

MacDonald mumbled. "Nor did the man who gave the rings to you."

"How do you know he gave them to me? That I didn't buy them?"

"These rings cannot be bought. They are both a blessing and a curse. You were chosen."

"Chosen? A curse?"

The man's look was hard. "Look at me. How old do you think I am?"

"I wouldn't know. Eighty-five?"

MacDonald laughed before beginning to cough. Between taking birdlike sips from a glass half-filled with a cloudy liquid, he answered in a raspy voice, "I'm well over a hundred and twenty."

He was obviously frail and in ill-health, but Will was doubtful. "How can that be?"

"Look," he said, leaning forward and holding out a gnarled hand. On the third finger of his right hand was a ring, a ring almost identical to the one Will was wearing. "This is my curse."

"I was told the rings bring power and success. And immortal love, whatever that means. How is it a curse?"

After drinking more of the sickly white liquid in his glass — Will was sure it wasn't water — he took a ragged breath. "A long time ago I was successful, admired and respected. I partied with royalty and dined with heads of state. I owned a townhouse in Belgravia, a villa in Spain, and a yacht in the Maldives. There were servants to take care of my every need. I had luxury cars, and my wife wore designer dresses, jewels, and furs. You see, I ran a powerful global investment empire that extended from London to Hong Kong. In my mind I had fulfilled, even exceeded, the promise of the ring. Not only did I support charitable causes, I was generous to my friends and all those in my employ. And yet, despite all my treasures," he wheezed, "I became greedy. I didn't think of it that way some sixty years ago. But, in truth, that's what it was."

"I'm not sure I understand."

"Then be quiet and take these words to heart." Looking down at the slip of parchment in his hand, he began to read:

"Whoever are given these stones are offered blessings beyond the realm of dreams in that they are immortal and carry through the ages. They arose through primordial portals from deep within the earth to emerge into the light and woe to the one who allows them to return. Who chances to wear the stones must use them wisely, to enhance their lives and those of others with love and without malice. Or be forever damned."

The old man suddenly looked angry. "It's my own bloody fault. I knew the warnings, and yet I still sinned against them. I stole money, lots of money. Oddly enough from my own company."

"Were you caught?"

"Yes and no. The ring saved me from prison, but in turn has caused me to live a long, painful life." He began to cough again and reached for his glass. After taking a long drink, he put the glass down with a sullen look in his wet eyes. "Because of me, my dear wife suffered and died in agony. My friends, such as they were, first deserted me and then perished, one by one. So, you see, I am indeed living the curse of these rings. I have tried to take my own life, but something always pulls me back. This is my warning to you: embrace the power, the success, but do not betray the gift." He replaced the parchment and the ring on its bed of velvet before handing it back. "It is essential you find the one this ring is meant for, for it must be given within your lifetime. When you do, you will find not only eternal love but also completion, for she is your one soul mate throughout time. Take my story to heart. I wish you the best, young man. I've said enough. It's time for you to go."

Will blinked. *Throughout time?* "May I ask one more question?"

MacDonald, looking even more haggard than before, muttered, "Be quick."

"How did you know your wife was, as you say, the one?"

"A fair question," he said, seeming to gain a little strength. "You see, unlike you, I never had possession of both rings. When Constance was young, she by chance walked into an antiques store, one she had never noticed before. She was looking for a gift for a friend when the owner, who she described as an elderly man with a stoop, invited her to try on a gold ring with a dark stone. She wasn't really interested, not until he told her stories of love and success, and, as she liked to say, it sounded like such a lovely fantasy that she decided to indulge herself and buy it. After picking out something for her friend, the man charged her only for the gift. When she asked him why, he answered: 'Take the ring with my blessings. I promise you will find love immortal.'"

Will smiled. "I imagine she couldn't say no to that."

"Who could?"

"But how did you know . . . ?"

For the first time, MacDonald smiled, revealing teeth yellowed and stained. He put his head back and closed his eyes as if envisioning the memory. "I was a carefree young man with no thoughts of marriage. Until one day, like Constance, I went into a shop looking for something. Whatever it was, I can no longer recall, but I was approached by an old bearded man with a stoop carrying a roll of tattered red velvet. I don't think I need to describe the rest."

Will nodded.

"A few months later, I met Constance at the house of a mutual friend. We laughed about the coincidence of having similar rings. I think I fell in love with her at first sight."

"You were lucky."

"It has naught to do with luck. It had already been foretold by fate. I promise you, you will recognize the one the ring is meant for."

"I'm not so sure. Not after what has already happened."

The old man sipped from his glass, and Will realized he would provide no answer.

"You said your wife died. Do you have her ring as well?"

"Yes and no," MacDonald answered, wiping away a tear. "I have the ring, but not the sapphire."

When Will looked back with a silent question in his eyes, McDonald sighed, "One of the mysteries of the sapphires is that when one passes, the stones are never found. Do not ask me why, for I have no answer for you."

Will hesitated before holding out his hand. "I was told this ring is silver with gold. Is that true?"

He shook his head. "The metals in these rings, like the sapphires, were forged by the solar winds and conflagrations that birthed this planet through countless millennia of volcanic fire, oceans of water, and more ice ages than have been told. What this metal is, and where it originated, is as yet unknown."

"And the sapphires?"

"You must go. I can say no more."

Will stood up. "I'll leave you. But please, at least tell me that."

With some hesitation, he nodded and glanced at Will. "There is a place called Callanish. Do you know of it?"

"I do. I was there on a school outing. Long ago, I'm afraid."

The man's eyes bored into him. "Then make sure that was your first and last visit. Heed what was written in the parchment; you must not allow the sapphires to return to their origins."

"At Callanish? I don't understand."

"I've already said too much. Remember, beware of that place."

"Are your rings and mine the only pairs?"

MacDonald sat back. "No. There are still, I believe, several more. And throughout the centuries, most, but not all, have been found in locations in Great Britain. Others, as far away as China, even Argentina."

"When was the parchment written?"

"At least two thousand years ago. The alphabet is *eyam*, what is now called Ogham. An example would be MAQ or MAQI which evolved to Mac. If you were CUNAMAGLI, you would have been a prince of wolves. Most of the original alphabet was found carved as inscriptions in stones or trees that were considered to be mystical. What is written on the parchment can only be interpreted by those in possession of the sapphires."

"Then I can read it?"

"I have given you the message. That is enough. Go live your life. The less you know about the rings, the better. I advise you to abandon your questions. Do not pursue them further."

"Why? Please tell me so I can understand your warnings."

The man sat still, as though making a decision. "These sapphires have influenced civilization throughout history. I don't know why one is given them, but they seem to end up in the hands of those who have some ability to impact this murky, chaotic world in which we exist. Think of Julius Caesar, who is always depicted with a large medal or pendant of power around his neck. Somewhere in such ornaments is a small, unimposing blue stone, more often than not surrounded by larger gemstones such as rubies, emeralds, and so on. The stones may look insignificant, and yet they have both manipulated and impacted the past. Caesar was a dynamic leader who extended Rome's reach well into Europe. But infused with power and weakened by his infatuation with Cleopatra, he betrayed the gift and thus was murdered by his rivals. And yet, look at Justinian who, along with his wife Theodora, built the powerful Byzantine empire. Both wore rings with such stones." He stopped and chuckled. "It is said that Catherine the Great stole and then hid her husband's ring, thereby rendering him more useless than he already was."

"How can you know they were in possession of the sapphires?"

"So it is told. The stones are to be used for good." His voice became harsh. "It is only when we overreach or become weak that they curse us. You should be aware that through the centuries there are those who have discovered the magic of the sapphires and, thinking they will create power and wealth, have attempted to seek them out. They are wrong. The gifts are granted only to those chosen. And yet, how or why that is, is not for us to know. In your case, you have a special talent; you create, and thus have the ability to enhance not only your life but the lives of those around you. I suggest you pursue your singular gift rather than trying to change the world."

"I have no desire to change the world. Just to understand why I was chosen or given this gift — if gift it is."

"In truth, young man, there is no apparent logic as to why one is chosen and another not. We humans are frail creatures who must make the best of our lives. In my case, I squandered the power I was offered. The wretched being you see before you is the result.

"May I ask how you know this?"

"I listen to the voices."

"The voices?"

"Surely you hear them."

"Yes. But to me they are incomprehensible. Like hushed whispers heard from a distant room."

"The voices you hear are those who have gone before. They live inside each of us. They speak of our journey through the millennia."

Will stared at the man, aware he was talking about the voices of the dead. "How is that possible?"

"How is anything possible?"

"What about the chants?"

"I have never heard chants, only muted voices."

Will shook his head, wondering if this could become any more bewildering. "How is it that you understand them?"

"Perhaps because I am about to join them." Obviously exhausted, he closed his eyes. "Maybe I am already a ghost." His voice was barely a whisper.

While it wasn't the answer Will hoped for, he knew better than to push any further. "May I come see you again?"

"I would advise against it." He stopped to take a breath. "Although you may think I'm mad, listen and trust my final words to you. There are entities, earthbound spirits who seek to return the sapphires to the earth from whence they came. In the time of the ancients they were no doubt influential and powerful men, likely Shamans or clan elders who were put to death by another, more powerful hand. Although they perished millennia ago, they never passed over and their spirits still wield a seductive yet deadly force. Be ever vigilant. Do not allow yourself to be drawn into their realm."

Startled, Will asked, "What does that mean?"

The old man sighed. "I can say no more. Stay far from Callanish and you will have no problems. Ask no more questions. Take care to keep the gold ring safe until you find the one it is meant for."

"How will I know?"

"I already told you, you will know."

Chapter 17

"Will." The voice was loud, shattering the dream. He awoke to his shoulder being shaken.

Opening his eyes to morning light, he wasn't sure where he was. "Oh, Cia," he muttered. "What time is it? I was really out."

"You were, indeed. It's just after eight. I was getting worried. Are you sure you're all right? Why did you stay up here?"

He wasn't about to tell her of his dream, or more realistically a half-awake trance—one he'd been unable to stop. Standing up, he felt a distinct pain in his back, no doubt from reclining in such an odd position. "I meant to come back to bed, but I guess I fell asleep." He looked at her. "Was I snoring?"

She made a face. "No. I've never heard you snore. But you were mumbling, and I had a hard time waking you."

"I was, ah, dreaming."

"About what?"

He shook his head, glancing beyond her to where two portraits, shining in the morning light, stared tranquilly back at him. Having no time to question why such heartrending memories were suddenly surfacing now, he took her hand. "Nothing important. Come, let's go downstairs. I could use some tea."

Later that morning, after Will went off to teach a class at St. Martin's, Patrick suggested they take the tube to New Bond Street to visit a couple of galleries. Before going to lunch, they stopped at Will's gallery where Patrick introduced her to the director, James Davies, a dapper middle-aged man with a sharply pointed goatee.

Cheerfully clasping Cia's hands, he walked her over to a couple of small paintings. "Will's not part of this show, but I always keep one or two of his portraits out."

"They're lovely."

With a self-satisfied nod, he reached over to straighten one. "Yes. They always attract attention."

Back on the street, Patrick suggested a small café in a nearby mews where they could talk in quiet.

As soon as they ordered, Cia asked if he was aware that Will had slept part of the night on the couch in his studio.

"I didn't know, but not to worry. I've been there many times when I've seen light in the middle of the night. Sometimes when he's unable to sleep he goes to the studio to work." He grinned. "Artists don't keep regular work hours."

"I guess," she sighed. "So, Patrick, you said there was more about Will that I needed to know."

Before answering, he took a moment to light one of his ubiquitous cigarettes. "For what I'm about to tell you, you must open your mind, because much of it won't seem real or even remotely plausible. It will sound like one of those fantasies written from times long past. Are the stories real, or is some writer making them up? In truth, much of Will's story does seem a fantasy. And yet here we are, it's almost 1975, and although we may not want to acknowledge it, I have come to believe there are mysteries that surround us; conundrums, if you will, beyond our comprehension."

"That sounds ominous. But, please, go ahead."

"So. Let us return to the seductive duchess with the beautiful daughter. Her name, by the way, was Carolyn. After returning to London, Will finished the portrait and shipped it off to the lady, who, by all accounts, was thrilled. But Will couldn't get the daughter out of his mind. When he rang her, she was delighted to hear from him, and they arranged to meet in Cambridge the following weekend. After that, she came frequently to London or he took the train to see her. She was about to return home to Edinburgh for the summer when he asked her to marry him."

"That was the engagement he mentioned." *As did Stefan.*

"He was twenty-six and she nineteen, and they were deep in the throes of young love. A day or so before she was to leave, he—supposedly by chance—passed an old, nondescript antique shop. I don't know where, perhaps Camden Passage, certainly not anywhere around Portobello Road. He once told me he no longer remembered its location. Inside he noticed two unusual rings set with dark stones that seemed to give off an odd luminescence. The proprietor was reluctant to take them out, but Will insisted. After Will asked a lot of questions, particularly about the stones, the man said they were sapphires, supposedly very ancient and set into rings of gold and silver. More important, he told Will the rings had unique powers that created an unbreakable, immortal bond between the two people who wore them. He also warned that the smaller ring would fit only one, and giving it to the wrong woman could have unforeseen consequences. When Will said he wanted to buy them, the man just gave them to him. Will told me he felt as though the man recognized him and was waiting to pass them on."

"The man actually told him the stones had *powers*?"

"He did."

"And do they?"

He held up his hands. "Be patient. Let me tell the rest of it."

"This is weird but fascinating, isn't it?"

Patrick smirked. "I'll let you decide. So, when Will got back from the shop he rang Carolyn. They met the next evening in Hyde Park where he asked her to marry him." He looked pointedly at Cia, whose only response was a nod.

"When she said yes, he put the ring on her finger. But it didn't fit, and Will promised to have it resized. Although disappointed, she asked him to bring it to her home in Scotland, where she said they could announce their engagement.

"While she returned to Edinburgh, Will stayed in London to finish some work. When he took the ring back to the shop, he was told the old man had died, and quite unexpectedly. His grieving widow not only blamed his death on the rings but reminded Will that the smaller ring was meant for one person and could not be resized. He left in shock and tried another jeweler who told him exactly the same thing."

"That must have been very upsetting for him."

"It was, Cia. Not only had the ring become a problem, he had also begun to worry that Carolyn's parents wouldn't approve of him. Still, he never expected what happened next." He stopped to finish his beer before waving to the waiter for another.

Cia put up her hands. "Don't stop now, Patrick."

"Apparently, when Carolyn told her parents about her engagement her mother became furious. She said she would never allow her to marry an artist, particularly that artist, and she was expected to marry a man of her own aristocratic status. Although her father agreed, he said if she was truly in love he would consider the possibility, but not until he met the young man. Her mother, however, remained adamant and refused to discuss it further." He paused and shook his head. "Until one day when she did."

Cia stared at him wide-eyed. "She told Carolyn she had slept with Will?"

He nodded, his face solemn. "That's exactly what she did."

"How could she do such a thing? Did Carolyn call Will to talk about it? To ask if it was even true?"

"No, Cia, she never did. She broke the engagement in a letter. When he called to try and speak with her, her mother hung up on him. A couple of days later, he took the train to Edinburgh and went to her house, only to discover she had passed away very suddenly."

Cia put her hands to her face. "How tragic."

"It was. But he still didn't understand how it all happened. Not until a couple of years later when, by chance, he ran into one of her friends. She was the one who told him the whole miserable story. Not only what the mother had done, but that Carolyn, grief stricken, had taken sick and died of some unknown strain of pneumonia. I'm not sure Will ever really believed it."

"Did he think the ring had something to do with her death?"

"Not at first. It was only when he returned to London that he began to blame himself for not taking the warnings seriously."

"That's crazy. One would have to believe in witchcraft."

"Not witchcraft, Cia. More like spirits."

"What's the difference?"

"Witchcraft has to do with black magic. Whether it exists or not, it's still, for better or worse, a product of human imagination. Spirits, at least these spirits, if one chooses to believe the legends, are said to have emanated from the earth at the time it was formed billions of years ago. The rocks in that area of Scotland are some of the most ancient on the planet."

She shook her head in disbelief. *Witchcraft? Spirits? Why not just fairytales?* The difference was these fairytales were being told far more from the perspective of the Grimm brothers than Walt Disney. Not to mention that Cinderella's stepsisters didn't exactly expire when the glass slipper didn't fit.

Patrick mashed out another cigarette in the already overflowing ashtray. "When Will returned a few days later from Scotland, he was a changed man."

"How so?"

He looked up as an impatient-looking waiter brought the bill. Cia realized several hours had passed and, except for the two of them, the café was deserted. "Let me share this with you," she said, picking up her purse.

Patrick shook his head. "No, Cia, I have it." Handing a few pounds to the waiter, he said, "We'll just be a few minutes more."

"Patrick. you said Will had changed. I would think he would have been in mourning."

"He was. He was also determined to discover how such a thing could have happened. With the death of the old man, his only recourse was to go back to the other jeweler who he was convinced knew more than he had said. Will must have been quite intimidating because he was finally given a name: MacDonald."

"MacDonald?"

"Yes. Although Will later questioned whether the man was real or some sort of spectral vision, MacDonald gave him valuable information about the rings and their power."

"Wait a minute. Did you just say 'spectral vision'? Are you serious?"

"It's too long to go into now, but trust me when I tell you this is neither joke nor fantasy. Although MacDonald explained how to live with the supposed 'gift' as well as the power of the stones, he also warned Will about something he called 'earthbound spirits,' and also to stay away from Callanish."

She stared at him. "This is sounding crazier every minute. What is Callanish?"

"An ancient stone circle in the Outer Hebrides. It was constructed over five thousand years ago, about the same time as the oldest pyramids in Egypt, and two thousand years before Stonehenge. No one knows anything about it. Whoever built it had no written language and left no trace of their existence other than a few rough burial cairns. It's stands in a cold, desolate plain of rain and wind. Not exactly where you'd go for a holiday."

"And 'earthbound spirits?' Did he ask about whatever they're supposed to be? The very thought makes my skin crawl."

133

"I asked Will the same question. He said he was so overwhelmed he didn't think of asking anything further."

"Come on. This is getting too weird."

"Any more weird than hearing those strange voices?"

"I guess not. And Will really believes all this?"

"He's taken it very seriously."

"Did he ever go back to MacDonald?"

"Actually, he did."

She looked at him with surprise. "And?"

As though requiring a moment to think, he stopped to light another cigarette. "The alleyway was boarded up, and the buildings were being razed. The jewelry store had closed, and when Will enquired in the shop next to it, he was told the owner had shut it down within one day and disappeared, leaving no forwarding address. He also questioned if anyone knew of MacDonald, or anything about an old man living in the third building in the alleyway. The clerk was dismissive, saying those buildings had been abandoned for years, and it was about time they were demolished. He confided that pedestrians had long steered clear of the alley due to rumors that it was haunted by an old man who had died decades ago under mysterious circumstances."

Cia sat back and shook her head. "Come on, Patrick. You're frightening me. I have to say that as a resident of the twentieth century, this entire story is off the wall. And yet, Will can't have imagined that conversation with MacDonald." She looked unsure. "Could he?"

He smiled. "Remember when I said you would have to open your mind? That much of what I was about to tell you wouldn't seem remotely plausible? Was there really an old man that no one knew about? Or was MacDonald really an illusion?"

"Or a ghost?" she said, with a shiver.

"And yet, despite his conversation with MacDonald, Will was still heartbroken. When he went home he took off his ring and put it in the box along with the other, gold ring. Then, as he tells it, he put the box on a table in his studio. When he went to get it later, the box was gone."

She made a face. "This is too much. Disappearing rings?"

"Well, it turned out the box hadn't really disappeared. It showed up under some papers he swore he never touched. After that, he put it safely in a drawer. He told me that after he did, the house took on an unearthly silence. When I called him a few days later, he sounded morose and refused to go out or see anyone, even his closest friends. He spent all his time in the studio trying to paint and becoming increasingly frustrated because he didn't think his work was any good."

Cia hesitated, thinking this was essentially the same as Stefan had told her. "Was he painting portraits?"

"No, Cia. His portrait work was drying up. He wouldn't leave the studio to go to parties or gallery openings where he'd meet people. He wasn't even making calls. When some of his lady friends rang, he would say he'd call back and never did. I told him he had to stop feeling sorry for himself and get back into circulation." He shook his head. "That time he hung up on me."

"That's crazy."

"He was out of his mind with grief and guilt. Within a few months, he was down to his last few pounds and becoming desperate. That's when he says he woke up in the middle of the night after dreaming of the old man in the curio shop. He was holding out the lacquered box, saying it was time to wear the ring; that it would bring him great love and even greater success. Although it was three in the morning and Will had vowed never to touch it again, he went to the drawer and took out the box. He later told me that the very moment he picked up the ring the voices returned and the house came alive around him."

Feeling a shiver, she said, "No way. I don't believe it. This is too much, Patrick."

He looked at her, his face somber. "No matter how you feel about what I've told you, you must never speak of it to Will. Particularly of the rings. He can never know we talked."

"I understand. Anyway, that's all in the past, isn't it?" Sounding more confident, she added, "I'm in love with the man he is today."

He stood up. "The waiter is glaring at us. We should get back."

"You mean back to the very popular *and* successful Will Jamieson?"

Taking her arm, he nodded. "And we're about to have dinner with some people who want to make him even more successful."

As they alighted from the taxi, Cia saw Will standing in the open doorway talking with a young woman in a frilly blue dress who was holding his hand and giggling. Patrick held her back. "Pay no mind,

Cia. He's been painting her portrait. She's the daughter of a very influential member of the House of Lords."

As the girl backed away toward a waiting saloon car, she blew Will a kiss.

Cia raised her eyebrows. "That was something I didn't need to see." While Patrick shook his head and mumbled something about "women," she marched in a huff past a bemused Will who tried to stop her. Ignoring him, she continued directly up to his bedroom which, to her relief, appeared undisturbed. When he didn't follow her, she waited a few minutes before going to the kitchen where he was speaking with Patrick, who immediately excused himself.

"What's wrong, Cia?" His look was open, innocent.

She took a breath. "Will, you know I'm not the jealous type, certainly not in our situation, but were you really with another woman while I'm here sharing your bed? I'll be gone in a few days. Couldn't you have waited until then?"

Seeing her eyes misting with tears, he took her in his arms. "Cia, my love, come with me to the studio. I'll be happy to show you what I was doing with her."

At the top of the stairs he took her hand and led her to a large painting of the same young woman she had just seen, except that she wasn't wearing the frilly blue dress. In the painting, she was dressed in a flowing Victorian gown, her pretty face looking out as though caressed by a morning mist. The colors were pale strokes of violets and blues, the style imagining the post-impressionists. Noticing the same Victorian gown thrown casually over a chair, she turned to Will. "I'm sorry. I didn't mean to think the worst. It's just . . ."

"Cia, I promise you it was nothing. She was delighted with the painting and was being a bit flirty. Most girls are." He put his finger under her chin, tilting her face up so he could kiss her lips. "Aren't you?" he whispered seductively.

"Where's Patrick," she asked, suddenly blushing.

"Upstairs in the loft behind the studio. I'm sure he'll be down shortly. Come to bed. We haven't much time."

Dinner turned out to be with the same two producers as well as a writer from the BBC, who explained with great energy that they were planning a series about artists past and present. After describing a format that would feature contemporary artists discussing their work in relation to past painters whom they admired or had influenced them, they said they wanted Will to host several segments. Although Will, low-key as always, asked to be told more, Cia couldn't miss the flicker of excitement in his eyes. After dinner, the conversation went on until last call when, reluctant to end the evening, they moved to the nearby flat of one the producers to continue their discussions.

It was well past midnight and many brandies later when, with handshakes all around and promises to continue the discussion, the three of them departed. Since they weren't far from Will's flat, he insisted that due to their inebriated state they required fresh air, and, despite Patrick's protests, they should walk. More than a bit unsteady, with Cia in the middle and their arms supporting one another, they wove their way down a quiet Chelsea street in the direction of Fulham Road. Without warning, Will broke into song, bellowing broken fragments of 'Che gelida manina,' an aria from *La Bohème*, at the top of his lungs. Startled, Cia tried to stop him, saying he was going to wake up the entire neighborhood. Suddenly, Patrick chimed in, and in exasperation Cia yelled at both of them to shut up. That's when they noticed the bobby watching from the faint glow of a streetlamp just ahead.

Tapping his nightstick against his thigh, he faced them. "What're you three doin' in the middle of tha road howlin' like stray cats at two in the mornin'?"

Will spoke up, taking care to enunciate his words. "Well, my good man. To be truthful we've just left our friends and are now on our way home."

Cia stifled a giggle.

"And where might that be?"

"Cresswell Place. Just a couple of streets away," Will said, trying to point while steadying himself against Cia who was shaking with barely contained laughter.

"Let's see some identification," he said, looking doubtful.

Trying to maintain a dignified balance, Patrick sniggered. "Please, sir. Who would be carrying identification on the street at this late hour?"

With a shake of his head, the cop took out a pad and pencil. "So wot's yer names, then?"

With a straight face, Will responded, "Ben Johnson." Holding back laughter, Patrick blurted out, "Christopher Marlowe," and Cia, in a moment of panic, croaked, "Zelda, um, Zelda Fitzgerald."

After licking the point of his pencil and carefully writing down the names, he shined his flashlight over the three of them. "Best be on yer way. No more caterwauling and disturbin' the peace."

"No, sir," Patrick muttered, his face appropriately solemn. After turning the corner and glancing back, they collapsed in laughter.

Chapter 18

The next morning, after Will—none the worse for wear despite a long night of drinking—left to meet with James Davies at his gallery. Patrick padded into the kitchen holding his head and yawning. "That was quite a night. Is there any coffee, Cia? Tea won't do today. That's the problem with staying with Will. Late nights and too much booze."

"Yes, of course," she said, spooning coffee into a French press. "I had to go out and buy this. Will won't even try it."

"He's a committed tea drinker. Always has been."

"Not entirely tea. I never drink this much at home. And yet it never seems to bother him the next morning."

"Too true. Unfortunately, I require aspirin."

She tossed him the bottle. "I already took a couple."

"Thanks. What are you doing today? I have a meeting before taking the train back to Yorkshire."

"I have to go to Arlington-York Press. The owner is a friend of the publisher I work for and he's asked me to check in to say hello. Whatever for, I have no idea. I really wish we could talk more."

"Is there anything specific?"

She poured coffee and handed him a cup. "After all you've told me, I'm still not sure what to think."

"Didn't you say just yesterday that it was all in the past?"

"I did. But it still keeps running through my mind."

"I wouldn't worry too much. I see the affection the two of you have for one another. And although you live on the other side of the pond, I have a feeling that things will eventually work out. I'm quite sure he's in love with you."

She put her hands to her face. "Oh, Patrick, do you really think so?"

139

"You have to understand that after what happened to Carolyn, he's overly cautious. Just be patient, Cia. Give him time. Under no circumstance can you even hint that we've talked. He must never know I betrayed his confidence, much less his friendship."

"I wish I didn't have to leave in a few days. Is there anything more you can tell me?"

"Not really. Nothing more than you already know."

She looked doubtful. "But there is more, isn't there? I don't know why, but somehow I feel it."

"There are things about Will that may seem otherworldly, and yet he's very much a product of his own time. Despite all that's occurred since he's had the rings, he lives firmly in this world and no longer seems to question those things that cannot be explained." He paused and thought a moment. "Until now, he's had no reason to."

"What are you saying?"

"Maybe I shouldn't say this, but I have the feeling he may be questioning his decision to keep the other ring hidden."

"That's good. Isn't it? You said it's supposed to be passed on."

"He tried that once. He doesn't want to repeat his mistake."

"Even if he thinks I'm 'the one'?"

He put his hand on her arm. "Please, Cia, give him time. He'll make the right decision."

Not letting it go, she shook her head. "I still believe there must be more. Maybe there are things I'm not supposed to know."

"Or perhaps I shouldn't have told you as much as I did. And yet as I said before, I do believe you are now a part of this."

She looked confused. "Part of what?"

"There appears to be more activity around him."

"You mean the voices?"

"Lately they sound more agitated. And those birds. They're something new."

"I've seen them, Patrick. Not only this time. I also saw two on a tree outside a pub in Lewes. It felt like they were watching me. That sounds crazy, doesn't it?"

He shrugged. "I don't know. Ravens, other than those that have populated the Tower of London for centuries, are very rare in Great Britain. What they're doing outside this house or a pub in Lewes, I have no idea."

"One or two have been outside almost every day. When Will was with me at my cottage in Massachusetts, two huge hawks showed up. I had never seen them before. It was creepy."

"Did you see them in Yorkshire?"

She shivered. "Yes."

He sighed. "Actually, I did as well. They may, indeed, have something to do with you."

She shivered. "Patrick, would you leave me your phone number? In case I ever want to call you?"

"Of course. Feel free to ring me anytime."

Arlington-York occupied an old Georgian building just off Bloomsbury Square. A secretary with white hair and a stern demeanor showed Cia to the office of Mr. Phillips, Sid's friend. A gaunt, dour-looking man, he nevertheless turned out to be quite chatty, dispelling any concerns she had about why she was there or what she would have to say to him. He told her about book-selling in London before asking about publishing in the States. Twenty minutes later, after an assistant brought tea, he asked specifically about her job. More relaxed, she told him about the authors she worked with as well as answering his questions regarding the book they were doing with Lanny Winters.

"I assume it has been printed by now? We're expecting a shipment from BookEnds for the holidays."

She smiled. "It has. Since I've been away, I haven't seen it yet. I do know that everyone is very proud of it, including Lanny."

"Your publisher, Sidney, told me you played a significant part in the production of it."

With a slight blush, she nodded. "That was nice of him."

Carefully placing his tea cup in its saucer, he looked at her with a serious expression on his face. "Miss Reynolds, have you ever considered working here, in London?"

She could hardly breathe. It was a thought that had been swirling in her mind for days; one she could never get up the nerve to discuss with Will. "Actually, I have," she stammered. "I would, however, need a work visa, and there's nothing special about what I do."

He shook his head. "Quite the contrary. I do believe it would be possible. I could use someone with your talent."

Feeling her heart beating wildly, she put her hand to her chest. "Thank you, Mr. Phillips. I don't know what to say."

They were interrupted by a light knock on the door as his secretary poked her head in. "Sorry to disturb you, sir. Your next appointment is here."

Cia stood up as Mr. Phillips walked around the desk and handed her his card. "Give me a call, Miss Reynolds, if you'd like to discuss this further. I doubt my friend Sidney will be happy, but I think you'd make a smashing addition to our team."

Thanking him again, she shook his hand and turned to go.

"You will think about it, won't you?" he called after her.

She smiled. "Yes. Definitely. I'll be leaving in a few days, though."

"No rush. Ring me from New York. The position will be waiting."

Cia arrived at the flat, once again finding ravens perched on the trees, this time in front. Seeing her, they began fluffing their feathers and cawing loudly. With a shudder, she quickly unlocked the door, and, hearing Dvořák's "New World Symphony" blaring, practically raced up to the studio. Hearing her, Will looked back. "Ah. There you are."

"I hope I'm not disturbing you."

"Not at all. Is something wrong?"

She shivered. "I just saw those birds again."

After lowering the music, he put down the fine brush he had been using to touch up an eye of his subject: a middle-aged woman this time, not the girl from a few days ago. "Ignore them," he said, putting his hands around her waist and giving her a kiss. "How was your meeting?"

"Oh. It actually went well."

"Tell me about it."

She shrugged. "There's not much to tell. We discussed publishing in London and New York. That's all."

He shook his head. "Come now, Cia. You're being too vague. I think there's something more than 'it went well,' isn't there?"

She looked back at him with questions in her eyes.

"He asked you to come work for him, didn't he?"

Surprised, she stepped back. "How can you know that?"

"Did you not intend to tell me?"

"I guess I would have. Right now, you're frightening me."

"I can't tell you how I know. I just do. These things happen from time to time."

"Are you clairvoyant?"

"More like intuitive. So, when were you planning to tell me?"

"I would have at the right time. I mean if there was a right time. It's a big decision. I was hoping you'd bring it up."

"You're right, Cia," he said with some hesitation. "But let's leave that subject for the moment." He glanced across the studio. "I want to ask something of you."

"What?"

"Will you sit for me?"

She looked up at him. "Sit?"

He smiled. "Not nude, if that's what you're thinking. I'd like to do a portrait."

She indicated the painting he had been working on. "What about her?"

"Lady Wyscombe can wait. I only have you for a few more days."

"All right. But isn't there another aspect to this conversation? Something you might want to tell me first?"

"What?"

Giving him a coy smile, she said, "Didn't you just say you were intuitive?"

"Yes, Cia," he said, looking into her eyes. "I do love you."

With joy flooding her entire being, she reached up to kiss him. "And I love you," she whispered, barely registering a soft current of air that, with barely a sigh, ruffled her hair.

After another late night out with Will's friends, a night, as always, filled with intense conversation and too much booze, Will woke up unusually early. Hearing him moving about, Cia mumbled, "Are you all right?"

"Did you hear that noise?"

She squinted up at him. "No. What is it?"

"I don't know," he said, going to the window. Opening the shade to the pink glow of dawn, he stepped back. "Bloody hell. There's a spot of blood on the glass. A bird must have flown into it."

Startled, Cia looked up. "Should you go down and look?"

"No. It's probably just a sparrow or something."

"I'm not so sure," she said. "I dreamed about those huge black birds last night. They were everywhere, watching us."

"That's strange. I had a similar dream. I was in some sort of a field talking with a man, but there was a mist and I couldn't see his face. Behind me, large birds were perched on a tall white stone." He closed his eyes. "I couldn't see them, but I knew they were there. And the man," he shuddered. "He felt like death . . ." his voice trailed off. He looked out the window again. "You may be right. I see a black bird on the sidewalk. It looks dazed."

Hearing the tension in his voice, she didn't mention that in her dream the birds had been watching from what looked like a white column. Thinking her dream had been far too similar to his, she shivered. "Is there a window open? Why is it suddenly drafty in here?"

"It's just your imagination."

"I'm not so sure," she murmured. "I think I felt something like that last night." *When you told me you loved me.* "Didn't you?"

"No," he said absently, still staring out the window.

She glanced at him in surprise. "Are you all right?"

Without looking at her, he muttered, "I think you should get up."

"Why? It's 6:30. Since when are you a morning person? At least as far as getting *out* of bed." She was surprised when she didn't get a response, not even a smile.

"Pack a bag for overnight," he said, his voice sounding flat. When she looked at him, he was already starting to get dressed.

"Are you kidding? What's going on? Why are you suddenly in such a hurry?"

He seemed distracted, distant. "We have to take a drive," he muttered.

She sat up, crossed her arms and glowered at him. "What if I don't want to?"

With a sigh, he sat down on the bed next to her. "Cia. Please. I need you. You are part of this. Of me."

She reached for his hand. "I don't understand, Will. I love the idea of being part of you, but why at this unearthly hour do we have to take a drive?" She looked down in surprise. "Why does your ring feel so warm?"

As he pulled his hand back, she saw the stone flash. At the same time, the voices escalated from hushed to shrill. "What's happening. And what are those sounds? You have to tell me."

He stood up. "Not now. Later. We have to go. Please, Cia. If you love me, trust me. We'll talk in the car."

"Can you at least tell me where we're going?"

With a glance at the bloody spot on the window, he nodded. "North."

She shook her head. "Didn't we just come back from the north? Are we going back to Patrick's?"

"Not Patrick's. Scotland."

"Oh. I've always wanted to go to Scotland. Where? Edinburgh?"

"No. The west coast. Stornoway."

"Stornoway? I've never heard of it."

"It's a town in the Outer Hebrides."

The Outer Hebrides? With curiosity rapidly morphing to alarm, she closed her eyes, recalling the story Patrick had told her. *Wasn't the Outer Hebrides the place Will had been specifically warned not to go to?*

"Why?" she whispered, trying to stifle a distinct surge of apprehension.

He looked again at the spot on the window. Sounding tense, he whispered, "We'll know when we get there."

Chapter 19

Becoming increasingly apprehensive about the drive to Scotland, Cia took her time getting ready while repeatedly trying to dissuade Will from going at all. Nevertheless, he was adamant, and by the time they left London he had become edgy and impatient. Whenever she tried to engage him in conversation, his only response consisted of an occasional terse word or two. She wondered if she should have stood her ground and refused to go, but something told her he wouldn't have let her. After several hours of pretty but repetitive countryside, she saw a sign for Liverpool. "Aren't we near Skipton? Why don't we stop at Patrick's?" *And maybe he can talk you out of this worrisome compulsion.*

"No time," he mumbled, making a turn at yet another roundabout. She glanced at him with concern. His expression had become serious, verging on morose. Although there had always been a certain intensity about him, this was a side of him she hadn't seen before.

"What is it, Will? If something is wrong, please tell me."

He shrugged.

Determined to break his silence, she asked, "How far is, um, Stornoway?"

"Still a long way." His tone was clipped. "We'll make a brief stop up ahead for lunch. Then it's a few more hours to Glasgow."

"Oh good. That sounds like fun," she said, trying to sound more optimistic than she felt.

"We won't be stopping in Glasgow. More likely Loch Lomond. That way there'll be less driving tomorrow."

"Tomorrow?" *Are you kidding?* He hadn't bothered to mention that this little jaunt would take more than two days. "What's at Loch Lomond?"

He shook his head as if annoyed. "Please, Cia, stop asking questions. I don't know what's at Loch Lomond."

"You mean we're driving hundreds of miles and you don't know why?"

Ignoring her question, he pulled over at the next roadside grill, where he said they could pick up sandwiches. Refusing to get right back in the car, Cia insisted they take them outside to a picnic table to eat. He agreed, although with reluctance.

Taking a sip of tea, she said, "Come on, Will. You have to tell me what's going on. This isn't like you. Why are we here?" Seeing only farmland and the road curving endlessly ahead, she shook her head. "Wherever here is."

"Cia, be patient. I need you to trust me."

"I do trust you. I just wish you'd tell me where we're going and, more importantly, why."

"I told you. Stornoway."

"What's so important about Stornoway?"

He appeared impatient. "It's not Stornoway. It's what's near there. Callanish."

The name hit with a force that took her breath away. Hadn't Patrick said that MacDonald had warned Will to stay away from not only the Outer Hebrides, but specifically the place called Callanish? Not about to betray Patrick's trust, she simply asked, "Why?"

"I wish I could tell you. Something is there for me, but to be honest I don't know what it is. All I do know is that you have to be with me." He paused to light a cigarette. "You've never been to Stonehenge, have you?"

"No, Will. How could I? Except for the writer's conferences, I've always been with you. Why didn't we go there instead?"

He looked toward the road, his voice distant. "It has to be Callanish. They're waiting for us."

Feeling a knot in her stomach, she stared at him. *They?* "Who? Who is waiting?"

"It was in my dream last night. And yours."

My dream? "We're going to Callanish because of a dream?" She felt she was trying to coax information out of a reluctant child.

"It was a message. By the way, those weren't columns you saw."

Becoming exasperated, she shook her head. "Come on, Will. It was just a dream. What does it matter if I saw columns or not?"

He looked away, to the horizon. "When you see Callanish, you'll understand."

He's chasing a message from a weird dream? It didn't sound like the grounded, pragmatic Will Jamieson she knew. Something else was at work here, something far more powerful and frightening than mere dreams or even nightmares. It was as if he was on some sort of quest—one he didn't understand, and one she knew, despite her questions and protests, he wouldn't abandon. Thinking again of fantasies and mysteries, she wondered what the hell they might be walking into.

They arrived at Loch Lomond at dusk and continued along the lake until Will spotted a small hotel. The proprietor, a jovial, elderly man with greying hair, explained they had arrived just in time; the tourist season was drawing to a close, and he was about to shut down for the winter. Although their room had a lovely view of the grey-blue lake, dark clouds obscured the last of the sunset.

They took dinner in a book-lined study, the main dining room having been already closed for the season. Trying to make conversation with a mostly silent Will, Cia took his hand. "This is so romantic. Don't you think so?"

He squeezed her hand before standing up abruptly. "You finish, Cia. I'm going back to the room."

Now what? "Is something wrong?" *Other than this insane trip?*

"I'm tired. It's been a long day."

She got up and faced him. "Look, Will. I still don't understand why we're here or why you need me with you. To be honest, it appears you don't either. I think it might be best if I go back to London tomorrow. If you choose to continue this quest, then you should go ahead. Alone."

With a sigh he took her in his arms. When she tried to back away, he held her tight. Looking into her eyes, his voice was low, urgent: "Please, Cia, I love you, and I need you. Especially now. There is something important for both of us at Callanish, and I have to find out what it is. I can't tell you why or what because I don't understand it myself. Not yet. All I know is, it's essential that we remain together. Please, my love. Stay with me."

With tears in her eyes, she put her head on his shoulder. "How can I say no to you."

The next day, they had another five hours of driving, mostly over rolling hills garlanded with rough gorse and the occasional stunted tree. The herds of sheep that had clogged the roads around Glasgow had all but disappeared and, in an occasional distant field, Cia pointed out large, shaggy-looking beasts that Will said were long-horned cattle. Low clouds hovered over a landscape that became ever more desolate as they approached the sea. At the small town of Ullapool, they boarded the car ferry to Stornoway. During the damp, chilly trip, Cia stayed inside, breathing in the tang of salt water and rotten fish. Huddled in her coat, she asked herself how she had ever managed to get herself to such a gloomy place.

Will, meanwhile, paced the deck, smoking and gazing out at the sea as if expecting some answer from the roiling waves.

They disembarked at Stornoway, a village of neat houses surrounding a thriving fishing port. As they drove from the ferry out to the street, Cia noticed a craggy-faced man sporting a well-worn tam glance pointedly at their car. Pulling up next to him, Will asked for directions to Callanish. After mashing out a cigarette, he leaned down. "Have ya been there before, sir?"

"Not in a long time. I'm in a bit of a hurry. Can you direct me which road to take?"

"Oh. There's no rush, sir. Them stones 'ave been waiting for thousands of years. I'm sure they'll be glad to welcome ya back." With a wink at Cia, he stood up and pointed to a road leading away from the port. As Will thanked him and put the car in gear, Cia looked at him in shock. "Did you hear what he said about the stones welcoming you back? What was he talking about?"

He shook his head. "It was nothing, Cia. He was just giving me directions."

She wasn't so sure. When she turned to look back, the man was nowhere to be seen.

Leaving the town behind, they drove several miles through pockets of low, drifting fog. As they crested a hill, the mist suddenly dispersed, offering a pristine view of what appeared to be white columns shimmering in the distance. Cia stared in disbelief; the image was far too similar to her dreams to be coincidence.

Will parked on the verge and went around to open her door. She stepped out, at once awed and terrified, and realizing that Will

149

had been right: what she was seeing weren't columns at all, but tall, jagged stones glowing white against a low, threatening sky.

"This is Callanish?" she whispered as if normal voices should not be heard in such a mystical setting. There were no cars or tourists. Except for the whine of the breeze, the place was silent and deserted.

Will walked a few steps ahead and nodded, his voice a flat monotone. "This is the place. Where we belong."

Glancing around, she shook her head. "Belong? What are you saying?"

He stopped, as if listening. "Something is happening. Do you hear it?"

"It's just the wind," she whispered, hugging her coat around her as fingers of fog began drifting across the circle of stones. And yet, underlying the moan of the breeze, she could hear the distinct cadence of chants. Doubting there was anything so mundane as a church nearby, she was sure it was the voices. *But why here? And why now?* "What is it, Will? What are those sounds?"

"Don't talk, Cia. Just listen," he whispered, beginning to move towards the center of the circle. "They want me to return. They say . . . in the season of warmth."

"Who, Will? There's no one here."

As though in a trance, he turned to look at her. "No. They're all here."

Barely breathing, she realized he wasn't looking at her, but through her. "Please tell me," she said, trying to maintain a semblance of composure.

"For the rituals." His voice was unnaturally low and coarse.

"Rituals? What kind of rituals?"

"Pagan," he whispered, reaching out as though to caress the stone. "These are over five thousand years old." With an expression of sadness on his face, he knelt down next to a shallow depression in the grass. Moving aside a few small stones, he said, "Take care where you step."

She watched him, having no idea what he was doing. "Why?"

Muttering what sounded like a prayer, he ran his hand gently across the grass. "This was a burial chamber. A cairn," he whispered, his voice devoid of inflection. "Long ago. An important man."

Before she could ask what that meant, he cut her off. "There is more. From long before these stones. There is more."

She felt her blood turn to ice. *There is more.* Isn't that what she had said to Patrick?

"How can you know?"

He narrowed his eyes. "I know."

She was shivering despite a shaft of sunlight that slashed through lowering clouds as if to shine on them alone. While she desperately wanted to leave, she was becoming too afraid to speak.

Without a word, he put his arm around her waist and led her closer to the center monolith. "This is our place," he murmured. "Where we began. Don't you remember?"

"Will, please. What are you talking about? I've never been here before."

His eyes were unnaturally bright, glowing violet in the reflected rays of the weak sun. "You have. You may not remember right now, but you will. Later." Before she could back away, he turned abruptly and grabbed her hand. "We must go now," he said in a clipped voice. "We're expected at the inn. We'll return at dusk."

He had booked an inn? *When?*

He drove silently and fast on narrow, winding roads. She wanted to ask how he knew where to go but thought better of it, doubting he'd answer. As they approached a weathered stone house on a hill, he made a sharp turn into a loosely graveled driveway partially obscured by large trees, their leaves tinged with the first autumnal oranges and reds. So far, they were the only trees of any size Cia had seen on the island. Seeing no other cars, Will parked next to a stone pathway bordered by late-blooming rose bushes. As Cia got out, she noticed the exterior of the house was almost entirely enshrouded by a thick blue-green vine. Above the front door, under a thatched roof badly in need of repair, a hanging sign swayed in the breeze. Carved into it was a fierce-looking hawk, its wings spread in full flight. She saw no name.

As though out of thin air, a plump, middle-aged woman suddenly materialized in the doorway. Swaddled in a white apron over a long, faded blue dress, she welcomed them with a smile that didn't quite match her small, sharp eyes. As soon as Will brought their bags inside, she said she had prepared sandwiches and pointed to a table next to a window so obscured by vines that daylight barely shone through. Thanking her, Cia glanced around, picking up a cloying mustiness, perhaps of aging furniture or the unusual scent of smoke emanating from the large stone hearth. *Probably both.* The entire place looked worn, even shabby; as her mother would have said, "slightly frayed at the edges." She touched a tablecloth that had certainly seen better days, or more likely decades. As for the heavy porcelain dishes with their faded patterns of dragons and flowers, she had found Imari such as these, albeit in far better condition, in antique stores on a brief excusion to Portobello Road. Even the oversized silverware was scratched and worn, as if left over from a past century. The entire room felt off, strangely empty despite the clutter of sagging chairs and scuffed wooden tables. She shook her head, thinking there had to be better, or at least newer, hotels in the area.

And yet the sandwiches turned out to be surprisingly fresh, mostly garden vegetables with some sort of mayonnaise, no doubt homemade. They had passed no towns in the immediate area, and she wondered if the woman had to go all the way to Stornoway to shop. After the strange morning, she was trying to relax, in no rush to leave the table. But Will ate quickly, and before she could finish her tea, he asked the woman to show them to their room.

Taking a ring of oversized, archaic-looking keys from the pocket of her apron, she led them down a narrow hallway lit only by candles to the last door on the left. For some unknown reason, Cia questioned the choice of rooms: *Why the one furthest from the main room?* She had the unsettling feeling that no one had stayed there in a very long time.

As the woman handed Will the key, she cast a narrow-eyed glance at Cia before closing the door silently behind her. Despite being grateful that a small fire had been set in the fireplace across from the bed, Cia tried to suppress a growing sense of apprehension. Seeing no lamps but only candles in tin holders, she realized the inn had no electricity. In alarm, she walked to a partially-opened door, relieved to find a long, narrow room—probably a dressing room that at some point in the past had been turned into what was, at best, a rudimentary bathroom. *Hopefully usable,* she thought, seeing a clawed tub, a toilet with a pull chain, and a chipped cabinet that had likely held a wash bowl, later replaced by a now-yellowed sink.

When she moved closer to the fire to warm up, Will threw off his jacket and reached for her. After two tense days, she was relieved, hoping he was at last being romantic. But when she put her arms around him, he drew back, his eyes again glazed. "I'm tired, Cia. I need to lie down."

As he lay back on the bed, she sat down next to him. "Please, Will. Can you explain what was happening at the stone circle? And, more importantly, why we are here?"

Closing his eyes, he murmured, "Later, Cia."

"Will, please . . ." she started to say, realizing by his heavy breathing that he had fallen asleep. "What the hell?" she sighed, shaking him gently. When he wouldn't wake up, she covered him with a coarse blanket before lying down next to him. She was still mystified, having no idea what had compelled him to drag her all the way to this forlorn island. He had asked her to trust him, and yet how could she when she had no clue to his increasingly erratic behavior? Becoming aware of an unexpected sound, she sat up. It was a low droning, as though coming from somewhere below, perhaps a basement. She first wondered if it could be some sort of washing machine, but then recalled the building had no electricity. Whatever it was, the dull hum just added to her frustration. Closing her eyes, she wished Will would wake up so they could talk. Or, even better, that she could prevail upon him to leave this wretched place and return to Stornoway.

Feeling her shoulder being shaken, she opened her eyes. "Come along, Cia. The sun is about to set. It's time to go." Will's voice was tight, urgent.

She blinked, trying to emerge from a deep sleep populated by fractured dreams. "Go? Where?"

He was already pulling on his jacket. "To Callanish."

She didn't move. "No, Will. It's getting dark. I don't want to go back there."

He shook his head. "You really want to stay here? Alone?"

She considered the option for about a second and, with a sigh of resignation, reached for her sweater. "What's that sound?"

Already at the door, he looked back at her with impatience. "What sound?"

"Like a humming noise."

"I have no idea. Come on." She wanted to ask what the rush was, but realized he probably wouldn't bother to answer.

When they reached the verge where he had parked that morning, he again led her towards the stone circle, now deeply shadowed in the rapidly fading light. Stopping in front of the center monolith, his lips moved as if in silent prayer. Frightened, she backed away, but he caught and held her in an unbreakable embrace. The sky seemed to be darkening faster than usual, and before she could take a breath they were both on their knees facing one another. She closed her eyes as he first touched, then kissed her lips. Rigid with fear, she felt him remove her sweater, his hands first caressing her face and then her breasts, all the while muttering in a harsh, guttural tongue. She had the distinct feeling it wasn't precisely her he was touching; that his desire was directed at something or someone far beyond this time and place. She wanted to beg him to stop but was unable to find her voice. As blue fire sparked from the stone in his ring, she flinched and fell back on the damp grass.

Throwing off his coat, he looked down at her. Seeing his eyes flash in the last glow of twilight, she cried out while attempting to scramble away, but he was too strong and held her down. "There's no reason to be afraid," he whispered, his breath soft on her cheek. "This is our place. Yours and mine. As it has always been."

The wind sighed as a huge, orange moon rose above the eastern horizon with an unearthly light that chased shadows in a ritual dance through the stones. At the same time, a deep guttural chanting began to echo around the circle, as though an ancient choir had surrounded them. Through eyes clouded with tears, Cia turned her face away. away. But it was no longer the circle of stones that she saw. Instead, they appeared to morph into a high, steep cliff, where, through swirling mist, a silhouetted figure stared down at her from a dim circle of light. As the figure receded, Will's mouth met hers, giving her no choice but to surrender to an overwhelming desire that surged through her mind and body, leading them both to the primal moment when sensation encompasses the entire universe and obliterates time.

She opened her eyes to shifting moonlight and the feeling of cold, damp earth. Half-naked and shivering, she stumbled to her knees. The moon, now high above the horizon, was smaller, though still tinted orange. The chants had died out, leaving only the soft moans of the wind. Trying not to panic, she found her sweater and looked frantically for Will, relieved to see his shadow falling across the center monolith.

"Will," she whispered, her voice hoarse with dread. She didn't think he had heard her, but he looked back. "Cia. Come here."

In a daze, she walked to him, her shadow joining his on the massive stone. He took her hand. "Do you remember now?"

"Remember?" she whispered.

"That we've been here before."

"No, Will. We haven't." *At least I haven't. Have I?* She was shaking, whether in shock or terror, she didn't know. Probably both. She tried to pull him away. "We have to go. I'm scared and freezing."

"There's nothing to be frightened of," he said, putting his arm around her and pulling her close. "Not anymore. Don't you feel a sense of peace? This is where we began."

She could hardly breathe. "Please, Will. I have no idea what you're talking about." Suddenly aware of deepening darkness, she looked up just as a cloud settled across the moon, obscuring the shadows. When she looked back, she saw Will shake his head and blink, as though awakening from a dream. In that fraction of a second, his eyes became clear, no longer glazed.

Seeing her shivering, he took off his jacket and wrapped it around her. "It's all right," he whispered.

"Are you kidding?" she snapped. "Nothing is all right. What the hell is happening?"

"Nothing . . ." he started to say. Stepping back, he glanced around in obvious confusion. Seeing the stones as though for the first time, he stared in awe. "Bloody hell," he whispered. "This is Callanish. What the fuck is going on?"

Cia looked back at him in disbelief. *He doesn't know where he is?* If nothing else, he finally sounded normal, far more lucid than he had all day. "Come on, Will. You can't be serious."

"I've never been more serious in my life. The only memory I have is driving off the ferry this morning. After that, the rest is a blur."

"What about our little drive from London to get here?"

Picking up the edge to her voice, he took her hands in his. When she moved away, he looked hurt. "Yes. I do remember that. And yet it seems a distant memory."

"You're saying you remember nothing about what happened earlier today? Or just now in front of that stone?"

"I gave you my coat and asked if you were all right."

Exasperated, she shook her head. "How about the inn? Or having sex in the middle of the circle? The huge moon? The chants? Standing in front of that stone as though it was an altar?"

He ran his fingers through his hair. "No. None of it. Why is it dark? Didn't we take the ferry in the morning?"

Trying to maintain whatever patience she had left, she nodded. "Yes, Will. We did."

"I'm sorry, Cia. I'm just as bewildered as you. My last memory is speaking with a man in Stornoway."

A man in Stornoway? The same man she had thought seemed out of place? "Look, Will, whatever the hell is going on, it's freaking me out. We need to get away from here."

"Where's the car?"

She shook her head; he really was in a state of confusion. "This way. I don't think we should go back to that inn. Can't we just go back to the mainland, or even Stornoway? If only for the night?"

"The inn?"

"Please, Will. Try to remember."

As they got in the car, he looked out at the stone circle. "It looks like there's a heavy fog rolling in. I don't think we'll make it to Stornoway. Do you remember how to get to this inn?"

He was right. A thick mist had already obscured the top of the stones and was beginning to settle around the car. Cia asked herself how the world could have suddenly gone so far off kilter; she dreaded having to return to that strange woman and the even creepier inn. Like the man in Stornoway, something was very wrong about it; something she felt but was unable put into words. And then there was that sound. With a shiver, she took a breath. "I think I do."

The fog appeared to be thickening, and Will was forced to drive slowly. By the time they reached the driveway, they could barely see the house. Sitting alone on its hill, it appeared eerily dark and deserted. As they drove closer, Cia clutched Will's arm and gasped in shock; the vines, leafy and green that morning, were now dry and shriveled. Looking further, she could see the sign with the bird was broken, dangling from one hinge while creaking ominously in drifting fog. Quite a number of stones from the walls appeared to have loosened and fallen to the ground. And yet, when Will stopped the car at the pathway, she realized that whatever she thought she had seen was wrong, or perhaps some sort of illusion created by the mist. The stones were, indeed, intact, and the sign still hung from its two hinges. Below it was a lantern, it's wavering light barely visible.

Leaving the car, she glanced again at the vine. If not quite the dried husks she had visualized, it had, indeed, withered; several thick stalks having already fallen away from the walls. Trying to suppress a wave of anxiety, she made her way along the path. Feeling a sting, she looked down, seeing rotting rose petals crushed beneath her feet. It was only then that she noticed the rose bushes. Healthy and replete with pink flowers that morning, they had not only become brown and desiccated but had spread thorn-encrusted branches across the path to tear at her legs. Trembling, she looked back at Will, her voice breaking. "I can't do this. There's something evil here. We have to leave."

He put his hands up. "Cia. Please. Look around you. There's no way to drive through this muck." Choking back fear, she didn't know if what they were seeing was real or if there was some sort of sinister magic to this place. She told herself it was better, and no doubt safer, to stop thinking such things.

The proprietress was waiting at the door, the forced smile from the morning replaced by a stern expression etched into her deeply lined face. Focusing on Will, she chided, "It's late. You know when the night mists descend, you should not be out. There are no streetlamps. You cannot even see the roads." She was right; the damp fog was now being engulfed by a white, foul-smelling mist that had already blotted out the anemic glow from the lantern at the front door.

"Dinner is long gone. But I saved some soup."

Grateful to be indoors, Cia sat down at a table in front of the fireplace where smoke from the fire mingled with the pleasant scent of freshly baked bread. When Will picked up a candle and went to their room, she sat back, attempting to convince herself that, despite her apprehension, everything would be all right.

The woman returned with bowls of thick, fragrant soup, placing them carefully on the table. "You must be freezing. You should not have been out so late. It's not safe." Picking up a heavy woolen throw, she draped it over Cia's shoulders. When Cia looked up to thank her, she caught her breath. The woman's hair, a mousey brown that morning, was now snow white. *What's happening here? And how long were we really gone?*

The woman looked at her with concern. "Are you all right, my dear?" Refusing to allow illusion to overtake logic, Cia responded that she was fine. She was about to ask what "not safe" meant when Will returned. Seeing her covered by the throw, he said in that worrisome flat voice, "It gets cold here at night."

The woman threw him a sharp-eyed glance before moving towards the kitchen. "Why yes, sir. You should know it does. We must not let the fire go out." He stared at her retreating form, a puzzled look on his face.

She returned with a plate of warm bread. "Come, sir. Have a seat. This soup will warm you. It's made from the last of the vegetables from my garden. I have plenty, now that the tourists have gone."

Cia put down her spoon. "I was surprised not to see any sightseers at Callanish. Are there no visitors at this time of year?"

The woman smirked. "Of course there are. They come, even in the snow." Her glance returned to Will. "That's because you are here, my dear," she murmured.

Cia jumped. "What did you say?"

"Just that the soup was made today."

Will put his hand gently on Cia's arm before saying the soup was delicious. When the woman returned to the kitchen, he leaned in. "I heard her as well. Are you all right?" His voice was low, hushed.

She looked back at him, her eyes wide. "No. I'm trying to keep from screaming. You heard what she said about why there were no tourists today. Why would it have anything to do with you?'

"I wish I could tell you. Unfortunately, I can't."

"Maybe I'm just tired, but do the walls in this room look blurry to you? Like they're not quite solid. And that pot of roses? When we arrived this afternoon, those flowers were in full bloom. Now they're dead, just like those rose bushes out front." She put her head on his shoulder. "I'm scared, Will. Why can't we just go home?"

He put his arm around her. "Cia," he whispered. "We can't leave. Not until morning. Look." He pointed to a front window, now completely opaque with white mist. "Trust me. I promise it will be all right."

"I'm not so sure," she said, unable to suppress a deep shudder. "Have you asked yourself how we came here in the first place? You told me something drew you here. But what? Everything that's happened today is beyond reality. That huge moon, the sound of chants, shadows moving over those stones; not to mention sex in the middle of it all. And this place? What is it? Is it even real? Are we real?" she whispered, scanning the room. "Let's find out." Before Will could stop her, she ran to the front door and flung it open. As malodorous mist began to creep in, the woman flew out of the kitchen, her raised hands like claws. "Close that door," she screeched. "Do it now!"

Cia slammed the door and glared at the woman, who all-too-quickly resumed her composure. "You must listen to what I tell you. You cannot open any doors or windows in the night. And the fire must be kept going. The mist is cold. It takes away the heat. Do you understand what I am telling you?" Her voice was low but firm.

Although she didn't understand at all, Cia nodded. The woman shook her head and, in a huff returned to the kitchen. Cia grabbed Will's hand. "This is madness," she whispered.

"We'll be all right."

"How can you say that?"

"I can't tell you why. I just know it. Whatever happened today is over. You'll feel better once we get to London."

"No, Will. I don't think it's over at all. This place wants something from us. Or maybe from you."

"You have to stop overreacting. We'll leave at dawn."

"I want to go back to New York. Tomorrow, if I can."

"Stop panicking, Cia. We have to talk about this."

"I don't know if we can. It's like we're trapped in some sort of alternate reality. How did we get here? And, more importantly, why can't you remember?"

"I've already told you I have no idea. If you love me, you'll help me find the answers."

"I do love you, and I hope I can be helpful. But something has happened to you in the last two days. From the moment that bird flew into the window, you became someone, or perhaps I should say, something else. And while I know stone circles are supposed to be sacred places, I have to tell you your actions were considerably more profane."

With a deep sigh, he shook his head. "I'm truly sorry for whatever I did." He reached for her hand, looking hurt when she pulled away. "We should go to the room. It's important we talk before you forget."

"Why would I forget?

"I don't know why. But I think you will, and soon."

"It's the rings, isn't it?"

He stopped moving. "What did you say?"

She put her hands to her mouth. She hadn't meant to say "rings." Or had she? Either way, she knew she had just opened a Pandora's box.

He stood up quickly, practically knocking over his chair. "Bloody hell," he said, his voice rising. "How do you know . . . ? It was Patrick, wasn't it? What did he tell you?"

Without a word, she jumped up and took her plate to the kitchen where the woman was fussing over an ancient cast iron stove. *Probably stirring up some sort of witch's brew.*

"Sleep tight, dear. Don't forget. You mustn't let the fire go out."

With an involuntary shudder, Cia managed to thank her. Picking up a lantern, she walked toward the hallway, Will close on her heels. They passed several closed doors before she stopped in front of one. With a glance down the hall to make sure the woman wasn't watching, she turned the knob. As expected, the door was locked, as were the next two she tried. "We're alone here, aren't we?" she whispered.

"Please, Cia, let's go."

"There are no lights. Did she snuff out all the candles?"

"It doesn't matter. We have our lanterns."

She looked back at him. "Why do I have the feeling it does matter?"

In their room, the fire had been set and a couple of candles lit. They flickered in a cool draft from the windows, creating staccato shadows on wallpaper so faded the pattern of pink and yellow roses was barely discernible. Cia sat on the creaky bed and looked up at the man she loved. A man she thought she knew. Now she wasn't so sure.

He was abrupt. "What did Patrick tell you?"

She shook her head. "He told me how you came to have the rings. That's all." *Well, almost all.*

Clearly agitated, he shook his head. "That's not a story you needed to know."

She got up and faced him. "Why not? I'm sure that ring you wear, and the other, wherever it is, have something to do with why we're here. I've known from our first night that there are mysteries around you. Those sounds in your flat are not the wind, nor are they the pipes or the house settling. And what about those birds that watch over you? If you really believe I'm part of this, then I deserve to know what's going on."

Looking exhausted, he shook his head. "How can I tell you when I don't understand it myself." After a brief hesitation, he added, "The ravens, however, have only appeared since I met you."

She stared at him. *Didn't Patrick say the same thing?* "Weren't you warned to stay away from here?"

He looked up quickly. "That was told to Patrick in confidence. He talks too much."

"He only told me because he knows we love each other. He said it was for my own protection." She reached for his hand. "You are in love with me, aren't you?"

"Cia, how can you ask?"

"It's not just saying the words. I'm sure you've said them plenty of times before."

He took her in his arms. "No, Cia, I haven't. What's important right now is for you to tell me what happened today."

With a deep sigh, she described their conversation at the stone circle that afternoon, where in a strange voice he told her he would have to return for the rituals in "the season of warmth," along with the odd phrase, "This is our place."

He nodded. "The season of warmth is obviously summer. Rituals may refer to ancient harvest celebrations. But 'our place'? I have no idea."

"That was scary enough. Then you said you had made a reservation at this inn when I was sure you hadn't. And yet you drove straight to it. Do you even know the name of this place?"

He thought a few seconds, then shrugged. "No. I don't."

"Neither do I. There's no name anywhere."

"Be that as it may. We're here. What else?"

She sighed. "We had sandwiches, and then we came to this room. Do you remember that?"

"No."

"I wanted to talk with you, but before I could even say a word, you fell into a deep sleep, and I was unable to wake you."

He sat on the bed and stared into the fire. "It's odd. I do remember wanting to kiss you but suddenly feeling terribly tired. Then it was dark, and I was standing in a field. Strange-looking people were running past as if they didn't see me. They were small and sinewy and naked. Some had tattoos on their bodies." He closed his eyes, as though trying to force the image. "They were carrying torches. When I looked up I saw a huge orange moon and felt like I was looking for someone." He shook his head. "I can't remember much else. I need you to tell me what happened at the stones."

She took a breath. "I'm not sure that was entirely a dream. When we were inside the circle, you practically raped me while mumbling in some unintelligible dialect. I'm sorry. That's the only way I can describe it."

Appalled, he got up and paced the room. "Did I hurt you? Why didn't you push me away?"

"I tried, but you seemed to have superhuman strength. And then, to be honest, I no longer wanted to. It was as though our bodies had become one. We were floating above the ground, and I was clinging to you. Your desire became mine, and our passion enveloped the entire universe." She shook her head. "That sounds crazy, doesn't it?"

He took her hand and kissed it. "No, Cia, not at all. Actually, it's quite poetic."

"Poetic?" She shook her head. "More like frightening. I also saw the moon you described in your dream. It was huge and orange and," she paused and closed her eyes, "that's when I saw shadows moving across the stones and heard that weird chanting."

"That's a sacred site. What the hell did I do?"

"Whatever it was, there were definitely more than two of us in that circle."

"I'm sorry, Cia. A thousand questions are surfacing in my mind. Questions for which I have no answer."

She touched his shoulder. "Do you remember standing in the moonlight in front of the center stone?"

"Yes. When I saw our shadows on the monolith, the most incredible sense of peace came over me. I felt so much love for you." He looked at her, his face serious. "I gave you my jacket because it was cold."

"And now?"

He put his arms around her. "How can you ask?"

"Maybe it's that I shouldn't be with you."

"No, Cia. This can only be happening because we're together. I need you to help me make sense of it." He hesitated, as though making a decision. "Since Patrick told you not only about my ring, but that I was warned to stay away from here, I imagine he must also have described at least some of my discussion with a man named MacDonald. Am I correct?"

"Yes," she admitted in a small voice.

"What you need to understand is that since that time, despite the voices and a few, let us say, odd moments, my life has been without incident. Only since we met have unusual things occurred."

"What sort of things?"

"Let's leave that for later."

She sighed and rubbed her eyes. "I'm so tired."

"Maybe we should try and get some sleep."

With a sudden shiver, she reached for the blanket. "Is it cold in here?" She tilted her head, listening. "I'm beginning to hear that weird humming sound again."

"It sounds like some sort of machinery, but I don't see how that's possible." He got up and opened the door to the hallway. "I hear it out here as well."

"Maybe you should go ask that woman?"

"There's no light. Not even under any of the doors."

"Then where is she? She never told us her name, did she?"

"No," he said, stepping back into the room. He was about to close the door when it suddenly flew from his hand and slammed shut. At the same moment, the room began to shake, as though the earth was shifting below.

Cia stifled a small scream. "What was that?"

"It felt like an earthquake."

She interrupted him. "An earthquake? Here? And why is it so cold?"

"I don't know," he muttered, glancing around the room. Seeing the fire burning low, he went to a basket holding a small pile of peat turfs and threw a couple in.

"What is that?" Cia asked.

"Peat. Scotland is covered in the stuff. There's little wood on these islands. Peat is cheap and burns about the same. It's been used for thousands of years."

"It smells funny."

As he started to speak, the room shook again, more violently this time, almost knocking him off his feet. As the drone rose to a heavier thrumming sound, Cia screamed and pointed to the floor that appeared to be undulating as if in waves.

"What the fuck? Come on, Cia. We have to get out of here."

Before she could move, the floorboards next to the bed began to shatter and lift. Trying to keep his balance, Will grabbed for her hand, "Cia, let's go."

She jumped off the bed just as he reached the door. "Bloody hell," he shouted, pulling his hand away from the knob, now coated with a foul, greasy residue. When it wouldn't turn, he pushed against the door, but it didn't move. "Shit," he muttered. "I can't open it."

Panicked, Cia looked back just as a putrid-smelling brown mist began to spiral up through a black, ashy hole that suddenly appeared in the ruptured floor. Will moved quickly, kicking a large splinter over it, but the mist burned through it, turning it quickly to ash. As the candles sputtered and died, the thrumming deepened. Waving away a fetid odor of rot and decay, she pointed. "Will. The bathroom." Before she could reach the door, it slammed in her face. When she tried to open it, it wouldn't budge.

Aware the room was becoming not only darker, but colder, Will shouted over the drone, now sounding like thunder in their ears. "Get back on the bed, Cia. Under the blanket. Do it now." Looking back at him in silent terror, she nodded. Seeing the fire had all too quickly burned down to ashes, he stepped cautiously across the broken floor. As the room again shook violently, he grabbed for the bedpost just as more floorboards bulged and cracked beneath his feet, as though trying to knock him off balance or, he thought, more likely to block him from the fireplace. Recalling the woman's warning, he knew their only chance at survival lay in keeping the fire going. Stepping carefully over the widening fissures, he grabbed more turfs and threw them on top of the dwindling embers, praying the flames would catch.

As the fire began to consume the mist, the vibrations ceased, and the droning reverted to a dull hum. In the dim firelight, Will could just make out Cia on the bed, shaking uncontrollably.

With her hands covering her face, she whispered, "There's something here. It's in the room with us. How can such things be happening? Is this some sort of hallucination . . . or are we in hell?"

Having no answer, he reached in his pocket for his lighter, cursing silently when he realized he'd left it in the car. Feeling his way to a wobbly chest of drawers, he found a tattered box of matches in a drawer that reeked of mildew. Worried they might be too old, he tried several before one finally caught. Relieved, he stepped carefully on what he hoped were solid floorboards to light the candles as well as the lanterns. Moving quickly back to the door, he saw the knob was still dripping with funky-smelling slime. Putting aside his disgust, he reached for it, shaking his head in frustration when it still wouldn't turn.

In the low light, Cia stared at him with wet eyes. "What does this place want from us? We're going to die here, aren't we?"

"No, Cia, we're not," he said in a firm voice that he hoped sounded convincing. Suppressing a grimace, he wiped his hands on the bedspread before wrapping his arms around her. "As long as we keep the fire going, I think we'll be safe. You're exhausted. Try and sleep now. I'll stay awake."

"How can I sleep when I'm afraid I'll never wake up? No. We'll both stay awake. At least that sound seems to have stopped."

She was right; both the shaking and the thrumming had ceased, and the room had become quiet again. Pulling the coarse blanket over her, Will hoped it wasn't too quiet. Stepping carefully across the fractured floor, he added more turfs to the fire. He didn't mention the pile of turfs was dwindling all too quickly and he'd have to be vigilant to make them last through the night. Returning to the bed, he propped a couple of leaden pillows against the wall. Behind the pillows he noticed a lighter area where a headboard—wooden, no doubt—had been. He tried not to question how it might have disappeared.

He looked down at Cia who was now snuggled against him, her eyes closed, her breathing soft and regular. Feeling his own eyes stinging, no doubt from the caustic mist mixed with smoke from the fire, he decided to close them for just a few seconds. Half asleep, he barely felt the room shudder and the thrumming start again, this time becoming deeper as though something was boring up through the earth below. Nor did he register the plume of stinking vapor rising through another sharp fissure in the floor next to the bed. Not until he became aware of a forceful tug at his hand.

"Cia," he mumbled, "let go." She opened her eyes just as the candles flickered out and the room reverberated with unearthly guttural screeches that drowned out her screams. Will's eyes flew open as a cloud of grey vapor began to enshroud the bed. With a shout of pain, he attempted to pull away from a thick, sodden membrane that rapidly encased his entire arm while invisible talons clawed his fingers and tore at his ring. In the dying glow of the dwindling fire, Cia saw slimy, ragged tissue thickening as it curled around his hand. Panicked, she grabbed for his arm. Using every bit of his strength, he wrenched his hand back as a shriek of rage erupted, the screams echoing off the walls around them.

As the vaporous mist dissolved, the room was now close—too close—to freezing. Despite his thudding heart and shredded fingers, Will moved quickly to throw more turfs on the fire. Waiting until the flames caught, he returned to the bed and put his arms around Cia until she stopped shaking. With more confidence than he felt, he tried to calm her sobs. "It'll be all right, Cia. Whatever it was, it's gone. I don't think it's coming back." With a glance at the window, he was relieved to see the first pale light of morning. "It's almost dawn. As soon as the sun burns off the fog, I'm sure we'll be able to get out of here."

Realizing Cia had gone limp in his arms, he rubbed her hands. Seeing her eyelids flutter, he whispered, "Cia? Wake up, my love. Talk to me. It'll be all right, I promise." Ignoring the pain of his bloodied hand, he tried to believe his own words.

As the room gradually brightened, Will again approached the door. Although the slippery goo remained, this time it opened without resistance. With a deep shudder he imagined that whatever evil had manifested itself – no doubt the 'earthbound spirit' that MacDonald had warned him about–had now, thanks to the emerging dawn, slithered back to whatever primordial hell it inhabited. Stepping with caution into the hallway, he saw faint sunlight seeping through the vines that still obscured the windows. Motioning for Cia to follow, he moved silently down the now cracked, sagging hallway to the main room and out the unlocked front door. So far, the woman was nowhere to be seen.

At the end of the path, Cia gratefully breathed in fresh, if slightly foggy air while noticing the vines had reverted to a healthy green. There was no remnant of the deadly white mist that had imprisoned them the night before.

Sensing a change in the atmosphere, she looked back at the house. The woman, still in the same faded blue dress and white apron, had just stepped out the door. Peering out at them with narrowed eyes, she walked with some difficulty down the path where the roses, now open to the faint sun, had pulled in their thorns and retreated to their beds. Cia didn't miss that her hair was, once again, brown.

With no more than a sharp glance at Will, who was throwing whatever clothing they'd been able to grab into the car, the woman moved close. Ignoring Cia's disheveled skirt and blouse and unbrushed hair, she murmured, "I hope we'll be seeing you here again, my dear. The legends say the most successful marriages are consummated within our sacred circle of stones. Something you have perhaps already discovered." Not believing she had heard her correctly, Cia backed away. But the woman merely smiled and handed her a paper sack. "Some sweets for your trip home. Don't forget what I told you."

In the light of day, the moment seemed all too normal, and Cia stepped into the car questioning if she and Will had somehow hallucinated the entire night. As he made the turn out of the driveway, she glanced back. The woman who had waved to them only seconds before had not only vanished, but, holding back a cry of terror, Cia saw the vines begin to curl and shrivel.

"What is it?" he asked, still sounding tense.

"Please, Will. Just get us away from here."

On the drive to Stornoway, they were both silent. Suddenly hungry, Cia looked for the bag of sweets the woman had given her. When she couldn't find it, she put it down to just another illusion, one that hadn't survived the end of the driveway.

Chapter 20

It was a couple of hours later, well after reaching the mainland, that Will stopped at a small hotel. By then they were both starving but had agreed to get as far from the island as they could. Now feeling they were, Cia hoped, safely away from the terrifying anguish of the night, she began to relax. Trying to avoid replaying the horror of it, at least for the moment, she asked Will if he had paid the woman for the room and their food.

Taken aback, he shook his head. "I never even thought about it."

"And she never asked, did she?"

"No."

Biting gratefully into a scone, she shook her head. "I would imagine money is meaningless in that place. That is, if it even really exists." Unable to hold back a tremor, she looked at him. "What's really frightening is, I wonder if we were ever expected to leave?"

He reached for her hand, his look and tone somber. "I know you're still scared, but we need time to talk, to try to come to terms with what has happened. I don't want you to leave. This isn't only me. It's something between us; something we need to sort out together."

"And yet, how can we? I've already told you what happened at the stones. After that, how can we ever explain what we just lived through?" She shrugged. "How did all this come about in the first place? And what was it that drew you there?"

Stroking her hand, he said, "You know I have no answer to any of those questions. Not right now, anyway."

"What if that thing comes after you again, Will?" she asked, wiping away a tear. "I'm frightened. Not only of what we just lived through, but of what could still happen. Aren't you?"

"That's why it's important we stay together and deal with our fears. We are still the same two people as yesterday. Or perhaps I should say the day before. If you care for me, as I believe you do, you'll help me work through this."

In the end, she had stayed. Sitting together on the love seat in his studio, they held hands while replaying the incomprehensible night for hours. Will mentioned MacDonald saying it wasn't only humans who might seek out the rings, that he should also be aware of "earth-bound spirits," which had sounded too outrageous to be true. At the time, he admitted, he'd considered it the ramblings of a bitter old man.

Cia shivered, recalling Patrick mentioning such a thing as well. "This is the stuff of nightmares and ghost stories." She shook her head. "How can that have been real?"

"In some sense, I'm not sure it was. And unless I can find some-one to ask, we may never know. If you can, try to put it aside, at least for the moment."

She looked at him wide-eyed. "How? Too many questions keep swirling in my mind, like why did it suddenly get so cold? And if that woman wanted us dead, why did she tell you to keep the fire going?"

"I don't know, Cia. Maybe she figured the peat would run out and that thing would come for us. MacDonald might have had an explanation, but unfortunately he's gone. That is, if he ever truly existed, which then raises more questions. I'm afraid the time has come, despite MacDonald's warnings, to find answers."

Sounding anxious again, she said, "Didn't MacDonald tell you that could be dangerous?" With a sigh, she shook her head. "And yet, there we were at Callanish, the very place he warned you to stay away from."

"Please, Cia. That, thankfully, is over. Now it's important to look to the future." He took her hands in his. "I'd like you to be part of that future. That is, if you still want to."

With some hesitation, she nodded. "You know I do."

"Wait one minute," he said, getting up and going downstairs. When he came back, he was holding a small, black lacquered box that he placed carefully on the table in front of them. As if out of nowhere the whispers, which had been mercifully silent, returned.

Looking nervous, Cia glanced towards the corner of the studio. "Why are they doing that?"

He smirked. "The voices? I never really know. Ignore them."

She frowned. "That's not so easy."

He glanced at the box. "You can look, but you must not touch."

"Why?"

"You already know these rings, or rather the sapphires, have caused the death of two people. Possibly more. I'm sure Patrick told you the other ring is meant for only one person in this life. While I have come to believe this ring is, in truth, meant for you, I'm not yet willing to take that chance. Not until I'm sure."

"Maybe it's not a good idea to open it."

"I think opening it is all right. Touching, however, is not." He barely tapped the lid which opened with a discernible creak. Cia could see the ring, with its intertwined strands of gold, was just a smaller version of his and, like his, had a tiny hinge.

She pointed. "What is that?"

"I was told that these rings fit together. That's what supposedly makes them immortal."

She blinked. "Immortal?" *Didn't Patrick mention something like that?*

"That's what I was told."

"If that ring fits me, does that make us immortal?"

He laughed. "A nice thought. Do you think we would tire of one another?"

"Not with what's been happening," she said, finally allowing herself a smile. She leaned in closer, never expecting the stone to suddenly spark a deep blue flame.

"Shit," he gasped, snapping the top closed. "Sorry."

Hugging herself, she murmured, "It's okay. I was about to say the same thing."

He picked up the box and took it back downstairs to his room. When he returned, he looked troubled. "I know we were going to talk about the possibility of you working here in London. Working, implying living together."

She sat still, thinking that three days before she would have joyfully jumped into his arms. Now, seeing his dark expression, she was sure less than positive news was coming.

He sat down and put his arm protectively around her shoulders. "However, as much as I love you, I think we have little choice but to put any plans on hold. At least until I can find out more. Maybe it was only Scotland, but I don't want you—or me, for that matter—to go through something like that again."

She nodded, knowing he was right, yet still unable to hold back sobs. With tears in his own eyes he gathered her into his arms. "Please, Cia, don't cry. I'll find someone, somewhere, who can explain this. Patrick knows a couple of professors at Glasgow University. Maybe they can help. Although explaining it might be a bit dicey."

She burrowed into his arms. "What happens now?"

"Now?" He looked confused. "What do you mean?"

She took a breath. "When will we see one another again?"

He looked surprised. "I've been so preoccupied with Scotland, I haven't thought about that."

Without thinking, she blurted out, "Would you want to come to New York for the holidays? We could go to the cottage."

Seeing him shake his head, she was suddenly drained of all strength, as though her heart had frozen.

"I'm sorry, Cia. The Critchlowes asked me to come to Majorca again for Christmas and New Year's." Aware of her sorrowful expression, he put his hand to her cheek. "I had no idea we'd become this close. That I'd fall in love with you."

She looked at him with tears in her eyes. "You can't get out of it?"

"I'm afraid not. You have to understand that much of it is work. Lady Critchlowe has become my friend as well as a patron. That may sound a bit archaic, but both she and her husband have gone out of their way to introduce me to new people, the sort who want to have their portraits painted."

Unable to hide her disappointment, she started to get up. "Don't be upset," he said, reaching for her hand.

She looked down at him. "Just how old is your Lady Critchlowe?"

He rolled his eyes. "In her sixties. She's like a special aunt."

"And she sees it that way as well?"

"Yes, Cia," he said with a grin. "I promise you, she does. Look. Maybe I can arrange to leave right after New Year's. If so, I'll come to New York in early January."

"What about the gallery? Will it be finished by then?"

"That doesn't matter right now. The last I heard from Steve, it was still running late. Either way, we'll plan some time together," he said, kissing her lips. "Let's leave this. At least for the moment. Right now, I'd like to ask a favor."

"A favor?"

"I'd like to do a few more sketches of you. Will you sit for me again?"

When she nodded, he caressed her cheek. "You may have been frightened to death in Scotland, but even with tears in your eyes, you've never looked more beautiful."

Part II

Love is our true destiny. We do not find the meaning of
life by ourselves alone—we find it with another.
—*Thomas Merton*

Chapter 1

Grateful to be home, Cia tossed her keys on a small table near the door, the sharp sound of metal hitting wood making her jump. While waiting for her heart to calm down, she glanced around the living room, the thought beginning to dawn that she was now safe. Here there were no hushed voices, no huge, angry-looking birds, no eerie standing stones that floated in unearthly mists, and, most of all, no deadly, grasping entities in an inn she was still too terrified to think about. The mere fact of walking through her own front door began to release the unbreakable tension that had held her firmly in its grasp since Scotland. This was what reality was supposed to be: the sound of hammering next door, the shouts and laughter of children on the sidewalk, the clatter of traffic on the street. Putting her shaking hands to her face, she feared the memories would never fade. She had no answer as to how they survived a night that had somehow existed beyond time; an amorphous, evil limbo somewhere between nightmare, hallucination, and death.

With a shiver, she recalled Sid's words that unless something "dramatic" happened with Will, she might want to rethink their relationship. She doubted the inn was quite what he'd had in mind.

Although Will had predicted her recollections would fade, he had been wrong, at least about the inn. Although parts of the day at Callanish were becoming vaguely indistinct, mirages wavering just beyond the grasp of recall, the horrific night still remained sharp, as though etched forever in her memory. In one sense, she knew she should consider herself lucky; what she and Will had lived through was so far distant from the realm of reality that she would never be able to tell it without others thinking she had either lost her mind or was conjuring up a fantastical ghost story. And yet, perhaps a time would come, sometime far in the future, when she would be able to write the unlikely events of that day and night.

Although in no mood to unpack, she opened her suitcase. While pulling out what seemed like reams of dirty clothing, her hand touched a box tied with a blue satin ribbon. Inside was a bracelet of delicate gold chain links. Her eyes filling with tears, she clasped it on her wrist. Will had not said a word, just tucked it into her already packed suitcase.

Will. In the few seconds after the membrane—or whatever other-worldly slime—released Will's hand and began to dissipate, she had been too exhausted to stop herself from falling into unconscious-ness. In those brief moments before he had woken her with anxious words, she'd had a frightening dream, one she had been too terrified to tell him: She was standing on a darkened corner in an unknown city, unable to find her way through a cold, white mist when sud-denly a tall, gaunt man with long black hair and coals for eyes mate-rialized in front of her. Instinctively, she recognized him as a man of faith but of no religion. Although she tried to back away, he held her with a dark, malevolent stare. In his hand he held a large knife, and when he spoke his voice was coarse. "If I were to stab you with this knife, you would surely die and be no more. Still, you would, as in a dream, see those who have gone before. And if you were to be born again and once more fated to meet your eternal lover—the one you desire but can never have—it will be with renewed belief. You may think you understand, but you must expect nothing." There was more, but the dream had been broken by Will calling out her name. That's when she'd opened her eyes, seeing the bloodied ring halfway off his finger. Although wishing it away, she knew it was another memory that would forever haunt her days as well as her dreams.

Chapter 2

Sarah was leaning on Cia's desk shuffling through a pile of papers when Cia came in. "Well? Did he pop the question? Are you about to become a resident of London?"

"First of all, please remove yourself from my desk." She laughed, all too aware of the lack of mirth in the last few days and that laughing actually felt good. "You are crushing potentially Pulitzer Prize-winning manuscripts. And before I say a word, I should see Sid."

"Not until you tell me all about it. Last time you made me wait until lunch."

She blinked. *I'm not sure you really want to know.* Attempting to make light of it, she said, "It was good, Sarah. We're happy together. But there are some, ah, problems that need to be worked out, not the least of which is that we live three thousand miles apart."

"Come on. I'll bet you could get a job there." Looking doubtful, she frowned. "Why do I think you're not telling me all of it?"

"Let me go see Sid, and then I will." *Well, some of it.*

"So, you're not engaged, or anything?"

"Or anything? You mean are we going steady? Is this high school? Come on, Sarah, get a grip."

"Oh well. A famous artist, attractive, sexy, nice house in London, what else could one want?"

If it were only so simple. "What I may want and what I can have may not be the same." She stopped, once again recalling her dream of the man with dead eyes and his chilling words: *the one you desire but can never have.* If, indeed, it was a message, she had no way to interpret it. Or perhaps it was simply a bad dream in the middle of a very surreal night.

"Now you are getting way too heavy for me. By the way, you'll be happy to know the Lanny books are here, and they look fabulous."

"Where are they?"

"In the conference room. First, go talk to Sid."

"Is there something I should know about?"

With a grin. "Maybe. As I said, go see Sid."

On the way to Sid's office, Cia stopped in the conference room, almost tripping over opened cartons scattered about. On the table, several piles of books had been stacked, their glossy jackets shining in the overhead spotlights. She had to admit the cover photo was compelling: Lanny in his cowboy hat sitting on a black horse and flashing his movie-star smile as the sun set perfectly pink and gold behind him.

Picking one up, she leafed through the pages with a growing sense of satisfaction, even pride. It had taken months, almost a year of painstaking work, and it showed. The writer had done his job, and Roz had created layouts with variously scaled, vibrantly colored photographs that balanced well with the accompanying text. She was anxious to call both, particularly Roz, who she knew would be waiting with baited breath, to thank them for a job well done.

Taking one along, she went to Sid's office. He looked up when she entered and held out his hands. "Welcome back, Cia. I see you've found our latest masterpiece. It just hit Barnes & Noble and has already sold out. You did a great job."

"Thank you, Sid. It wasn't all me, far from it. Still, I have to admit I'm proud of it."

"As is Lanny, his agent, and hopefully millions of his fans. Although we were told he's in the middle of a new movie, he's agreed to do book signings in New York and LA."

She smiled. "That's great, Sid."

"Tell me, how was London? Did you have a chance to see Phillips at Arlington-York?"

"I did. He was quite pleasant. We had tea."

"That's it?"

She shrugged. "He told me a little about his company and asked what we were doing. He was excited about the Lanny book." It wasn't the moment to mention his job offer.

He raised an eyebrow. "Anything else you might choose to impart?"

Aware where this was headed, she shook her head. "Everything went well. Not to worry. I'm not about to run off to England." *Not quite yet, anyway.*

"Good," he said. "Because I have some news you might find interesting. We're promoting you to senior editor, which, ah, entails a rather nice raise as well."

Breathless, she tried to quell her surprise. "Oh. Thank you. I'm thrilled that you believe in me." With a brief hesitation, she asked, "What about Sarah?"

He nodded. "Sarah as well. Although I'm afraid you will still have to share an office." With a grin, he added, "I'm surprised she didn't tell you as soon as you came in."

"No. Only that I should go talk to you."

When he got up to shake her hand, she couldn't stop herself from giving him a quick peck on the cheek.

Sarah jumped up and hugged her. "You've heard the news? That we were both promoted? Not to mentioned getting raises?"

"Yes. My head is still spinning." She held out the Lanny book. "And this is beautiful."

"It is, and we're getting fabulous reviews. About time, I'd say. With all we do and the crap we take from our authors, we deserve this." As Cia laughed, Sarah turned to pick up a thick manuscript. "Here," she said, her smile turning to a grimace. "I don't want to ruin your day, but have a look at this. It's a new novel by our own Maury Robbins. I usually like his work, but this one will be a bear." After dropping it with an ominous thump on the desk, she glanced back at Cia. "By the way, are you going to the cottage this weekend?"

"I think so."

"Want company?"

"What about Mike?"

"I'm supposed to see him Saturday." She shrugged. "But I could use a break."

"Thanks, Sarah. I should probably go by myself. I need some time to think through some things." *If that's even possible.*

She looked worried. "That sounds ominous. Are you sure something didn't happen with Will?"

Quite a lot of things, actually. "Not to worry," she said, trying to sound lighthearted. "I promise I'll tell you the good stuff later."

Friday turned out to be even more hectic than Cia anticipated; not only were two novels due to be released to the printer, the public relations department was screaming for more information from both the editors and their authors.

By the time she arrived at the cottage it was almost ten and Sonny's store was shut tight. After lighting a fire, she lay down on the sofa, her thoughts drifting, as always, to Will.

She wished there was someone she could find who could explain about Scotland. And yet, like Will, she wouldn't know where to start. At least Patrick had contacts in Glasgow. She would just have to wait for Will to get back to her, which, she was well aware, was unlikely to happen anytime soon.

A scratching noise woke her from a light doze. The fire had burned down to embers and the lights, usually bright, had for some unknown reason dimmed to barely a glow. Hearing the sound again, she went to the door, wondering if perhaps a cat or dog was on the porch. No stray animals were camped on her doorstep, but seeing a tree branch scraping against a front window, she went to find shears to cut it off. As she reached to snip it, she noticed the leaves had already begun to change, oranges and yellows overtaking the deep greens of late summer. Even with the branch gone, she still felt tense, that maybe she shouldn't have come alone. *Get over it. Everything is fine.*

Back inside, the lights had brightened again, but she became aware of a slight sighing sound. Although the night had been still before, she put it down to a freshening breeze.

After scrambling a couple of eggs with some Havarti and chives, she made coffee and returned to the living room. While she ate, she looked through a newspaper she had brought along. The Watergate scandal was intensifying, and now that Vice President Agnew had resigned and been replaced by Gerald Ford, there was even more pressure on Nixon to produce the White House tapes. Wondering if the so-called investigations would ever end, she took her dishes to the sink.

Suddenly feeling tense and very much alone, she picked up her jacket, thinking the cool air might help her unwind. As she walked down the driveway to the road, she was surprised to see a few houses nearby were already shuttered, their owners gone for the winter. She couldn't imagine why. She loved autumn; the crisp days and nights fragranced with drying leaves and wood smoke.

A flash of lightning suddenly split the darkness and, as though with an exhale of breath, the wind gusted. *It's nothing*, she told herself, *just a distant storm.*

As the sky lit up with another streak of lightning, she stopped, experiencing a distinct stab of fear. The wind died as quickly as it had begun, and the light of a lone streetlamp sputtered before returning to cast a pale ochre glow. About to turn back, something drew her glance to the house across the street, to an outdoor light that shone brightly at the center but faded to a soft haze through the dense bushes below. The light flickered as a gentle breeze sighed through the trees, raining down a cascade of rust-colored leaves. Feeling an unexpected chill, she ran back to the house.

Although it was only about ten, she was suddenly exhausted. After locking the doors and scattering the ashes in the fireplace, she picked up Kurt Vonnegut's *Breakfast of Champions*, climbed into bed, and began to read.

It was well past midnight when something woke her out of a deep sleep. Opening her eyes to complete darkness, she felt a twinge—an instinctive sense that something wasn't quite right. Feeling around the quilt, she touched the book, which still lay open at her side. That meant she'd fallen asleep while reading, and unless the electricity had gone out, the bedside lamp should still be on. She was about to reach for it when she felt a current of cold air caress her skin. Sensing movement, she looked up as a whitish mist began to rise at the end of the bed. Too frightened to move, she stared as it swirled into an amorphous shape, slowly forming an appendage that reached out to her as if in supplication. Behind the translucent figure, she could make out the shadow of another face: one with light, luminous eyes. Not knowing if she was awake or dreaming, she tried to scream but no sound emerged. With her heart pounding and her eyes never leaving the shifting vapor, she fumbled for the lamp. As her finger hit the switch, the room jumped into sharp focus. She watched in horror as the apparition uttered a shrill, plaintive cry and began to dissolve.

Collapsing on her pillows, she lay back, trying to calm her thumping heart. After a few minutes, she glanced with foreboding at the door, sure she'd left it open. Now it was closed. Quietly moving the covers aside, she forced herself to sit up, the touch of her feet on the cold floor making her flinch. Shaking with apprehension and holding her breath, she stopped to listen at the door for any sign of disturbance. Not hearing anything, she opened it cautiously and peeked out, seeing only darkness broken by the pale light of the setting moon. Although the house was cold, she hardly felt it. It was only after turning on every light in every room that, still trembling in fear, she ran back to bed. Pulling up the covers, she looked at the spot where she had seen . . . what? Was this the ghost Sonny had jokingly mentioned? She had owned this house for over a year, so why had it suddenly appeared now, particularly after just returning from those terrifying days in Scotland? And hadn't Will said it had been something between the two of them that had created all that horror? Will was currently three thousand miles away, no doubt having a peaceful breakfast about now. No. This had to be some-thing else—something to do with her alone.

Convinced that sleep was no longer possible, she picked up her book, hoping it would distract her. The next thing she heard was the jarring sound of the phone ringing. Shaking off the cobwebs of ragged dreams, she ran to the living room to pick it up.

"Cia? Are you all right? I called earlier, but there was no answer. I was becoming worried."

"I'm fine, Sarah. I had some weird dreams last night. Sorry. I must not have heard the phone."

"You're sure?"

She yawned, trying to sound convincing. "Yes. I'm freezing. I have to put the heat on and take a shower. I'll call you later." Hang-ing up, she ignored the heat and ran back to the bedroom. Grabbing her jeans and a sweater, she dressed quickly She could shower later; first, she needed to talk with Sonny.

Fortunately, she was in the store. In her haste, Cia had forgotten it was Sunday, and many Sundays the store was either closed or open only in the afternoon.

Practically leaping out of the car, she ran coatless into the shop. Seeing her, Sonny stepped back in alarm. "Cia. What's wrong? You look like you've seen a ghost." Seeing the expression on Cia's face, she nodded. "I think maybe you have seen a ghost. Come, sit at that table near the wood-burning stove. I'll bring coffee."

Cia sat, feeling haggard and glad the shop, which smelled deli-ciously of baking bread was, at the moment, empty. Sonny yelled to someone in the back, probably Charlie, her sixteen-year-old son, to go out front in case any customers came in. Bringing two cups of black coffee along with a couple of warm blueberry muffins lightly frosted with confectioner's sugar, she sat down. "This should help. Tell me what happened."

Taking a much-needed sip of coffee, Cia began to relate what she had seen the night before. "I don't know if it was a dream or if I was really awake. Am I going mad?"

Sonny patted her hand. "Not at all. You're not the first to tell that story. In fact, you'll find quite a few old newspapers with articles about sightings in our local library. I'm pretty sure, however, that most are about one apparition, not two."

"I'm afraid to go back. Did you see the lightning and hear the wind last night?"

"No, Cia. It was calm all night. Maybe it was part of your dream. Next time you might want to bring a friend."

"I promise I will. Meanwhile, is there anything more you can tell me about my house?"

Sitting back, Sonny sipped her coffee. "I've already told you, the girl—I believe her name was Cecelia or Isabelle, something like that—was waiting for her fiancé to return from England when she took sick and died. Most likely of pneumonia. From all accounts, it was a brutal winter that year. There was also a rumor about a ring he supposedly brought her. And yet when she died, no ring was found. It's thought that perhaps it didn't fit, and he took it back to have it made smaller. That may be true, or not. Either way, it must have been very sad."

Cia put her hands to her face. The story was far too familiar. "Did he ever return?"

Sonny shrugged. "I really don't know. Why are you looking at me like that?"

"Is it possible there could be more information? Anything written, or maybe drawings or paintings that might still exist? If not, I'll try the library."

Sonny thought a moment. "Actually, I do have a few old journals and diaries from around that time. People occasionally find hidden letters and even decades-old newspapers in the older houses, usually during renovations. They often bring them to us."

"Why?"

"My great-grandfather opened this store back in the 1880s. Since then, our local residents have come to us with all sorts of oddities they've found, and also to relate stories of unusual things they've seen, or imagined they've seen. Through the years, my family has become the keepers of the history of this town." She stopped abruptly and looked at Cia. "Now that I think of it, there may be one or two notebooks that were found after the original house burned down. They were in a box under the ashes. No one understood how they survived the fire."

Cia held her breath while Sonny went upstairs. A couple of women walked in, the bells on the front door jingling and rousing her out of a trance. Picking up a bottle of maple syrup, a basket of apples, and a few local cheeses, they went to the counter where Charlie rang them up.

Sonny returned with a couple of ancient-looking, leather-bound journals wrapped in oilcloth. Gently unwrapping them, she handed one gingerly to Cia, who put it flat on the table and opened it, the spine cracking as if in protest. The earliest date was from 1810 and it appeared to be some sort of ledger. With a sigh of disappointment, she shook her head. In the next one, the writing was a small, labored cursive, difficult to read. After gently turning a few pages, the brittle paper flaking even at her touch, Cia saw the date, 1799. With an intake of breath, she murmured, "This could be the one we want."

The following page described the harvest of 1798 that appeared to be abundant. After a few more pages, most dealing with the buying and selling of produce, the writing became larger and rougher, saying the winter, which had come unexpectedly early in November, was dreadful and freezing, with several feet of snow already on the ground. They were afraid of running out of wood and food had become scarce. After a couple of blank pages, Cia was becoming worried, but the next page she turned was dated, February 1799. After reading a few lines, she stopped. "Sonny. Look at this," she whispered, pointing to a smear—perhaps from water, or possibly tears:

Today during another snowstorm our darling daughter Cecily died. We were unable to take her to a doctor as the roads have become impassable. My wife has no more tears to shed and all we do is pray for this damnable winter to end before another of our children falls ill. May she rest in peace.

Stuck between the next two pages was a faded slip of parchment. Cia removed it carefully and placed it on the table. It was a drawing of a girl with large eyes and dark hair cascading around her face. She had been sketched gazing directly out at the viewer with a shy, sweet smile. At the bottom, written in an archaic cursive script, was, *To darling C. from W.*

Sonny whispered a prayer and crossed herself. "She looks like you, doesn't she?"

Hardly breathing, Cia looked back at the page in the journal.

> *We have no way of getting news of this sad event to Mr.*
> *Williams, her fiancé, and he won't return to us until spring.*
> *We know he will be devastated, as he was to be bringing her*
> *a marriage ring.*

Mr. Williams? A ring? And a C. and a W. on the drawing? It was too much. Trembling, she handed the book back. "Put it away, Sonny. I can't tell you why. Just promise you will never show this to anyone. Not unless I ask you to."

Sonny, wide-eyed, put her hands to her face. "Oh, Cia, I think I understand."

Shaking her head, Cia murmured, "I wish I did."

Returning to the cottage, she lit a fire and sat down to think. No spirits, weird sounds, or even scary apparitions were going to drive her away. It was almost 1975 — real life, not fantasy, and she refused to accept that last night had been anything other than a disquieting dream, more likely a nightmare. She was alone in an old house with few, if any, neighbors, and it was possible her imagination had gotten away from her. And yet, what about the journal? The story it told, along with the drawing and the initials, was all too familiar, and she began to wonder, despite that Will was far away, if it was their interaction that had caused the ghost to appear. Either way, she had to agree with Sonny: next time, she would ask Sarah to come along.

Chapter 3

After taking Cia to the airport, Will returned to a flat that felt surprisingly empty without her. While he would have liked her to have stayed longer, he knew it was important for both of them to stop the never-ending questions and discussions; to take time away, if only to regain some semblance of their normal lives.

Although he entered to silence, he knew it wouldn't last long. The voices usually came through when he was inside for only a short while, as if by the mere fact of unlocking the door he woke them up. And yet they had awakened quite a bit sooner when Cia had been there.

He put the kettle on for tea and brought out a bottle of brandy; he was going to need it. Taking both upstairs, he left the lights off; it wasn't yet noon and the studio was flooded with late morning light.

Settling himself on the loveseat where he and Cia had spent hours talking only the day before, he poured a good spot of brandy into the steaming mug. Despite that his mind was still reeling, he had to try to make sense of what had happened. Although Cia had described in raw detail his behavior at the stone circle more than once, he remained mystified. Those actions weren't his; he would never be that forceful with a woman. If one rebuffed his advances he always backed off without rancor, which, if memory served, usually resulted in the lady eventually having a change of heart and mind. He smiled at the thought before focusing his attention back to Cia and her confession that his overwhelming passion, if that's what it could be called, had sparked hers. As hard as he tried to recall those lost hours, he found only an abyss filled with dark shadows that caused him to feel queasy and offered neither answer nor respite.

The phone rang, startling him out of his reverie. Picking it up, he heard Patrick's all too cheery voice.

"Am I calling at a bad time, Will? Is Cia still there?" He chuckled. "I don't want to interrupt anything."

"Not at all, Patrick. She left this morning."

"Sorry I missed her. How did you leave it? I think she was hoping for some kind of, ah, relationship discussion. After seeing the two of you together, I can understand why."

"I'm afraid it's become a bit more complicated than that."

"You don't sound very well. What happened?"

"It's a long story. Not for a phone call."

"That's not doing it for me. I want to hear more."

"We went to Scotland, Patrick. To Callanish. While we were there some, ah, rather dodgy events occurred."

"Callanish?" he sounded surprised. "Didn't MacDonald specifically warn you not to go near the place? If you wanted to show Cia a stone circle, you could have taken her to Stonehenge."

"It's not quite that simple, I'm afraid." He stopped to light a cigarette. "There are, however, a few things you and I need to discuss. Like why you told her about the rings."

Will heard him hesitate. "Please don't be angry. I did it for good reasons. For her and for you. Look. I called because I'm planning to drive down to London tomorrow and wanted to ask if you could put me up for the night. Now I'm concerned. I haven't heard you sound like this since Carolyn died. Forget tomorrow. I'll leave here in an hour." Without waiting for a response, he hung up.

Will looked at the phone, curious to hear why Patrick considered his reasons to be valid; at least he should have told him. He wasn't sure he could even begin to relate the bizarre events at Callanish and the inn, particularly how Cia had come to tell him about the rings. Then again, maybe it would do him good. If nothing else, drinking with Patrick was better than drinking alone. Taking one last sip of tea, he went back downstairs to change into jeans and an old shirt. Maybe working on his paintings would ease his mind.

By the time Patrick arrived, it was already evening. When he suggested they have a drink to clear the air, Will went to the kitchen and opened a new bottle of scotch. "My brother sent this. I think it's as good a time as any for a twenty-year-old single malt." Picking up two glasses, he led the way back to the studio, which seemed to have become the place to talk.

After pouring a couple of shots, Will asked, "You told her about the rings. Why?"

"I thought it was important. You know she's in love with you."

"And she's aware I feel the same. But what can I do? When she was here, the voices never stopped. One would have thought a conference was going on." He looked down at his hand, his face serious. "This ring, and the spirits that inhabit it, have supposedly guided my life for more than twenty years, and yet all, since Carolyn, has been relatively quiet. Until now."

Patrick frowned. "What are those scratches on your hand, Will?"

He shook his head. "We'll get to that."

"Then you really do accept that there are spirits."

"How else can I explain what has happened in my life? You were the only one who knew. And now you've told Cia. Tell me why."

"Because she's the first woman since Carolyn you haven't just toyed with."

"You know the reasons for that. I'm afraid to become too close to any woman. I can't take the chance. Are you implying that I'm not good to the women in my life? I've always gone out of my way to be honest, making it clear that what I have with them can never go any further: that all the love and sex is transitory and will never lead to marriage. Some walk out in tears while others choose to enjoy the moment." He sipped his drink. "More of those, fortunately."

Patrick held up his glass. "To you, Will. A man of great seductions. You are a star as well as an inspiration."

"Thanks, Patrick. But you know as well as I that it's not all me. They are just as seductive, maybe more so. And as for being a star? Such things, at least in human terms are all too fleeting." He snapped his fingers. "A flash, and then it's gone. One day you look in the mirror and ask what happened to the years."

Patrick nodded. "All too true, my friend. But now you have Cia. Don't you want more with her?"

"I would give up all those women if I could only get past the fear of harming her. But let's put the ladies aside. The rings are what started this and, in truth, I hadn't thought much about them until I met Cia and unusual things began to happen. So, once again, I have to question what it was that brought me to that curio shop and how that old man knew they were meant for me, not someone else. For years, it really hasn't mattered." Closing his eyes, he took a breath. "Not since Carolyn. She was a beautiful, heathy girl who died too soon."

"Are you still convinced it was the rings? Her parents said it was pneumonia."

He shrugged. "I'm sure it was pneumonia. But how did it happen so fast that she died before I got there? It's a question that has lingered in the back of my mind for years. Now, after what happened with Cia in Scotland, I'm afraid the time has come to look for answers."

"Before you get to searching for such things as answers, why don't you tell me about what happened, and how Cia came to tell you about the rings?"

Will poured a couple of more shots. "Hold on tight, Patrick. You've known about the strange things happening in my life, but this belies belief."

The twenty-year-old single malt was down to the last couple of shots by the time Will finished the story of Callanish and the inn. Patrick sat through it wide eyed, drinking heavily and mostly speechless until Will held out his scratched hand.

"You must be bloody kidding. You're telling me a vapor did that?"

"It wasn't precisely vapor, Patrick. I assume it was what Mac-Donald described as an earthbound spirit. Call it what you will, but something ancient and evil arose through the earth that night, something that craved that sapphire with an all-consuming greed. I still don't understand how we survived." He stopped to refill his glass. "I will never forget the terror of being trapped in that room."

Patrick shook his head before mashing out his cigarette in an already overflowing ashtray. "And the woman at the inn? Do you think she knew you? It sounded that way. But then, how could she?"

"Good question."

"Where did you get the name of that place? Did someone give it to you?"

"No. And I never rang for a reservation. In fact, I never saw a name or, for that matter, a phone. And yet, the woman knew we were coming. She was waiting for us in the doorway." He stopped and took a breath. "What's worrisome is the possibility that something like that could happen again. That entity, demon—whatever it was—didn't get what it wanted. Before it tries again, I need to find answers. I can't commit to Cia or anyone else in this life until I know more."

"This is bloody incredible. So now what?"

He took a breath. "What I'm about to tell you will also sound strange, maybe even more so. Since returning from Scotland I've been suddenly recalling certain moments—experiences, you could say—from the past. I believe they must be connected to what happened to Cia and me."

"Such as?"

"You really want to hear this?"

"After what you just told me? I'm afraid I must."

Will sat back before taking a long drink. "I was eight when my parents took my brother and me on what they described as a family vacation. To Egypt, of all places. It was winter. I remember because we boarded the ship in heavy coats, and when we arrived, my mother let me off the ship wearing short pants."

"Lucky you. My folks never took us anywhere but Bath."

Will smiled. "We took a train to Cairo and stayed at Shepheard's. In those years it was considered a grand hotel, and it was, in truth, all of that and more. There were tall men, impossibly tall from the viewpoint of an eight-year-old. Nubians, I imagine, in white robes and turbans looking after one's every need." He laughed. "That first day, while my mother was unpacking, I snuck out to go exploring. After an hour or so, she realized I was gone and began frantically searching for me. Meanwhile, I was having a hell of a time running around all the salons and restaurants. One of those nice, tall men brought me back after he found me hiding behind a palm tree. The best, though, were the pyramids. They were pure magic. I begged my parents to let me ride a camel until they finally gave in. In those days, guests brought picnic lunches and sat around being served by waiters from the hotel. While they ate, I climbed on the pyramids and the Sphinx." He looked at Patrick. "You may wonder why I'm telling you this, but I promise it's not your typical 'My Trip to Egypt' story."

Patrick grinned. "I already had that impression."

"A couple of days later, we boarded a boat in Cairo to take us up the Nile to Luxor. Before we even checked into the hotel, my father insisted on going to the Valley of the Kings. He wanted to visit Tut-ankhamun's tomb. You know the story, that when it was opened, all those involved with the excavation died mysterious deaths."

Patrick nodded. "I do remember that from school."

"My father was told, however, that it was a long, hot trip, and better left until the next morning. An older man with a long, white beard came to collect us in an ancient black saloon car with a driver dressed in typical Egyptian robes. I think my mother was nervous, but my father, in his white suit and safari hat, was anxious to get going. I remember driving though empty, featureless desert for miles. I was bored, and my mother kept telling my brother to stop fidgeting. But as we approached the Valley of the Kings, I had this odd feeling of déjà vu, as if I already knew what I was going to see there."

Patrick shook his head. "C'mon, Will."

"Listen to the rest of it. Then tell me what you think."

Patrick shrugged. "Go on."

"Our first stop was the Temple of Hatshepsut, a massive, two-tiered, colonnaded tomb with a ramp leading up to it. It looked gigantic to me, and I remember running up the ramp and turning left, as though I knew I would find something familiar. While the guide walked with my parents explaining the wall paintings and hieroglyphics, I went ahead, weaving in and out of the columns until I saw a kneeling statue that stopped me. When the guide arrived with my folks, I asked him if the statue was Thutmose and why he was not only in this tomb, but opposite Amon-Ra. My parents didn't even register it and continued on. But the guide, looking like he'd seen a ghost, stopped and asked me to repeat what I had said. When I again said the names, he asked how I knew the statues were Thutmose and Amon-Ra. I told him I had no idea, I just knew it was odd that they were both there. He turned so white I thought he was going to have a heart attack. He ran to my mother asking if I had learned about ancient Egypt in school. She shook her head, saying we wouldn't study it for another couple of years. I know it sounds crazy, but the entire place, along with the sculptures and paintings, seemed to mean something to me, as if I had been there before. When we returned to the hotel, I even started drawing some of the hieroglyphs from memory. They were probably just scribbles, but they looked real enough to me. What's even more odd is why these memories are suddenly returning now. I haven't thought about that trip in years."

"I would agree that it's well beyond strange. Did your dad get to see King Tut's tomb?"

"Yes, although we were only permitted to go partway in." He shrugged. "It didn't have the same effect on me. I think the guide, who kept watching me, was relieved by that."

"Did your brother react the same way?'

Will snorted. "He was six. He was oblivious and bored."

"What do you think it all means?"

"I wish I knew."

"Did it ever happen again?"

He nodded. "A few years later, my parents rented a villa in Greece, on Mykonos. I think I was about fourteen. Like Egypt, it was not only fascinating but eerily familiar. When we arrived, I asked our guide where the sheep were. He looked at me like I was from another planet. Apparently, there had been no sheep on Mykonos for decades, maybe centuries, although he did say there were still a few on the nearby island of Rhenea.

"When my father asked where I got the bizarre idea about sheep, I told him I didn't know. One day, I went down to the dock and asked a bunch of fishermen who were taking a boat to Rhenea if I could come along. One of them wanted to know why I wanted to go to an island where there were only dead people. Much of it is an ancient cemetery. When I answered that I just wanted to see it, he looked at the others, who simply shrugged, and said to jump aboard. I spent the day wandering the ruins and the cemetery until it was time for the boat to leave. And by the way, there were sheep on that island."

"Did anything happen?"

"Not really. And yet, like Luxor, it was as though I'd been there before. I felt I was looking for something, or someone, but I didn't know what."

"You were fourteen? Don't you have a, um, friend you visit on Mykonos?"

"Oh yes. Olympia," he said with a small smile. "Now there's a name for you. I met her that year. She was older, all of seventeen. We're still friends."

"From your look I won't ask anything more," Patrick said with a grin.

Will's smile was wistful. "She may have been my first real crush."

"Were there any more trips with such, ah, incidents?"

"No. Just Egypt and Greece." He stopped abruptly. "Although . . ."

"What is it? You look like you're in another world."

As if in a trance, he nodded. "There was a school trip to Glasgow. On the way, we stopped in the Outer Hebrides to see the Callanish Stones. That was the only time I was there until a few days ago. I can't believe I didn't think of it before. I remember the teacher explaining that the stones were over five thousand years old, older than Stonehenge, though not connected in any way. I interrupted her—rather rudely, I'm sure. I told her she was wrong, that there was a connection with Stonehenge." He smirked. "You can imagine how that went over. She became quite indignant and asked how I could possibly know such a thing. I simply replied that I had been there a long, long time ago. When all the other kids laughed, thinking it was a joke, she yelled at them to stop, saying it wasn't funny. Still, I had the feeling she was a bit freaked out by it."

"Did you realize what you were saying?"

"Not until after I said it. But in my mind, I knew it was so."

Patrick lit a cigarette. "I believe you, and yet between your déjà vu and the recent encounters at Callanish, I'm not sure anyone else would."

The phone rang, startling them both. Will got up to answer. "Annabelle, my love. Good to hear from you. When did you return?" he asked, his solemn demeanor morphing to one of seductive charm. "Yes. Of course, but not this week. Come next Wednesday. We'll have another sitting for your portrait." He stopped to take a breath. "Yes, my dear. We'll have all afternoon. I'll open a bottle of wine. You know I always make time for you."

He hung up, seduction reverting to sullen. "I didn't need that."

Patrick laughed. "The ladies just won't leave you alone, will they?"

"I have no patience for any of them right now."

"So, Will, what does all this add up to?

He shook his head. "I wish I knew." He got up and paced. "I told you about what happened when we went to a jazz club in Canada. When Brother Luke didn't want to shake hands or have a drink, I should have realized something was off. It wasn't until I asked about him that I found out he had died twenty years ago. That I saw him

193

is one thing; that Cia did as well made me wonder what the hell was happening. He also mentioned she would be special in my life."

Patrick grinned. "Maybe fate was giving you a gentle push to get on with it."

Will shrugged. "You could be right. And yet, there's something else in the back of my mind. A vague memory I can't quite grasp." He looked at his watch. "Let's go have dinner. Some place where we won't run into the usual blokes. Maybe a couple of pints will help trigger it."

Patrick shook his head. "A couple of pints after all that scotch?"

"I'm totally sober, Patrick. Nothing seems to obliterate those memories."

They had to walk several streets down Fulham Road before finding a pub on a side street where they were unlikely to run into any of their friends. Nevertheless, the place was crowded, and they had to wait until a table of four paid the bill and left.

"You're patient tonight, Will. Usually you walk out if a place is too busy."

He shook his head. "I need to keep these thoughts going, Patrick. There's something more to this. Something I'm missing."

"Now you're creeping me out. You're beginning to sound like that American writer. Stephen King, I think his name is."

Seeing Will's blank gaze, Patrick looked worried. "What is it?"

"That name, Stephen. There's something about it."

"Take your time."

After a couple of minutes, Will lit a cigarette and looked at Patrick. "When we returned from Egypt, there was a man—a youngish man— who came to our house. His name was something like Stephen."

"Who was he?"

Will glanced around, not seeing the restaurant, but reaching for something far beyond it. "My mother had a dinner party. She met this man, a historian or perhaps an Egyptologist, before the trip. I'm sure she invited him to regale him, along with her friends, about our adventures. During dinner, she joked about me going up to a statue and knowing not only the name, but also asking about the god Amon-Ra. She actually giggled, saying I had made our guide very nervous."

He stopped to light a cigarette. "After dinner, this man took me aside and asked how I recognized Thutmose and Amon-Ra. I was embarrassed and told him I didn't know, that the names had just come to me and maybe I shouldn't have said them. He said it was all right, and if anything like that happened again, would I please call him. He even gave me his card. I recall thinking he had a very odd first name. Something like Stephen, but more unusual."

"What did you do with it?"

"The card?" He shrugged. "Who knows. I was a kid. I think he was pretty young at the time. If he was in his thirties, he'd be in his late sixties, maybe early seventies today."

"Why don't you try the library. If he's an archaeologist or an historian, maybe you can find him by papers he's published."

"That's pretty thin, Patrick. All I remember is it's something like Stephen."

"If you see the name, maybe you'll recognize it."

Will signaled for another drink. "Let me think about that."

When there was no letter or call from Cia in the following days, Will began to be concerned. As nervous as she had been before she left, he was sure she wouldn't ignore the bracelet he had placed in her luggage. When a letter thanking him arrived a few days later, he was relieved, not only that she had found it, but that she sounded more her normal self. Although, he mused, it could also be the simple fact that she was now safe in New York, far from the voices, not to mention the rest of it.

As the holidays approached, Will was too busy to think much about the man who had been to dinner at his parents' house those many years past. One afternoon, after a lunch with the BBC producer who was still pursuing him for their proposed artists' series, he picked up a call from Patrick. After covering the latest gossip, Patrick mentioned he'd put the word out to a few of his friends at the University of Glasgow. "I asked if anyone might know of a professor of archeology or psychology, or perhaps a combination of the two if, indeed, there was such a thing. And, by the way, whose name might be Stephen or something like it. They thought I had gone bonkers but agreed to ask around."

"Thanks, Patrick. I appreciate it."

"Are you off to Majorca again? What about Cia?"

"I'm afraid I screwed up. When Lady Critchlowe invited me, I said yes without thinking."

"Is Cia upset?"

"Unfortunately, she is. But it was too late to change anything."

"I will then be thinking of you drinking and partying with the various aristocracy and royals, both current and defunct, who flock there to escape the worst of the winter chill."

"Please don't make me feel more guilty than I already am. Anyway, you know it's work for me."

Patrick guffawed. "Is that what you told Cia?"

"Whose side are you on? I promised her I'd come to New York in January. It'll also give me time to catch up with Steve about the gallery. When will you be in London?"

"Not before the first week of February. There's an opening at the Tate. I expect you will be going?"

He laughed. "You know I'd never miss it. One never knows whom one might meet. Have a good holiday, Patrick. And let me know if you have any luck with those names."

Chapter 4

Cia turned up the collar of her coat against the light flakes that had just begun to fall. Sarah, her eyes scanning Park Avenue for a taxi, was already in the street with her hand raised. Seeing one stop up the block, she raced for it, determined to beat out two men in dark overcoats frantically dodging traffic in an attempt to cross against the light. Grabbing the door, she held it open as an elderly woman emerged as if in slow motion. With a smile of victory, she glanced at the men, who glared back in obvious irritation. Never shy, she shouted, "So much for chivalry."

With a laugh, Cia slid in next to her.

"Great," Sarah said. "Cia is smiling. At last."

"Those men couldn't believe you beat them out."

"Yeah. I know. Like they would have given it to us. Ever since the day I ran for a taxi in a downpour outside Lord & Taylor and two men cut me off, it's been war."

"Where are we going?"

"Fifty-Sixth and Third."

"Tell me again why we are going to a competitor's party?"

"It's not the entire company, Cia," she huffed. "Just the art department and a few editors. My friend June works there. She asked us to stop by for a drink."

As they left the cab, a young woman ran for it. Sarah told the driver to wait. Cia wondered if she would have done the same for a man.

Brushing snow off her coat, she glanced at the building. "I'm really not in the mood for a party. Why don't we go to a movie? *The Godfather II* just opened at Cinema One. It's only a couple of blocks up the street."

"Come on, you'll have a glass of champagne, meet new people and then we'll be off to Bloomingdale's for some last-minute Christmas shopping."

"Why are you pushing me to meet, as you say, 'new people'?"

"Look. I know you adore Will. But after what you told me about Scotland, I feel like there are too many unanswered questions. Not to mention him going off to Majorca and leaving you alone for the holidays. It's hard to believe you will ever have a real relationship with him. Time, as they say, is passing."

In truth, Sarah didn't even know the half of it. "Look. You know we love each other. Whatever is happening around us, I'm sure we'll work it out."

"You don't mind that he's out partying in Majorca?"

"I try not to think about it."

"See? That's why you have to move on with your life. He's running around all over the place, and here you are without even a date for New Year's Eve. And what about Ian? Any word from him?"

"No. Thankfully," she said with a grimace.

"Come on. Archer is on the twelfth floor."

"I'd rather go home."

"No way," Sarah said, pulling her into the elevator.

The doors opened to a wide reception area decorated with a huge Christmas tree blinking with colored lights. The reception desk had been abandoned, and they followed the sound of laughter as well as the faint scent of grass down a hallway to the art department where a pretty blonde ran to Sarah and embraced her. "I'm so glad you could come." Turning to Cia, she held out her hand. "You must be Cia. I'm June. Come meet everyone."

Cia glanced around, aware the art department was quite a bit larger than the one at BookEnds. Sarah had told her that Archer designed all their book covers in-house, unlike BookEnds who freelanced them out.

June handed them plastic glasses of champagne and introduced everyone. Cia had just begun talking with an editor when a tall man with green eyes and sandy hair walked in. As someone handed him a glass of champagne, his eyes met hers. Feeling unexpected anticipation accelerating her heartbeat, she looked away.

Seconds later, he was standing next to her. With a warm smile, he held out his hand. "You must be Cia. I'm Mark. Sarah has mentioned you often. I hear you both worked with Lanny Winters on his book. Congratulations. It should be a best seller."

She hoped he didn't notice her blush. "Thank you. We hope so. How do you know Sarah?"

"I met her through Mike, her boyfriend, a couple of months ago. At least I think he's still her boyfriend. What day is it?"

They both laughed, and he touched his glass to hers. "Unfortunately, I'm about to leave. I hope I'll see you again."

Cia smiled. "Nice to meet you."

A few minutes later, Sarah sidled over, whispering that it was getting late and Bloomingdale's would be closing soon. After saying their goodbyes, they walked to the elevator. "What was that about, Sarah? A quick drink? Be straight with me."

She grinned. "I wanted you to meet Mark. And since you refuse to go on a blind date, I figured this was as good a time as any. I've invited him to join us for Christmas dinner."

Cia shook her head. "You blindsided me. You know I have no desire to date."

"So you keep saying. However, just think about it." Sarah pulled off a glove and started counting on her fingers. "He's attractive, successful, he's straight, and best of all: single. He doesn't have chattering voices or large birds following him around. Nor does he, at least as far as I know, have rings that glow and kill people. Not even ex-society wife hang-ups like some people we know." She looked at Cia with wide eyes and a broad smile. "He might just be normal. Can you, of all people, deal with normal?"

She laughed. "I don't know if any man can be considered normal."

Christmas at Sarah's had been pleasant despite missing Will and trying to avoid agitating thoughts about how he might be celebrating. Since her return from London, he'd been writing almost every week; lovely, heartfelt letters that usually ended with slightly erotic musings of how he wanted to kiss or caress her—images that always elicited a rush of breathless desire on her part. Occasionally, he'd include a quick sketch of something he imagined or saw; one of her favorites was a sweet drawing of a very large man walking a very small dog.

Although he had also called several times, he still hadn't mentioned anything about finding someone who could help explain the events in Scotland. At the same time, she was well aware that they both tended to avoid any mention of those days. In his last call before leaving for Majorca, he said he regretted having accepted the Critchlowes' invitation, admitting he'd been thoughtless and would much prefer to be spending the holidays with her. Her momentary flicker of hope lasted until he added that, unfortunately, it was now far too late to cancel. Once again, he promised to call the minute he returned to London, saying he would come to New York as soon as possible.

Putting her concerns aside, she spent much of Christmas afternoon talking with Mark, who was attentive as well as charming. She also discovered he wasn't just the executive editor at Archer; his last name was actually Archer. His grandfather had started the company in 1910, eventually handing it down to his father, who had built it into a significant publishing house. After his father's death, he and his sister, who handled the financial end, had taken it over. Along with Sarah's other guests, all in publishing, they spent a lively, albeit wine-soaked evening trading humorous stories about the eccentricities of their authors and publishers—including Mark, who took it all with tongue in cheek. Later, when he offered to take her home, she thanked him.

She was surprised when a cab came by so quickly. After all, it was Christmas night.

"Good karma," Mark remarked with a grin.

As she alighted from the cab, he started to get out with her, but she stopped him. "I'm fine, Mark. Good night."

He shook his head. "No, Cia. If nothing else, I'm a gentleman. I'll walk you to your door."

She was about to say good night again when he looked deeply into her eyes. "I'd like to see you for New Year's. Unfortunately, I have plans to go skiing. Would it be all right if I call when I return?"

She had looked back at him with some regret. "Mark. I'm sorry. I'm afraid Sarah hasn't been exactly fair. You see, I'm involved with someone, and although I had a lovely time tonight, I don't want to waste your time."

"I understand," he said, sounding a bit disheartened. "Well, whoever he is, he's a lucky man. I wish you the best." With that, he gave her a kiss on the cheek and, before getting back into the cab, turned to smile at her.

Chapter 5

New Year's Eve in Majorca was always an event. Between the parties in the grand houses, a costume race, street parades, and fireworks in the main square, the festivities went on for days.

The sun had just begun to rise on New Year's morning when a somewhat-plastered Will returned to the villa from his last stop of the night. That party, at the home of an artist friend, had been heavily fueled by booze and wine along with intense discussions of painters, both living and long gone. As he approached the Critchlowes' villa, he noticed two ravens perched on a nearby tree. With their yellow eyes focused on him, they cawed back louder than he would have imagined. Feeling an unexpected chill, he pushed open the unlocked front door and walked quickly through the massive living room still littered with empty champagne bottles, overflowing ashtrays and the usual New Year's detritus of discarded paper hats, masques, and confetti. After almost tripping over one of the more effete Critchlowe sons sprawled on a wine-stained damask sofa, he silently climbed the curved marble staircase to his room. When he opened the door, he stepped into an unexpected cacophony of sound. He had heard the voices, usually sighs, on and off since his arrival more than two weeks before, but he didn't have to be inebriated to realize they were in frantic discussion. Shaking his head in exasperation, he shouted, "What the bloody hell? Shut the fuck up!" He was both amazed and gratified at the abrupt silence.

"Thank you," he murmured. As he got into bed, he suddenly pictured Cia with her arms around him. Whether it was the birds or the voices that prompted the vision, he suddenly realized how much he missed her. Although he had danced and flirted with more than a few pretty girls, he had chosen to return to his room alone. He fell asleep quickly—not unusual after a long night of heavy drinking. His dreams were fractured and mostly forgettable, but one was frighteningly clear:

He was in a field, walking through tall grass while small creatures — squirrels, hares, voles, badgers, and other strangely unfamiliar furred animals —scurried back and forth, ignoring him. A cloudless cobalt-blue sky shimmered above emerald green birch trees that swayed in a gentle breeze. In the distance, he saw a cross-shaped stone that appeared to have some sort of archaic characters carved into it. As he started to move toward it, the animals began making fretful noises and ran off. Bewildered, he looked around, seeing a large brown fox standing not two meters away. He stood motionless as the animal stared at him with a fierce intelligence in its fathomless eyes. Suddenly it blinked, and, without a sound, moved past him to the cross-shaped stone where it stopped, and, with a quick glance back, disappeared into a dense copse of trees beyond. He followed it as far as the stone, afraid to venture further. Looking down, he tried to make out the carvings . . .

He woke up in a cold sweat, knowing there was a message within the dream, though still too groggy to grasp it.

Looking forward to a quiet New Year's Eve, Cia, Sarah, and Mike drove to the cottage. Since it had snowed a few days before, almost every car on the road held ski racks. Deciding to make a quick stop at Sonny's store, they waded through several inches of fresh snow before entering to the always pleasant scent of baking. While Sarah picked out some groceries and an apple pie, Sonny pulled Cia aside. "No apparitions this year. Promise?" They both preferred not to acknowledge her as "the ghost."

Cia shook her head. "Unfortunately, I doubt that I have much say about it. Other than the occasional flickering light, it's been pretty quiet. But please, feel free to stop by one dark night and have a friendly chat with her. She's, um, pretty transparent."

Sonny laughed. "If it's all right with you, I'll pass on that. By the way, I wanted to ask if you and your friends would like to join us tonight to ring in 1975. Come around nine?"

Cia glanced at Sarah, who nodded. "We'd love to."

Outside, Mike looked back. "What was that all about?"

"Just Sonny inviting us to her house." Although Cia had confided in Sarah about the apparition, they hadn't mentioned her to Mike, who no doubt would have pronounced them both, at the very least, delusional.

The evening was spent making coq au vin while consuming too many glasses of pinot noir. At nine, they piled into the car and drove through falling snow to Sonny's house, a stunning Swiss-type chalet festooned with flower boxes currently filled with colorful holiday lights. Leaving their boots and coats in the entry, they entered a two-storied living room complete with a large Christmas tree glittering with white lights.

Connor, Sonny's tall, grey-haired husband, offered glasses of champagne and introduced them to several of their friends, including Maureen and Bob, the couple who lived across the way from Cia's house.

She shook their hands. "I'm so glad to meet you. The light on the side of your house always attracts me. Especially when all the other houses are closed for the season. It's sort of become a beacon."

Maureen nodded. "We keep it on a timer. I hope you'll come by next time you're here."

"Thank you. I will."

A couple of women, already tipsy on champagne, wandered over to ask if Cia had seen the ghost. Barely managing to keep a straight face, she said, "I hate to disappoint you, but we've been, um, apparition-free."

Sonny, who had overheard the question, caught her eye and grinned. Cia shrugged as one of the women turned away and muttered, "So far."

Connor laughed. "Don't worry, Cia. Our ghosts, unlike some of our guests, are pretty friendly."

She had thought that was the end of the discussion until he yelled out, "When was the last time anyone saw her? The ghost, I mean." Cia cringed, thinking she could have given him the time and date. She wished they would all stop talking about it.

One of the women chimed in. "Oh. It had to be long before our time. But definitely after the new cottage was built. I'll bet she's still there." She winked at Cia. "Maybe you'll have a chance to see her."

"Actually, I'd rather not," she said, as everyone laughed.

"It's three minutes to midnight," Connor shouted while frantically attempting to adjust the rabbit ears on the television. Cursing under his breath, he cleared the fuzzy picture just as the ball began to drop in Times Square, accompanied, as always, by the frothy music of Guy Lombardo.

When everyone had finished kissing and wishing one another Happy New Year, the three of them reclaimed their coats and drove home on roads blanketed by several inches of newly fallen snow.

While Cia went to the kitchen to finish up the dinner dishes, Sarah dragged an inebriated and half-asleep Mike off to bed.

The night was unusually silent, any sounds muffled by falling snow. Not yet ready for bed, Cia sat down on the sofa and stared at the still-glowing embers, her thoughts turning to Will and wondering what he was doing that night. *Probably better not to know.* Still, she smiled inwardly at the old phrase, *Absence makes the heart grow fonder.* In her case, it was all too true. Her only wish was that he still felt the same. She no longer cared about the voices, the ghosts, or even the rings. She did know, however, that she would be more at ease with answers, if, indeed, there were answers.

As she moved to tamp down the ashes, the lights flickered. With a quick glance around the deeply shadowed room, she whispered, "I'm sorry, Cecily, for what happened to you. I believe we both know your Mr. Williams is now my Will. But this house belongs to me, and no matter what you do, you're not going to frighten me into leaving." Suddenly a cool breeze sighed through the room, ruffling the ashes and leaving her skin tingling. "So be it," she said aloud.

Though she seldom dreamt of Will, that night he occupied her dreams. Through a white mist, she saw him walking though the stones at Callanish as if searching for something. As he moved closer to the center monolith, a shadow of an animal began to follow him. She watched as he picked up stones with strange markings and then dropped them. She wanted to call out but was unable to find her voice. Distracted by a sound, she looked away. When she turned back, he was gone. It was dawn when she awoke hearing snow hitting the window. Or perhaps the faintest of whispers.

Unable to ignore a rare morning-after headache, Will sat up and put his hands to his face. He could hear sounds of activity downstairs, no doubt the housekeepers setting up for a New Year's open house. Wishing for a Bloody Mary, he settled instead for the glass of water on the nightstand. As he drank, the dream from the night tugged at his mind. Closing his eyes, he tried to force a replay. The images came slowly: he had been in a field with small playful animals. At first, he didn't understand why they had suddenly become fearful and vanished. Then he remembered; it was the fox. He had stared into its eyes until it had walked on, halting at a stone carved with odd hieroglyphs. *Gaelic. The characters on the stone were ancient Gaelic.* He had no idea how he could possibly know such a thing, and yet he was sure it was so. As the dream became clear, he took a breath. Fox in Gaelic was *sionnach*.

With a shock of recognition, he dropped the glass and whispered, "Sionn."

Part III

We must be willing to get rid of the life we've planned, so as to
have the life that is waiting for us.
—*Joseph Campbell*

Chapter 1

A couple of days after New Year's, Sid called Cia into his office. "I have a proposition for you. One I believe should make you happy. Phillips, who you met at Arlington-York, called this morning. He asked if I would be so kind as to send someone to London to assist on a rather significant international project that we will be collaborating on. You must have made quite an impression since he specifically asked for you. It'll be for a couple of weeks, perhaps a little more."

Flushed with excitement, she jumped up to kiss his cheek, causing him to immediately blush. "Yes, Sid. Thank you. That would be fantastic."

"I know it's short notice, but I'm afraid you will have to leave this weekend."

"Not a problem. I'll organize everything with Sarah."

"They will be happy to book a hotel. Unless," he grinned, "you wish to make other arrangements."

About to answer, she stopped abruptly and stared at him. She'd had a couple of hastily scribbled postcards from Will, but so far, no mention of when he'd be returning to London. Now it would be her turn to surprise him. "Can I tell you in a couple of days?"

"What's happened to your friend?"

"He's been away for the holidays and hasn't returned yet. I'll try to call him tonight."

"Whatever works. I know you're the right person for this job."

The front door had barely closed before she picked up the phone to call Will. When there was no answer, she considered writing a short note but realized she'd likely beat it to London. After trying the next two nights with no response, she found Patrick's number in Yorkshire and rang him. Although happy to hear from her, he said he'd had no word from Will but expected him to be home within the next couple of days. When she asked if he knew how to reach him, he hesitated. "No, Cia. I'm sure he'll call you as soon as he returns."

It wasn't until she hung up that she realized she had forgotten to mention she'd be coming to London that weekend. She briefly considered calling back, but not wanting to sound desperate, she reconsidered. Assuming Patrick was right, it might not matter. She reminded herself to tell Sid she would need a hotel, if only for a few nights.

Chapter 2

Mr. Phillips's secretary at Arlington-York had booked a small hotel not far from the office. Cia could hardly believe the room was even more cramped than the one where she'd stayed in Knightsbridge on her first trip to London. With a sigh, she hoped Will would return within the next day or two.

On her first morning, Mr. Phillips, welcoming her with a warm smile, showed her around the office and introduced her to the editors she'd be working with on a series of books for both the English and European markets. The offices, occupying what had once been an elegant Georgian residence, were pleasant enough despite creaking hallways and small, cluttered rooms that tended to mustiness. At the end of a somewhat chaotic day of meeting new people with unusual names and various accents, she was handed a couple of manuscripts to edit. That night, with one of the manuscripts in hand, she returned to her room where she again rang Will. When there was no answer, she put aside a queasy stab of emptiness and turned her attention to her work.

The next couple of nights became a frustrating repetition of the first; repeated calls, all to no avail. And yet each morning she woke up feeling optimistic, not only with the thought that this was the day Will would call, but that the work with her co-editors, Cynthia and Gwyn, was going so well. The three of them had even shared a few laughs trying to understand Gwyn's heavy Scottish accent. It was only later in the evening, after more unanswered phone calls, that she again found herself drowning in anxiety.

One evening, hurrying back to her room through an unexpected snowstorm, she heard the unsettling sound of cawing. Looking up, she saw two large ravens staring down at her from a darkened lamp post. As they fluffed off a frosting of white, the lamp flickered on. Convinced it was a sign that Will had at last returned, she practically ran the rest of the way. And yet when she called, there was still no answer. Unable to hold back sobs, she stared at the phone as though it had become her enemy. *Didn't he say he'd try to get back just after New Year's so we could meet in New York? Well, here I am in London, and it's now well into the second week of January, and why the hell isn't he here?* In the unlikely case he would call her office before she could reach him, she had made sure to leave the numbers for both Arlington-York and her hotel with Sarah as well as at the reception desk.

Brushing away tears, she questioned how this could be happening. She'd arrived in London happy, her mind filled with dreams of nights spent in Will's warm embrace. She'd even pictured his thrilled surprise at seeing her. But with each passing day those dreams had soured, leaving her miserable and lonely. Even working was becoming a chore; Gwyn had actually snapped her fingers in front of her face to get her attention that morning. She considered ringing Patrick again, but to what end? No doubt he would just reiterate what he'd said before. Or, knowing Will had returned, what could he say that wouldn't devastate her?

She touched the gold bracelet Will had given her, recalling the sweet memory of finding it in her suitcase. She'd worn it every day since. Now a million doubts spun unhappy webs in her mind, not only about Scotland but the fear that whatever had been murmured at their last kiss was no longer true.

That same night she had a dream: Will was standing on a shadowy street holding a large portfolio while laughing with a woman with blonde hair. When she called to him, he looked up, staring not at, but through her, as though she didn't exist. When she woke up, her pillow was damp and her eyes red-rimmed.

The next afternoon, Cynthia asked if she would like to join her and Gwyn for dinner. Having no plans other than returning to her claustrophobic hotel room to fret about Will, she thanked them.

They took a taxi to a narrow, dimly lit lane in Soho, alighting in front of a Chinese restaurant, the entrance garishly decorated with colorful, thrashing dragons. About to follow her friends inside, something caught her eye. Down the street, a large saloon car had just come to a stop in front another restaurant. She watched as an aristocratic-looking woman, her blonde hair upswept in an elegant chignon, stepped out and, with obvious excitement, waved to a man approaching from the other direction. *It's nothing*, she told herself, reaching for the door. Hearing a joyful shout, she once again glanced toward the woman, this time seeing the man embrace her. With a sharp intake of breath, she recognized Will. In shock, she spoke his name.

Although he couldn't have heard her, he stepped back, and, with a look of disbelief, his eyes met hers. After saying something to the woman, who glanced back and shrugged before going inside, he approached Cia.

Before she could say a word, he reached for her hand. "Cia. What are you doing here? Why didn't you tell me you were coming to London?"

She flinched at his touch, her posture tense, her eyes narrowed. "I've been here almost a week, Will. I've called your flat every day and every night. I even wrote to let you know where I'd be staying. From the look of things, it appears you now have other interests." Her eyes welling with unavoidable tears, she whispered, "At least you could have told me."

"No, Cia. Don't get the wrong idea."

"From what I just saw, how can I not? I was sure you would have called or at least read my letter by now. I thought you were avoiding me."

Still looking bewildered, he shook his head. "How can you even imagine such a thing? Please. Tell me why you're here."

"No," she snapped, stepping back. "Why bother? I have to go."

"Stop it, Cia," he said in a sharp voice. "This is my fault. I only returned from Majorca a few days ago. There was a freak snowstorm and all the flights were canceled. I've been calling your apartment and your office for the last two days. Your receptionist repeatedly told me you were out. She never said you were away."

Not convinced, she said, "What about Sarah? You could have asked for her."

"I did, twice. She was either out or in a meeting. I even left a message for her. She never called back."

Putting her hands to her face, she whispered, "I had one of those strange dreams last night. You were talking with a blonde woman, and now this. It's happening again, isn't it?"

He put a hand to her shoulder. When she didn't back away, he said in a softer tone, "No. You mustn't say or even think such a thing." He looked down with a sigh. "I'm sorry. By the time I got home, I was so overwhelmed with work and three weeks of mail that I decided not to answer the phone. I haven't even spoken to Patrick. The one time I did pick up a call, it was Lindy, the woman you just saw. She's an old friend and when she invited me to a birthday party tonight, I couldn't refuse. Now I'm glad I didn't. It's the first time I've been out other than teaching a class this afternoon." This time when he took her hand, she let him. "Now Cia, please tell me why you're here."

"There's no time right now. I'm supposed to be having dinner with some people from my office."

He looked surprised. "Your office?"

"I'm working here for a few weeks. At Arlington-York."

With confusion turning to comprehension, he nodded. "Now I understand. Where are you staying?"

"The Alcott. In Bloomsbury."

"Not the most elegant place."

She shrugged. "It's near the office. And to be honest, I didn't think I'd be there this long."

"And now you won't have to be." He looked at his watch. "I'll meet you at the hotel, say, ten-thirty? I should be able to escape by then."

"I don't know…" Before she could say another word, his arms were around her and his mouth on hers. This time when she looked up at him, tears of relief were evident in her eyes.

Tucking a few stray hairs behind her ear, a tender gesture that she loved, he murmured, "I love you, Cia. Don't ever forget that. When you get back to the hotel, check out and we'll go to my flat. That is, if you want to."

Are you kidding? This time it was she who reached up to kiss him. "Go to your party," she whispered. "I'll see you later."

He hesitated. "I can't believe how we found one another."

She looked at him with renewed concern. "Why do I think this whole thing has something to do with the rings?"

He squeezed her hand. "I don't think so, Cia. Sometimes it's fate that trips us up."

"You'll have to explain that to me," she said, looking doubtful.

"One day I will."

214

It was just past ten thirty when Will pulled up to the entrance of the hotel. After waiting a few minutes, he turned off the motor and went inside to the small reception area. Surprised Cia wasn't downstairs, he asked a sleepy-looking clerk to ring her. She answered, asking him to come up to her room.

The door was ajar and she was sitting on the bed, her eyes red from crying.

"What is it, Cia?" he asked, putting his arm around her.

She turned to face him. "I'm not sure this is a good idea."

"What isn't a good idea?"

"Me, staying at your flat."

"Why is it any different than a couple of months ago?"

She wiped away a tear. "Last night I dreamt of you laughing with a blond woman."

He tried not to look suprised. "So you were being a little pre-scient, that's all."

"To be honest, I'm scared."

"Of what?"

"I saw ravens the other day, Will. It felt like they were waiting for me. That's when I was sure you had come back."

"I thought I explained what happened."

She nodded. "You did. And yet, why do I have the feeling it isn't quite so simple? What if I go back to your flat and something happens again? If you had no control over it then, why would anything be different now? As much as I love you, I don't think I can survive another version of Scotland."

Holding her close, he whispered, "I'm sure it will be fine. Nothing has changed. I love you, and I want you to come home with me."

She moved away. "When I saw you with that woman, I thought about you and your life. I'm afraid we live in two different worlds."

"Cia, please, you're overreacting for no reason. I already told you she's just a friend. One of many."

"One of many?" she looked pointedly at him. "So what am I to think?"

With a sigh, he stood up. "All right. Let's try this. Tell me what you did New Year's Eve?"

"Why?"

"Humor me."

215

She shrugged. "Sarah and Mike came to the cottage. We went to a party at Sonny's."

"Did you have a date?"

She hesitated. "No, Will, I didn't."

"Why not?"

"I wasn't interested in getting involved with anyone. Why are you asking?"

"Because, Cia, I was alone as well. Despite there being plenty of opportunity, as I'm sure you've already imagined."

"Okay. I'll bite. Why were you alone?"

"Because there's an American woman with whom I'm very much in love. Now, Ms. Reynolds, shall we go?"

Looking into his eyes, she relented. "How can I ever say no to you? You have no idea how much I missed you."

"Yes. I do," he said, cupping her face in his hands. "You are so beautiful," he murmured. "I never want to stop touching you, making love to you."

She moved into his arms. "I was afraid I'd never see you again."

"I promise that will never happen. Right now, all I want is to kiss you all over, touch you in every place you've ever imagined or thought you've imagined." His voice was low, seductive. "I can't tell you how many nights I pictured you lying in my arms. Please, Cia, come home with me."

With a sigh, she reached up to kiss him. "Only if you promise to do all those things."

"Why do I think that won't be a problem?"

A couple of days after settling in at his flat, she decided to surprise him by making dinner. He was accustomed to going out every night, if only to one of the local pubs, and she wasn't finding the offerings very interesting. She asked Gwen if she had any idea where she should shop.

She looked doubtful. "You're cooking? I thought you were staying in a hotel."

"Well, no. Not anymore. I'm, ah, now staying with a friend. He was away the first few days I was here."

She smirked. "I thought you seemed happier. Where does this friend live?"

"In Chelsea. Cresswell Place. Just off Fulham Road."

"Cynthia knows that area better than I do. Come with me." Cia followed her to Cynthia's office, where they waited until she was off the phone.

"Cia wants to know where to shop around Fulham Road near Creswell. She's making dinner for a friend."

Cynthia looked surprised. "You've been here a week and already snagged a bloke?"

"We met two years ago. We've been having what I guess you would call a long-distance relationship."

"That can't be easy. What does he do?"

"He's an artist."

"Well, that explains Chelsea. Would I know his work? What's his name?"

She hesitated. "Will Jamieson."

Gwyn stared at her. "Will Jamieson? The Will Jamieson? Are you kidding? It took a Yank to get to him? You do know he has quite the reputation."

"So I've been told."

"And you don't mind? I mean, don't you wonder what he's up to when you're three thousand miles away?"

"I try not to."

"Is this serious?"

"I hope so."

"You know he's from Edinburgh."

"Yes, Gwyn. And when you have the time, I'd like to ask a few things. I mean, about Scotland."

Cynthia extended her hand. "Have a seat and ask away."

"Thanks. I know this may sound weird, but I wanted to ask about, um, haunted places in Scotland. Like stone circles, the Loch Ness monster and such."

Cynthia looked at Gwyn and frowned. "That's a funny question. Why?"

Cia shrugged as if it was no big deal. "Will talked about going for a visit, and I hear there are lots of mysterious places, particularly stone circles."

Gwyn thought a minute. "Interesting question. Let's see. It's said that Edinburgh Castle has been haunted for over a thousand years. Not really all that unusual. In almost every part of Scotland there are houses, castles, churches, and graveyards where people swear they've

217

seen ghosts. We've had, you could say, a rather turbulent history, and people imagine all sorts of things. I would say most of it is myth." She paused as if to think for a moment. "And yet, maybe not all. What stone circle are you talking about? There are quite a few."

"Callanish."

Gwyn sat back in surprise as Cynthia exclaimed, "Blimey! That's a scary one."

"Why?"

"Below the big center stone, there's a burial chamber. It's empty, but you don't want to be there after dark when the fog rolls in." She gave an exaggerated shiver.

Before Cia could ask anything else, Gwyn cut in. "There are also quite a few cairns, burial chambers, in that area. There's even a hill that's said to be haunted. At one time, a house was built on it, but it burned down. No one knows why, although some say it was hit by lightning. If I were you, I'd tell your Mr. Jamieson to take you to Stonehenge. It's a lot closer and not nearly so creepy."

Unexpectedly, Cia felt Gwyn pat her arm. "Are you okay? You're white as a ghost."

"Sorry. I'm fine. I just felt dizzy for a minute."

"I wish I was in your high heels. Jamieson is quite the catch." She paused to give Cia a wicked grin. "Oh, right. You'll be going back to New York soon, won't you?"

"Very funny, Gwyn."

With a quick glance at her watch, Cynthia stood up and said she was meeting a friend at a pub in Chelsea, not far from Cresswell. "If you're ready, Cia. We can go together."

Cia nodded, trying not to think about a haunted house sitting on a hill.

They took a taxi to Fulham Road, where Cynthia pointed out a supermarket along with a green grocer nearby.

When she walked into the flat with two bags of groceries, Will, who'd been painting in the studio, came down to the kitchen. He stopped and stared. "What is all this?"

"Dinner. I've had about enough of shepherd's pies, fish and chips, and the like. And you always end up being surrounded by friends. I thought we could have some time alone."

He pulled her close. "Are you happy? I told you nothing weird was going to happen."

So far, anyway. She hugged him. "I only wish I didn't have to leave."

"Go ahead and make dinner. We'll talk about that later."

She blinked. "About what?"

He gave her quick kiss. "Be patient, my love," he said, picking up a cream-colored envelope from the counter. "By the way, I've been invited to a rather fussy sort of party Saturday night. Have you, by any chance, brought along a cocktail dress?"

She looked up from peeling an onion. "Actually, yes. But wouldn't you rather go alone? I don't want to cramp your style."

"Absolutely not. I want you by my side."

She leaned over and kissed him. "Thank you."

After taking the roast chicken out of the oven, she made a salad while Will opened a bottle of cabernet. During dinner, with the voices barely audible under a classic recording of Sonny Rollins's "The Bridge," he told her he might have the name of someone to talk with about what happened in Scotland.

"Seriously? I was afraid to ask. I thought you'd given up on it."

"To be honest, I almost had. That is, until I had a very strange dream."

She stared at him. "Tell me."

Taking a sip of wine, he began to describe the scene in the field and seeing the fox.

Startled, she shook her head. "Will. You're frightening me. I had a similar dream. You were at Callanish, and an animal was following you. I only saw its shadow, but I'm sure it was a fox." She stopped and took a breath. "Do you think it's possible that our minds, or at least our dreams, are somehow communicating? After Callanish, nothing would surprise me." She was about to tell him about the night she saw the apparition but stopped. That could wait.

"I'm curious. Do you remember when you had that dream?"

"Yes. It was New Year's Eve."

"At what time?"

She shrugged. "I went to bed about one, I guess. Sometime after."

219

He took a deep breath. "Mine was the next morning. Given the time difference it's possible we had those dreams about the same time."

With an obvious shiver, she stood up. "I was talking about Scotland with a couple of the girls at my office today. One of them mentioned that Callanish is a very scary place. When I asked why, she said there were quite a number of burial cairns nearby. She specifically mentioned a hill with a house that burned down." She reached for his hand. "It was said to be haunted."

He got up and put his arms around her. "Stop thinking about that. I know it upsets you. What's important is that Patrick should be getting back to me in the next day or so. He thinks he may have found the man I'm looking for."

She stared at him, her face serious. "That's good, isn't it?"

He nodded. "Yes, Cia. Stop looking so worried."

Forcing a smile, she changed the subject. "Speaking of Patrick, will he be coming to London?"

"There's an opening at the Tate in a couple of weeks. Do you think you'll be able to stay until then?"

"I don't know. We'll be finished with this project in another week. It's already gone on longer than expected. I can ask, but I know Sid wants me back."

"And what if I want you here?"

She stared at him. "What are you saying?"

"Look, my love, I'm not exactly getting down on one knee and asking you to marry me. Not yet, anyway. However," he paused, "I'd, ah, like you to come live with me. Assuming you want to."

Putting her hands gently to his face, she kissed him. "Will, there's nothing I would like more." She smiled, realizing how difficult that request must have been. She'd never seen him so awkward before. "As long as you don't wake up one morning and drag me off to another frightening stone circle."

"No," he said, his face serious. "Since you've been here, I'm sure you're aware the voices have been unusually quiet, and I haven't seen even one raven. Nevertheless, I'd still like some answers."

"To be honest, I no longer care. I did before, but what's past is past. Every time I think of that inn, my skin crawls. Maybe you should just let it be."

He shook his head. "I'm afraid I can't. If you're going to be here with me, we need to be certain that nothing will happen again. Particularly now that we're so close to finding someone who may be able to explain it. You must also understand that I have to be sure before I give you the other ring."

She could feel butterflies stirring in her stomach. The ring meant he believed she was the timeless love that Patrick had mentioned. It was the final step; one she knew in his mind transcended even marriage. And if, by some strange chance, the stories were to be believed, it would bind them for all eternity. If nothing else, it was a lovely thought, one she could only wish was so. "Tell me how you know about this man you're looking for."

"It's a long story, beginning when I was eight years old." He went on to tell her of his experience of déjà vu in Egypt and then meeting the man with the unusual name of Sionn at his parents' dinner party. "It was only on New Year's, when we both had similar dreams about the fox and the carved stones, that I remembered it. The dream was obviously a message, one I had to decipher."

By the time he finished explaining what the fox and the stones symbolized, she was staring at him wide-eyed. "I had no idea. Do you think that your déjà vu is why the rings came to you?"

"I don't know, Cia. That's one of the things I hope to find out. Now, however, you have to answer my question."

Fluttering her eyelashes, she said, "You mean about living in London? Let me think about it."

"Absolutely not. It's now or never." He laughed, taking her in his arms.

She snuggled close to him. "Well, Mr. Jamieson. This has been quite a night. At least so far. Maybe I'll consider coming to live with you after you remind me what I might expect."

Taking her hands, he brought her to her feet. "My pleasure."

The next afternoon, Cia, along with Gwyn and Cynthia, were called into Mr. Phillips's office, where he informed them their part of the joint project with BookEnds would be complete in just a few days. He added that he considered it a great success. After the meeting, he took Cia aside. "You know my job offer is still waiting."

"I appreciate it, Mr. Phillips. I'm afraid I can't answer you right at the moment, but I think I may be ready to discuss it in the near future."

With a rare smile, he nodded. "The sooner the better. Although, I wouldn't choose to be there when you inform Sid."

Despite being excited about the job offer, by the time Cia arrived at the flat she was practically in tears. She told Will she had spoken to Sid that afternoon, and while he'd agreed to let her stay the weekend, he wanted her back in the office by Tuesday at the latest. Without a word, Will took her in his arms. "Come, Cia, let's have a drink. I also have some things to tell you."

Taking a couple of glasses of scotch, they went upstairs to the studio where they took their now-familiar places on the loveseat. "Patrick called earlier. He finally located the man I told you about. His last name is McKenna, and he lives in St. Andrew's, near Edinburgh. I've already phoned but was told he's away and won't be back before late March. I'll make an appointment to see him as soon as he returns."

"I guess that's good news, Will. Although, it still worries me."

"The bad news, however, is the gallery is still not finished. Steve is now saying it will likely be May before they can open, although he's committed to having my show before summer."

When she looked back at him with an unasked question, he shook his head. "While I'm not unhappy about having more time to complete more paintings, I'm afraid I may not get to New York until then."

"That's almost four months, Will," she whispered.

Seeing her eyes mist with tears, he held her close. "Don't be sad, Cia," he said, kissing her nose. "It will all work out for us. I promise."

Promises or not, Cia was becoming increasingly anxious about the upcoming society party that Saturday night. This was Will's bailiwick, and she was convinced there was no way she would fit in. When she put on her black cocktail dress, Will kissed her neck and told her she looked beautiful, which made her smile but did little to diminish her anxiety level.

The taxi let them off in front of an understated, white stucco townhouse on a quiet street in Belgravia. Cia had expected something a bit more elaborate until Will explained that the wealthier one was, the less one tended to flaunt it. "In this case," he said, "the address is enough."

Once inside, however, the placid exterior belied an extravagant interior. That they were greeted by a butler in full livery was daunting enough, but entering into a lavishly decorated salon populated with titled men and their equally titled wives, many in long gowns—with even a tiara perched on a couple of well-coiffed heads—only added to Cia's apprehension. She wanted to beg Will to stay by her side, but already knew that wasn't going to be possible.

Their effusive hostess, Madelaine, bejeweled to the gills and dressed in the latest Saint Laurent, flew to greet Will with an exaggerated hug. With an appraising glance at Cia, she welcomed her with a mere semblance of a smile.

Will had just taken two glasses of champagne from a passing waiter when a squat woman wearing a somewhat dated silk Chanel and dripping diamonds, presented herself for cheek kisses. While offering a vacant smile as he introduced her to Cia, she grabbed his hand and, in a squeaky voice, demanded, "Come along, darling. There's a baroness who is simply dying to meet you." He looked at Cia, who could only murmur, "Go ahead."

"Are you sure?"

Do I have a choice? "Not to worry. Do your thing."

Watching a gaggle of middle-aged women surround Will like feeding sharks, she wandered around the sumptuously furnished room looking at the impressive artwork; a nice-sized Renoir along with two large Picassos and a small but lovely Matisse. But it was the flattering portrait of their hostess hanging prominently above the fireplace that drew her attention. As expected, it was signed: W. Jamieson.

Hearing a bell chime, signaling dinner was about to be served, Will came over and took her hand. "How are you doing?"

"Fine. How was the baroness?"

He smirked. "Tedious. She wants to discuss a portrait."

"Are you sure it's just a portrait she's interested in? She looked like she was about to devour you."

With a glance at the table, he squeezed her hand. "It appears you're sitting between Lord Williston and Donald Smethers. He's an industrialist."

"Why can't I sit next to you?" she whispered.

With a sardonic grin, he shook his head. "It's just not done."

Dinner turned out to be an endless affair of one tasteless course after another broken by brief, grueling bursts of conversation with each of her seatmates, neither of whom had the slightest interest in a book editor from New York. The only attention she did receive was a doughy hand groping her knee from the rather portly lord to her left. She immediately brushed him off.

After dinner, the ladies drifted back to the salon while the men retired to a wood-paneled library for brandy. One of the younger women came over, introducing herself as Sydney. "I can see you're feeling a bit awkward here. You must realize Will is extremely popular. Most of these ladies are less than pleased that he brought along a date."

A date? Although tempted to say she was a tad more than a date, Cia simply nodded. When Sydney asked what she was doing in London, she mentioned her job at Arlington-York. Sydney nodded absently as a waiter passed by with a tray offering a spot of Drambuie. Cia took a glass while Sydney indicated a loveseat where they could sit down and continue to chat. After about twenty minutes of Sydney nattering on about her horses in Sussex—or was it Surry— Cia was relieved to see the men return. She hoped Will would say they could leave soon, but, after mingling for only a few minutes, she groaned inwardly as he, along with the other men, moved to a cluster of oversized armchairs to continue drinking their brandies and smoke their foul-smelling cigars.

Shortly thereafter, no doubt due to the vast quantities of champagne and other spirits already consumed, the conversation rose to a fever pitch of tinkling glasses, laughter, and gossip. Giggling and giving one another knowing glances, two of the younger women got up and approached the men, who continued to ignore them. Doing her best to pay attention to Sydney's incessant chatter, this time about a recent hunt, Cia saw her suddenly sit up straight and her eyes fly open. She looked back just as one the prettier socialites launched herself into Will's lap and proceeded to give him a rather overzealous kiss. With unanimous guffaws, the various lords, barons, and so-called industrialists raised their glasses.

Cia didn't know if he somehow intuited her stare or just came to his senses. But with a sobering glance back at her, he put down his drink and moved the girl, albeit gently, off his lap. Giving him a narrow-eyed scowl, she flipped her hair and made a beeline for a grinning baron.

Before Sydney could resume her conversation, Cia felt Will come up behind her.

"We should go," he said in a soft voice. "We both have a busy day ahead of us tomorrow."

Sydney looked up at him. "On a Sunday? Dear boy, you work too hard. And what about Cia?"

"He's right. I'm leaving in two days. It's been lovely talking with you, Sydney. Good luck with your horses."

"Yes. Well. I hope we'll be seeing you again. Sometime."

Sometime? Trying her best not to grit her teeth, she preceded Will to the entry where the butler was already holding their coats. After a mostly silent taxi ride back to his flat, she went directly to the kitchen.

"What's wrong?" Will asked, following her.

"Nothing."

"Then what are you doing?"

"Making tea."

"Why?"

Her response was terse. "Because I feel like it."

Fully aware that when a woman says nothing is wrong, something always is, he shook his head. "Cia, please. What is it?"

She didn't look up. "It's time for me to go home. I don't belong here."

"Stop this," he said, sounding exasperated. "You're overreacting again."

"Look Will, it was difficult enough being blatantly ignored by those people all evening, except, of course, at dinner when Lord whatchamacallit started rubbing my thigh with his fat paw. But watching everyone try to keep from laughing while that girl threw herself at you was a bit too much."

Coming up behind her, he kissed her neck. "I'm sorry. I should have realized it would upset you. To be honest, this happens all the time. No one thinks anything of it."

Somewhat mollified, she turned to face him. "I do. I love you. But I doubt I will ever be accepted by your friends. Not those friends. They want you to themselves."

"They were jealous that I was there with someone outside their circle."

She grimaced. "A commoner?"

225

"What do you think I am?"

"Court painter?"

He laughed, breaking the tension. "A couple of hundred years ago, perhaps. As far as I'm concerned, they'll just have to get used to you."

"I hate to say it, but that won't happen."

He took her hands in his. "If you have a ring, it will."

She stopped moving. "What are you saying?"

"Does it require an explanation?"

"I thought we weren't pursuing that discussion right now," she said, trying to calm her suddenly accelerating heartbeat.

"Look, my love, let me go to Edinburgh and meet with McKenna. That's important to me; to us. I'll be in New York in a few months. Before, if at all possible. We'll talk more then. All right?"

She hesitated. "Are you sure?"

He put his arms around her. "By now, you should know I will never betray your trust. Nor do I say things I don't mean."

The next morning, the phone didn't stop ringing. Several of the party goers from the night before called, not to ask about Cia, but to inform Will that soon after he left, a small fire had broken out. The story was that one of the men had stood too close to a curtain with his cigar, and, although it had gone up in flames, it had been quickly extinguished. After hanging up the third call, he looked at Cia. "What do you think?"

"Why are you asking me?"

"Because I have the distinct feeling that you better not get angry anymore. At least when we're together."

Chapter 3

A young woman hefting an armload of books pointed Will in the direction of Dr. McKenna's office at the end of a long corridor. Seeing a small plaque on the door with his name, Will knocked. Hearing a deep voice shout, "Enter," he opened the door just as a sprightly, white-haired man with a plaid woolen muffler wound around his neck rose from behind his desk and reached forward to shake his hand.

"Thank you for seeing me. I hope this isn't an imposition."

"In truth, Will. If I may call you Will? I've been waiting for you."

"Waiting? For me?"

"Yes. After that night at your parents' house those many years ago, I was sure we would eventually meet again. Please. Have a seat. I'll ring for tea. I have the feeling there's much to talk about."

Will sat down on a well-worn leather armchair facing a massive oak desk, scarred from years of use and strewn with papers. Around him, books overflowed wooden shelves that lined every wall, and on the floor more books, many with cracked leather bindings, had been stacked as high as a meter. On one shelf, he noticed a glass case containing shards of ancient pottery and broken mosaics, and on another a row of clay oil lamps, small pots, and several bulbous fertility goddesses, all of which no doubt predated Christianity by millennia. Behind McKenna's desk, a few large, decorated urns sat at the feet of a graceful, if headless, sculpture. Will guessed she was the Greek goddess Aphrodite.

The older man cleared his throat. "I'm curious to know how you found me. You can't have saved my card from all those years ago."

"I wish I had. I located you through a friend who knows someone at the University of Glasgow. That, however, was only after I finally remembered your first name."

He nodded. "Not many Sionns around. Most people think it's Sean, but it's pronounced more like 'shoon.' After all this time, I'm impressed that you remembered me."

"I remembered because you appeared to take an eight-year-old seriously."

Mc Kenna leaned forward on the desk, his fingers intertwined. "Tell me about your parents. I recall they were good, solid people. You have a brother, don't you?'

Will smiled, feeling a bit more at ease. "Yes. He now runs the distillery in Aberdeen. My father brought him into the business before he died. Unfortunately, my folks are long gone."

"So, tell me what has brought you here."

Will shifted in his chair. "I think you may already know the answer to that."

McKenna nodded. "In truth, I thought I would have seen you here long before this."

"Why?"

"If you recall, I asked you to have your mother ring me if anything like what you experienced in Egypt happened again. I'd have been surprised if it didn't. Now I imagine by your presence that it has."

"Yes. Twice more, actually. But that was years ago. Now . . ."

McKenna put his hand up to stop him. "Let's begin with the past. Can you tell me what happened each time?"

Since he already knew about Luxor, Will began by telling him about Mykonos and asking their startled guide about sheep. "The man thought I was daft. He said there had been no sheep in Mykonos for centuries. And yet I knew there had been."

"That's a hard one to pin down. It could have been anytime from the Middle Ages to the nineteenth century. Anything else?"

"Not really. I did go to Rhenea. Nothing much changes on an island of the dead. The locals said it was haunted and yet it didn't seem haunted to me. It felt familiar."

"I understand. I've been there. But you said twice?"

He took a breath. "There was a school trip to Glasgow. With a stop in the Outer Hebrides."

The Professor's eyes went wide. "Callanish?"

"Why do you look surprised?"

He shook his head. "Tell me what happened?"

"When we arrived, I made the mistake of telling the teacher I'd been there before. She thought I was either lying or showing off."

"What do you remember about it?"

He shrugged. "Like what?"

"Did the moment come as an image or a feeling?"

"A hazy image, along with the feeling I'd seen those stones before. But they had seemed larger, and one or two had been horizontal, as if not yet put up into position."

"And after that?"

"Nothing. That was the end of it. That is, until a few months ago."

They were interrupted by an elderly woman bringing a tray with tea and biscuits. While she fussed over setting out the cups and pouring the tea, Will looked around the cluttered office. "What is it that you teach? Are you an archaeologist?"

McKenna put his hand out, indicating the bookcases. "Actually, by definition, I'm an anthropologist with an advanced degree in psychology. In that regard, I'm more of what you might define as an explorer into the mysteries of ancient civilizations. I have spent my life trying to make sense of certain individuals' ability to recall the past. Not recent, mind you, but the distant past going back centuries, even as far as the Bronze or Stone Age. I've traveled the Middle East and Europe seeking out those who have experienced profound and often extended episodes of déjà vu. You must understand that while almost everyone has an occasional flash, most put it off as meaningless. Then there are others, like you, who have had intense and often disturbing visions and seek to find answers. I spoke with one man — an American — who, on a family trip to Athens, suddenly recalled standing inside the Parthenon while it was being built. Since the man was a dentist with little interest in anything but teeth and golf, his wife thought he was putting her on. When he began describing structural elements in detail, his wife, in a fit of pique, brought him over to a couple of archeologists who were working nearby. There are always a few archeologists on the Acropolis, you know. They just can't seem to stop digging. Anyway, it turned out that whatever the man told them were facts that only a trained architect or archeologist would know."

Will laughed. "You must enjoy this."

He offered a slight grin. "I do. What's most important for me is to unravel where these memories are coming from and why, without warning, they are manifested. It takes hours of discussion, occasionally even hypnosis. Recently, a woman from Liverpool came to me in serious confusion. On a visit to Israel with a tour group, she suddenly knew her way through the ancient alleyways of Old Jerusalem and, despite the guide trying to stop her, she insisted on leading the entire group directly to the underground tomb in the Church of the Holy Sepulchre. Out of nowhere, she suddenly recalled being there as a child and watching a Christian church being constructed over the Roman temple that previously occupied the site. She remembered her mother trying to drag her away."

"She was that specific?"

"Yes, Will. Just as you were about Egypt. The church she described was built by Constantine, the first Christian emperor, in the year 326, ostensibly to hide the burial cave of Jesus's resurrection. No one on her trip took her seriously, some saying she must have read about it and wanted to show off. That wasn't the case at all. She was a widow with three kids and little interest in the Middle East. The trip was a gift from her sister who had been there and loved it. From her account, she said she experienced a flash of recognition and the sense that she was living it again, albeit for a brief moment. Right here in our own small country we have an inordinate number of people who report such occurrences. Not all are real, of course, but those that are, are compelling. Scotland is quite the spiritual place despite, or perhaps due to, our rather tempestuous history."

Will grimaced. "I guess I'm not alone in this."

"Not at all. Were there any more incidents after Callanish?"

"No. That was the last. At least as a child."

McKenna paused to sip his tea. "That's not unusual. When we are young, our minds are open, and we absorb knowledge like sponges. More children than you might expect experience such moments. I constantly hear from rattled parents who tell me little Mary said she had a nice conversation with Aunt Sophie who, by the way, has been dead for thirty years. They want me to explain how she could know about her. All I can tell them is that it's a moment and not to fear; it's unlikely to happen again. I always add that if it does, to please bring her back. As we get older our life experiences take over, and although we may have those moments, they're not as strong or as frequent as when we are young. This is not to rule out those children who demonstrate a unique extrasensory clairvoyance and often grow up to have psychic empathy. You, as I recall, had a very powerful reaction in Luxor. That's why, when I met you, I asked you to contact me when it happened again. For I knew it would. I'm pleased you found me after all these years."

"Are you some sort of psychic?"

McKenna lit a pipe, the fragrant scent of tobacco overtaking the musty scent of well-worn books. "Maybe a little. I'm more of a searcher, you could say, who is seeking answers."

"Answers?"

"Answers to why some of us remember past lives while others don't."

Will stared at him. *Past lives?* MacDonald had mentioned *ancient lives*, but never *past lives*. At least not specifically. That he could have lived a past life was incomprehensible, far beyond his realm of belief; there was no logic to it. He wanted to get up, thank the man and leave. And yet he didn't move, the idea beginning to form that the possibility might not be quite as far-fetched as it sounded.

"What was it that made you decide to find me?"

He shrugged. "I'm also looking to find answers."

"To what?"

Will held out his hand. "One is this ring. Another involves a woman I've become close to which seems to have provoked some rather unusual occurrences."

"Rather unusual?"

Will smirked. "I was understating it. More like extremely bizarre."

"I noticed your ring, particularly the sapphire. Perhaps you should begin with that."

Will related the story, from the old man in the curio shop to the sudden death of Carolyn and his subsequent conversation with Mac-Donald, which, despite later circumstances, he still considered to be real. When he finished, McKenna stood up and walked to the window. "You are a rare specimen, Will. You have no idea of your power."

"What are you talking about?"

"Much of our lives are governed by time and place. It was no accident that you walked into that shop on that particular day. I would have to say you were meant to. What do you know of the man who gave you the rings?"

"Nothing more than I've already told you. When I went back, he was dead."

"That's because you weren't meant to return to him. He was what is known as a messenger. Messengers such as he have existed in one form or another throughout the ages. Think of the Greek god Hermes who is described as having a foot in two worlds: the mortal and the divine. What is essential is that in each generation there are those, sometimes perceived as old men with beards, who transfer the sapphires from one soul to another—that's how it continues. You were likely the last visitor to that shop the old man encountered. I'll wager there were others before you to whom he passed on either trinkets with the stones, or the sapphires themselves. He was waiting for you."

Will sat back in surprise. "How can you know this?"

"Early in my studies I found a few vague references to sapphires. They were always obscure, but I eventually figured out that in some ancient cultures, such as have existed in our own islands, sapphires represented not only love but power as well. What surprised me is that they were often mentioned not as single stones but as pairs. I didn't understand why until I met a couple of men who, like you, were in possession of such sapphires. That's when I went back even further, to ancient Gaelic manuscripts. Although sapphires are seldom referenced, whenever they are, it is always with warnings to beware of 'pale entities,' which I assume are what MacDonald referred to as earthbound spirits."

"Do you know why?"

"All I can tell you is they are said to be the spirits of those who passed long ago and yet lingered on, whether through fear of passing over, guilt, or possibly to complete some task. I imagine the being he cautioned you about was not your common, everyday man. He would have been a powerful tribal leader, possibly even a shaman who died unexpectedly or was put to death for some transgression. Either way, he may not have had time to appease his gods. If a man was an authority figure in his lifetime and through the centuries, never passed from the earthly realm, his spirit may have gained even more strength. There are gravesites all over the British Isles that are considered dangerous, even evil, and therefore thought to be haunted. I'm assuming you've come into contact with such a spirit?"

Will tried to suppress a shudder. "Let's wait on that. I promise I'll return to it later. MacDonald also said we are chosen. Why me?"

"I'm afraid I don't have an answer for you. MacDonald obviously had far more knowledge than I. As I mentioned, however, I have met two others in possession of such stones. Like you, they each experienced intense moments of past lives that began as déjà vu. Interestingly enough, they were both struggling around the time they were given the stones, and both, to my surprise, mentioned an old, bearded man such as you described. And yet, once the sapphires were in their possession, they became highly successful in their fields. And each, upon meeting their soulmate, fell in love and so passed on the second ring without incident. One is a well-known musician and the other, surprisingly, a banker who is much respected by his peers. That's when I began to understand the manuscripts mentioning sapphires as pairs, in that they represent not only love but immortality."

"How did they know exactly who was the 'one'?"

"I would imagine one would intuit a special connection. I have the feeling you may have already met the woman who connects with you through time. Although you are currently uncertain, at some point you will have to accept her. Have faith in yourself, Will. You will know who she is and when to give her the other ring."

Will sighed. *Connects through time? Here we go again.* "It's obvious that Carolyn wasn't that person, and she paid for it with her life. I'm sure you understand my reluctance."

"The ancient spirits, those that are said to inhabit the sapphires, can be harsh. And yet, despite your loss, they have been good to you. I made a few calls and know how successful you've become."

"I won't deny that. And yet, perhaps I would have come this far without the rings."

McKenna shook his head. "There's no way to know."

"What about the voices?"

"Voices?" he looked startled.

"They are muffled, indistinct, as though whispers heard from down a hallway, or perhaps a distant room. Usually it's just murmurs, but there are times they sound like faint medieval chants."

McKenna stared at him. "If I were a religious man, this is where I would cross myself. That is extraordinary. Can you understand them?"

233

"Not at all. They sound garbled to me. MacDonald said he heard them clearly. That's how he knew so much. They're not in my head. Others have heard them as well."

McKenna got up and paced. As he opened a window, mystical medieval chants from a nearby church drifted into the room. Obviously taken aback, he glanced at Will, who shook his head. "Those voices sound a hell of a lot more spiritual, if that's the right word, than the ones nattering on around me."

"Voices," McKenna whispered. "In truth, I have heard muted whispers such as you describe, usually late at night when all is quiet and I'm half asleep. Like MacDonald, I often imagine them to be the muddled murmurs of past generations." He smirked. "Of course, it could just as well be that someone left the telly on in another room. I actually got up once to check, but all was silent. In that respect, they may act as spirit guides, although I've never heard of guides being vocal. Do you hear them only in your home?"

"I've heard them in other places. Even New York."

"Perhaps," he said, returning to his desk, "you should tell me about the woman you mentioned. Has she heard these voices as well?"

"Her name is Cia. And yes, she has."

"Cia? An unusual name. A variation of the ancient Greek Kynthia, the mythological goddess of the moon. But I digress. Have you noticed any unusual birds?"

Looking startled, Will said, "There have been ravens outside my flat for months."

"But only since you met her?"

"Actually, yes. I don't recall ever seeing them before."

"Ravens are often considered messengers. Also totems; symbols of time, place and transition. If they only appeared after you met Cia, she may represent such a transition." He stopped to relight his pipe. "I don't think you came here just to tell me of sapphire rings and Cia."

Will shook his head. "What triggered all this is Callanish. When MacDonald told me it was dangerous, that the sapphires seek to return to their origins, I had no idea what he meant."

McKenna suddenly looked pale. "That's what I read in the ancient manuscripts. Callanish has long been thought to be a vortex."

"A vortex?"

"A point of energy that emanates from deep within the earth. Where energy circles a spot and flows out, around, and back into it. Although virtually nothing is known about Callanish, over the centuries it has been thought to be both sacred and profane. What is known is that some individuals have gone there and experienced unusual insights, even saying they've been able to communicate with the past. Whether this is real, wish-fulfillment or even fantasy, I have no clue. For most, it's just an interesting tourist site." He paused. "Obviously not for you."

"No."

"And Callanish is where you came into contact with this so-called earthbound spirit?"

"No, Professor. It was at the inn."

He sat back, a look of surprise on his face. "An inn? You mean there's another part to this?"

"When I tell you the rest of it, you can decide."

"You mentioned that MacDonald died not long after you spoke to him."

"So I believe. When I went back, I was told he had never been there at all."

McKenna nodded, a serious expression on his face. "Whatever. Illusion or not, he passed on information that went against natural laws. It may have been his way of ensuring his death."

Will sat back in surprise. "What are you saying?"

He glanced at his watch. "It's getting late. What say we break for a bit and then meet for dinner? There's a pub near here called the Hounds. We can regroup there at seven."

Will took a deep breath, the fresh breeze working to clear his head. The afternoon with McKenna had been revelatory but troubling, and he was almost afraid of what was to come. It was only around three, and with hours of daylight left, he decided to drive to Croft Moraig, a stone circle on a bleak moor northwest of Perth. As he parked, he was relieved to see groups of tourists milling about with cameras.

Taking his time, he strode at a leisurely pace through the oddly stunted stones, feeling nothing of the compulsion that had drawn him inexplicably to the far more majestic site at Callanish. Nevertheless, experiencing a vague sense of timelessness and unease that might cause even the most hardened sightseer a shiver of apprehension, he left quickly, returning to St. Andrews in time to meet McKenna at the pub. He was already sitting at a table, the pint of Guinness in front of him half gone.

Taking a double scotch from the bar, Will joined him. "Sorry. Am I late?"

"Not at all. You look refreshed. Did you have a nap?"

"I drove to Croft Moraig."

"Why?"

"I wanted to see if it would have any effect on me. It didn't."

"Then I suggest we pick up where we left off. You were about to tell me about Cia and Callanish. Oh, yes. And an inn."

Will sat back and sipped his drink. He began with meeting Cia at the gallery and feeling there was something special about her. He described their subsequent trips to New York and London, and their growing affection for one another.

McKenna shrugged. "Sounds like a nice story. Boy meets girl, albeit a bit long distance."

"Except that, on our first night together, she picked up on the voices and wanted to know what they were. She surprised me. Particularly since most of the, ah, ladies who have spent time at my flat never heard, or at least never mentioned, them. I told her it was the wind, pipes, whatever. She never quite bought it, but it didn't come up again in any meaningful way until last October when she stayed for ten days. I was in love with her by then and quite certain the feeling was mutual. She had just been offered a job in London when I had this crazy compulsion to take her to Scotland."

"Callanish."

"Yes," Will said, finishing his drink before waving to the barkeep for another round. "I had no idea why, but I drove like a maniac. By the time the ferry docked in Stornoway, I was already envisioning the stones shining white against an indigo sky. It was as if I had been there yesterday, not all those years ago as a school boy." He paused before shaking his head. "And that, unfortunately, is all I remember. At least until that night at the inn."

Looking incredulous, McKenna stared. "Then how do you know what happened?"

"Because Cia was aware and awake. And terrified. As she described it, we drove straight to the stone circle where I began mumbling in a strange language she didn't understand."

McKenna nodded. "Go on."

"That evening at dusk, she said I acted as though I was possessed; that I practically dragged her back to Callanish where
I apparently prevailed upon her to have sex in the middle of the
stones." He stopped to take a breath. "Not only do I not remember,
I cringe when I think of it."

"Later, when I woke up from whatever fugue state I was in, I
was standing in front of the center monolith with no memory of the
entire day. By then, Cia was justifiably panicked and didn't want
to go back to the inn, but a heavy fog had rolled in and we had no
choice. That's when we became aware of peculiar things going on."

"What sort of things?"

Will described the heavy fog that rapidly became an opaque, white
mist, essentially trapping them, and also the rosebushes that scratched
at Cia's legs. "That was just the beginning. Once inside, the atmosphere
felt thin. Only when I stared at something did it come into focus. I rationalized that I was tired, or perhaps it was the combination of candle-
light and shadows. The inn had no electricity, but that wasn't it . . . It
was that the entire place felt used up, like it existed in another time.
When we spoke, I could hear echoes of our voices. And yet, there we
were, eating and talking, actually living in a room warmed by a fire. It
was eerie, as though reality had somehow shifted."

"I assume you were alone? No other guests?"

"Cia tried several doors in a hallway. They were all locked."

McKenna closed his eyes as if trying to clarify a thought. "Was
there any sense of recognition from the woman?"

"She spoke as if she knew me; that I should have known it wasn't
safe to return so late. There was more, but I just assumed she was
being strange."

"You never considered that it could be an illusion?"

"Illusion?" He shrugged. "We were eating soup, drinking tea.
We stayed overnight in a room with furniture and a fire in the fireplace. These are all tangible things. That is, until the fire started to
go out. That's when everything went to hell."

McKenna put his hand up. "And yet, perhaps it was something
more than what you were seeing. It could have been an illusion
generated between the two of you. In theory, the place might have
existed as a nice little modern inn, and yet you perceived that day
and night as though it were a hundred years ago."

Will shook his head. "With all due respect, Professor, that's not possible. When I tell you the rest, you'll understand. The woman had already warned us not to let the fire die out. What she didn't tell us was what would happen if it did. We were trying to sleep when the flames burned too low. That's when the room began to vibrate and the floor started to buckle."

With a look of disbelief, McKenna started to interrupt, but Will put his hand up to stop him. "After I tossed some peat into the fireplace, it stopped." He closed his eyes as if reliving the moment. "But not for long. That's when I went to the door."

"Let me guess. It was locked."

"Not the first time. We should have got out then, but that fog — or whatever it was — made it impossible to leave. It was quiet for a few minutes before the shaking began again, this time with a heavy thrumming sound. When the floorboards began to crack, I grabbed Cia and ran for the door. By then, some sort of disgusting slime had coated the knob, and I knew we were trapped. How or why the fire kept us safe, I have no idea. If we had run out of peat, I doubt I'd be sitting here today."

"Was that the end of it?"

"After a few minutes of quiet, I tried to convince Cia to try and sleep. The next thing I knew, she was screaming and something was tugging at my hand. It wasn't her. Something, I have no idea what, was in the room with us. We could smell its vile odor and hear the deep sound of it boring through the floor, but all we could see was some sort of weird vapor. That's when I felt bony, slimy claws trying to tear my ring off." With a shiver, he stopped to drain his glass.

McKenna also took a long pull of his drink before staring out the window. Shaking his head, he whispered, "I've read of demonic manifestations in ancient texts, but considered them simply part of the magic at the core of primitive tribal beliefs. Shamans, for example, instilling fear of the gods in order to control their clan." He grimaced. "Then again, maybe not so primitive. Magic and fear are still prevalent in most contemporary religions. You must have been terrified."

Will held out his scarred hand. "Still think it was an illusion?"

"That's from the vapor?"

"Or whatever it really was."

He shook his head. "It's likely your so-called inn masked a hidden grave in an ancient, possibly Neolithic burial site. If not a vortex, it had to be a channel that went deep into the earth. Something in the spirit realm reached out from that channel to find you. Call it an earthbound spirit, demon, or whatever, there's no doubt it was after your sapphire."

"Are you saying that some man who died thousands of years ago lured us to that place so he could take the stone in my ring?"

"No longer a man, I'm afraid. Something far more powerful. And although you felt drawn to Callanish, it was the demon in that cairn that enticed you. There must be a connection between it and the stone circle."

Will stared at him before shaking his head. "A connection?"

"You lived it, Will. How else would you explain it?"

"I can't," he sighed. "I'm not sure I'd even believe it, any of it, except for these scars."

"This inn. Was it close to Callanish?"

"Within a couple of kilometers." He paused for a few seconds. "Now that I think of it, I told you that someone in Cia's office described a house built on an ancient burial mound. She said it had burned down. It couldn't have been the inn." He looked at McKenna. "Or could it?"

"It's entirely possible. Paranormal activity is associated with temperature change, particularly cold. I would bet it's happened before; this can't be the first time. It's possible that someone in possession of the sapphires was lured to the inn and, in a panic, started the fire that destroyed it. And yet, the woman went out of her way to warn you about the fire. That's odd, since she had to be part of the illusion." He hesitated before looking at Will. "You said she recognized you, which implies you must have been there in a past life."

"She seemed to know me, but how?"

"Not by your face; more likely your aura."

Aura? What the hell? Once again, he wanted to get up and leave. And yet, there was nowhere to go; not if this so-called spirit could find him again. "How would whatever it is know we were there? Or should I ask: How did it manage, as you suggest, to lure us there in the first place?"

"It likely began the very second you met Cia. It was waiting, knowing the two of you had found one another before and, through time, would again." He paused to tap out his pipe in an ashtray. "Try to understand it's your soul, your energy, and your spirit that have, over the millennia, been reborn. And, it appears, quite a few times. Cia's as well. I believe that through the centuries you searched for one another and connected, probably thanks to those sapphires. If, in past lives you sought answers as you have now, you likely became vulnerable, easier for the entity to reach."

He put up his hands. "No, Professor. This is too impossible to believe."

"Listen to me, Will. While it may sound inconceivable, you seem to have lived almost twenty-four hours from a previous life. Something we are not allowed."

"Allowed? By whom?"

"The basic doctrines of natural law and physical reality. By consciously living through that day, you have, in effect, transcended time, possibly even death. That you survived may indicate that you, and Cia as well, may have gained some sort of power."

Will shook his head. "This is too much."

This time it was McKenna who got up to buy another round. "I think we both need another drink, maybe more. I've never heard anything like this."

After touching glasses, Will took a moment to light another cigarette while McKenna revived his pipe.

"Let's put the inn aside," Will said. "What's also important is that in the middle of all this, Cia suddenly brought up the rings. I hadn't told her about them and, until there was a good reason, I never would have. I realized it had to be my good friend Patrick who, against my wishes, confided in her."

"And you are now questioning if you should give her the ring?"

He nodded. "When we returned to the flat, I felt a strong urge to have her try it on. I even went so far as to show it to her. It was as if it was tempting her to touch it."

"All the signs point to it, Will. As long as you love her."

"I do," he said in a soft voice. "I feel she's become part of me."

"Certainly part of your past. Since you never felt this compulsion with any of your other relationships, it would confirm the ring belongs to her."

"Could something like this demon, as you call it, happen again?"

McKenna sat back and sipped his drink. When he finally spoke, his voice was firm. "I wish I knew. Since you thwarted it once, it may be too weakened to try again. At least in this life."

Will looked skeptical. "In this life? What are you saying?"

"Right now, I'm thinking out loud. Follow me, and let's see where this leads." When Will nodded, he went on, "I would postulate that you have encountered this spirit before, perhaps several times, which means it's influenced your life, your very existence throughout who knows how many centuries. It also implies that it knows you; that it has the ability to intuit your current patterns by how you acted in the past."

Will closed his eyes. "That is a truly terrifying thought."

"What's more terrifying is that it's not only this life, or even your past lives. It's your future as well."

Suddenly looking pale, he whispered, "Are you saying this could continue?"

McKenna put down his pipe, the tobacco gone cold. "Why wouldn't it? As long as the demon exists, this will go on, just as it has, for centuries. Think about it."

"I'd rather not."

"And yet, what if you could do something about it?"

"You mean change the future?"

"Essentially, yes. Except the only way to change the future is by impacting the now, the present. If this thing has stalked you and Cia through thousands of years, maybe the time has come to stop it."

"Are you kidding? How the hell . . ."

"Kill it."

Will put his hands up. "That's crazy. How do you kill a spirit? It's formless. At best a slimy vapor. What would you suggest? Exorcize it?"

McKenna shook his head. "You can't exorcize it. It's not Christian. It's pagan. Far more ancient."

"It's nothing more than air."

"Not quite. It creates its own form. You should know; you've experienced its power, felt its touch, heard its voice."

"How does one kill such a thing?"

"'Kill' may be the wrong word. Send it to another realm; somewhere beyond where it can no longer wield its power."

Will could only stare. "That is truly insane."

McKenna actually cracked a smile. "And yet, why not try?"

"How would one even begin?" He shook his head. "It'll probably end up killing us before we can send it to some other hell."

This time it was McKenna who put up a hand. "Let me do some research. There are several ancient texts I haven't looked at yet. One reason is that they deal with such subjects as possession, demons, and death, which wasn't something I was interested in at the time. I have no idea of what I'll discover; it could turn out to be just occult fairytales. If I can find a way, what would you think?"

"If you do find anything, then we can discuss it. I understand what you're saying, but to me it seems far too removed from reality to make any sense. After what happened in Callanish, or should I say, the inn, wouldn't this demon sense that we were coming for it?"

"That's what I want to find out. Speaking of Callanish, and, although I'm loath to mention it, there may be more for you there."

Will shook his head. "Why? Or, more importantly, what?"

"I'm afraid with your logical mind, and despite what you experienced, you may need to take a leap of faith. I believe something significant must have happened there. To Cia as well."

"How can that be?"

"Think about it, Will. What other answer is there? The sapphires must be connected to the stone circle as well as the inn. And all of it is connected to something primal, beyond our knowledge and understanding. It may be that the sapphires were found about the same time the stones at Callanish were being erected."

"Are you saying I was there a thousand years ago?"

"More like five thousand. Callanish is said to date from 3000 BCE. On your school trip, you said you had the impression the stones were larger, and some were lying on the ground. That means the circle was not yet complete. By the way, did you know that, over the centuries, those huge monoliths were submerged in peat? It was only in the mid-1800s that they were discovered and unearthed. That's likely when the inn was constructed. Whoever built it probably didn't know, until it was too late, what lay beneath."

When Will, looking suddenly pale, shook his head, McKenna went on, "I would imagine some spiritual power, a special karma, has guided you through time and kept you safe from the demon. Up until now, anyway. The inn aside, I believe you were drawn to the stones to receive some sort of knowledge."

Will stood up abruptly. "Karma? The idea of past lives isn't enough? I need another drink. This is giving me a headache."

"Bring another for me, as well. Then ask yourself why you are here? It was you who came to me searching for answers."

"That's true."

"You mentioned that Cia was with you again in January. I assume nothing more occurred?"

"All was quiet until I took her to a party where some lord felt entitled to, ah, stroke her thigh at dinner. The next day I was told that after we left, a small fire broke out. The asshole who caused it was the same who made the mistake of touching her during dinner. It was quickly extinguished. But I wondered."

"What did I tell you about power?"

"Is it possible?"

"We've already agreed you may have thwarted death. After that, I would imagine just about anything is possible."

Will raised his glass. "That is actually a frightening thought."

McKenna laughed. "I would suggest you try not to make her angry. Now I have a question. How did your friend find me? You said you had forgotten my name."

Will nodded. "As soon as Cia returned to New York, I confronted Patrick. As I suspected, it was he who told her about the rings. After apologizing, he wanted to know how the discussion had come up. When I told him about what happened in Scotland, despite finding it hard to believe, he agreed to help me locate someone who might have an explanation. While we were talking, I also mentioned that old memories of Egypt and Greece had suddenly begun to surface. That's when I remembered meeting you, but couldn't recall your name. Not until I had a dream. I was walking in a field and saw a fox standing near a stone with Gaelic hieroglyphs. You have to understand that I know nothing about such things.

"Fascinating. And yet, one wonders how you made the connection that sionnach is Gaelic for fox. I'm sure you are now aware that dream was a message, though one you had to parse." Relighting his pipe, he said, "I didn't think you came here to discuss your youthful experiences of déjà vu, but I never expected to hear such a story."

Less tense now, Will sipped his drink. "Let's get back to messages. Perhaps there really is more, and I should go to Callanish again. Alone this time."

"Tell me why you think so."

"Because you could be right. Look at what happened at the stone circle. If that wasn't connected to the entity, what was it and why did it happen?"

McKenna looked unsure. "Good question, but even if you were to go alone, you may be taking too much of a risk with fate. There are mysteries of life and death we are not meant to know."

He shook his head. "I still need to know more. That is, if there is anything more. I can't take the chance of this happening again. Not for me, not for Cia."

"That's your power talking, Will. Don't allow it to place you in harm's way. That spirit is still there, waiting. Let me have some time to look at the texts. Maybe we can find a way to deal with it."

"We?"

"I have the feeling this isn't a one-man job."

Chapter 4

Despite her rush to get home, Cia stopped to pick up a bunch of yellow tulips and a bottle of Sancerre, Will's favorite wine. When she had spoken with him the night before, he had sounded rushed, only telling her what time he would arrive and that he couldn't wait to see her. With a happy smile, she'd told him the same, not mentioning her renewed anxiety about his meeting with McKenna a few weeks before.

He had called as soon as he returned from Edinburgh. Although it was well after midnight in London, and obvious that he'd had a few drinks too many, he'd said he had things to tell her that, even after Callanish, would be difficult to believe. When she asked him to be more specific, he had merely answered that she'd just have to wait until he could hold her in his arms before revealing the Professor's secrets. His other news was that Steve had already mailed the invitations for the gallery opening. "In fact," he laughed, "they sent them out before they even called to confirm that I would be there."

"What about your paintings?"

"They were already crated and ready to go. They should arrive, hopefully, tomorrow. I miss you, Cia. It's been too long. I won't let that happen again."

She closed her eyes. "What does that mean?"

"I'll tell you when I get there."

Cia glanced out the window just in time to see Will alighting from a taxi. Unable to suppress a welling of emotion, she ran for the door and down the stoop, practically leaping into his arms.

"Whoa," he said with a laugh. "Before you knock me over, let me put down my suitcase."

After a prolonged kiss, she became aware of several neighbors passing by. "We probably shouldn't be making out on the street. Let's go inside."

"Then may I show you how much I missed you?"

"Love first, talk later?" she asked. When he nodded, she blushed. "How sweet of you to ask."

The door hadn't closed before he took her hand and led her to the bedroom. Looking back at his suitcase, she murmured, "I'm guessing you don't want to unpack?"

"As I said, we have other, more important things to catch up on."

It was well after nine when, starving, they agreed it was time to get out of bed. At a nearby bar Will ordered a hamburger with the reluctant admission that on his last trip he'd developed a taste for them, but was still unable find a decent one anywhere in London.

She giggled, licking his fingers as he fed her a French fry. The last months began to dissolve as they touched hands, kissed, and caught up on one another's lives.

"There are so many things I have you tell you, Cia. I loved reading the stories you sent and, although I looked for the Lanny Winters book in London, I was told they had sold out."

"So I heard. They're still back-ordered. Not to worry, I have a couple at home and also at the cottage. If you'd like, we can go there for the weekend."

"I was going to suggest that. We need some time to talk without anyone interrupting us. Anyway, I want you all to myself."

"And why would that be?"

With a leer, he whispered, "You'll just have to wait to find out what evil deeds I have in mind when there's no one around to hear you scream."

She gave him a coquettish smile. "I have to wait?"

"Actually, no." He signaled the waiter for the check.

The next morning, he called Steve to let him know he had arrived.

"Glad to hear your voice, Will. I just got word that your paintings cleared customs. I'm expecting them to be delivered to the gallery later this afternoon. You should plan to get here by three at the latest. Also, there's a dinner tonight with the public relations people and some of our investors. This opening is going to be a big deal, and we're excited to have you be part of it."

"I'm looking forward to it. Is it all right if Cia joins us?"

"Yes. Of course. I'm glad you two are still together." Will nodded, thinking the same thing.

The dinner was at Raoul's, a new and already trendy restaurant in Soho. After cheek kisses from Steve and Carl, they introduced her to two men from their public relations agency. Both looked up and nodded absently before returning to outline their plans for the opening. Will listened carefully to their explanation of whom had been invited and why, and which newspapers and magazines had promised to send reporters—or, preferably, art critics—the *New York Times* and *ARTnews* being primary. As well known as he was in England, this was his first show in New York, and if the PR guys were to be believed, it promised to be a major art-world event.

The night of the opening, Cia arrived at the gallery around five. Although there was at least an hour before the doors were to open, she was surprised to find quite a few people already milling around outside. The public relations agency had apparently done their job, and Will had been told they were expecting over three hundred people to attend—by invitation only. As she pushed open the heavy glass door she noticed several attractive young women in little black dresses huddled together over clipboards, no doubt lists of invited guests. Across the vast open space, a similarly attired redhead tossed her hair while chatting—or, more realistically, flirting—with Will. Noticing Cia come in, she patted his arm and, with a sniff of deep disdain, swanned over to confront her. "I'm sorry, miss. The gallery isn't open yet. Please wait outside."

Cia glanced briefly at Will, who had already started walking towards her with a wicked grin on his face. Leaning close to the girl as if to confide in her, she whispered, "He's my invitation."

As Will put his arm around her waist, the girl backed away, her face scarlet, her attitude evaporating. "Oh, sorry. I didn't know . . ."

Cia glared back at her. It wasn't the moment for subtlety. "Now you do."

Will steered her away. "I've never seen you like that before, Cia. You're a tiger."

Fluttering her eyelashes, she said, "I like to protect what belongs to me. At least what I hope belongs to me."

"I believe you already know the answer to that. Right now, I want to show you what I've been working on these last months." Taking her hand in his, he began to circle the gallery. Most of his new work were the sensuous nudes he was known for. Each one had been placed with practiced care, juxtaposed for maximum impact; in one case, two young women staring out with a look of ennui next to another canvas of a woman looking back with a distinct attitude of superiority. He had also included several lyrical landscapes.

Surprised, Cia commented that she had never seen anything even resembling a landscape in his studio. "I don't paint them very often, but I wanted to see how they would go over in New York."

"I like them. You should do more. I see you brought the portrait of the girl in the Victorian dress."

"Steve said someone has already asked to buy it. I reminded him that it's only on loan. All the portraits are."

"I assume you're showing them in order to receive commissions here?"

He nodded. "That's the point."

At the bar, he handed her a glass of champagne before taking one for himself. As they touched glasses, a photographer stopped to snap a couple of quick shots. When he finished, he looked at Will. "Later I'd like a few of you in front of one or two of your larger paintings. Not sure the paper will print a photo with tits, though. Maybe a portrait."

Will suppressed a smile. "No tits, then. Not a problem."

Cia noticed a couple of men come in and walk directly to Steve. Giving them an effusive welcome, he motioned to Will to come over. Cia kissed his cheek. "Go ahead. It's your night. Don't worry about me," she said lightly. "I'll be here doing my best not to be jealous of all the ladies who will be chatting you up and inviting you to their dinner parties."

"No worries, Cia. You are my only love." As he walked away, she closed her eyes, savoring the moment and feeling a shiver of exhilaration that warmed her heart.

Fortunately, it was a pleasant spring evening, and a fashionably dressed, if somewhat impatient crowd had already formed a ragged queue between the red velvet ropes. At six o'clock sharp, the young women in little black dresses moved as though choreographed to the entrance where they began to tick off names on their clipboards, allowing only invited guests in while turning away those whose names were not on their lists. Cia noticed that those rejected, mostly young people, were likely artists from the neighborhood. Will had insisted that once the invited guests, which included many potential buyers, departed and the crowd thinned, they be allowed in. Seeing Will's name stenciled on the tall glass windows, she felt a sense of pride. Closing her eyes, she prayed for the evening to be a success.

Looking back, she saw Will in discussion with a tall man in a black suit. Black suits were unusual; most men considered them attire for funeral directors. But this man, most likely an art critic, carried it off with elegance. Watching his face, she was pleased to see him nod and smile. After they shook hands, he put on glasses and started around the gallery, making notes on a small pad. Within seconds, Will was surrounded by three grey-haired men and their much younger wives.

On her way to the bar for another glass of champagne, she saw several small, simply-framed sketches she hadn't noticed before; they had been blocked by the bartenders setting up. Moving closer, she recognized two portraits Will had done of her in London.

"So, lady. You going to buy those?"

She turned around with a laugh. "I don't know, Sarah. I'll have to ask the artist. If I play my cards right, maybe he'll give them to me." As they hugged, she whispered, "I'm so glad you're here. I don't know anyone."

"Coralie came as well. She's standing near the door keeping an eye on Will."

"What does she think he's going to do? Levitate?"

Sarah smirked. "I have no idea, but she still insists she has to read your cards. And soon."

Cia glanced at Coralie. Sarah was right, her eyes were following Will's every move.

"You look happy, Cia. Will seems to have that effect on you."

"When I'm with him, the world becomes a wonderful place." She swept her hand, indicating the rapidly filling room. "And this is amazing. I'm so happy for him."

"You should be. He's attracted some important names here tonight."

Later, as the gallery began to thin out, Coralie came over, admitting that she liked Will's paintings, but it was time to go home to feed her cats and, by the way, her husband as well. "Please, Cia, come talk to me. It's important that I read your cards."

Cia thanked her, promising she would. With a nervous glance at Will, who must have sensed her presence and nodded to her, Coralie caught her breath and scurried out.

"Perhaps she's just attracted to him," Sarah quipped.

"You never know. I'm sure you noticed that she placed her cats before her husband."

"Maybe that's what happens after eight years of marriage."

With a laugh, Cia shook her head. "I like cats, but I doubt they go well with oil paint. Whatever. I guess I should let her do her psychic thing one of these days. Maybe after Will leaves."

As the last of the guests departed, Will came over and kissed Sarah on the cheek. "Thanks for coming."

She glanced around. "How could I ever miss this? Looks like it went really well."

"I believe it did. We'll leave soon. Steve says we're going to a place called Fanelli's. It's an old bar that was a speakeasy during prohibition. I hope you'll join us."

"Sounds perfect. Thank you."

"Walk around with me," Cia said, taking Will's arm. "I want to see the red dots."

Circling the gallery, she counted eight dots. He'd not only sold five nudes and three landscapes, he'd also been asked by a couple of well-dressed men to discuss portraits of their wives.

"That sounds like good news. Does that mean you'll stay longer?"

"I'm not sure I can. Davies, from my London gallery, rang here earlier today. It appears they require my presence by late next week."

With optimism turning to disappointment, she stopped. "Please, Will. You just got here. Can't he wait a few more days? We never seem to have enough time together."

Putting his arm around her, he said, "I promise we will. Meanwhile, you and I have a lot to talk about."

"We'll go to the cottage tomorrow."

"It may have to be late. I've been invited to a soiree tomorrow night."

She felt a stab of frustration. "A soiree? How chic."

"In a penthouse on Fifth Avenue. They bought one of the big nudes and insisted I see their collection and meet their friends. I couldn't very well have declined. I told them we would stop by for a drink."

"We?" she looked surprised.

"Of course, Cia. Why are you even asking?"

Despite being relieved, she was also disappointed; not mentioning that she'd arranged to take the afternoon off so they could leave early. It turned out to be moot anyway; he had also been asked to lunch by one of his new American "patrons," and had made an appointment later in the afternoon with another.

It was close to three in the morning when they left Fanelli's and stumbled back to her apartment. Despite the euphoria that accompanied a successful exhibition, not to mention the many, many drinks after, they fell into bed in one another's arms and were asleep in seconds.

Cia woke up first. Seeing it was almost eight thirty, she ignored the expected hangover and got quietly out of bed. She was just pulling on shorts and a T-shirt when Will rolled over.

"Where are you going?" his voice was hoarse.

"I'll be right back. Go back to sleep. You deserve it."

"No. Come back. I want you."

"You can have me in a few minutes. I'm running down to the newsstand."

"Aha. Make sure you bring only the papers with good notices."

She returned to find Will in the kitchen drinking orange juice.

Throwing the newspapers on the dining table, she kissed him and put on water for coffee and tea.

He sat down and opened the *Times* gingerly, leafing through it until he found the Arts section. Not hearing anything, she looked at him. "Well?"

"Let's see. He respects the fact that I don't follow trends. Also, that I have a somewhat retro style in an era of rapid and too-often vapid change. He's complimentary of the nudes and particularly admired the portraits. He called me a fresh face, particularly in a downtown gallery." He looked up. "Not bad. I suppose."

"Are you kidding? Kramer? That was great. You're a star." Positive she had seen Dorothy Schiff in the crowd last night, she began flipping pages in the *Post*. "Look, Will, there's a picture of you with a couple of those society ladies. 'Brit Brings Style to Soho'." She read through the blurb before passing the paper to him. "They mostly talk about who-was-who. That's typical. But they also really liked your paintings."

He shrugged and stood up. "Time for a shower?"

"You don't care about the reviews?"

"Of course I do. Good notices are important."

"Go ahead. We'll get the *Voice* in a few days and the *Daily News* later."

He grabbed her hand. "Forget the newspapers. Come with me."

She looked up at him. "You've seen my shower. We'll drown."

"It is a distinct possibility. But not before I make love to you."

Chapter 5

Sarah had been gossiping all morning; less about Will's paintings and more about the crowd, a mix of wealthy art patrons, upscale New York society, a few celebrities—mostly of the Broadway theater variety—and many fashionistas with their hangers-on. The editor of "Vogue," along with Norman Parkinson, her favorite photographer, had been seen chatting with a recently hired young British assistant at arch-rival *Harper's Bazaar*. When Marge, who was not only the romance editor, but prided herself on being the most fashion-savvy woman at BookEnds, stopped by to ask who she was, Sarah sniffed. "Oh yes. I was standing right next to her. I'm not sure, but it sounded like she was a Brit. Think her name was something like Winter." She glanced at Marge with a frown. "You weren't there. How do you know who was talking to whom?"

Marge winked. "Gossip, my dear. And a few close friends at *Vogue*."

With barely a pause, Sarah went on to describe several middle-aged society women who had practically come to blows while endeavoring to get close enough to meet the artist whom they had been told was "personable, charming" and, if the chat from London was correct, "talented in more ways than one." Many of those same ladies had dragged their reluctant husbands along—as it was they who controlled the checkbooks—while other spouses, arriving directly from Wall Street, alighted from their personal limos. Within an hour an impressive column of shiny, black, chauffeur-driven Cadillacs and Lincolns had lined up along the cracked and crumbling curbs of Greene Street.

Cia arrived at the office a little after ten, bringing along the newspapers. Her first stop was Sid's office.

"Late night, I assume?" he asked.

"Yes. Very," she said, handing him the *Times* already opened to Will's review. Glancing at it, he nodded. "I'm happy for him, Cia. I like his work, especially the small portraits of you. You seem to be very, um, compatible. My only worry is that he lives in London."

She felt her face redden. "Don't worry, Sid. We have no plans." *Not yet, anyway.*

Ignoring the pile of pink phone message slips on her desk, she put them aside for later. There were more important things on her mind, such as asking Sarah what to wear to such a thing as a soiree.

Sarah made a face. "How would I know? Ask Marge. She's always going to those society things."

Marge was on the phone but indicated the chair in front of her desk. Cia sat down, glad to be off her feet after the night before.

Finally hanging up, Marge ran a hand through her unruly red curls and lit a cigarette. "Heard your friend had a successful show. Sorry I couldn't make it. School night, you know."

Cia didn't know. Instead, she smiled and asked her for advice.

Exhaling volumes of smoke, Marge rasped, "Since you say it's at six, it's definitely a cocktail party. Do you have anything like a dressy jumpsuit or palazzo pants?"

Cia rolled her eyes. "No. I don't do much entertaining at home."

Taking another drag of her cigarette, she shrugged. "These days you can wear them out at night. They're a hot look at clubs."

Of course they are, she thought sardonically. "How about a sleeveless coral sheath?"

"Maybe. Simple may be best. You don't want to be wearing bell bottom hip-huggers or anything like that."

Cia thanked her. *I could have figured that out on my own.* Will, however, being an artist, could wear anything he wanted, probably even bell bottom hip-huggers. His look, fortunately, veered more to dark sport jackets, often corduroy, over colorful shirts and knit ties. She had never seen him in a suit.

Will had told her he'd meet her at the apartment at five thirty. When he arrived, she was clad only in lace panties and a bra while sorting through her closet. "I still have no idea what to wear. Which one of these dresses do you like?"

When he didn't answer, she turned to look at him. "What is it?"

He nuzzled her neck. "Do you think I can just stand here with you looking like that?" His voice was deep, seductive.

When he put his arms around her, she whispered, "We're going to be late." Feeling him silently unhook her bra, she stepped back and took a breath. "I guess I should get those dresses off the bed."

"Do it quickly," he said, throwing off his jacket. "We don't want to be *too* late."

A short time later, she retrieved the dresses and held them up. "Which do you prefer?"

"Honestly? You look good in anything. How about that one?" he said, pointing to the coral number.

"Good. I was thinking of that one, anyway." Turning back to the closet, she bent over to search for heels that matched.

Watching her, he groaned. "Please, Cia. Put some clothes on. You're driving me crazy."

She looked back at him with a grin. "Good for me."

A liveried doorman showed them to an elevator where another similarly attired attendant took them up to the penthouse. The door opened to a long gallery hung with several Impressionist paintings. Cia stopped abruptly. "That's a Cézanne," she whispered, "and a Corot." Before Will could utter a word, their effusive hostess, wearing green silk palazzo-pants with a matching chiffon top, glided up to Will and took his arm, leaving a flustered Cia to follow.

The first thing she noticed, other than the magnificent view of Central Park, was Will's painting prominently displayed on a gold easel. Although it was customary for paintings to remain in the gallery until a show ended, the woman had obviously leaned on Steve to have it brought uptown. As she introduced Will to her guests, Cia trailed along, murmuring her name and shaking hands.

While Dom Pérignon and hors d'oeuvres were being passed by butlers, the women gathered around Will and his painting of two nudes. One by one, they turned to appraise Cia, as though speculating that she might be one of the models. Taking a glass of champagne, she escaped to the lavishly planted terrace.

Inside she heard the lilt of laughter, more from the women than the men, who had removed themselves to a corner, no doubt lamenting the recent stock market crash.

Hearing one of the women squeal, "Oh. Look at his ring," Cia moved to the terrace door just as their hostess took Will's hand.

"Where on earth did you get this?" she asked, peering at it.

"It was given to me many years ago."

"It's gorgeous. So different." The last spoken by a tall, red-haired woman in a Pucci jumpsuit. Moving closer, she reached out to touch it. Suddenly the stone lit up with a bright blue spark. With exclamations of surprise and nervous laughter, the women jumped back.

"What was that? Magic?" the Pucci jumpsuit asked, keeping her distance.

"Not at all. The stone is a sapphire. Sometimes it, ah, catches the light and reflects it." By now the women were practically jumping up and down. "What kind of design is that? Where can I buy one?" two women asked at the same time.

"The design is Celtic, very ancient," he said, sounding a bit distracted. "I'm afraid I don't know where one would find another like it."

The hostess looked disappointed. "You mean there are no more? Anywhere?"

"Not that I know of," he said. "I do have a smaller one." Looking directly at Cia, he added, "But that is meant for one special person."

The women turned as if noticing her for the first time. "Ohmygod. Is that a proposal?" one of them shouted.

Cia stared wide-eyed, her hand going to her open mouth.

With an almost imperceptible nod, Will murmured, "Why, yes. I think it could be perceived as such." Extending his hand to a scarlet-faced Cia, he led her back inside. As everyone gawked in stunned silence, he turned to their hostess. "This evening was lovely. Unfortunately, we have to leave."

"Not before we toast you both," she responded graciously. She motioned to a butler to bring more champagne.

Will stood aside as the women, downing a few more glasses of champagne, congratulated a shocked Cia, who barely murmured back to them while glancing at him as though to make sure he, as well as the moment, were real. After thanking their hostess, who said she and her husband would be in London later in the summer and hoped to see more of his work, Will handed her a card with his address and phone number.

As they were leaving, Cia overheard one of the women whisper, "Lucky girl. I'd take just one night with him." The giggles continued until the elevator doors closed.

Outside, she stopped, still stunned and unsure what to say or how to react.

Without a word, Will took her hand, leading her across Fifth Avenue and into the park. Finding a tree in full flower, he got down on one knee. "Cia. That wasn't planned. In fact, I wasn't even thinking. Nevertheless, will you marry me?"

"Will," she said, with a bemused laugh. "Get up. Of course I'll marry you. But why now, and in the middle of all those people?"

He stood up and brushed off his pants. Taking her in his arms, he shook his head. "When I saw the ring spark, it was as though everything suddenly came together. I knew then that it was right, just as I had been told."

Wiping away tears of happiness, she whispered, "Other than thinking I was going to faint, it was definitely the most special moment of my life. You have to admit that had to be one of the crazier proposals." She glanced around. "In Central Park, no less."

"It doesn't matter where. Just know I love you and always have."

Her eyes widened. "Always?"

"Come, Cia," he said, taking her hand. "Let's go. We'll talk more about it tomorrow." Giving her another quick kiss, he murmured, "I'm just pleased you didn't get pissed off at anyone."

It was late by the time they arrived at the cottage. As they drove through the small town, Will glanced out the window. "That's your friend's store, isn't it?"

"Yes. We'll stop by tomorrow." She considered mentioning the journal with the sketched portrait but decided midnight might not be quite the best time for such a revelation.

When they got out of the car, Cia reached for a flashlight. With no moon and no outdoor lights, they were encased in inky darkness. Will stretched his back while breathing in fresh air. "Look," he said, putting out his hand. Where there had been only the deepest night, the air around them suddenly lit up with thousands of fireflies.

Astonished and a little frightened, she moved towards him where a few, blinking frantically, were circling his hand. "What's going on? I didn't see any fireflies when we drove in."

"Neither did I. It's amazing."

"There are so many. Where did they come from?"

"Maybe they were waiting for us."

Or maybe fate has sent us light instead of darkness. Taking the flashlight, she began walking to the front door. Suddenly, hundreds of fireflies surrounded her and, blinking in unison, guided her to the front porch. Hoping the bugs were indeed friendly and not some sort of evil portent, she glanced back at Will, still standing as though enthralled. Finally taking their bags from the car, he followed her inside, the insects glittering as he walked. A few seconds later, when she looked out, the blinking lights were gone.

While turning on a couple of lamps, she glanced at Will. "Have you ever seen anything like that before? I mean those fireflies?"

"No, Cia. It's probably just another one of our mysteries. A pleasant one, at least." He put an arm around her. "This has been an incredible week, hasn't it? The exhibition, the reviews, the commissions, that silly soiree . . ."

She hugged him. "And those bugs?"

He kissed her gently. "I was going to say my proposal."

"Oh, yes," she whispered. "Particularly that."

The next morning, she awoke first, listening closely for the voices. Aside from the chittering of birds and the usual buzzing insects, the house was silent. Sliding on Will's shirt, she went to the kitchen to make coffee and put on water for tea. A few minutes later, Will padded in, put his arms around her waist, and gave her a kiss. "Let's have breakfast. Then I'll tell you about my conversation with McKenna."

She nodded, beginning to feel a knot of apprehension in her stomach.

While she finished up the breakfast dishes, he went to get dressed. Still wearing his shirt, she put on a pair of shorts, and, handing him another cup of tea, followed him out to the porch.

The day was warm with only a few puffy white clouds marring an otherwise perfect blue sky. She sat down on the steps next to Will who, appearing to be deep in thought, sipped his tea. "I'm not quite sure where to start, Cia. I've already explained about my incidents of déjà vu."

"That you knew things when there was no way you should have?"

"Essentially, yes. McKenna explained that he's met with quite a number of people who have had similar experiences. Do you understand what I'm saying?"

She nodded, recalling the journal in Sonny's store. "I think what you're saying is you have lived a past life."

He looked surprised. "How did you come to that?"

"You first."

He took his time lighting a cigarette, as though considering what to say. "All right. Except that it's not only me. It's also you. Both of us, according to McKenna, have had several lives, maybe more. Some, but not all, together. He feels those moments of déjà vu were actually deeply held, long-suppressed memories; memories at the core of our genetic makeup that are never meant to surface."

With a sardonic laugh, she said, "Does that mean there have been other women in your past lives of whom I should be jealous?" *Actually, I think I already met one.*

"Please, Cia. Be serious."

She shook her head and stepped off the porch. With a sigh, Will followed her to the pond where she stopped to watch a pair of ducks paddle in circles. "If I, as you say, have lived before, why is it you have those memories and I don't?"

"Do you recall what you said about that first night at the gallery? That you had the feeling we'd met before?"

"That's nothing new. People say it all the time. Whether they mean it or not."

"In our case, it was a connection. We were fated to meet."

"And what if I hadn't come to your exhibit that night?"

"We would have met some other place. It wasn't random."

She put up her hands. "Will. This is too much. Too hard to believe." *Or is it?* Turning away, she watched the ducks flutter their wings and fly off.

"I know you're having a difficult time with this. It's not easy for me, either." He paused before continuing in a soft voice, "Last night when you asked me why I proposed to you in front of all those people, there was something I wanted to tell you, but couldn't."

"What?"

"It wasn't just the ring flashing, Cia. Nor was it you standing in the doorway with the sun setting behind you. It was both you and me and our entire past that I saw, if only for a split second." He took a breath. "It was all the things we were and have now come to be."

She shook her head. "How is that possible?"

"That's a question I keep asking myself. McKenna feels we were drawn to Callanish to receive a message. But so far, other than the entity, we don't know what it could be. Something profound happened within that stone circle, but I still have no idea what it meant or why."

"A message? From who? No one was there." Suppressing a tremor, she whispered, "At least no one we could see."

"I'm just trying to explain what he and others have told me. Those rings were meant to come to me . . . and you. And they are somehow related to that stone circle as well as the inn."

"So it wasn't only you, but me as well, that created all the craziness in Scotland?"

"Apparently."

She sighed. "All those women in your life, and I'm the one that made you go to Callanish."

"This isn't a joke, Cia."

"Have we really had those rings before? I mean . . ." she paused and shook her head, "in other lives?"

"Not necessarily the rings. The sapphires."

She felt a chill come over her, as though a cloud had obscured the warmth of the sun. When she looked up, the sky was clear. "What happens when we die?"

He stopped to think for a moment. "MacDonald told me they are never found, but he didn't say why. Perhaps in this, as well as our previous lives, we were fated to be in possession of them in order to find one another. "

"So each time we have to meet and start over?"

"I really don't know, Cia. But, my love, that's not for us to worry about. Not now, and hopefully not for a very long time."

With his arm encircling her waist, she put her head on his shoulder. "And the voices?"

"McKenna thinks they're a manifestation of the spirits in the rings. They may also be guides who watch over our, well, my life. Possibly yours, as well."

"So we are being ruled by these supposed spirits?"

"I don't think 'ruled' is the right word. They may be an intrinsic part of us. Perhaps, as MacDonald said, they really are the voices of our ancestors, or the universe trying to communicate with us. This could be true for many people. It's just that we are more aware of them."

She kissed his cheek. "You may be more aware, but I'm never getting naked again."

He laughed. "Then I'll have a chat with them. Tell them to look away. Come on. It's getting hot and buggy out here. Let's go inside."

"I think it's time to visit Sonny."

"Do we need anything?"

"Not really. There's something I think you should see."

Sonny's store was as busy as Cia had ever seen it. Although it was too early for local tomatoes and corn, customers were anxiously grabbing the first lettuces and herbs from her garden. Even the shelves, normally filled with baked goods, were close to being empty. Charlie, looking harassed, acknowledged her with only a brief nod. After working her way through the line, she asked where Sonny was.

"Mom went to Tanglewood. One of the hotels wanted to talk with her about making pies for their restaurant. She'll be back tonight."

Disappointed, Cia said they'd stop by tomorrow. She turned to leave, seeing Will balancing a baguette while trying to drop a couple of scones into a brown paper bag. With a grin, he held them up. "Breakfast tomorrow."

When they returned to the cottage, Cia noticed two ravens perched on a low branch near the pond. "Why are they suddenly here?"

"McKenna says they're messengers. Of what, I have no idea."

"Why would they show up now? I haven't seen them since returning from London. I hope nothing strange is about to happen."

"Lunch is about to happen. Ignore them."

Will had brought a bottle of chilled Riesling to go with a lunch of Black Forest ham, Brie, the baguette, grapes, and a couple of apples. Biting into one, he said, "I suggest we leave past lives where they belong: in the past." When she nodded, he poured two glasses of wine. Touching his glass to hers, he smiled. "Now tell me, my love, when would you like to get married?"

261

Startled, she looked at him. "I don't know. This has all happened so fast, I've had no time to think about it. Next spring?"

Putting his hands to her face, he kissed her. "That's too far away. I know there's a lot to do, particularly for you, but all I want is to wake up every morning with you next to me."

Unable to hold back tears of joy, she hugged him. "I never imagined I could be this happy."

"Would you want to get married here? Or London?"

"Which would you prefer?"

"Perhaps London. Either way, we should keep it small. Only family and close friends. If you want Sarah to come, I'll be happy to buy her a ticket."

"You would do that for her?"

"For you, Cia, I would. She's your best friend."

"How did I ever get lucky enough to meet you?"

He kissed her nose. "I'm not so sure you felt that way last fall. However, as we now know, it had more to do with fate than luck." Holding her close, he kissed her lips. "Think about what you'd like to do. All I desire is having you with me. For all time."

"Maybe we should go inside," she whispered.

Unbuttoning her shirt, he shook his head. "I want you right here." He looked up. "The birds have gone."

"And the spirits?" She giggled. "Won't they be watching?"

"Maybe they'll learn something."

The day had been perfect. That is, until Cia realized the next day was Sunday and Will would be leaving in another two days.

Later, after grilling steaks, Will said he wanted to go for a walk. The sun was just setting in a display of glorious pink, as, hand in hand, they walked down the driveway. On the street, Cia noticed the outdoor light from Maureen and Bob's house go on, obviously on a timer set for dusk.

"Do you know the people who live there?"

"I've met them a couple of times. Once at Sonny's New Year's Eve party. They're nice. She's a well-known photographer, and he's in the music business."

"Classical?"

She laughed. "More like rock and roll."

Without warning, the fireflies returned, flickering through the trees and circling around them. It wasn't as if one or two appeared first; they all descended at once as if in a happy swarm. While they lent a certain magic to the night, Cia had to wave them away as they made their way back to the cottage. Suddenly Will stopped and reached out his hand. Before she could ask what he was doing, several of the glowing insects hovered over his ring before one alighted on his outstretched fingers.

She caught her breath. "It actually landed on your hand."

"I think they're putting on a show for us."

As soon as they returned to the house, the fireflies vanished, leaving them once again to a dark, moonless night.

Cia didn't know what had awakened her. The night was quiet, unusually hushed; the insects and night birds eerily silent. Feeling a chill, her first thought was to get up and close the window. Instead, she pulled up the covers and turned over to snuggle with Will. Touching an empty bed, she opened her eyes, surprised to see him sitting up, his eyes still closed. It was then that she saw the vaporous cloud shimmering in front of him. In stunned silence, she stared as it slowly morphed into the translucent shape of a woman. As though in a trance, Will began to extend his hand to the indistinct figure that swirled and shifted just beyond his reach. Not knowing if she was awake or if this was another nightmare, Cia tried to scream. When no sound emerged, she tried to move forward to wake him but found herself unable to move, as though some invisible force was holding her in check. The apparition floated closer, a skeletal face crowned with snaking tendrils materializing out of churning mist. Seeing spectral fingers reaching out to Will, Cia lurched forward and with a scream, freed herself from the unseen, vise-like grip. As Will opened his eyes, the wraithlike figure recoiled in fury and with a shrill shriek of rage, began to dissolve into formless mist. But not before pointing a long, withered finger at Cia as well.

Barely awake, Will blinked before lying back on his pillows. Cia moved next to him. "Will? Are you all right?"

When he didn't answer, she saw he had fallen asleep. Feeling the cold abating and the night sounds return, she let him be. Although her conscious mind told her there was no way she'd be able to sleep, she was suddenly overcome with exhaustion. When she woke up again, it was almost noon. Her first impression was that it was another lovely day, her second, that she was alone in bed.

Trying not to panic, she threw Will's shirt on over a pair of shorts and walked quickly through the house. After calling his name without any response, she ran outside, relieved to see him sitting on an old log at the edge of the pond, sketchbook in hand. Putting her hand to her throat, she waited until the thudding in her heart subsided. Moving quietly, she walked up behind him and kissed the back of his neck. He grabbed her hand. "I tried to wake you. But you appeared to be in a deep sleep."

She sat down next to him. "How long have you been up?"

"I don't know. A couple of hours. It was a weird night with strange dreams."

Dreams? "Tell me."

"I don't remember much except that I was in a darkened room. It was cold, and I was looking for something. Then I saw some sort of vision. A woman, or maybe a girl, who wanted to tell me something."

"What did she look like?"

"I couldn't see her very well. It was foggy."

"Were you scared?"

He put down his pencils. "No. It felt like she was someone I knew."

She squeezed his hand. "It wasn't a dream."

"What are you saying?"

"I saw her as well."

He raked his hair with his fingers. "Tell me this isn't happening again."

"We have to go see Sonny."

He looked confused. "Sonny? What does she have to do with this?"

She took his hand, pulling him to the car. "It's a little hard to explain. You'll see when you get there."

Fortunately, Sonny was in the store helping a young couple pick out some homemade jams. When she finished ringing them up, she came over and gave Will a peck on each cheek.

"Sorry I missed you yesterday." She glanced at Cia. "Uh oh. I know that look."

Cia steered her away from three women who were browsing. "I want you to show Will the journal," she whispered.

Looking surprised, she whispered back, "Don't tell me it's happened again." When Cia nodded, she shook her head. "With Will?"

"Yes."

"This is unbelievable. I'll get it."

The shop was busy, the few café tables occupied by couples drinking coffee and reading newspapers. Sonny beckoned them into the kitchen where she brought out coffee and tea along with a plate of warm scones. Will watched her go to a darkened stairway.

"Where is she going?"

"To get a journal that was found in my house. I mean, the house that burned down before the cottage was built." She explained about Sonny, her grandfather, and their history in the town. Sonny returned with the journal, and making sure Charlie had everything under control in the store, she sat down next to them at a well-worn pine table. Cia unwrapped the oilskin covering and found the page she wanted. "Start reading from here."

Will glanced at her with unspoken questions before looking down. A few minutes later, he stopped and shook his head. "This is incredible. If I hadn't seen this with my own eyes, I wouldn't have believed it."

"There's something else," Cia said, pulling out the small sketch she had carefully placed between two pages. "Look at this."

"Bloody hell," he whispered, taking it. "From what you first told me, I was afraid this had something to do with that accursed inn. This, however, appears to be something else."

"I agree. I heard no whispers last night. It was almost too silent."

"Do you understand what this means?" When Cia nodded, Sonny, who was looking more uncomfortable with every second, stood up. "I'd better check to see what's going on in the shop."

Cia waited until Sonny left before turning back to Will. "When I first saw these pages, I wasn't sure. I think Cecily was our, ah, visitor last night."

He looked at her in disbelief. "How can you know that?"

"I saw her once before. When I told Sonny, she found this journal. I'm sorry. I should have told you sooner."

"What may be more important is how you came to buy that particular house. It can't have been coincidence. You must have felt something. Or maybe it was waiting for you."

She shivered. "Please don't say such things. Remember, that's not the original house. And no, I never felt anything special. That is, other than liking it."

"And last night was no dream."

She shook her head. "No. It wasn't. Not only that, but when I tried to wake you, something held my arm as if to stop me from touching you." She sighed. "When I finally woke you, she pointed at me before disappearing. By the time I could move and speak again, you were in a deep sleep."

"Did I say anything?"

"Only that you were tired."

"When did you see this . . . her, the first time?"

"Last spring. When I returned from London. There was also another figure, at least part of one, behind her."

He stared at the drawing. "Do you think those apparitions were you and me?"

"Don't you?" she whispered. "Maybe she's looking for the ring Mr. Williams promised her."

"This book dates from 1800. The inn was one thing, but this, this has to be tangible proof that we've been together in past lives."

"It's nice to know we've loved one another before. And yet you must admit, it feels a little weird."

He turned to her abruptly. "Is there some place we can make a copy of these pages and the drawing?"

"I'll ask Sonny. The library has a Xerox machine, although I'm sure it's closed on Sunday."

"I want to take the copies to show McKenna the next time I see him."

She looked surprised. "McKenna? Why do you need to see him again? Didn't you get all the answers you wanted? Besides, I thought we agreed this has nothing to do with Scotland."

He took her hands in his. "It mentions a ring, Cia. That means it has to do with the sapphires, which again comes back to Callanish. Do you know anyone else who has evil entities and heartbroken ghosts interfering with their lives?"

"Very funny."

"Still. I feel I need to go back."

"Just to see McKenna, right?"

He shook his head. "To Callanish as well."

She backed away. "No, Will. I don't like that idea at all."

"It will be all right," he said with a grin, as though trying to take the edge off the moment. "I promise I won't stay at the same inn again."

266

"This isn't a joke. Assuming there is or was an inn at all. But why go again? What do you expect to find?"

"That's what I don't know. I'll only stay a couple of days."

She stood up. "No. I love you, and I don't want anything to happen to you. Callanish scares me."

"We'll talk about that later. Right now, let's see if we can find a copier."

Sonny was talking with a couple of customers in the shop, and Cia waited until they left. "The only other copier in town would be at the police station," she said. "I know the chief. I'll give him a call."

By the time they returned to the cottage it was early afternoon, and Will went straight to the bedroom to look for any signs of ghosts. Cia followed him. "Stop saying that; you're creeping me out. The voices are bad enough, but ghosts?"

"It shouldn't. Aren't you at least happy to know we've loved one another before?"

"I'm not sure 'happy' is the right word. And if we don't remember, what's the point?"

"Only that the stories may be true, and our love really has transcended time."

She hugged him. "That's almost too much to grasp. I wish you didn't have to go back Tuesday."

"I'll only be a few weeks, Cia. And when I come back, I'll bring the other ring to you."

She was just as happy to return to her apartment in the city. At least there was no chance of any apparitions showing up in her bedroom. Will spent those days in meetings and making plans with his American ladies for their sittings later in August.

It seemed to Cia they couldn't stop touching, kissing, and talking about the future. She told Will she wanted to wait until he returned before saying anything to Sid about getting married and moving to London. Meanwhile, she'd have to swear Sarah to secrecy.

When she drove him to the airport Tuesday night, she was unable to stop weeping. "I feel like you're leaving too soon, that we need more time. Now, not later."

Taking her face in his hands, he gently ran his finger across her lips. "Just know that you are my eternal love, Cia. There's no need to be sad or worried, not any more. It's only a few weeks." Kissing away her tears, he whispered, "Keep thinking about us, about our life together."

Nuzzling his neck, she closed her eyes. "I promise I will."

The next morning, Sarah was waiting to pounce. "Okay, Cia. Now you have to tell me. Everything. What happened over the weekend and, more importantly, are you getting married? Come on, no more saying you don't want to talk about it."

"Only if you promise, actually swear, not to tell anyone."

She crossed her heart and held up three fingers. "I swear by the Girl Scout oath."

"I thought you were thrown out of the Girl Scouts."

Sarah made a face. "Well, that's actually true. They have no appreciation for individual leadership." She grinned. "But I swear anyway."

Closing the door, Cia told her about the soiree and how, first in the middle of a gaggle of women and then kneeling in the park, Will had proposed to her. Sarah stood up and clapped.

"Stop. It's supposed to be a secret."

"Yes, I know. But this is great. Unconventional, but still great. What else?"

Cia shrugged. "We had a lovely weekend together."

"That's it? That's all you can say?"

"Just how graphic would you like me to be?"

"C'mon. No weird incidents?"

Not about to say anything about the apparition, Cia shook her head. "It was very loving."

Since she hadn't mentioned Sonny's journal the first time, there was no reason to mention it now to Sarah, or, for that matter, anyone else. Besides, who would believe her? She was having a hard time herself. Whenever she thought of the ghost, no doubt Cecily reaching out in despair to her lover from a past life, she could feel her skin prickling. They had, however, been lucky that Sonny had been able to reach the police chief, who had let them make copies of the pages and the sketch.

"Are you going to let Coralie read your cards?"

She shrugged. "I guess."

Chapter 6

Will hadn't been in his flat more than fifteen minutes when the phone rang. Not in the mood to talk, he ignored it. When it rang again half an hour later, he shook his head and went to answer it.

The persistent caller turned out to be a reporter from the *Daily Mail* who had picked up Will's reviews from the *New York Times* on the international wire services and wanted an interview. Never minding good press, Will agreed to a meeting the next day.

Setting himself to the irritating task of unpacking, he heard the phone ring again. This time, it was Lady Adele from Lancashire. The wife of a member of Parliament, she had, over the past year, continually beseeched him to paint the portrait of her now sixteen-year-old daughter. He had demurred several times—particularly after meeting the girl, who was pleasant enough, but like Lady Adele in need of good dentistry and perhaps a small chin implant.

"I'm sorry, Lady Adele, I've just returned from New York and have no plans to be in Lancashire until the fall."

"Yes. Well. That's hardly a problem," she huffed. "I've just got word of your success in the States. Brilliant. That's why I'm calling. My little Beatrix is on summer holiday, and we will be more than happy to travel to London."

Will put his hand to his head. Flying always gave him a headache. Now Lady Adele was doing her best to exacerbate it.

"I'm planning to be in Scotland sometime in July. If you'd like, I can stop by your, ah, home on the way, and we can begin some preliminary sketches." He was always tempted to say "castle," which, although extensively renovated in the centuries since the 1600s, it truly was. There was even a moat, now filled with Lady Adele's prize-winning rose bushes.

Thanking him profusely, she finally rang off. As he went in search of aspirin, the phone rang again.

"Ah, good. You've returned," McKenna said, his voice unusually upbeat.

"Actually, a few days earlier than I would have liked."

"How was New York and your exhibit?"

"It went very well. Thanks for asking."

"And Cia?"

Will couldn't help a grin. "That went even better. I asked her to marry me."

"Great news. Congratulations." He hesitated. "Now that you've taken that leap, I hope my research of the last weeks hasn't been for naught."

"I assume you're talking about the, ah, earthbound spirit?"

"Yes, Will. I was able to procure access to several ancient manuscripts. None, of course, going back as far as one would like. Nothing exists before 300 AD, and then only Ogham inscriptions carved into trees or stones. It's only from the eighth century on that we have texts, written primarily by Irish monks who were ferreted away on mostly uninhabited islands. They copied Christian manuscripts brought to Ireland from churches across Europe, which, as you know, was in chaos at that time. While they do reference demons and evil spirits, they are, of course, Christian. I was more interested in the old Gaelic texts written in Sean-Ghaeilge, 'Old Irish'."

"There are no ancient Scottish manuscripts?"

"Unfortunately not. The Scots didn't catch up until much later. Our language is a hodgepodge of Germanic, Anglo-Frisian; throw in some Gaelic, French, whatever. We've had a lot of influences."

"So, everything you found was basically ancient Irish?"

"Yes. But considering we're only separated by twelve miles you can understand the exchange of information."

"So much for the history lesson. I'm still not convinced this is a good idea. Attempting to send a demon to some netherworld isn't something one does every day."

"Think about it, Will. It's likely this entity has been interfering with your life for millennia. I would think you would want it destroyed. Wouldn't you, now that you have Cia, want to be quit of it?"

"Obviously. At the same time, I prefer not to endanger what I have right now."

"And yet there may have been others through the ages who attempted such a thing and probably did perish in the process. The difference is, we now have the knowledge and the tools to accomplish this. I recall you mentioning MacDonald saying there were several pairs of sapphires out there. Millennia ago, when all this began, I would bet there were many more, and through the years as the demon grew in strength, it managed to retrieve them by luring unwitting individuals into its trap."

"Didn't you say the area was covered by peat moss for centuries?"

"If it can show its power through dirt and stone, peat would not have been able to stop it."

Will paused to take a much-needed breath. The fiction, at least as far as he was concerned, they had discussed only months before was suddenly becoming far too real.

"With the help of a Gaelic scholar, who can 'read' Ogham and Gaelic, I was able to find several obscure passages in some of the texts that I mentioned in our last conversation. There are a few that not only reference ancient spirits and demons but . . . how can I say this . . . also describe how to banish them."

"You really think I have the ability to exorcize this ancient demon?"

"I believe, given the right intentions and a few necessary implements, we can."

"We?"

"You can't do this on your own, Will."

"Why would you, Professor, even consider this?"

"My gut instincts are telling me it must be done."

"Why would you put yourself in danger? Researching déjà vu and demon hunting are very different things."

"This is a unique situation. And while I must admit it is daunting, the idea of actually confronting something from the spirit world, something we have only glimpsed through hypnoses, is exhilarating. I am convinced we will prevail."

"Or die trying."

McKenna actually guffawed. "That too."

"This isn't funny."

"No, Will. Far from it. Tell me. Are you still planning to go to Callanish?"

"Yes. Most likely the last week of July."

"Then I suggest you stop here first. Whether we end up trying to accomplish this or not, you need more information before you go."

It was close to eight and, with nothing in the fridge, Will was about to go out to a nearby pub for a quick dinner when Patrick rang, curious to know how his trip had gone.

"I wish you had been there, Patrick. I wasn't sure about the reaction of either the citizenry of New York or the press, but it worked out very well."

"So I've heard. Word even got to us here in the hinterlands. Did you pick up any commissions from that very same citizenry, as it were?"

"I did. From a few members of the social set, which easily rivals our aristocracy. At least in wealth."

Will could hear the smirk in Patrick's voice. "That's not saying much, considering some of those old titles are barely subsisting in their crumbling manor houses. By the way, tell me about Cia."

"What can I say, except I sort of proposed to her with a group of other women standing around."

After he described the cocktail party and the weekend with Cia, Patrick, expressing surprise, said, "I guess congratulations are in order. I'm happy for you, Will. I don't think you would ever have got this far without McKenna."

"That's probably true. And, although it sounds beyond strange to say it, if this is just one of our lives together, at least we'll both be happy in it."

"You're sending chills down my spine. But I do get the point."

"Are you coming to London anytime soon?"

"I don't think so. The summer is too lovely up here. One of your BBC producers rang me last week after calling your flat several times. He wanted to know where you were. I told him you were in New York and would be back this week. They're anxious to start filming in a couple of weeks. He wants you to pick an artist or two to discuss on the show."

"No worries. I'll ring them tomorrow."

"Maybe you should look into one of those new telephone answering gizmos that take messages while you're out."

"I don't think so. If somebody wants to reach me they can try another time. That's too intrusive for my taste."

"Understood."

"I may be up your way in late July. I'm thinking of going to Callanish again."

Patrick was silent for a few seconds. "Why?"

"I need answers."

"I thought you got answers from McKenna."

"Those added up to more questions."

"Have you considered there may be no answers?"

"I have to find out."

"What about McKenna?"

He hesitated. "I intend to see him first. Before I drive to Callanish."

"I don't like the sound of this. You don't even know what you're looking for. It's too dangerous. You have Cia now. Why can't you let it be?"

"Because it feels like something I have to do. I still have a few classes to teach before the summer holiday. I'll stop at Lady Adele's first, then I thought I'd come to you for the night. If I do stop to see McKenna, the drive from Edinburgh to Ullapool isn't so long."

"You can still get those heavy fogs up there, even in summer. I wish you would just skip it."

"No worries, Patrick. As I told Cia, it will be fine."

Chapter 7

Cia put down the phone and closed her eyes. She wished she could have convinced Will not to return to Scotland. Just the thought of it gave her the creeps. And yet she knew him well enough to understand that once he decided to do something he wouldn't stop until it was accomplished.

Sarah had brought in a couple of bridal magazines one day at lunch and left them on Cia's desk. When she returned from a meeting that afternoon, her eyes went wide. "Sarah. What is this?"

She had merely grinned. "It's July, Cia. Will is coming back in August. I think it's time we look for a wedding dress."

"We?" Cia picked up the magazines and shoved them in a drawer. "What if Sid or Marge—or worse—Coralie had come in and seen them? No one is supposed to know. Not until Will and I make some decisions."

"Lighten up. Everyone in the office has pretty much figured it out. Don't worry. They're on your side."

"Still, I have no intention of wearing a white wedding dress. I did that once before, and look how well that worked out."

"This is different."

"If I showed up in one of those frothy numbers, Will would be on the next plane to China, or wherever. And rightfully so. No. It has to be understated, elegant. Maybe cream-colored, short, or calf-length."

"There are dresses like that in there. Of course, they're for the mother of the bride."

Cia balled up a piece of paper and threw it at her. "Very funny."

"Seriously. Have a look. I did see a nice cream-colored, bias-cut silk in one of them."

"You did?"

When Sarah nodded, she took one of the magazines from the drawer. "Well. Maybe just a quick look."

"That's better," Sarah said, getting up and peering over her shoulder. "When are you going to have Coralie read your cards?"

"She's on vacation. I think she'll be back Monday."

A couple of days later, Steve called to tell her Will's show was closing and that he and Carl were more than satisfied with how it had gone. "He sold very well, Cia. "

"I'm glad to hear that."

"I'm calling because we have a new exhibition about to begin, and we're moving Will's unsold canvases to the back. I'm sure we'll have more interest in them. Before Will left, he told me he wanted you to have the small sketches. Two, I believe, are of you."

Trying to keep the emotion out of her voice, she said. "Steve, thank you. He never mentioned it to me."

"He wanted to surprise you. When can you come?"

"It is that. How's tonight after work?"

"Perfect. I'll see you then."

"What was that about?" Sarah asked.

"Do I have to tell you everything?"

She frowned. "Of course. By the way, Mike said he'd join us at the cottage this weekend. It's supposed to be nice."

Cia nodded. As far as she was concerned, the more people in the house the better. "Steve asked me to come down to the gallery tonight. I had no idea Will had told him to give me the small sketches from behind the bar. Want to come?"

"Sure."

When they arrived at the gallery Will's paintings had already been taken down and stacked along a wall. Brushing away a stab of sadness, she watched two of Steve's assistants move crab style across the floor trying not to drop a very large, garishly colored canvas. Taking deep breaths, they set it down with obvious relief against a side wall. Noticing her for the first time, one of them said he'd go find Steve.

"Look at that," Sarah said, pointing to the front window where Will's name had been replaced by the name of an artist she didn't know; no doubt the creator of that same large painting. A few minutes later, Steve came out holding a small carton. "I had these wrapped for you, Cia. Will never meant these to be sold. He sent them along just for you."

She gave him a peck on the cheek. "Thank you, Steve. These are special."

"So is Will. I wish you both the best."

She looked surprised. "He told you?"

"You don't remember? I was there, albeit in a corner. I wasn't sure what I'd heard. After you left, Mrs. Stutts was overwhelmed that Will proposed to you at her, um, soiree, as she called it."

"Actually, so was I."

Chapter 8

It was the last week in July. Will's classes were over and after completing a portrait he rang Patrick to say he'd see him in a couple of days.

Unwaveringly skeptical, Patrick said, "I still don't like the idea of you going to Callanish again. What does Cia say?"

"She doesn't want me to go. And yet I must. I'm hoping it will close the loop on my understanding of all that's happened."

"You've accepted the concept of the sapphires and past lives, not to mention living with those annoying voices. You're successful, about to get married—something, by the way, I never thought I would see—and everyone adores you. And soon we'll be seeing you on the telly. What more do you need?"

"I'll let you know once I get there. See you in a few days. After I stop in Lancashire."

"Oh yes. Lady Adele." He smirked. "Good luck staying out of her clutches. And, by the way, I'm considering having a show in September. Sort of an introduction to the season. It will be all small works. Do you have anything just, ah, laying around?"

He thought for a minute. "Actually, I may."

Before leaving London, Will called Cia, who again expressed apprehension about his trip.

"Please, my love. There's no need to worry. I'll be stopping at Patrick's for a night and ring you from there."

"Promise you'll be careful. And stay away from that inn."

He laughed. "I have no intention of going anywhere near it. Nor do I plan to spend much time at the stones. McKenna suggested I wander around the island, get some other impressions. I'm taking my camera."

"Will you go see him from there?"

It was the question he'd been trying to avoid. "Actually, I'll probably stop and see him first."

He picked up the tension in her voice. "Why?"

"He wants to discuss a few things before I go."

"You're not telling me all of it. There's more, isn't there?"

"Just a few things that McKenna found in his research on Callanish." He hated lying to her, but to keep her from worrying there was little choice. "I'll try to call you from Stornoway. Although the phone service there could be dicey."

"Please, Will, I wish you wouldn't go."

"Stop worrying, my love. I promise I'll have you in my grasp soon enough."

He could sense her smile. "I can't wait. I love you, Will. Please take care."

Seeing the blue mini drive up the lane, Patrick met him outside.

"Glad to see you," he said as Will exited the car and stretched. "How was Lady Adele?"

"Not quite as annoying as I recalled. I did a few sketches of her daughter, who, I'm pleased to say, did look a bit better. Lady A told me she can't wait to come to London to have her sit for the painting."

"When? Aren't you going to New York in September?"

"Actually, at the end of August. Steve has even arranged a studio in Soho for me." He laughed. "He said everything is set. I only have to bring my brushes. I told Lady Adele I'd ring her when I return."

Seeing Patrick peer inside the car, Will tossed him the keys. "The paintings are in the boot. I brought you three small nudes."

"Brilliant. How long will you stay?"

"I'll have to leave early tomorrow morning. I told McKenna I'd meet him at his office by noon."

"Why do I have the feeling there's more? That you're not telling me what this is really about."

Will shook his head. "It's really nothing."

"If it was nothing, you wouldn't be going back to McKenna or, for that matter, Callanish. There's no way to talk you out of this?"

"What is it with you and Cia? I'll only be in the Outer Hebrides for two days. It's not a big deal." He looked at his watch. "Would it be all right if I ring Cia? Otherwise, I can call from the post office."

"Not at all. I'd like to congratulate her. In fact, perhaps you'd like to think about getting married up here."

Will looked at him with a smile. "You're a good friend, Patrick. I'm sure she would like that."

Chapter 9

The blinds were drawn with only a single lamp illuminating McKenna's office. When Will walked in he could barely make out the desk, now littered with open leather-bound books and what appeared to be scrawled sheets of paper.

McKenna jumped up to shake his hand. "I'm glad you're here, Will. We have much to discuss."

"Good to see you, Professor. Why is it so dark in here?"

"It's these books. They contain copies of some of our most ancient manuscripts. Normally, they're not allowed out of the research library. I had to chat up the librarian, who made me promise to return them later today." He picked up a few of the papers. "These are what I've been copying by hand."

"You don't have a copier?"

"Not allowed. The books themselves are old, and the pages too brittle. You can't touch them without cotton gloves, and they can't tolerate light." He gently closed the books before opening the blinds. "Have a seat. I have a lot to tell you."

Will shook his head. "That's what I'm afraid of. I still don't think this is a good idea. In fact, I'm sure it's a very bad idea. I should probably just go to Callanish and see what, if anything, happens. I'll stay away from the inn. If there's anything unusual, I'll call you."

"And that may very well be what you will end up doing." He leaned forward on the desk. "However, I'd like you to listen to me first."

"That's why I've come. I respect the time and effort you've put into this."

"Are you hearing the voices much these days?"

"Now that you mention it, not so often."

"Then be attentive on the island. If you begin to hear them, it could be a warning."

He shrugged. "Fine."

Ignoring Will's indifference, McKenna went on, "I've already told you that I found quite a few references on demonic possession in my research. Most, however, are from the early Christian era. There's very little about pagan demons and, as you are aware, nothing from the Neolithic period. I'm making the assumption that this entity wasn't what we would describe as 'possessed' in life, that only due to some sort of catastrophic event or unexpected death did he resist crossing over and so become evil. Although it may be that my assumptions are fallible, I'm afraid we'll have to work within that construct."

"Is it possible this, uh, entity could be female?"

"It's possible, but somehow I doubt it. From what we know of our local primitive cultures, they appear to have been male-dominated. And yet, how can we know? Male or female, the entity still exists."

Will nodded. "Go on."

McKenna took a breath. "There's not much more I can tell you. I'm afraid we're on our own."

"There you go with 'we' again. This should just be me. It's my problem, not yours."

"I've already told you it's not a one-man job. In fact, it will be necessary to bring in at least a couple of other, ah, participants."

Will shook his head. "No way. It's crazy to put others at risk, much less to even attempt such a thing. We know the entity is far stronger than we are."

McKenna put up his hand. "Not necessarily. This goes far beyond déjà vu and into the realm of fundamental human instincts, those hidden in what some scientists refer to as our reptilian brains from hundreds of thousands of years ago. How we have evolved over the last five thousand years is no more than a drop in the evolutionary bucket."

"And that means what? We have to think like a man from five thousand years ago?"

"What I'm saying is that, in his lifetime, this entity's primary motivations were likely not very different from ours today."

"Motivations? Not to be disrespectful, but are you kidding?"

"Not at all. Our history is full of men who have been consumed by power, not to mention lust and greed. Perhaps that's what led to his demise and refusal to cross over. Besides, we already know what it's after: the sapphire in your ring. And I have no doubt it'll eventually go after Cia's as well. For reasons we can never know, it's motivated to seek out those gemstones and will continue to do so in this life and into the next."

Will got up and paced. "This is impossible."

"You can't let it destroy your life. At least not this one."

"It found me. I'm still here."

"What if it tries again, particularly when Cia has the ring? And what about your future lives? It's time to think about that."

He stared at McKenna. While it seemed too far out, too surreal, he had to acknowledge there was an underlying logic to the Professor's thinking. *Kill it and it will no longer haunt my dreams or threaten my very existence. Or, more importantly, Cia's.* "Tell me what this will involve? Certainly not crosses and garlic."

McKenna offered a small grin. "No, Will. It's not a vampire. And yet, despite having no corporeal body, it still has a long reach. Also, I'm not ruling out what I have read of Christian exorcisms, about the use of holy water and oil. And it wouldn't hurt for us, as well as our various tools, to be consecrated."

"Consecrated? You mean in a church?"

"Yes. As I said, it can't hurt."

With a sigh, Will sat down again. This was sounding crazier every minute. "What sort of 'tools'?"

"Smudge bundles of white sage and thyme to purify the space. Candles, salt. Black salt if I can get it. Matches, oil, and a hemp rope. A broom if we have to sweep rubble from the area where the channel comes through. And we'll have to come up with some incantations."

Will rolled his eyes. "This is insane. Incantations? Matches? It's already survived a fire. Probably caused it."

The Professor shook his head. "We'll discuss that later on. Are you still set on going to Callanish tomorrow?"

"Yes."

"Then, as before, I suggest you stay away from the inn. Maybe take a drive up the east side of the island first, just to get a feel for it. It's far more serene, and there are some scenic beaches. It will help to clear your mind. Meanwhile, I'll look further for what more can be done." With a glance out the window, he stood up. "Meet me later at The Hounds. We'll have dinner and discuss this some more."

"You're really convinced you want to do this, aren't you?"

"Never more sure of anything. It must be done." He looked pointedly at Will. "What's more important, however, is you. You are the one who must believe."

Chapter 10

The drive had taken longer than anticipated. Not due to traffic; there were few cars or lorries on the road. Once Will passed Inverness, the weather turned nasty with squalls of cold rain that swept across the roads, making visibility difficult. Despite the storms, he still managed to arrive at Ullapool in time for the last ferry.

After disembarking at Stornoway, he took a few steps around the port, relieved to be out of the car after the long drive. Strangely, as bad as the weather had been on the mainland, here the sun was shining, and barring any incoming fog, it would be until well after ten. The Outer Hebrides weren't considered much of a garden spot, and despite that it was the beginning of August he was sure the hotels weren't overly booked. Bypassing a few small inns along the port, he decided to look further. At the very end of the marina he found one more, The Royal, which appeared to be the largest hotel in town.

He was greeted effusively by a sprightly middle-aged man in a tartan kilt who told him he, indeed, did have a room with a lovely view and, should Mr. Jamieson be so inclined, the dining room was open just across the lobby. Before having dinner, he went to his room and decided to lie down for a few minutes. When he awoke, bright light was shining through the window. A glance at the clock told him he'd slept almost twelve hours.

Along with his camera, he brought a guidebook down to breakfast. He'd already made up his mind not to start with Callanish. For his first day he planned to drive north along the east coast of the island where, as McKenna had said, he would find picturesque coves and beaches, although the sea was far too icy for swimming. Swimming wasn't exactly what he had in mind; he was looking for a location, or possibly several, where he might feel the same magnetism that had drawn him to this bleak, windswept island in the first place.

He had just gotten in his car when he noticed a tall, craggy-faced man in a faded tam walking towards him.

"Good day, sir," he said, mashing out a cigarette under his heel. "I thought I recognized you. We don't get many visitors twice within one year." Seeing that Will didn't register the connection, he said, "You don't remember? I gave you directions to Callanish last October. You were with a bonnie young lady."

"You have quite a memory."

"Then you're off to the stones again?"

"Not until tomorrow. Today I plan to drive around this side of the island."

He began to back away. "Then have a nice day."

"May I ask you a question?"

"Yes, sir. What can I do for you?"

"Last time we stayed at an inn not far from Callanish. I, ah, don't remember the name. Do you by any chance know of it?"

The man looked perplexed. "Nay. There's no such place, sir. Not anymore. There was, but that was many years past. I mean about a hundred, just after the stones were dug up out of the peat. Lots of folks came by in those days. At one time there were quite a few inns and small hotels, but they've been long abandoned or lost to the elements. This is a harsh place, as you know."

"This is an old stone house on a hill. With a few tall trees at the entrance."

"Aye. I know of what you speak. That house still stands, or I should say, the charred shell of it. It's said to be haunted by an old woman."

Before Will could say he didn't want to hear any more, the man leaned in as if confiding a secret. "You see, sir, there was this young couple who came to see the stones. Much like you and your lady, interesting enough, and about the same time of year. It's said there was an unusually dense fog that night. No one could see through it, and those who lived nearby spoke of it as foul-smelling, like sulfur, as though the devil himself had come up through the earth. It became so cold that everything froze up and the poor young couple burned everything they could find until the entire place went up in flames. It took more than a week before the townsfolk could get close to it. And when they did they all ran off in horror."

Will was beginning to feel uneasy. "Did they find anything?"

He shook his head. "Other than the stone walls, they found nothing."

"Nothing? How can that be?"

"Everything inside had burned to a crisp. Sorry, sir. That wasn't proper. But, unfortunately, true. Not even bones were left from the flames. Just ash surrounding a pit in the ground. When a few men were sent to look into it, as I said, they ran away saying it had been a grave under what was once a rocky cairn. Truth is, it turned out the entire hill was an ancient burial mound, likely from thousands of years past and possibly going back to the time of the Callanish stones themselves. Some say that pit went deep into the earth, all the way to the schist, the primeval rock below. And it was through that pit that the demons reached up to retrieve something they wanted. So, sir, do ya know what that could be?"

I think I have a pretty good idea.

As if reading his thoughts, the man nodded. "Sorry, again. I wasn't being quite truthful. Actually, two things were found under the ash. A charred metal band, like a ring, and the remains of what looked like a lady's brooch. I don't know of any metal that could stand such heat, do you?"

Will shook his head. Didn't MacDonald say his ring wasn't silver at all, but something as yet unknown?

"Well, sir, whatever gemstones they held, if indeed there were such stones, disappeared in the fire. Odd that the metal survived and the gemstones vanished, don't you think?"

Will stared at the road ahead. "I really wouldn't know."

The man stepped back to light another cigarette. "So now you know a bit of our local history. As for the inn, or what's left of it, the townsfolk still believe it's haunted. No one goes near it. Sometimes on nights of heavy fog, strange shrieking sounds are heard along with foul odors. It just stands there on the hill, abandoned and crumbling."

Trying to keep his wits about him, Will nodded. "That's quite a story."

"So you see what I mean, sir. You couldn't have stayed there, could you?"

"No. I'm sure you're right."

"I suggest you stop by the cove at Mangersta. You've come at the beginning of August, midway between the summer solstice and

286

autumn equinox. This is the time of the ripening of crops; the ritual of Lughnasadh, the wedding of the sun god and earth goddess. These are ancient and sacred beliefs. I think tomorrow you will find the sunset especially pleasant. Make sure you go, sir. It's not far from Callanish."

Will watched the man, if man he was, walk off. It was obvious he had delivered not one, but two messages; the first that he and Cia had, indeed, inhabited an illusion manifested by an entity that had reached beyond the grave to reclaim a coveted sapphire. And, if he was to be believed, not for the first time. The second was that there was something for him at Mangersta.

With a deep shudder, he again acknowledged that he and Cia had been lucky to have escaped death. As he put the car in gear, he began to be plagued by misgivings, questioning if the time had come to not only abandon McKenna's wild quest, but his own search for answers. Since he'd come this far, however, he decided to keep to his original plan; tomorrow he would visit the stones, and if there was time he'd make a brief stop at Mangersta before leaving this place, hopefully forever.

Taking the road north, he came upon a broad, sandy beach where a dark, foamy sea lapped the shore. With camera in hand, he strolled along the edge. Other than the breeze off the frigid water, he felt no disturbance; the place was decidedly tranquil. He drove on to Tolsta, a beach populated by ragged stone pillars that looked to have gouged their way through the earth. After taking a few photos, he returned to the car and continued on to his ultimate destination, the lighthouse at the Butt of Lewis, the most northern point of the island.

Braving harsh, biting winds, he looked down to where tempestuous waves crashed with fury over huge, craggy rocks. Through icy sea spray and low, threatening clouds he could barely make out the ghostly shapes of desolate islands in the distance. Clutching his jacket around him, he returned to the car and headed back south in search of a warm pub.

He found one along the road to Stornoway. With only a few dented and dusty cars parked in front, it didn't appear to be a tourist destination. Inside, he breathed in the comforting scent of decades, perhaps even centuries, of beer and whiskey blending pleasantly with tobacco smoke. Although it wasn't crowded, he was aware that every weather-beaten face turned to appraise him as he walked in.

He took a local beer from the bar and, having noticed the area was dotted with smokehouses, ordered a plate of smoked salmon. With most of the patrons either sitting or standing at the bar, few tables were occupied, and he chose one near a window with a view of the sea. The place felt vaguely familiar, but then, he mused, most old pubs did. Beginning to unwind, he realized it was a feeling he hadn't had in quite a while. Perhaps it was because he'd felt no pull from the stones, even as close as they were. Instead, he was enjoying the serenity, the actual aloneness of the rugged, sparsely populated island. The thought crossed his mind that he might even want to bring Cia back again. He imagined McKenna would advise against it.

He downed the beer quickly, and as he returned to the bar to get another, he sensed a presence, as though he was being watched. With a quick glance around, he noticed an elderly man with a face as weather-beaten as the island staring at him from a darkened corner. When he returned to his table, he watched the man get to his feet with obvious difficulty. After adjusting a threadbare tam, he picked up his pint of Guinness and hobbled over. "D'ya mind if eye join ya, yung mon?"

Will nodded, curious as to what a local man would want of him.

Making small talk, the old man asked where he was from. Hearing London, he asked what he was doing in the Outer Hebrides.

"Just visiting. This morning I drove north. Tomorrow I'll go to the western side."

The man nodded while lighting a well-worn pipe inlaid with what looked like ivory. "So yur a tourist? Odd, you don't seem like one. You've been here before."

It wasn't a question, and Will once again began to feel a vague sense of unease. "Yes. I have been here before."

He nodded. "Ya said yur from London, but ya have a wee bit uf a Scot accent."

"I'm originally from Inverness," he answered, with the unsettling suspicion that the man already knew where he was from as well as why he was here. In the ensuing silence, he lit a Rothman while watching the man casually sip his Guinness. Placing it on the table, he glanced at Will's ring.

"Tha's a sapphire. I've seen others like it before."

"I understand this is the region they come from."

A smile creased the old man's face. "Aye. Lots wer found here, in caves. But yers is older. Nothing like wot you've got there has been found for centuries, maybe more."

"What do you mean, 'maybe more'?"

"Tha hills there," he pointed west, "around Loch Roag. They're ancient rock, formed in the fires when the earth was born."

Aware the conversation was now verging on the surreal, Will asked, "How can you know that?"

The man puffed on his pipe. "I know."

"Where is this place?"

"Loch Roag? No' far from here. In fact, just below our Callanish stones." He paused, as if waiting for a response. When Will didn't respond, he pointed a gnarly finger at his hand. "Yur sapphire comes from there."

Beginning to feel his skin prickling, Will again asked the man how he could know.

He winked. "I know lots. But I'll wager ya 'ave already figured that out."

"Not at all. Please, tell me."

"Nay. I cannae do that. Just take care, sir. This island is filled with magic, not to mention memories that go beyond the centuries, and spirits from beyond time itself." With great effort he stood up, his pale, watery eyes glaring down at Will. "Visit your stones at Callanish and leave here. Do not attempt to overstep the boundaries again." This time there was no heavy accent; his words were clear as day.

Before Will could say another word, he hobbled to the door. By the time Will registered what he had said and got up to follow him, the old man was gone. Outside, he looked left and right, seeing nothing more than empty road and low, rolling hills. He went back to the bar. "The old man who was sitting at my table. Do you know his name?"

The barkeep looked perplexed. "An old man?"

"He was drinking Guinness and appeared to be somewhat crippled. He was smoking a pipe, inlaid with ivory or something."

"No, sir. There was not such a man here. Poor Mr. MacFarland used to have a pipe like that, but he passed some twenty years ago."

Will nodded. *Why am I not surprised?* First the man that morning in Stornoway going on about the inn and now this one talking about sapphires. There was no peace for him in this place. Perhaps he should have heeded Cia's and Patrick's warnings, but he was here now, and he had to finish it. While the old man in the curio shop and MacDonald had claimed the sapphires came from the Outer Hebrides, this man, or whatever he was, had now told him where; and almost at Callanish itself. Wasn't that what he had come for? Suddenly, he wasn't sure.

He decided that if all went well at the stones tomorrow, he'd drive to Mangersta, take in the sunset, and that would be the end of it. The very idea of killing the demon was becoming more outrageous by the second. It was all too evident, not to mention terrifying, that powerful entities, even beyond the accursed inn, could reach from beyond the grave to make themselves seen and heard. For mere humans to attempt to challenge something so formidable verged dangerously close to insanity. He couldn't wait to get home.

The next morning, he stopped at a petrol station near the hotel, finding it far more costly than on the mainland. That had been expected but, low on fuel, he'd had no choice. Seeing the craggy-faced man from the day before strolling toward him, he paid the attendant and drove off before he could get close enough to chat.

The road looked vaguely familiar and, after passing several signs, he saw one with an arrow pointing to Loch Roag. Knowing that nothing awaited him there, he continued on, recognizing the turn to the inn not far ahead. After forcing himself to drive past it, curiosity overrode apprehension. Ignoring a sharp stab of foreboding, or more likely primal fear, he turned back.

What had been a defined gravel driveway last fall was now a deeply rutted dirt track choked with weeds. He drove only several meters before deep grasses and tangled bushes blocked the way. It was clearly the same place he and Cia had stayed except, as the man in Stornoway had said, it was now a crumbling shell of scorched stones. Putting aside his fear by convincing himself it was just a decaying ruin—one of many on the island—he left the car and began to work his way closer. The thatched roof was long gone, but the sign with the carving of the hawk was still discernible. He could see it hanging by one rusted hinge, swaying and squeaking, the sound eerie in a restless breeze. The rosebushes that had reached out to scratch Cia's legs were either dead stalks or massively overgrown, effectively blocking the remainder of the path to the blackened rect-angle that had been the front door.

Transfixed, he asked himself how this skeletal structure could have existed with rooms, a kitchen, fireplaces, an old woman, and, most frightening, a bedroom where he and Cia had fought for their lives against a malignant spirit. And yet he wasn't prepared to accept the concept that they had inhabited an illusion so powerful that, as the old man in the pub (no doubt an illusion himself) had said, it had ripped the boundary of time itself. And yet, how or what had he overstepped? The inn, at least as he and Cia had perceived it, was there waiting, beckoning them to its doorstep.

The wind gusted, ripping desiccated leaves off decaying trees; trees that had appeared green and healthy last fall. He was about to return to the car when he chanced one last glance back. Stopping abruptly, his felt the hair on his neck bristling. In one window there was now a faint light, as though a candle had been lit. A shadow moved through it, a vague shape with no eyes. He felt a push and then a whisper, as though the wind was summoning him. The overgrown rosebushes shiv-ered and parted, opening a narrow corridor. As he made his way along what was left of the path, the sky turned to indigo and the wind began to whine through shriveled branches. He could smell it now, the fetid odor of decay and burnt flesh. Staring up at the window, he was drawn by the flickering and the shifting shadow. Despite sensing a malevolent presence, he no longer cared; he saw only the light, felt only the magic. Entranced, he walked slowly up shattered stone stairs to the scorched doorway. Something inside whispered, enticing him forward. As his foot began to cross the threshold, a vaporous appendage reached out to welcome him. Abruptly, a sharp crack shattered the spell, awakening him with a jolt. A truck had passed, backfiring as it disappeared up the road. Breathless, Will gazed with horror into the blackened pit of hell where the light flicked out and the beguiling whispers turned to screams of rage. With adrenaline fueling his body, he stumbled back.

Regaining his balance, he ran through the dense, cloying rose bushes, unaware of thorns raking his hands and clothing. When he dared look up, the window was again dark, devoid of light. Knowing evil had once again reached beyond the grave, he had little doubt that this time he'd avoided certain death.

He backed the car out quickly, the odor of putrefaction still stinging his nostrils. He was anxious to hear what McKenna would have to say about this little moment, although he doubted that he or anyone else in the corporeal world of flesh and blood would have such a thing as an explanation.

Seeing the stones come into view on the horizon, he pulled over. He had to compose himself, to quiet the tremor in his hands and the thudding of his heart. Looking at his fingers, he expected to see blood. Despite the rose bushes closing in as though trying to prevent his escape, his hands as well as his pants appeared unscathed. He considered returning immediately to Stornoway; he'd had enough terror for one day. And yet, as fear and tension subsided, he became surprisingly calm. He decided he could use a pint to further tranquilize his senses, but recalled no pub this close to the stones.

Taking a breath, he drove on to Callanish, the monoliths shimmering white against an unusually clear sky. He parked on the verge, relieved to see several cars, a bus, and groups of tourists wandering, cameras at the ready. For the first time, he became aware of stones to his left and right, and realized that sometime in the millennia preceding Christianity, they had been placed in the shape of a cross. As he walked he assessed his feelings, but other than curiosity he felt nothing; no magic, no desire, no hint of the surge of kinetic energy that had defined his earlier trip.

Like any tourist, he strolled casually, watching others snapping photos. He had purposely left his camera in the car; he required no more memories of this place. He flinched when an older man with bushy hair stopped him, asking if he would take a photo of him and his wife in front of the center monolith. Pointing, he said to make sure to include the remains of the rocky cairn at its base. As Will took the picture, he was unable to banish the memory of Cia shivering next to him as darkness shrouded the same stone.

By the time he left, it was mid-afternoon. Passing several pubs, he made sure to choose one with a tour bus outside; he didn't need any more elderly Scottish ghosts intruding on his lunch. More important, it was time to think about what had happened at the inn. Somehow the demon had recognized him at his approach, mesmerizing him and all too quickly drawing him into its lair. Realizing it would never leave him in peace, he put aside his earlier doubts and made the decision to call McKenna.

Chapter 11

McKenna, along with what he jokingly called his "crusaders," arrived the next day at Inverness. Will joined them that afternoon, still questioning why they couldn't have met in Stornoway, or even Ullapool. When he'd called McKenna to tell him what happened at the inn, he had actually sounded excited, again insisting the demon would never give up and the only choice was to go ahead with his plan.

Still undecided, Will had stared at the phone. For a man who had always been in command of his own life, he was finding it difficult to cede any sort of control to someone else, even McKenna. And yet, despite all their discussions and McKenna's explanations, this was a situation that remained far beyond his comprehension. That McKenna had grasped the deep significance and taken it upon himself to remedy it, if remedy was even the right word, was something he considered at once admirable and foolhardy. If, however, this was the only road to be taken, he could hardly refuse.

When he arrived at the hotel, he was shocked to see Patrick and Bobby, his assistant, drinking with McKenna in the bar. "What the hell . . . ?"

"Join us, Will," McKenna said with a broad grin that lit up his normally serious countenance.

Clearly agitated, Will snapped, "Bloody hell! What have you done? How did Patrick and Bobby become part of this?"

Patrick put up his hands. "Cool it, Will. After you left, I began to question not only why you would choose to return to Callanish, but why you would also need to see the Professor. I was sure there was more you weren't telling me, so I took it upon myself to call and ask. I figured if it was just a quick trip, as you said, then there was nothing to be concerned about. When he told me about his plan, my first thought was that he had gone bonkers. After hearing his explanation, I said I wanted in."

"No. This isn't right. I can't be putting all of you in grave danger."

"Understand, Will, that I asked to do this. When McKenna said the two of you weren't enough and it would take at least four men to banish this, uh, entity, I told him there was no need, that I would join you. Better to have friends than strangers. Bobby overheard me and asked to come along as well. If you and Cia are to have any life together now, or as McKenna says, at some future time, this must be done. And done properly."

Will looked at the three men. "Since none of us have any idea of what 'properly' may be, all I can say is thank you. Now, however, I suggest we all have a drink, or maybe two, and then go home."

"No way," Bobby shouted. "We're going to kill it, whatever the bloody thing is."

Will looked at McKenna. "He has no idea, does he?"

"On the contrary. We have not only discussed it in grim detail, we have come prepared."

Unconvinced, Will shook his head. "How prepared can you be? We have no real idea of what awaits us."

"I believe I do. All we need is for you to have faith."

Bobby nodded. "When I asked to come along, Patrick first said no. But I insisted. I admire you, and I intend to help." He was a slight young man in his late twenties with a shock of unruly black hair that fell below his ears.

"Look, Professor, I appreciate all this, but let's be real."

"I am determined be very real," he said, indicating two canvas bags on the floor. "What's in those will do the job."

Will grimaced. "Your demon hunting kit?"

He nodded. "Before we leave tomorrow morning, we'll stop at East Church to pick up holy water and have our implements blessed."

"What power can a Scots church have against a pagan demon?"

"We need to take all the precautions available to us, Will."

Still not convinced, Will rolled his eyes. "How about us? Shouldn't we be blessed as well?"

"I've already spoken to the priest. Although he was doubtful, he agreed to do as I asked."

"He didn't think you were daft?"

"Not at all. Almost everyone in Scotland has some belief in ghosts and spirits. You should know that by now."

"You are very convincing, McKenna."

"Not at all, Will. Just driven to do what's right."

The church was old, dimly lit, and suffused with chilly cross drafts. Candles flickered, throwing jittering shadows across plaster walls adorned with faded religious paintings. They met the priest, an older man in a dark cassock, in front of the altar where he sat with them to discuss their quest. After saying prayers over bundles of sage and thyme, candles, salt, and the rest of McKenna's supposed "armaments," he glanced at Will, asking if it was he who had become the focus of the evil spirit's attention.

"Unfortunately, yes. And yet I still question why we are here. This entity is ancient, pagan. Its gods, if gods it did worship, were of sea, earth, and sky. Why would a Christian church hold any sway over such a being?"

The priest nodded. "I understand your concern. And yet Professor McKenna has done extensive research and truly believes that what we are doing here today can only help; that whatever blessings you take with you will enhance your efforts. I can't say that I disagree with him." He picked up three vials. "Take this oil and holy water and use it wisely." He glanced at McKenna. "Have you decided on your incantations?"

McKenna nodded. "We have."

He made the sign of the cross. "Then go in peace and accomplish your goal. May God, the angels, and the forces of light be with you."

After thanking him, McKenna turned to Will. "You should leave your ring here."

Perplexed, he looked back. "Why?"

"I believe the demon recognizes you by that sapphire. If it doesn't sense it, it will make our job easier. If only to get inside the house."

"Why leave it in a church?"

McKenna shrugged. "Why not? Better here than taking it to Stornoway. You seem to wake the ghosts there, as well."

"No. I'll put in in the safe at the hotel. I have a feeling I may need it when all this is finished. That is, if 'finished' is even possible."

"Why?"

"Call it intuition."

In Stornoway they first stopped at the hotel where Will had arranged an additional three rooms. When McKenna got out of his car, he looked around. "It's been many years since I last came here. I'd like to see the stones, but that will have to wait. Perhaps later." He glanced at his watch. "It's almost two. Although we still have hours of daylight, we should go straightaway to the inn." He stopped and looked at each of them. "Are you sure you're all up for this?"

As Patrick and Bobby murmured prayers and crossed themselves, Will shook his head. "I don't know how anyone can be ready for such a thing. However, if you're convinced, let's get to it. Better in daylight than darkness."

McKenna shrugged. "Day or night, I doubt it will make much difference. Still, make sure you have your torches."

Patrick got into the car with Will while Bobby, holding rosary beads and still muttering Hail Marys, went with McKenna. McKenna glanced at him. "You don't have to come with us, Bobby. Not if you're afraid."

He shook his head. "I'm not afraid. I want to help."

"I understand. At the same time, you must understand the danger."

"I do, as much as I can."

McKenna reached over to squeeze his shoulder. "And we all thank you."

Bright sunlight that had played hide and seek with puffy white clouds all morning appeared to weaken as they approached the inn. Will pulled into the driveway and stopped in the same spot as a couple of days before. McKenna parked close behind him. Leaving their cars, they all stared up at the inn. McKenna blew out a breath. "Looks innocent enough, doesn't it? And yet even from here you can sense the menace, that underneath there's something dark."

Will, feeling sweat run down his back despite the cool day, could only nod. "How do you want to proceed?"

"We must be very quiet. Without your ring we have to go in with the belief that the spirit doesn't know you're here. Not yet, anyway."

"I can only hope you're right." Will pointed ahead. "Watch out. Those bushes are dangerous. They may look dead, but they're full of thorns."

"You said they parted for you?"

"When I was being lured in. I have a feeling they won't be so accommodating right now."

"Let's get our gear out. I brought heavy gloves. Those should get us through the worst of it."

Bobby, with Patrick's help, had taken the two canvas bags from the cars. To Will, they looked small, insignificant. Certainly not enough to scare, much less banish, a demon.

Patrick handed out the gloves, and they silently pushed their way through the heavily spiked bushes, each swearing under their breath whenever a barb bit through their pants. The sign with the hawk, which hadn't been moving when they had left their cars, began to sway and creak ominously at their approach.

Seeing Will look up in alarm, McKenna whispered, "Pay no mind. Let's just get to the porch, or whatever is left of it."

"Can you smell it?"

McKenna nodded and turned to Patrick and Bobby who were taking short, shallow gasps. "Keep breathing through your mouths," he whispered. Following Will up the broken stairs, he put his hand up, indicating for them to wait.

Beyond the charred doorway the darkness was complete, the stench of death and decay overbearing. "How can there be no light?" Will whispered, looking up. "There's no roof, no windows. It was like this the other day as well. I didn't even realize it, not until now." He shivered, recalling the blackness before him as he was about to heed the demon's song. *In truth, I was beyond thinking, even seeing.*

"This place should be flooded with daylight," McKenna said. "The entity must be powerful enough to block it. I've never seen or heard of anything like this." He turned to the others. "Follow us in with your torches lit, but stay close to the door."

"I can hardly breathe," Bobby muttered.

"Then wait outside until we need you."

He shook his head. "No. I'm staying with you."

McKenna followed Will inside, the light from their torches raking the walls. The interior, as the man in Stornoway had said, was charred, which only added to the unnatural darkness. Will pointed his light to a scrawl of graffiti on the walls flanking what was left of the fireplace; red and blue paint having dripped down to a couple of aerosol cans either thrown or dropped in haste. In the corners he saw debris, old newspapers torn up along with a couple of smashed bottles and rusty tin cans, perhaps left by some poor soul who tried to use the place as a shelter or kids exploring what they considered a haunted house.

McKenna came up behind him. "Kitchen?"

Will nodded, his flashlight picking the mangled remains of an old iron stove and blackened utensils: a large iron fork, partially melted, lay next to a crushed pot. Feeling a tap on his shoulder, he jumped.

McKenna shone his light around. "No droppings. No evidence of mice or rodents of any kind." He hesitated. "There's an underlying vibration, do you feel it?"

Holding back a tremor, Will glanced back at him. "I don't like this. We have to find the channel."

"Where is it?"

"Probably the bedroom. That's where it trapped us," he said, taking a tentative step towards the corridor, which looked choked with fallen stones. Moving closer, he saw it was still passable. "This way," he whispered.

The rooms in the hallway were, as expected, empty of anything but fallen stones coated with ash. When he reached the last doorway, Will hesitated before taking a step inside. Both he and McKenna shone their lights on the floor, which appeared slightly less scorched than anywhere else in the house. The fireplace had collapsed, and as his light moved over the walls, Will caught his breath at seeing a narrow strip of yellow and pink wallpaper still clinging to singed plaster. Outside the window he could still see daylight, and yet this room, like the others, was as black as night.

Moving dirt and dust aside with his shoe, McKenna whispered, "We'll need the broom. I'll go."

"If the channel is in here, we'll need a hell of a lot more than that," Will said in a low voice. Hearing a noise, they looked back. Patrick and Bobby, looking anxious, were standing in the doorway, holding the canvas bags and the broom.

"We were getting worried," Patrick said.

"So far so good," McKenna said, taking the broom and handing it to Will. "While Will starts sweeping, you and Bobby take the white sage and thyme bundles and begin smudging the main room and kitchen. When you've made three complete circles, place the bundles in the dirt at the corners. Don't skimp. Make sure they're smoking. Then do the same with the candles. I'll do this room."

Kicking aside a heavy coating of ash, Will swept around the spot where he remembered the floor buckling and the vapor coming through. "I don't see it."

As McKenna lit his bundles of sage they felt a tremor. Startled, Will stopped and glanced at him.

"You must be close," he whispered. "Keep going."

Looking down, Will saw several large splinters under an accumulation of dirt and stones, one piece with blackened spots. Kneeling down, he picked it up. *Blood. My blood.* Below it, he could just make out a small crevice. Feeling the hair on the back of his neck rising in fear, he said, "McKenna. Over here."

Still holding the last bundles of sage, McKenna nodded before placing them in the corners. As he began unpacking the canvas bags, Patrick and Bobby reappeared. "We're done."

"Good," McKenna whispered.

"Even with the sage burning it still stinks," Patrick muttered.

Bobby pointed his light at Will, who was still staring down at what appeared to be nothing more than an insignificant fissure. With a shiver, he looked up. "This has to be it. It smells of death."

Motioning for them to stand back, McKenna took a large bag of salt and began to sprinkle it in a ring around the channel. After circling three times, he glanced at Will. "Something is happening. Do you feel it?"

Straightening up, Will held out his hand. "There's a breeze, like the air is eddying around us."

McKenna turned to Bobby. "It's time. Light the candles."

His hand shaking, Bobby lit the candles and moved quickly to place them on the floor in four quarters around the outermost circle. As he set the first one, the floor suddenly shifted and the walls shuddered with a loud crack. Patrick, his eyes wide, pointed wordlessly to an almost imperceptible hole where a thin spiral of fetid white vapor was slowly beginning to rise.

"Get the holy water. Now!" McKenna shouted. Obviously, there was no longer any reason to whisper.

Patrick grabbed two of the vials from the bag and, murmuring a prayer, began sprinkling it just beyond the circle. The shaking increased and the vapor, now a heavy white mist, began filling the room. The earth beneath their feet vibrated as a deep thrumming sound filled the space and echoed off the walls. Moving quickly,

McKenna took a length of rope from one of the bags and motioned for them to form a circle. As they joined hands, McKenna looked at Will, who began the incantation:

> *"Our Father who art in heaven, hallowed be thy name. Thy kingdom come, thy will be done on earth as it is in heaven. Give us this day our daily bread, and forgive us our trespasses, as we forgive those who trespass against us, and lead us not into temptation, but deliver us from evil."*

With a brief pause, they tightened their grasp before speaking again.

> *"Yea, though I walk through the valley of the shadow of death, I will fear no evil: for thou art with me: thy rod and staff they comfort me."*

As they repeated it twice more the thrumming escalated to a deeper drone, loosening stones that fell with dusty thuds from the walls.

This time it was McKenna who, in a loud, authoritative voice, began a chant of his own, with phrases he had taken from Dante's *Inferno*:

> *"Hope not ever to see Heaven. We negate your powers, the powers of darkness and the forces of evil. In this we banish you to the endless chasm of eternity; beyond fire and into ice."*

As he repeated it three times, the ground convulsed and began to split open, almost knocking them off their feet. Breaking the circle, McKenna grabbed quickly for the rope. Dousing it with oil, he put a match to it as though lighting a wick. Trembling in fear, but still rasping out prayers, they stared in disbelief as a more viscous vapor rose from the pit and appeared to form a shape: a translucent face with colorless eyes that revolved as though in slow motion and focused its malevolent stare directly on Will.

McKenna shouted, "Will," and handed him the smoking rope.

Trying to avoid staring at the writhing cloud in front of him, Will stepped forward and, holding his breath, lowered the rope into the pit. Moving back, he felt Patrick and McKenna reach for his hands, now cold with clammy sweat. As they resumed their incantations the image slowly began to disintegrate, and with an ear-split-ting shriek of rage that reverberated off the crumbling walls, it was sucked back into the fiery hole.

Through the dissipating mist Will looked up, seeing the sky above had turned a deep indigo edged with orange. Feeling the earth again shake violently and the already fractured walls begin-ning to collapse, he shouted, "Break the circle. Everyone out. Now."

Patrick and Bobby required no further urging and ran through the falling stones, their hands covering their heads. Will started out but looked back at McKenna, who had moved within the circle and was emptying a bag of black salt into the smoking hole. Despite the salt, they both watched in disbelief as a plume of fire suddenly erupted, singeing the earth just inches from McKenna's feet and opening another fissure that began vomiting out a heavy residue of slimy muck, stinking of decay and permeated with hundreds, even thousands, of dark-blue sapphires.

Seeing McKenna staring as though in a trance, Will shouted, "Back away. Don't touch them! They will kill you!" When he didn't move, Will grabbed his arm, pulling him away from the slimy ooze and through the doorway, barely clearing it before two large stones fell, pinning McKenna's leg.

Looking up in pain, he rasped, "Go, Will."

"No," he said, trying to move stones that seemed far heavier than they should have been. Finally heaving them aside, he could see McKenna's left ankle was shattered and bleeding. Half-lifting and half-dragging him, he managed to get through the crumbling hallway.

Seeing them, Patrick and Bobby ran in from the porch, help-ing Will carry McKenna out just as the walls imploded and with a screech of unearthly fury, a column of fire shot up as if to split the sky.

With ash falling around them, they moved as quickly as they could down the path through the rose bushes, which had already wilted and appeared to be dying. Ignoring the frenzied screams behind them, they managed to get McKenna into the front seat of Will's car. The last thing he said before he passed out was, "We did it, Will. We did it."

Looking back, Will saw Bobby, again clutching his rosary beads, suddenly sprint around the car and begin to retch. Patrick, not looking too well himself, went to help him. Realizing they were all covered with slimy black soot, Will grabbed a towel from the back seat and wiped his face just as Patrick reappeared and pointed to the street.

"We have visitors."

Two cars had stopped just beyond the driveway; the occupants gaping in open-mouthed horror at the scene before them. Grateful to see local people, Will ran down to ask how to get to the nearest hospital. One of the men, appearing confused, asked what had happened and why they were there.

Having neither the time nor the inclination to give a forthright answer, Will said he and his friends had simply gone up to look at the ruins when the ground unexpectedly shook. "That's when we saw the flames. Look, my friend, ah, tripped, and I think he broke his leg. Can you tell me where the nearest hospital would be?"

The man's wife looked dazed. "No one's gone near that place in a hundred years. You should have stayed away."

Trying to maintain his patience, he said, "Yes, ma'am. Now, please tell me how to get to the hospital."

A tall, stocky man carrying a black bag walked over from another car. "I'm a physician. Has someone been hurt?"

"Yes. Our friend. He's in my car."

With a brief, albeit curious glance at Bobby and Patrick, who were frantically trying to rub black ash off their faces, he looked inside and shook his head. Taking out some cotton strips, he wrapped McKenna's leg to make a tourniquet. "This man requires immediate medical attention. He has quite a few abrasions, and his ankle is broken."

Stepping away, he glanced at Will. "I have no idea what's going on here, but whatever it is, there's no time to explain right now. Follow me. The hospital is ten minutes away."

It was only when Will started his car that he realized the day had turned to dusk. He was sure they had gone to the inn just after two, so how, he questioned, had it suddenly become night? *Just how long were we really in there?*

Chapter 12

Despite a long night heavily laced with far too much booze, Will was unable to sleep. The few times he did doze, he woke up in a cold sweat, the image of dead eyes staring at him and screams of fury penetrating his brain with renewed terror. It was close to dawn when he gave up and walked to the window. There wasn't much to see; the harbor was shrouded in a thick fog.

Returning to bed, he still hoped for sleep but found himself continually questioning if they had, indeed, succeeded in either killing the entity or had at least sent it off to the furthermost level of hell. He knew he would never rest until he returned to the inn, or whatever was left of it, one more time, if only to make sure it was gone. *And yet that was just the structure. More important is what lies beneath. How can I ever truly know?*

The truth was, he couldn't. If, however, they had managed to achieve their goal, then his life and Cia's should be now freed of threat, at least from the spirit realm. In that regard, a weight would be lifted from his mind and all would be possible, not only within the present, but in whatever the future would hold for them in this life and beyond.

His thoughts shifted to McKenna and the doctor who had mysteriously shown up at just the right moment. After they brought McKenna to the hospital, and while his ankle was being assessed by a resident physician, he had looked for the doctor, wanting to thank him. He wondered why the man would just disappear or, as unlikely as it seemed, if he was just another apparition. If so, he was one ghost he'd like to thank.

Silent and deep in their own thoughts, the three of them had paced anxiously in the waiting room until the resident returned, informing them that he wanted to keep McKenna overnight. He suggested they take him to Inverness or even Edinburgh as soon as the next day for further evaluation. When Will asked to see him, the doctor shook his head. "He was mumbling unintelligibly about what sounded like vapors and salt. Is he, by any chance, a chef?"

While Patrick and Bobby glanced at one another, Will, holding back a laugh, answered straight faced, "Ah, perhaps at one time."

The resident nodded. "Well, we've just given him a sedative." After a moment of hesitation, he asked, "By the way. How did he break his ankle?"

Will repeated essentially what he'd told the first doctor about going to look at an old house that, without warning, began to crumble around them.

Not looking entirely convinced, he nodded. "That must be the fire everyone's talking about. It's good that doctor happened by."

"I wanted to thank him. Is he still here?"

He shook his head. "I was looking for him as well. To tell you the truth, I don't think I've ever seen him before."

It was enough, and Will backed away. "Thank you, doctor. We'll see you in the morning."

It had been full dark by the time they returned to the hotel, and Will went immediately to the bar where he asked for an entire bottle of single malt. It wasn't until each of them had drained their third or fourth shots that they could even begin to address the afternoon.

Holding up his glass, Will said, "To McKenna, may he heal quickly. And to us. May we never speak of this day again."

Patrick stared back at him. "You must be bloody kidding. How does one forget such a thing?"

"It will fade. I promise you."

Looking doubtful, Bobby slurred, "I don't know. I keep seeing those weird eyes. They were looking at you, Will. Do you know why?"

Pouring three more generous shots, he shook his head. "How can I? How can any of us understand . . ."

He was cut off by three boisterous men entering from the lobby. Taking drinks from the bar, the first one raised his glass. "Here's to whatever caused that bloody house to finally give up the ghost, as it were."

304

The other two guffawed, one touching the first man's glass. "By the time the fire brigade got there, the whole place had collapsed. Can't say I'm sorry, but I wonder how it happened."

"Who gives a damn?" the third one said, making the sign of the cross. "Too much dicey stuff went on up there for way too long. Folks hearing screams and such in the night. Good riddance to it. Do ya think there'll be an investigation?"

The first one shook his head. "Nah. Why bother? Still, I won't let my kids go near it."

Realizing they weren't alone, all three glanced at Will's table. "Didya hear about the excitement today? Out near Callanish?"

Patrick glanced at Will, who answered. "Sounds like a bad fire."

One of the men held up his drink. "Couldn't be bad enough."

The next morning, haggard from lack of sleep, not to mention too much booze, they drove to the clinic where another resident explained that their friend would likely need surgery before his leg could be properly set. By the time a groggy McKenna was wheeled out from the hospital, it had been decided that Patrick and Bobby would drive him directly to the hospital in Edinburgh.

With the help of a nurse, they were able to get him into Patrick's car. When he was settled somewhat comfortably in the back seat with his leg propped up on a pillow, he grasped Will's hand. "You're not coming with us?"

"No. I need to stay here. At least another day. I want to make sure it's really finished."

"Then I should stay as well."

"That's not possible. Your ankle needs surgery. I'll only stay one night, two at the most and see you in Edinburgh. You're in good hands with Patrick and Bobby."

"Don't tell me you're going back there."

"I have no choice."

"Then please be cautious. There could still be activity around whatever is left."

"I promise I will."

As Patrick was about to close the door, McKenna held up his hand. "Why did you stop me from touching the stones that were gushing from the pit?"

305

"To be honest, it was more instinct than conscious thought. The place was infused with evil. That entity must have hoarded those sapphires for centuries and they felt lethal to me. It took three showers before I could get the stench and slime off."

McKenna nodded. "I know. The nurses kept asking why I was covered in ash and what that awful smell was. They finally sponged me off. I'm curious if you'll see any sapphires in what's left of the place."

"I hope not. I wouldn't like to think of kids picking them out of the rubble. As you said, we did it. It's over, and I owe you my life."

Despite his pain, McKenna's eyes flashed with anticipation. "It was remarkable, wasn't it?" He rubbed his hands together. "I can't wait to get started on writing this up."

After several somewhat awkward hugs, slaps of the back and expressions of gratitude, Will watched them drive off. About to return to his car, he became aware of movement to his right. It was the craggy-faced man with the faded tam. Not entirely surprised, he waited, curious to hear what the man might have to say.

"I take it you've heard about our wee bit of excitement yesterday?"

As Will nodded, he lit a cigarette. "That inn, 'twas an, ah, interesting place. Townsfolk were scared of it, and rightfully so. Would ya, by any chance, know how it could'a happened?"

"Why are you asking me?"

"Cuz I know ya, sir. You've been here before. No' just last fall, but long ago."

Will felt an all too familiar shudder. "Before? When?"

The man shook his head. "Many times, sir. And once or twice with yer bonnie lady as well. Course, ya didn't look the same but we, uh, I knew it was you. This time you've made yer mark. We don't expect to be seeing ya again."

"My mark?"

The man shook his head. "Don' think I need to tell ya any more. What ya came here for is finally, how can I say, accomplished." He made a point of glancing up at the sky. "Fog's clearing, sir. It's midsummer's eve, a good day to stop by Mangersta. Wouldn't miss the sunset, if I was you."

"Why is that?"

"Well, sir, as I told ya, you'll find it very special. Truth is, it's what ya came for." After crushing out his cigarette he looked back at Will, his eyes luminous in a ray of sunlight. "And then I suggest ya leave this place. There's nothing more for ya here. We don't expect to be seeing ya again, either in this life or the next." Before Will could again ask who "we" were, the man turned on his heel and walked across the road where he disappeared in a whorl of shimmering dust.

Chapter 13

Sarah looked up from her typewriter.

"Hi, Coralie. Is there something you need?"

"I just wanted to ask if you and Cia would like to go out for lunch."

"Is today something special?"

"Well. How about that it's August first and summer is half over. We keep saying we'll go out, so why not today? It's really nice. Not too hot."

Sarah glanced at Cia, who looked up from marking up a manuscript. "Sure. Why not? I can finish this later."

Coralie hesitated. "Good. I have a suggestion. Cia, why don't we do your Tarot card reading now, before we go out?"

She shrugged. "All right. Since we never seem to get around to it, I guess today is as good as any. How long will it take?"

Coralie looked a little put out. "About half an hour."

"Where?"

"My office."

Cia, avoiding looking at Sarah, who was rolling her eyes, nodded. "Just give me a minute."

Sarah watched Coralie leave. "Maybe this isn't such a great idea, Cia. Who knows what she'll come up with? She's still nervous as a cat around Will."

"It'll be all right. They're just cards, aren't they?'

She was halfway to Coralie's office when she picked up the distinct aroma of incense. She was sure Coralie knew Sid was out. Otherwise he'd be in her office in a flash, yelling at her to get rid of it. In truth, Cia didn't particularly like the stuff either, but this was sandalwood and not entirely unpleasant. At the doorway, she picked up another scent, almost like grass. She asked what it was.

Coralie held up what appeared to be a small bundle of dried grey leaves tightly tied with rope. "Sage. I use it to clear the air of negative energy."

Sage? Negative energy? Cia sighed. "What do we do now?"

"Have a seat in front of my desk." Coralie snapped off the overhead lights, leaving only the glow from a lamp on her desk, which she then covered with a sheer pink scarf. Cia looked doubtful, hoping the scarf wouldn't catch fire.

After carefully opening a metal box decorated with vines and odd, intertwined figures, Coralie handed the cards to Cia. "I'd like you to shuffle them."

"They're large."

"Just do the best you can."

When she finished, she started to hand the cards back, but Coralie shook her head. "Break them into three piles, face down, and put them on the desk. Then place one pile on top of the other. In any order you want."

Cia stacked the cards, and Coralie reached out her hands, palms up. "Put your hands on mine."

As soon as Cia's hands touched hers, Coralie closed her eyes and began to whisper an unintelligible chant. When she finished, she asked her guides to help her understand the cards.

Cia watched, wondering why she wasn't feeling a bit weirded out by all this. After what she'd already experienced with Will, not to mention the ghost, she realized not much could faze her any more. Certainly not guides or, for that matter, Tarot cards.

Taking a deep breath, Coralie began laying out the cards, making a rectangle of four on a side. After completing it, she sat still and silent, her eyes moving over the colorful images in front of her.

"The top row represents you, Cia," she said in a soft voice. "It shows you are intelligent, and yet you tend to hold on to things, especially the past." She pointed to the Seven of Swords and the King of Pentacles. "These show deception, betrayal. But here, The Fool indicates change or possibly a new beginning. Now may be the time for you to put something from the past behind you. Try to see the whole picture, not rush into things. There will be new opportunity, but you must choose carefully."

"Do you think the past could be Ian?"

"Actually, it could." She looked down at the cards. "This, on top—the Queen of Wands—is you, and this—the Knight of Wands, on the bottom right—represents Will. These indicate a good match. They show that you are confident, enthusiastic and optimistic. You believe in yourself, but you can also be fiery. His card shows creativity and energy. He is not only sexual and seductive, he can also be daring and impulsive. If I didn't know better, I would say to beware of him. But I no longer think that is the situation here."

"What do you mean, 'no longer'?"

"As I told you, the first time I saw him I felt a sense of recognition. It wasn't his physical being as much as his spirit."

"I know the feeling." *More than those cards know.*

"He is very charismatic, isn't he?"

Changing the subject, Cia pointed to the Queen of Cups next to the Knight of Wands.

"What do the Cups represent?"

"Here they show love and energy. The Cups and Wands flow into one another, indicating that he is moving into an emotional, loving partnership. This, the Queen of Pentacles, represents serenity and nurturing. Along with the Queen of Cups, these are two energies that suggest that some sort magic has occurred." She stopped and looked over the cards. "I'm not clear on this. Do you understand what I'm talking about?"

Cia nodded. "I do."

Coralie waited a few seconds. Realizing no further explanation was forthcoming, she pointed to another card. "The Priestess is spiritual, intuitive. It indicates a strong sexual aspect."

Cia smiled, wondering if she was expected to elaborate.

With a sigh, Coralie turned back to the cards. "Ah," she murmured with a look of satisfaction. "He seems to be tuned in to his guides. That's rare."

Cia stared at her. This was becoming a bit more serious than she'd anticipated. She pointed to the Devil card. "What does this mean? It looks evil."

Coralie picked it up. Turning it back and forth, she said, "This card, the Devil, is not what you may think. It deals with illusion and looking beyond superficial appearances. There's also a shadow side to it. It's possible that sometime in the past Will was possessed or, more likely, obsessed with something. It could have been self-doubt or guilt that he tried but was unable to suppress. He may have become despairing, even self-destructive at some point. He's had to make difficult decisions." She stopped and looked over the cards. "Look. Here's the Fool. That may have given him the motivation to put the past behind him; to begin something new in his life."

Cia took a breath, thinking of the story of Carolyn's death and the aftermath when, overcome with guilt, Will had, indeed, hidden himself away, unable to work.

"When is his birthday?"

"Early February."

"He's an Aquarius. I'll bet anything his moon is in Scorpio."

"I wouldn't know. What does that mean?"

"It means he prefers not to accept the status quo. He does what he wants, as opposed to what others want for him or think he should do."

Like going back to Scotland.

Coralie put out two more cards. "The Hanged Man reinforces what I said about stopping to think about whatever you may be planning. It's not a good time to rush into something permanent. You might want to look at things from a different viewpoint."

"Are you saying I shouldn't be thinking about marriage?"

"Oh. I didn't know you were," she said, sounding flustered. "What I'm telling you is what the cards are saying right now. By autumn it can change." She quickly laid out four more. "The Ace of Wands. This is good. You are in the hand of God, and your relationship should blossom. But look at the moon on the card. It indicates that you may come to a crossroads, which refers back to the Hanged Man and thinking in a different direction." Looking perplexed, she shook her head. "And yet I'm not sure. There's not enough information here. Sometimes it's not as clear as we'd like."

Cia pointed to a card depicting a man with swords piercing his back. "What is that? It looks ominous."

After a brief hesitation, Coralie said, "The Ten of Swords. It means a decision will be made. There will be an ending to one path, one way of life, and another will begin. And yet the next card, the Five of Wands again indicates choices and opportunity."

"So tell me, what does all this mean?"

"Essentially that you and Will are basically suited to one another. You complement him, and he you. While there are things you should put behind you, you should also leave yourself open. This isn't the moment to rush into anything." She turned two more cards. "The Ace of Pentacles is interesting. It signifies abundance, seeing your efforts flourish. And this, the Six of Pentacles, indicates you will be receiving something of value. Has Will given you anything recently? A gift?"

"Not in the sense of jewelry or a ring." She held out her wrist. "He gave me this bracelet, but that was a while ago. Last week he surprised me with some drawings from his show, including two small portraits he had done of me. I guess those would be considered a gift."

She nodded before again peering at the cards. "While all this appears positive for you, it still suggests you should wait; not have too much expectation. I don't think you should jump into marriage, if that is what you are considering. Listen to the cards; perhaps give yourself a little more time."

With a stab of apprehension, Cia pointed to the Ten of Swords. "Tell me again about this card."

"As I said, it signals abrupt change. A decision will be made. It's very black and white. There is no grey area."

"What does that mean? What will happen?"

Coralie shook her head. "I wish I could tell you, but it's unknown. And yet the highest good will come of it." As she laid down the last card, the Five of Swords, she nodded. "At the end of the day you will come to terms with your spiritual gifts and what the future holds."

Looking up, she signaled the reading was over. "Cia, please understand the cards show what is influencing your life right now, not the future. And yet what is occurring now does affect that future. I hope this reading will help you make clearer decisions and gain some perspective about what is currently happening in your life."

"All right, Coralie. But exactly what is it that I should be thinking about? I'm confused."

"It appears there will be change in your life. Most likely that is Will. It's obvious you are a pair. The Queen and the Knight tell us that. And yet they indicate that you should proceed slowly and with care. Take time to know, to understand one another. And what has existed before, you must put behind you."

"I already have. Can I ask you one more thing?"

"Of course."

She pointed to a card on the bottom left corner. "You never said anything about this card. What is it?"

"The Knight of Swords. I didn't mention it because I'm not sure what to make of it here. Is there someone else in your life?"

Cia shook her head. "No. The cards must be wrong."

"Not necessarily. It could be someone you met a while ago. Someone with a keen intellect, who can make sense of confusion. He is honest and expects it of others."

She grinned. "Sid?"

Coralie frowned. "I doubt it."

"Well. Thank you, Coralie," Cia said, getting up. "Shall we go to lunch?"

"You go ahead. I'll be right down."

Coralie waited until Cia left before looking at the cards again. She was glad Cia hadn't noticed the card depicting a woman holding her head in anguish. The Nine of Swords was only one card away from the Ten of Swords; a card that, as she had told Cia, portrayed something final and irrevocable. What worried her was the Nine was far too close in that it represented not only grief, but also the abandonment of joy. Despite that it was also next to one of the last cards she had laid out, the peaceful and nurturing Ten of Cups, she was afraid that card alone would not be powerful enough to overcome the other two Sword cards.

Putting her hands to her face, she wished she hadn't insisted on the reading. Her early concerns about Will had softened to admiration, particularly after seeing him at the gallery. While it was true there were powerful spirits surrounding him, she considered him a good, decent man. Despite that the last cards had shaken her, she had been honest in telling Cia she was unable to predict the future. And yet, as she gently laid the cards back in their box, she questioned whether she should have spoken of her fears.

Sarah was on the phone when Cia returned. Saying she'd call back, she hung up quickly. "So? What did our resident psychic have to say? Any diamonds in your future?"

Cia sat down and shook her head. "It was all very confusing. The nice part was that she saw both Will and me in the cards. Apparently, we go together in temperament and love and whatever. I don't need cards to tell me that. What's worrying is that Coralie kept reit-erating that I shouldn't jump into anything too quickly, such as mar-riage." She shrugged. "She also said Tarot readings tell you what is happening now, not so much about the future. They don't give you any real answers. At least those cards didn't."

"Did you have any questions for her?"

"Actually, no. If you recall, this was her idea. Although she did say she now has a less scary view of Will."

Sarah laughed. "Don't we all."

Chapter 14

A car went by, throwing up a cloud of dust and rousing Will, who was still fixated on the empty space across the road. Although he no longer sensed any sort of presence, he still would have liked to have understood who "we" were. And yet, he could likely surmise the answer. While there was no question that he had to leave this place, a suggestion — or, more likely, a command — that echoed the old man at the pub, he still wondered why this ghost had again told him to stop by Mangersta.

He left the parking lot feeling nothing more than a vague sense of apprehension. As he approached the turn off for the inn, he passed a long line of parked vehicles and groups of local residents pointing, exclaiming, and, no doubt, conjecturing about whatever it was that finally caused the haunted ruin to catch fire and implode with such force.

Taking a breath, he left the car and walked to the pitted driveway. A few people turned to glance at him, and one man called out, "Place burned down yesterday."

"So I heard," he said, surprised there was no trace of odor or, for that matter, smoke.

The man shouted again, "Best not to go any further, sir. Might be dangerous."

"It's all right," he said, reaching down to pick up what appeared to be blackened ash. When his hand met the surface, he drew back in surprise. It wasn't ash that he touched but a hard, granular surface. When he tried, to no avail, to chip some off, he realized the stones, salt, the muck from the channel, and even the sapphires had somehow liquified and then congealed, bonding together to blanket the entire hill in an impenetrable black carapace.

A burst of laughter shattered his reverie, and he stood up just as two boys raced by yelling to one another while attempting to clamber up the slippery shell. Hearing the same man, likely their father, shout at them to come back, he began circling the mass until large stones and ash-strewn underbrush blocked further passage. With a final glance up to where the inn had stood, his instincts told him the place had been purified; that whatever unearthly spirits had occupied the hill would no longer haunt it. Murmuring a brief prayer of thanks, he started back to his car, unaware that one of the boys had run to his father, excitedly saying that he'd found a tiny hole, and when he poked at it a thin spiral of acrid smoke had suddenly appeared.

Before going to have a look, the boy's father glanced back in the direction of Will's car, seeing only an empty space.

In no rush, Will stopped at yet another old pub for lunch and a couple of beers. By the time he reached Mangersta, it was late afternoon. Since there were still a few hours before the sun would set, his intention was to have a brief look at the stacks of chiseled rocks that jutted from the roiling sea, take a few photos and then leave. If he missed the sunset, so be it. Maybe he could even return to Stornoway in time for the last ferry to the mainland.

Trying for a good vantage point, he walked out on a rocky ledge about five meters above thundering waves that threw crystalline veils of sea spray over the jagged formations below. Although he'd been told this was a popular spot, he was surprised to see no tourists.

Looking down at the thrashing sea, he wished he could translate the spectacular drama of it into a painting. And yet he believed that some scenes were meant to be purely visual, to be seen and recalled only in the mind's eye, not for rendering in pigment. Even Turner's moody storms couldn't compare to the majestic violence of these waters.

Finding a flat, grassy surface, he sat down, snapped a few photos, and let his mind drift. After what he had seen at the remains of the inn, he was now convinced the demon that had manifested the illusions was gone. While he was relieved to be free of it, that meant he would still leave with unanswered questions, not only about his, and Cia's, connection to Callanish, but the sapphires as well. Maybe the time had come to acknowledge there were, in truth, no answers.

As images of Cia drifted across his mind, he couldn't wait to go back to her. He'd never considered marriage before, the circumstances of his life necessarily precluding the possibility. Even if what McKenna had said about their past lives was true, it was this life that counted. They would have each other to love and cherish; and that was all that mattered to him.

Mesmerized by the incessant ebb and flow of waves crashing against the rocky outcroppings, Will was unaware his surroundings had begun to blur and soften, the churning sea gradually dissolving into a grassy field that appeared through a curtain of drifting mist. As it cleared, he recognized the place from his dream; it was where he had seen the fox. In the distance, the grove of birch trees shone white, their emerald leaves fluttering in a gentle breeze. Nothing happened for a few seconds, minutes, even hours. Time floated into twilight. Slowly becoming aware of flickering shadows, he began to glimpse what appeared to be young men and women moving rapidly through the trees. They were small and sinewy, many with what looked like circular or striped markings on their bodies. Instinctively, he knew they weren't Picts, nor were they Druids; this gathering was of an earlier, far more primitive generation of humans who predated both groups by centuries, maybe tens of centuries. As the scene came into focus, Will could see the young men, many carrying flaming torches, had heavy brows with dark, knotted hair and scraggly beards. The females, mostly young girls with flowers and feathers entwined into wild, windswept hair, wore thin layers of a flowing transparent fabric that looked to be a finely spun wool. The scene again became hazy before rematerializing in another, larger field where huge white stones glowed in the last rays of the sun. Some were vertical, others lying prone, as if waiting to be raised to an upright position. The same young people now shuffled along a well-trod path through the partially completed column of monoliths leading to more stones roughly configured in a circle.

Abruptly, all movement ceased as they turned to face the horizon where the sun joined the sea in an eruption of red fire. Chanting in alternately shrill and guttural tones, they bowed before extending their arms above their heads. As the last waning rays cast long shadows on the center monolith, the girls joined hands. Forming a circle, they began weaving in and out of the vertical stones. Moving faster, they threw their heads back in abandonment and, with high-pitched cries, worked themselves into a frenzy as their shifts swirled around them.

Outside the circle, the young men, naked except for colorful strips of cloth tied around their waists and upper arms, observed, their dark eyes flashing in the light from the torches. As the sun sank into the darkening sea, a bloated orange moon began to rise. Those who still carried torches shoved them into the soft earth and began running in a circle counter to the entranced girls. As the dancing accelerated, the young men stepped toward the girls, and with shouts of exaltation, began carrying them off. Whether this was a dream or hallucination, Will knew he was witnessing some sort of primordial mid-summer fertility ritual. He watched as one young man reached for a pretty, dark haired girl of no more than fourteen or fifteen and focused on them. The young man had the same sort of strips of cloth wrapped around his arms and waist as the others, although Will could make out a slight difference in the pattern. The girl he chose had matching bits of cloth wound around one ankle and braided into her hair.

When the boy embraced her, she appeared to awaken from a trance and, with a seductive giggle, ran away toward a stand of trees. Taken aback, the young man stared, an expression of surprise evident on his face. Chasing after her, he found her hiding in a copse of trees and surrounded by hundreds of flickering insects. Waving them away, he grabbed her hand and pulled her back to the now deserted stone circle. With a shake of her head, she resisted, glancing back to the lights in the trees. Will saw their shadows cross the stones as the boy led the girl, now trembling in fear, to the center where the soil appeared to be recently disturbed. There he spoke to her, caressing her face and soothing her in a quiet voice. Will was surprised he could hear him, but whatever he said was a language he didn't understand — one only spoken and never written — a language lost to the ages.

Reassured, the girl stopped struggling. Moving closer, she watched with curiosity as he withdrew something from the pouch at his waist. Taking her hand, he placed a handful of pebbles in her palm. She stared, enthralled, as he closed her fingers around them. After a few seconds, she opened her hand and, with a squeal of delight, threw the pebbles into the air where they flashed blue and white fire. Will watched in disbelief as the stones fell to the ground, still sparking with an unearthly glow.

Her eyes closed, the girl stood in acquiescence as the young man removed her shift and lowered her down in front of the moonlit monolith. For a brief moment, they knelt face to face until, with a sigh, she lay back. With a shock of recognition, Will knew without a doubt what he was seeing was identical to what had happened between him and Cia.

Becoming aware of shadows moving along the stones, he saw the young people had returned to form a circle around the pair. Hearing their incantations, a low singsong that sounded all too similar to the voices, the young man moved over the girl who, beguiled by the chanting, arched her back in desire. As she opened her arms to receive her lover, her face turned toward the cliff. Across the eons, her dark eyes met Will's and he heard her whisper: "All your days follow from here."

Before Will could grasp her meaning, the image blurred again, this time to a whitish fog where amorphous shapes moved as though in slow motion through an indistinct distance. As the image came into a sharper focus, Will saw several boys running past what appeared to be the Callanish stones. And yet this had to be many centuries later; the circle was not only complete but overgrown with weeds and strewn with debris. Ignoring it, the boys ran quickly, as if in a race through heavy woods, obviously far later growth. Reaching a hill covered in rocky burial cairns, they stopped abruptly, several nervously clutching coarsely worked metal amulets hanging from leather strings around their necks. In each, Will could plainly see a glittering blue stone at the center. Suddenly, the scene began to speed up as though fast-forwarding to brief, staccato images that looked like an old, scratchy silent film—except this film wasn't silent. Underlying it were whispers of conversation, a little of which Will was able to understand. He watched as one of the boys seemed to hesitate and then broke away from the others, who shouted to come back . . . the same boy running up the hill, laughing and dancing, beckoning to his friends . . . unaware of a swirl of vapor rising behind him ... not until skeletal fingers wrapped around his neck and, in one motion, tore off his amulet . . . the boy falling as the others fled, shrieking in terror . . . except for one who chanced a run up the mound to pull his bleeding friend away from danger, a foul mist chasing them as far as the woods beyond.

The scene shifting again . . . to a grassy field bathed in sunlight . . . a boy and girl clad in loose tunics tied at the waist chasing sheep away from a steep cliff that plunged into a shimmering blue green sea . . . then to a bustling marketplace where an old man placed rings with a glittering blue stone in each of their hands. The man drifting away . . . the boy and girl embracing, murmuring promises of love everlasting. The marketplace dissolving to a sandy pathway where several important-looking men in kilt-like garments rushed past swaying palm trees towards a long boat . . . one, who looked to be the leader, carrying what appeared to be long rolls of papyrus. In the distance, several pyramids grew from the desert. . .

As one dizzying scene morphed in rapid succession through light and dark, he briefly glimpsed villages, cities, and seas rising and falling until it slowed to naked men tattooed in blue symbols thrashing through woods, brandishing sticks and hurling rocks while screaming at the top of their lungs as they chased terrified Roman soldiers across a rocky escarpment. Then Callanish again, and the burial mound where a man, also marked with tattoos and holding two rings, stood next to a woman cowering in fear . . .

The scene spun to dark, murky skies: men in rough clothing tilling the soil below a crenellated castle as color-draped war horses carrying knights bearing the cross of the Crusades galloped by . . . then light again, to men and women gathering in what appeared to be the courtyard of a castle . . . the colors of Mary of Scots flying from a tower . . . a seductive man in a feathered hat leading a well-dressed lady to the corner of a garden as an old man holding a roll of red velvet observed . . . and then water and a ship, a young girl in front of a farmhouse . . . the man before her pointing . . . to what . . . To a ring on his finger and taking her hand while promising her another. A chaste kiss, a declaration of eternal love . . . another ship, not to London as promised but to Glasgow and then the Outer Hebrides . . . the man never seen again. The images speeding forward to a dense forest rising then receding to a windswept plain of low grasses and gorse . . . the scene slowing to a smiling young couple riding ponies among the Callanish stones, newly unearthed from their shrouds of peat and glowing in autumn light . . . the same couple entering a newly constructed inn built on a hill not far from the stone circle . . . greeted by a woman in a blue dress with a white apron . . .

The image faded, dissolving into the mist and thunder of the raging sea. Will blinked, suddenly aware of an enormous grey hawk squawking on the rock next to him. He flinched as it flew off, its huge, grey wings sending a gust of cold air against his face.

Stumbling to his feet, he tried to make sense of what had just happened. Had he really been suspended in a dream state between two realities—one, the long-forgotten past, and the other, today, the eve of Lughnasa in August of the year 1975?

Unable to move, he stared beyond the rocks until the last glimmer of twilight disappeared into the dark, ancient sea.

Chapter 15

Awakening to bright sunlight falling across his face, Will opened his eyes to bland, white walls hung with pictures of fishing boats floating on placid seas. Unsure of the time or where he was, he sat up, awareness slowly dawning that he was in his room at the hotel in Stornoway, still wearing the same clothes from the day before, although he did register that he'd at least had the foresight to hang his jacket over a chair.

With a quick glance out the window, he saw the first ferry of the morning chug into the port. Although the events of the night before were beginning to penetrate his foggy brain, there was no time to think—not yet. He had to get moving; his intention was to make it to Edinburgh by that afternoon, which meant he had to catch the next ferry out. Throwing his clothes in his suitcase, he checked out and ran for his car, grateful the craggy-faced ghost in the faded tam was nowhere to be seen.

By the time he stopped in Ullapool for breakfast, the night before had already taken on the quality of a distant memory. While scenes of the dreamlike kaleidoscope continued to linger, it was the image of the girl throwing the sapphires in the air and the look in her eyes as she bestowed her message, a message that would remain with him forever. He desperately wanted to talk with Cia, but in New York it wasn't yet dawn.

Back on the road, he encountered little traffic and the sky remained unusually clear. Forcing himself to focus on driving, he put off any thoughts about how he would describe to McKenna what he'd imagined, or in truth, had seen.

On the way into Inverness, he drove along the lake, unable to stop himself from an occasional glance. Although he had driven this same road a hundred times before, there was still no way he, or anyone else, could pass the mysterious lake without the unlikely expectation that the fabled monster would magically appear. He remembered his early years growing up not far from this place; happy mornings in the small, rural school, and afternoons chasing dogs and sheep across the moors. Seeing him trying to draw what he called his favorite sheep, his father had brought him a pad of paper and colored pencils. It had been a joyful time.

He stopped at a petrol station and, seeing a phone booth, rang Patrick who told him McKenna was still in the hospital but anxiously awaiting his arrival.

"Why did you stay the extra day, Will? Did something happen after we left?"

"In a way. But it's far too difficult to explain in a phone call. In fact, I think it will be difficult to explain in person as well. I can only tell you it was very strange. But then, everything on that island is."

Patrick sniggered. "Not for everyone, Will. Probably only for you. It sounds like you found your answers."

Will hesitated. "I believe I did. Right now, I'm on my way to see McKenna. I'll stop by tomorrow on the way back to London."

"Why don't you stay? You sound tired. Take a load off for one night."

"I need to get back."

"Actually, I'm afraid you do. The BBC guys called again. They seem to think you're very elusive. Apparently, the screen test you did with them came out well, and they're anxious to start filming in a couple of weeks. Nevertheless, I think you should stay tomorrow. It's a long drive, and I want to hear what more could possibly have occurred up there."

"I wish I could, Patrick. Even without the BBC I'm swamped with work. I have a portrait sitting next week and then I have to get ready for New York." He laughed. "Be patient. We'll have plenty of time to talk about the mysteries of Callanish."

"Have you spoken to Cia?"

"It was impossible to call from Stornoway. The phones were from the dark ages." He paused, amused at his reference. "I'll call her when I get to Edinburgh. It's still too early in New York."

"Think about staying tomorrow night."

"Thanks, Patrick. I'll let you know."

By the time he arrived at the hospital in Edinburgh, it was early evening. He found McKenna in his room with a heavy cast on his leg, grumbling to a nurse.

Shooing her away, he embraced Will. "Thank God you're here. I was worried. Are you all right? Did anything else happen?"

"Quite a bit. But first, how are you doing?"

"Well enough to leave this place. If you can get me out of here tonight, we'll have plenty of time to talk tomorrow."

"Not a problem. Let me go find the nurse."

Despite the initial difficulty of getting McKenna into his car, Will drove him home and helped him into his old, but elegant townhouse on a narrow street not far from his office in St. Andrews. They were met at the door by an attractive, middle-aged woman who hugged McKenna before thanking Will. Since McKenna had never mentioned a woman in his life, Will was surprised, not knowing if she was his housekeeper or something more. More seemed likely from the look of it.

After agreeing to meet the next morning, Will left to go to his hotel where he immediately rang Cia.

"Thank God, Will. I was terribly worried. Are you all right? Where are you?"

"Calm down, Cia. I'm at a hotel in St. Andrews. I only left Stornoway this morning. It was too early to call. Not to worry, my love, I'm fine, and I have quite a story to tell you."

"Can you tell me some of it?"

That was something he had been mulling over since leaving the island. He was afraid if he told her even a small part of it she would become anxious, which was the last thing he wanted. "Not right now. I'm tired and it's far too complicated. Anyway, I want to be able to hold you in my arms and see your face when you hear it. I'm meeting with McKenna tomorrow morning. Afterwards, I'll probably stop at Patrick's on the way home."

"Was it very strange? Just tell me that."

"I think one could call it, ah, otherworldly."

"But you found what you were looking for?"

He took a breath. "Yes, Cia, I believe I did, and more, much more. Although it will be hard to believe."

"And things will be better now?"

"Cia, stop worrying. All that matters is you and me. We belong together. In truth, we always have."

"What does that mean?"

"I promise to explain it. Right now, just tell me you love me."

"I love you. More than you can possibly know. I only wish you were here."

"Why?" he teased. "Did you have anything in mind?"

"Oh, well," she said in a lighter tone. "I'm sure we can think of something. That is, other than talking."

He was glad to hear relief and happiness in her voice. "I'll be there before you know it, and I promise never to leave you alone again. Not until you become tired of me."

"That will never happen. By the way, do you have the copies of Sonny's journal?"

He didn't mention that with all the excitement of the last days he'd forgotten about them. No doubt they were still buried in his bag. "I'll show them to McKenna tomorrow."

"I love you, Will. I can't wait to see you."

Feeling his own eyes become moist, he said in a soft voice, "I love you, Cia. For longer than you can possibly know. I'll call you from London."

The next morning, Margaret, McKenna's companion, greeted him at the door. Since it was impossible for McKenna to get to the office, they had decided to meet in his study.

Looking up, he indicated a chair. "Have a seat, Will. Why do I have the feeling we once again have, ah, unusual things to talk about."

"I think it's safe to say that."

"I assume you returned to the inn?"

"I did, and more."

They were interrupted by Margaret bringing a tray with tea and biscuits. When she left, McKenna searched through a drawer and brought out a tape recorder. "Do you mind if I record this conversation?"

"Not at all," Will said, lighting a cigarette.

McKenna turned on the recorder. "Ready?"

"As much as I will ever be."

"One question. When we were leaving the hospital, Patrick looked back. He said it appeared as though you were talking with someone, but no one was there."

Will nodded. "And yet there was. Someone only I could see." He went on to tell McKenna of his all-too-frequent interactions with the apparition who he finally came to realize was some sort of ghostly messenger, adding that their conversation in the hospital parking lot was likely the last.

McKenna smirked. "Interesting that you were told to leave by not one, but two ghosts. We must have made quite an impression on the, ah, spirit population there."

Will laughed. It seemed easier now in the safety of McKenna's study. "I believe we did. It was getting to the point where I wasn't sure who or what I was conversing with. After he delivered his message and, um, disappeared in a whirlwind of dust, I drove to the inn."

"I would have paid to have seen that," he sighed. "More to the point, what did you find?"

"All that remains is an impervious blackened shell that covers the entire hill."

"How odd. I figured you'd find a heaping pile of smoking stones, but a shell?"

"There was nothing; no smoke, no smell. It looked like everything had melted together. I only hope it remains that way."

McKenna shook his head. "I guess the four of us were more formidable than I imagined. How do you feel?"

"Thankful. To Patrick and Bobby, but mainly to you. You were the one who believed we could do it."

McKenna's eyes lit up. "It was quite the experience, wasn't it? Trouble is, it'll be difficult convincing people to believe it. Particularly the scientific community." He sipped his tea. "Was there anything else?"

"Yes. Mangersta."

He looked surprised. "I've heard of it. It's supposed to be a spiritual place."

"You don't know the half of it."

It took a couple more pots of tea before McKenna sat back, his eyes wide. "Are you telling me this girl from more than five thousand years ago looked you in the eye and actually said those words? And you heard her?"

"It's not something I could very well make up."

"And you saw the sapphires."

"I did. Very clearly. Maybe twenty or thirty of them."

"What about the stone circle?"

Will took a breath. "It was unfinished, exactly as I envisioned it when I was there as a schoolboy.

"How did you feel?"

"To be honest, I didn't. I was in some sort of trance. Things were happening fast, as if in a dream."

McKenna sat back and thought for a moment. "Very little is known about Neolithic Scotland. Over the millennia, diverse groups of inhabitants crossed what were then land bridges from Europe to what today is Great Britain. After that, depending on climate changes and their ability to adapt, they either thrived or died out. They left few clues to their existence and nothing in the way of written language. All that remains are the mysteries of the stone circles, some cairns, or burial chambers, and middens; mounds containing shells, shards of pottery, horns, probably used for vessels or hunting—basically, objects that were discarded. In that regard, Callanish remains an eternal enigma. And yet one you seem to have pierced."

Will laughed. "Thanks for the history lesson. But all that matters is having seen that boy and girl in the same place and, um, position in the stone circle that Cia described to me. Whether it was a dream, a hallucination or a message from the distant past, it explains what happened at Callanish, and also how the sapphires connect to us today, in this life." He stopped to light another cigarette. "The only question still unanswered is how that demon came to be and why it craved the sapphires."

"Which is something we will never know."

Seeing him reach over to stop the tape, Will put up his hand. "That, however, isn't quite the end of it."

"There's more?" he looked surprised.

"It's difficult to describe. It was as if I was looking through a kaleidoscope of rapidly changing images of what could only have been past lives." He shivered. "My past lives."

McKenna touched the tape recorder, as if to make sure it was still running. "Tell me," he said, his voice wavering.

After Will related whatever he could remember about scenes that flashed by all too quickly, McKenna asked if there was anything he saw that was specific, particularly the sapphires.

Closing his eyes, Will took a few breaths. "Now that you mention it, I did see rings. Other than the group of boys wearing amulets, the only time I noticed them was when I, or the man I assume was me, was with a woman." Opening his eyes, he again looked at McKenna. "While that must have been Cia, everything went by too fast; there was no way I could see it all. I'm sure I wasn't meant to. Two things, however, stand out. One was the old man with the stoop. I saw him more than once. The other was Callanish and how it appeared over the centuries."

"Did you see the stones covered by peat?"

"No. The last was of a couple riding through them, the stones looking as they do today. That was before I saw the same couple enter the inn." He shook his head. "I don't want to think about that."

"You said you could understand some of what was being said."

"A little, not much."

McKenna nodded. "You may have found the origin of the voices you hear; the whispers of your past."

With a sigh, Will looked at him. "Maybe they'll shut up now."

McKenna turned off the tape recorder. "This is beyond extraordinary. I believe you, but I don't know if anyone else would."

"I don't care about that."

With a deep sigh, McKenna sat back. "This may be the moment to thank your fates for granting you a unique gift: a glimpse through the veil of time to the very root of your, and Cia's, existence together. You must now understand that those delicate strands of memories, the same innate memories that predestined your flashes of déjà vu, were not mere accidents of time and place; they were, in truth, your history. If more of us were so blessed as to have such a moment, perhaps we would have more respect for our past."

Will stared at him, his face serious. "Somehow it all fits, doesn't it?"

"I would have to say it does. And yet, it requires far more thought, not to mention research."

"To be honest, Professor, I'm tired of thinking about it. I'll take the other ring to Cia in a couple of weeks with the wish that all the other stuff will just disappear. My greatest desire right now is to love her and spend the rest of our lives together." He smirked. "At least this one."

"And I wish the best for you both. Although it will take some time, I'll begin transcribing all this."

"I hope you'll come to the wedding."

"I wouldn't miss it. Even if I have to be there on crutches. But please, be vigilant."

"Vigilant? Why? What are you saying?"

McKenna's voice became low, guarded. "I still fear for you, Will. You have witnessed something no man has been allowed before. You have not only transcended death but transgressed natural laws."

"And yet, here I am," he said with a grin. "Thanks to you, we were able to vanquish one spirit, and now I've left the rest to their island."

"I can only hope you have. Something, however, still nags at the back of my mind. I'm not convinced this is quite as over as you may think. Are you absolutely sure the inn and surroundings were as impenetrable as you described?"

"Yes. And remember what the, ah, ghost said. That what I came for was accomplished."

Looking doubtful, he said, "And you believe a ghost?"

"Come on, Professor. I was told in no uncertain terms to leave the island."

"But you did walk around the shell."

"Yes. As I told you, it was buried under what looked like thick, impervious rock. Why? What's bothering you?"

"Of all the substances we used—the smudging bundles, salt, and so forth—there was one I didn't think was necessary. Since we were dealing with such an ancient entity, I felt the elements of its own time combined with the holy water and oil was enough. But there was one more."

"I'm not following you. What else could we have done?"

McKenna sat back. "I should have brought petrol."

Startled, Will stared. "That could have caused a massive fire."

"That's the point."

"But we saw the demon succumb to the flames."

"My only concern, and I may very well be wrong, is that the demon not only instigated fires in the past, but survived them, perhaps by somehow shielding itself. What was different this time is that it was unable to evade the flames from the oil-soaked rope that you dropped into the channel. At least we must hope so." He stopped, as though gathering his thoughts. "I know this is wild conjecture, but what if it took more, such as a real conflagration, to kill it?" With a barely perceptible shiver, he shook his head. "Maybe I should have brought petrol along."

"No, Professor. As I said, I believe we accomplished what we came for."

"Still, I must caution you to be vigilant of your surroundings, and although I hate to say it, Cia's as well."

"I promise I will. Of her in particular." He reached into his jacket pocket. "I almost forgot. I'd like you to have a look at this."

"What is it?"

"Copies of a couple of pages from a journal. It was found in the States, in another house that burned down about a hundred years ago. What's significant is that a few years later a new house was built on the exact site. The house Cia now owns."

Obviously surprised, McKenna said, "That has to be more than coincidence."

With a nod, Will proceeded to tell him about the apparition and going to Sonny's store to see the journal.

After reading through the pages, McKenna picked up the copy of the drawing. "Is this Cia?"

"It's Cecily. The girl in the journal. But there is a resemblance. Look at the signature on the bottom."

Throughout all the stories and explanations of life and death, he had never seen McKenna turn even more pale than he already was. "The message and the signature at the bottom," he whispered, "it's the same script as yours today, isn't it?" When Will nodded, he stood up and limped to the window. "This is an incredible find. Along with what you've described, it's the most tangible proof of past lives that has ever come to light."

"Do you think it's in any way related to Callanish and the inn?"

"When you saw the apparition in Cia's bedroom, did you feel any sense of threat?"

"Not at all. I thought I was dreaming."

"Then I tend to doubt it. I'm afraid Cia, by bringing you to the cottage, alerted a past love." He laughed. "You appear to be a popular guy. Watch out where you travel with her. On a more serious note, can this journal be made available if a researcher wants to see it?"

"I'm sure it can. They'll probably have to go to the States, though."

"There are those who would swim the Atlantic to get their hands on such a document. You must tell Cia's friend to be very careful and make sure to keep it in a safe, dry place. I need to consider how to handle this." He looked down at the tape recorder. "If you want a copy of the tape, let me know."

"Thank you. Right now, I'd just be happy for it to stop playing in my mind."

"Will you join me for dinner?"

"I'd like to, but I think it's best that I get on the road. Patrick is expecting me in Yorkshire tonight. And, to be honest, it's time to stop reliving this and get on with my life."

McKenna glanced out the window. "I think a storm is predicted. Perhaps you should stay."

"If I leave now, it should be all right."

McKenna reached out his hand. "Then, Will, may luck and the fates be with you. Go in peace."

Bidding goodbye to Margaret at the front door, Will stepped outside to a cool afternoon where bright sunlight was being overtaken by rapidly encroaching clouds. She followed him out, thanking him for bringing McKenna home from the hospital and visiting that morning. Looking down at her placid face, Will was sure she had no knowledge of the last few days, or even how McKenna had come to break his ankle.

"Perhaps you shouldn't leave just yet," she murmured, her worried eyes scanning the darkening sky.

"It'll be fine," he said in an assuring tone. "You know the weather here changes quickly." With a brief nod back to her, he started to get into the car, which seemed cooler than he expected, particularly since the day was hardly what one would consider cold.

As he headed south towards Yorkshire the sunlight began to fade, filtering through a light mist. *No problem. If that's the worst of it, I'll make it to Patrick's by dark.* What concerned him more were McKenna's last words about the demon. He questioned if it was possible that he had left the remains of the inn too quickly, that maybe those kids playing behind the hill had found something he missed. Considering it unlikely and weary of dwelling on McKenna's cautions, he turned the radio to a classical station and relaxed into the drive. Seeing a sign for a service area ahead, he suddenly had an intense desire to speak to Cia, if only to hear her voice and tell her how much he loved her.

Turning off, he picked up a large cup of tea and went to look for a pay phone. The only one in the entire place was taken by an older woman who glowered at him while nattering on, obviously in no rush to end her call. Seeing what appeared to be a storm approaching, he returned reluctantly to the car resolved to try either from the next service area or Patrick's house.

When he unlocked the blue Mini, he again felt a chill, as though a cool breeze had escaped the confines of the car. Rather than taking his jacket off, he kept it on.

So far, the traffic had been light, with few cars or lorries. Aware of a heavier, whitish fog overtaking the road ahead, he slowed, again feeling an unexpected rush of cold. About to put the heat on, he first glanced in the rearview mirror, startled to see what looked like a coating of frost on the rear window. With creeping dread, he sensed rather than saw a shadow form in front of it. His first reaction was to slow down and pull over, but the car didn't seem to be responding. Fortunately, there were no cars nearby, although through the thickening mist he could see several large lorries in the far distance. With fear gripping his mind and knotting his gut, he flashed on McKenna's warnings while again questioning if that shell was as solid as he had imagined. Out of nowhere the voices awoke with garbled whispers and fractured words that seemed to be trying to communicate with him. Suddenly he pictured Cia; that first moment of seeing her in the gallery, her eyes shining in summer sunlight at the cottage, her happiness at his exhibition and her smile filled with love as he asked her to marry him. He instinctively murmured her name as a cold, slimy shadow slid over his shoulders, encasing his chest. Over the agitated voices, he heard another; a foul, guttural exhale of what he was sure was "Cia." With his heart pounding in terror, he shouted, "What the hell do you want of me?" while attempting to pull away from blackened membranous talons that slithered down his arms and clamped his hands to the wheel in an unbreakable grip. The membrane began compressing his chest as fetid breath repeatedly hissed *Cia, Cia* over and over as though mocking him. Still trying to free his hands from the rigid grasp, he realized the entity, despite being blackened and damaged, had somehow garnered the strength to reach out to extract its vengeance. A thousand memories flooded his mind: childhood days roaming the moors, his early life of wild days and nights as a young painter . . . the sweet scents of summer .

. . the tang of the sea . . . but most of all, Cia; regretting they would not have more time; that as in past lives, fate had again decreed against them. His eyes brimming with tears of sorrow and despair, he knew that, even by his death—a fact that now seemed inevitable—this thing would, ring or no ring, hunt her; not only now but in some unknown future. Attempting to remain lucid, he could feel the car gaining speed while heading straight for the lorries, now looming perilously closer. *No*, the voices whispered, as though trying to penetrate his fogged brain. *This thing cannot be allowed to live on . . . you know the way . . . you know . . .* Gasping as the demon squeezed the breath from him, he suddenly envisioned McKenna saying he should have brought petrol to the inn. By now, the car was all too rapidly approaching the hulking lorry ahead, but fighting through a haze of pain he glimpsed another truck next to it; this one long and tubular with a dusty placard that warned DANGER on its tarnished back. He was no hero, but if dying was the only way to save Cia and their future lives, he was sure as hell going to take this fucking evil entity with him. Whispering Cia's name and picturing her in his arms, he gathered his last remaining strength and, with one final burst of energy, tore his hands from the wheel. As his ring ruptured the slime, the shadow flew back, releasing him with a shriek of fury that ripped through his mind. With his hands freed, he yanked the wheel to the right until the car was heading straight for the petrol truck. Out of the corner of his eye he glimpsed the grass verge and whispering Cia's name, reached for the door handle...

Rolling free of the car, he felt a searing pain as the day lit up with a flash and the ground shook with the thunder of the explosion. Hot air washed over him as dots of white lights began a flickering dance in the distance.

Chapter 16

Cia was becoming restive, moving papers around for no apparent reason.

"Stop fidgeting, Cia. What's wrong with you?"

She rubbed her eyes. "I have a headache."

"Come on. Tell Sarah what's going on."

Cia glanced at her, then back to the chaos on her desk. "It's been two days since I've heard from Will."

"That's what you're upset about?"

"He said he would call from London. He must be back by now."

"You know guys never call when they say they will. When Mike says, 'I'll call you tomorrow,' it always means two or three days. It's in their genes. I'm sure he's busy catching up. After all, he was away for almost a week. Probably had to sweep the ladies off the front stoop."

"Very funny."

"Relax. It's early. I bet you'll hear from him before the day is over."

"I hope so. I miss him terribly."

"Ah," Sarah crooned. "Nothing like young love."

Seeing Cia roll her eyes, Sarah laughed. "Stop your usual overreacting and get your shit together. We have a meeting with a new author who could be big for us."

After a day that passed all too slowly, Cia returned home, resolved to call Will. She let it ring eight times, thinking it was midnight in London and perhaps he was out with friends. When she tried again an hour later with no answer, she rationalized he might still be in Yorkshire with Patrick.

Doing her best, as Sarah continually said, not to overreact, she went to her address book to look for Patrick's number.

Although she'd called him in January, she couldn't find it; for some reason, it wasn't on the same page as before. Trying not to panic, she turned a few more pages, relieved to see Patrick's name near the bottom of one. And yet when she looked closer, she let out a cry. Originally written in ink, the number had smudged and was now undecipherable. Throwing the book to the floor, she put her hands to her face, unable to stop the tears leaking between her fingers.

The next morning, she arrived in the office early. She was just about to dial Will's number when Sarah came in. "What is it, Cia? What's wrong?"

Putting the phone down, she shook her head.

"Still no word?"

"No. I called his flat a couple of times last night. When he didn't answer, I tried to find Patrick's number in Yorkshire." She looked up at Sarah with wet eyes. "But the ink was smudged, and I couldn't read the numbers. Maybe Will has changed his mind."

"Don't be silly. What's Patrick's last name? You know where he lives. We can call information."

"That's the problem," she said, reaching for a tissue. "I can't remember his last name or even the town where he lives. It's as if my mind has gone blank."

Sarah hesitated. "You're not hearing those, ah, voices or anything are you?"

Cia shook her head. "No, Sarah. Maybe if I did hear them, this wouldn't be so weird."

She put up her hands. "Okay. I'll get coffee. Then we'll figure it out."

Holding back sobs, Cia nodded. When Sarah returned, she looked up. "I tried calling again while you were out. The phone just rang and rang."

"Try to calm down. You're stressing yourself out. We have a big meeting with Sid and a couple of the promotion people this afternoon. You need to prepare for it."

"I know," she said, with a ragged sigh. "I'll be ready."

Just before two o'clock, Sarah made a show of picking up her folders for the meeting. With a pointed glance at Cia, she said, "Shall we go?"

"No," she said, wiping her red-rimmed eyes. "I can't get past the feeling that something is wrong. I want to stay here in case Will calls. You go ahead."

"Look. Coralie is filling in at the front desk today. We'll stop by and ask her to forward any calls for you to the conference room."

She nodded. "All right."

"Get your notes; I'll go ahead of you." While Sarah was trying to make light of a stressful situation, she had also begun to worry. At the front desk, Coralie was just hanging up the phone. "Coralie. If there's a call for Cia, can you transfer it . . .

"Oh," Coralie interrupted, "I just put a call through to her. I think it was from England."

As Sarah ran back down the hallway, she heard Cia cry out, "Patrick?" as if a question. By the time she got to the office, Cia was slumped against her desk with her hand to her mouth. "Please, Patrick. No . . ." Sarah caught her, afraid she would fall. Her eyes glassy with shock, Cia appeared to look through her.

Sarah grabbed the phone. "Patrick? This is Sarah, Cia's friend. What is it? Has something happened?"

Through a crackle of static, he said, "Sarah? I . . . I don't know how to say this. There was an accident."

She glanced at Cia, who was now sitting on the floor, her back against the desk, her hands covering her face. Sarah was afraid to ask if he was dead; she couldn't say the word. Taking a breath, she finally spoke. "What happened?"

His voice breaking with emotion, Patrick said, "He's in a hospital near me. Here in Yorkshire. In a coma. I think Cia should come as soon as possible."

"Hold on, Patrick. Wait. Give me your number in case we get disconnected. Cia told me she tried to call you, but she couldn't read the number you had given her."

She heard him hesitate. "The same thing happened to me. I couldn't find anything with her work or home number, and my mind went blank when I tried to recall her last name or where she worked. It was only just now that I did. There's no time for these mysteries right now. She needs to get here."

Sarah kneeled in front of her. "Cia, he's in a coma," she said softly. "Can you get on a plane tonight?"

"Yes. I want to go to him."

Sarah helped her get to her feet. "Patrick? Where should she fly to?"

"The best is Heathrow. I'll have a friend meet her and drive her here."

"I'll call you with the arrangements as soon as I can. There's a travel agency downstairs. Will you be at this number?"

"I will be until you call. I want to return to the hospital as soon as possible. Thank you, Sarah. You're a good friend."

After giving him Cia's home number, she hung up and took a breath. "Cia? Can you function?"

"I have to, don't I?" The words came out as a broken sigh.

Although it was tourist season, Sarah managed to wheedle a seat on the ten o'clock British Airways flight. At the airport she paid the taxi driver, and with Cia's small suitcase in hand—there hadn't been time to pack very much—walked her quickly to the gate. Cia was still in a haze of shock, and as Sarah handed her ticket and passport to the gate attendant, she whispered, "If you have any cancellations in business class, can you please upgrade her? This trip is an emergency. Her fiancé was in an accident." The attendant, an attractive woman in her forties, glanced at Cia, who was mopping her eyes with a wilted tissue. With a nod, she began tapping away.

"The flight is full. But we're about to close the gate and one person still hasn't checked in. Let's wait five minutes. If he doesn't show, I'll get her a seat."

A few minutes later, the woman handed Sarah a boarding pass for business class. "She has to board now."

Sarah thanked her profusely. "Can I go with her on the plane? Just for a minute?"

With a quick glance around the now empty waiting area, she whispered, "Be quick."

When they reached Cia's seat, Sarah hugged her. "Try and call me. Let me know how he's doing."

"I will. Please, if you have ever prayed, this is the time."

Sarah squeezed her hand. "I'll get a group together."

A young man in a frayed Beatles T-shirt and faded bellbottoms was waiting outside customs holding a sign. Brushing strands of damp hair away from her eyes, Cia ran to him. "Are you Bobby?"

He nodded and took her bag. "Patrick sent me to collect you, Miss Cia. Do you want to stop for coffee or something? It's a five-hour drive, although we can stop along the way."

"No. Let's just go."

She followed him to the parking garage where she was surprised to see a fairly large car. When she started to climb into the front seat, he opened the back door. "Patrick said you might want to sleep. There's a pillow, if you'd care to lie down."

"Thank you," she said, getting in the back. Not only was there a pillow, but a soft mohair blanket as well. There had been no respite for her on the plane. Her mind had raced ahead with every mile. But once in the car, she fell into a light doze.

Feeling the car come to a stop, she sat up and blinked. "Are we there?"

"Not quite. Patrick asked me to call when we were an hour away. Are you feeling better?"

"I guess. I was able to sleep a little."

While he made his call, she went to the restroom where she was shocked at her reflection in the mirror. Her skin was pale and blotchy, and there was nothing to be done about her red, puffy eyes. After throwing cold water on her face, she brushed her hair and put on lipstick.

Bobby was waiting by the car with coffee and a package of biscuits. "I thought you might be hungry."

"Thank you. Did Patrick say anything about Will's condition?" He shook his head. "No."

"Are we going straight to the hospital?"

"He wants me to take you to his house. I guess it's easier to meet there."

She nodded. If there were any changes, she was sure Patrick would have told him. "How much further is it?"

"Not far. Maybe forty minutes."

Patrick was outside, pacing the pebbled driveway. Seeing the car approach, he walked quickly toward it and opened the door, taking Cia's hand as she stepped out. "Patrick . . . how is he? Can we go to the hospital now?"

His face told her all she needed to know and, sobbing, she fell into his arms, "No. Please. No."

She could feel his tears as he hugged her. "What can I say? I loved him as well."

Wiping his eyes, Bobby asked if there was anything he could do.

"Not right now, Bobby. Thank you. I'll ring you later." Putting his arm around her, Patrick began moving toward the house. "Come, Cia. We'll go to the kitchen. There's tea and sandwiches."

When she was settled in a chair at the kitchen table, he brought her a box of tissues before busying himself with making tea. If he was going to be able to deal with her, he had to try to keep his own emotions under control.

"Can we go to the hospital and see him at least?"

He turned to her, his eyes misting again. "No, Cia. It's better you don't. Let me finish here. When you're a bit more calm, we'll talk."

"I don't think I'll be much more calm than this. Please. Can you tell me what happened?"

He looked out the window at the bright summer afternoon. Fluffy white clouds floated lazily across a blue sky while finches and robins squawked in competition around a feeder hanging from a flowering tree. Life was continuing despite the grief inside. He put two cups and the tea on a tray. "Bring the sandwiches, Cia. I suggest we go outside."

Picking up the plate, she followed him to a shaded terrace.

He poured the tea and handed her a cup, steeling himself for the questions he knew were coming.

"Patrick? Please. Tell me."

Rubbing his eyes, he nodded. "When did you speak to him last?"

"He called from St. Andrews. He said he was stopping to see you on the way back to London. Why didn't you call me before yesterday?"

"Evidently, you and I had the same thing happen. Your friend, Sarah, told me you couldn't read my phone number, nor could you recall my last name. As soon as I was notified of the accident, I went to ring you, but your number had somehow been erased. I know I never touched it, and yet do I dare question how it happened? Then suddenly, out of nowhere, I remembered the name of your company. That's when I called."

She shivered. "It's all so strange, isn't it? We seem to be at the mercy of things we don't understand."

"And yet once the two of you found one another, it was as if nothing could stop you. Not the voices, not that inn, not Callanish. You got through them all."

"Apparently not quite," she whispered.

"I spoke with McKenna yesterday. He was devastated. He had asked Will to stay the night, that a storm was predicted. But you know Will. He said he'd only be driving as far as Yorkshire to see me."

"Was there a storm?"

Patrick put down his cup; this was the part he had been dreading. "Not in the sense of what one would define as a storm. From what the police inspector told me, a thick fog rolled in so rapidly that no one on the road could see. It created a massive accident; a chain reaction that began with the explosion of a petrol truck. Every one of the drivers the police were able to interview, of cars as well as lorries, said that within seconds they were blinded by a fast-moving white mist that obscured their windscreens so completely they had no time to stop."

With a sob, she put her hands to her face. "Oh god, please don't tell me he was burned."

"No, Cia. It appears he was thrown from the car." He had already made up his mind to stop there. She didn't need to know what the police inspector had told him; that they'd found traces of an unknown substance in the conflagration that, when touched, shredded to ash. He'd added that it was unlikely they would ever discover its origin.

Wiping away tears, she whispered, "That was no ordinary fog, was it?"

"No. I don't think it was."

"But why?"

"How can we know? Perhaps you should call McKenna. That's more up his alley."

"Did you tell him about it?"

"Yes. He said if you have questions, he'll be glad to talk with you."

"Me? Should I go to Scotland?"

"No. Definitely not. I don't want to lose you too."

She was startled by his terse answer. "What are you saying? Did something else happen? Am I in danger?"

Regretting his words, he put his hand to her shoulder. "Not at all, Cia." *And hopefully never again.*

He got up and paced. "I was thinking of having a memorial service in London. At Will's gallery. I'll have to ring Davies, but I'm sure he'll agree. It will be nice with his paintings all around. I'm sure McKenna will come."

"I don't know if I can do that."

"Cia." He sat down again and took her hands in his. "You must. Besides, I need you to come back to London with me. We have to go to his flat."

"Aren't there some legal aspects to this? Can we just walk in? With all that artwork?"

"I can. I'm his executor. I have power of attorney and all his instructions, as well as some additions he left with me on his way to Scotland. I'll have to stop by his solicitor in London to make sure everything is in order."

"Why would he leave you more instructions?"

"I don't know. He handed me an envelope and said to keep it with his other documents. If you think he was anticipating his death, I would say he wasn't. I imagine it may have had to do with you and your impending marriage."

Unable to stop weeping, she put her hands to her face.

He touched her shoulder. "Look, Cia," he said in a soft voice, "there's nothing more to be done here. I've, um, taken care of the preliminary arrangements. I'd like to go to London tomorrow. We need to spend a few days to make plans with the gallery and let everyone know. Will didn't want a formal funeral; his instructions were to be cremated. There are so many people who will want to pay their respects."

"I don't know them, Patrick. It will be awkward."

"You know a lot of his friends, Cia."

"Only to have dinner and drinks with."

"They are the ones who were closest to him."

She got up and took a breath. "I can't think now. Whatever you want."

Chapter 17

For Cia, London had been a happy place. She had met Will and fallen in love with him there. Now the city seemed grey and sad to her, or perhaps it was just the day.

Soon after leaving Yorkshire, dark, angry clouds obscured the sun, and by the time they arrived at Will's flat a sodden drizzle had begun to fall. Cia rushed to unlock the front door while Patrick found a parking space.

The flat, as always, was clean and orderly, but after being closed up for almost two weeks, she noticed a faint coating of dust as well as a musty odor underlying the perpetual scent of oil paint and turpentine. Trying to keep herself focused, she first opened the shutters on the front windows, letting in dim light. Forcing herself to bypass the stairway to Will's studio, she went to the kitchen and cranked open the windows, breathing in fresh, albeit damp air. With a quick glance at the trees, she saw no ravens.

She heard Patrick at the door, dropping their bags and shaking water off his umbrella. "It's dreadful out," he said, glancing first at Cia and then at the staircase. "Look. Why don't we make tea and get settled before we go upstairs."

"I guess tea takes care of all things."

"In England it certainly does."

She put on the kettle, but as she reached for the pottery cups she was unable to stop the tears leaking from her eyes. Finding some packaged biscuits, she brought everything to a table in the parlor where Patrick was beginning to spread out what looked like legal papers.

"What is all this?"

"Will's instructions. I have an appointment to see his solicitor tomorrow. You know there's a fortune in artwork here and in the gallery."

"What about New York?"

"Steve already shipped the portraits back. They were only on loan, and by now they've been returned to their owners. There are still five nudes and one landscape at the New York Gallery. I imagine they'll go for significantly higher prices now. I'll be in touch with him about that. When you go back, I'd like you go down there to see what's happening as well."

She sighed. "This is hard, Patrick. Isn't it?"

He patted her hand. "We have to do our best for him, Cia."

"I want to go upstairs."

"Are you sure you're ready?"

"Does it really matter?" She walked to the stairway and looked up into weak afternoon light, at the same time becoming aware that, except for the sounds from the street, the house was silent. Too silent.

It was only when she snapped on the light that the emptiness hit her. Without Will the studio was just a room filled with paintings. Closing her eyes, she willed herself to feel his essence, his energy; some tangible evidence of his presence. With a deep sigh, she opened her eyes, her glance going directly to one of the large easels. With a sudden intake of breath, she moved toward it. "Patrick . . ."

She heard him come up behind her. "Cia?" He sounded startled. "Did you know he was painting this?"

"No," she whispered. "He did some sketches, but he never told me he was painting my portrait." She moved closer. "Look, Patrick. In the painting. Behind my shoulder."

"I see it. It looks like he was going to add in his portrait as well. And yet, it's as though he was undecided."

She stared at the canvas, suddenly recalling the first apparition she had seen: the shifting vapor of a woman with an indistict face behind her, a face with luminous eyes.

"Maybe you should go downstairs. We can do this later." He paused. "That painting belongs to you, Cia. That is, if you want it."

"You know I do. Especially with the hint of his image." Unable to stop herself from weeping, she turned to look at it again. "It will always be unfinished, just like our love." She grimaced through her tears. "That sounds maudlin, doesn't it? Like a silly romance novel."

Patrick laughed. "I'm glad you still have your wits about you. Will would have appreciated that."

After looking through several finished and unfinished canvases, they agreed they were both becoming too emotional and it was time to stop, at least for the moment. Downstairs, Patrick suggested she put her things in Will's bedroom while he went to look for more documents. They had discussed sleeping arrangements in the car, he having to convince her that, despite her misgivings, it was best to stay at the flat. With a deep sigh, she walked reluctantly to Will's bedroom and sat down on the bed. Picking up a pillow, she held it to her face, inhaling his scent while recalling their last night together in this room. It had been last February. They had made love, holding one another for hours as though never wanting to let go.

Before laying her clothes out on the bed, she glanced around the room, suddenly sensing there was something she was missing. When her eyes landed on the dresser, she realized what it was. She opened the top drawer, seeing the black lacquered box. Lifting it carefully, she carried it back to the bed and sat down. When she tried to open it, the lid stuck. She felt around, trying to find a seam. Finally, with a click, the cover opened.

In shock, she jumped up and ran to the parlor. "Ohmygod. Patrick. The ring is gone. I found the box in Will's dresser. But it's empty. Do you think he had it with him?"

"Sit down, Cia."

"Why? What is it?"

"When I spoke with McKenna, he told me Will was definitely wearing his ring when he left Edinburgh. And yet no ring was found on him or at the crash site."

"I don't understand."

He shook his head. "When Will met MacDonald, he told him that when the one who possesses the sapphire dies, it disappears and is never found again. Not in this life. What supposedly makes them immortal is that they reappear over centuries and find their way back to the same, reincarnated souls." He looked at her. "I guess that's you."

She tried to hold back a shudder. "Will mentioned something like that once. I really didn't take it seriously."

"I understand, Cia," he said, with a nod. "Will also said that MacDonald still had his wife's ring, but not the sapphire. So maybe it happens that the rings, or whatever ornament holds the stones are, in some instances, and for whatever cosmic reason, left behind."

"How is such a thing possible? His ring was gold and silver with a sapphire, that's not exactly something that goes up in smoke." She held out the empty box. "And this just evaporated?"

He held up his hands. "How is any of this possible? Sapphires that flash fire, hushed voices, ravens, demonic spirits, ghosts, Callanish?"

"If I don't have the ring, does that mean we'll never find one another again?"

He put his arm around her. "He told me he was going to bring it to you in New York. That may be all that matters." He pointed to the box. "What's that?"

Looking closer, she carefully took out what looked like torn paper. "It's some sort of parchment. I wonder what happened to the rest of it?"

"It may be better not to."

"I don't know, Patrick. After all this, I no longer know what to believe."

"Cia, I think we need to get out of here, at least for an hour or two. A few of his old friends are meeting us at the pub. We could both use a drink or two. Tomorrow we'll go to his gallery to arrange the memorial."

"I'm still not sure I should stay. I'm afraid it will be awkward. All those coming have known him for many years. I never had the chance."

"We both know he would want you there. And I'd like you to help me catalog his paintings. Please. You must stay."

The following morning, while Patrick went to talk with the director of the gallery, Cia took a taxi to Harvey Nichols. Although Sarah had put out a black dress for her to pack, she had stubbornly refused to take it, convinced it would have been a bad omen. After looking at wedding dresses only days before, she was still finding it difficult to grasp that she would now be wearing black. She finally chose the simplest black sheath they had and paced with impatience while the salesgirl rang it up. The night before, she had called Sarah to tell her she'd be a couple more days, and that she regretted leaving her with all the work. Sarah had told her not to worry, to stay as long as she wanted or needed. With a smile in her voice, she promised there would be plenty to do when she returned.

The morning of the memorial service, Cia put on her new black dress, but barely glanced at herself in the mirror. With a sigh, she put on the bracelet Will had given her and took the pink scarf from her bag. Before leaving with Patrick, she went upstairs to look at the portrait. Reaching out her hand, she lightly touched the image of Will's face. "I will always love you and forever miss you," she whispered, not even bothering to stop the tears. As she turned away, something caught her eye. On a partially painted finger there was now a gold ring with a dark stone at the center. She was sure that when she and Patrick had looked at the painting the first time, the ring had not been there.

By the time they arrived at the gallery it was already a mob scene. Every chair had been taken, and people were standing at the back. Over hushed conversation, she could hear Will's favorite arias playing softly in the background, this one from *La Bohème*. Strangely, it was the same one he had been bellowing the night the policeman stopped them. She wondered at the coincidence.

After speaking briefly with James Davies, the director, who kept daubing a sodden handkerchief to his red eyes, Patrick took Cia's arm. The room was a sea of black, with many women also wearing veils and hats. As Patrick guided her down the center aisle, the sobbing began to be overtaken by whispers, no doubt from the rows of women, both young and old, asking one another who she was and, more importantly, why she was on Patrick's arm. Gripping his hand, she tried to stop herself from thinking this wasn't the aisle she should be walking down.

Two chairs had been reserved in the front row. As she sat down, Patrick introduced her to Will's brother, Scott. Looking bereft, he whispered that he was grateful to have spoken briefly with Will before he left Edinburgh and had hoped to meet her on a happier occasion. She thanked him.

Patrick squeezed her hand before proceeding to the podium. As he began to speak, the room was once again filled with the sound of overwhelming grief. Cia tried to stay focused on Patrick, avoiding the metal urn surrounded by yellow flowers.

As soon as Patrick sat down next to her, a man she didn't know got up and began to speak, and after him, another. It seemed to go on for hours; so many people having so much to say about Will.

There were almost too many memories, anecdotes, and stories, as well as praise for him as a man and a gifted artist.

When it was over, she and Patrick departed to more whispers. Outside, he introduced her to several of Will's friends she hadn't met before. Most looked at her with surprise, hearing for the first time that Will had planned to marry. Scott came over, again murmuring condolences. "I'm so sorry. I didn't know until he called that he was getting married," he said in a quiet voice. "I never thought he would; he waited so long. You must be very special." Although he was tall and nice looking, he seemed somewhat diffident, with little of the charisma and confidence of his older brother.

"To me, it was Will who was special," she said, wiping away an inevitable tear. "I hope you'll join us at the pub tonight. Quite a number of Will's friends will be gathering there. In fact, Patrick seems to think we'll be taking over the entire place."

"Yes, of course I'll be there. I'll leave for Edinburgh in the morning, after meeting with Patrick and the solicitor."

Suddenly, Gwyn and Cynthia wrapped their arms around her, murmuring their condolences. Brushing away tears, she thanked them for coming.

As the crowd thinned, a young woman took her hand. "I remember seeing you as I was leaving Will's studio last fall."

"Yes. I do remember." She was the pretty girl she had been jealous about. The one he had painted in the Victorian dress.

"At the time, I had no idea who you were. I must tell you how fortunate you were to have had his heart and his love. Many women adored him. And yet we all knew he was unattainable, that he would never truly love any of us." She squeezed Cia's hand before turning away towards a waiting car, all the while dabbing at her eyes with a lace handkerchief.

Cia noticed a slight man on crutches navigating his way through the still milling crowd. Reaching out one hand, he said in a soft voice, "Sionn McKenna."

She shook his hand, already intuiting an otherworldly aura about him. "Nice to meet you, Dr. McKenna. What happened to your leg?"

With a quick glance at Patrick, he said in a low voice, "Just, ah, a small accident. Fractured my ankle." He looked into her eyes. "I think I would have recognized you anywhere."

"How is that?"

"You are just as Will described you. I understand his attraction."

She was a bit taken aback. "Thank you." *I guess.*

"I'm sorry. I didn't mean to sound seductive. It's just that he spoke so much about you, I feel like I know you. I wish I could stay and talk further, but I must return to Scotland this afternoon. Perhaps you'll do me the honor of visiting me in St. Andrews."

"I doubt I'd be of much use to you. It was Will who had the memories, and the magic, as it were."

"I'm not quite so sure. I think you have deeper intuitions than you realize. Particularly when it comes to your house; not only how you came to buy it, but also what has occurred there. You might discover more under hypnosis. I do that with quite a few individuals who come to me. Those who wish to understand more of their past lives."

"Perhaps one day I will. Right now, I need some time to cope with . . . with this."

"I understand."

Patrick shook his hand. "Thanks for coming, Dr. McKenna. Glad to see you're doing better."

Although Cia had noticed McKenna's glance at Patrick, she had put it aside. This time, she looked from one to the other. "You've met before?"

Patrick hesitated. "I'll tell you about it later."

"About what?" she asked, sounding suspicious. "Another mystery no one has bothered to tell me about?"

McKenna put his hand to her arm. "Cia, dear, this isn't the time."

In an effort to defuse what was becoming a tense situation, Patrick cut in. "Cia was curious about what you thought of that sudden fog. If you think it had something to do with Will."

Looking somber, he nodded. "Unfortunately, I do. It was too sudden. I followed up with the police, who admitted they'd never seen anything like it before. Will was well aware of my concern that he may have discovered too much in Scotland. He saw and experienced things that we, as mortals, are never meant to know. Although the entity is gone, we have no idea what other evil may have existed. On the other hand, this may be an instance where fate steps in and throws the proverbial wrench into the workings of our lives. I never imagined Will would have been able to communicate so intensely with the past and, in truth, live to explain it. He was awed by his experiences, and they gave him incredible insight into his life. I know he couldn't wait to tell you, Cia. Especially since you were such an integral part of it. I'm just gratified he made it back to Edinburgh and was able to tell me the story."

She stared at him. "The entity is gone? What are you talking about?"

"I'll have to leave that for Patrick to explain."

Looking bewildered, Cia took out another tissue. "To be honest, I'm too exhausted for any more enigmas. Since, however, you seem to know about my cottage, I assume Will showed you the pages from the journal we found?"

"He did. And I'd like to talk further with you about it. Perhaps you could give me a call before you return to New York. In the meantime, please tell your friend to keep it well hidden and not give it to anyone before discussing it with you. It's an extremely valuable document." When she nodded, McKenna put his hand in the pocket of his jacket and withdrew a small rectangular box. Handing it to her, he said, "This is for you, Cia. It's a tape recording of my conversation with Will. It may seem unbelievable, but I promise it's not. He really did find the answers he was seeking, and his telling of it is incredible. Please. Keep it safe." He glanced at Patrick. "I think you should listen to it together. But perhaps not tonight. I suggest you wait another day or two until the grief of this day subsides."

"Thank you, Professor," Cia said. "I have one more question before you go."

"I'll be glad to answer anything I can."

"Will once told me we are on some sort of journey to either achieve or discover something about ourselves, and that is why we return."

"Yes. That is what we believe. It's possible that when you were together before, in your past lives, it was, as now, all too brief. Although there may have been many reasons for that, Patrick will explain how at least one has been eliminated. Hopefully, at some future time, the two of you will meet again, and thus have the chance to achieve a life together. That may be the ultimate cosmic, or spiritual goal. It also might complete, and therefore close the circle of your interactions with one another. Despite your grief, you must continue to have faith. As I said, I do believe you will find one another again."

"But with no memory."

"That, dear Cia, is the way of life and death." After a glance at his watch, he kissed her cheek. "Take comfort in what you had with him. Both of you."

The next morning, to Patrick's relief, Cia said she wasn't quite ready to hear about the entity or listen to the tape. Instead they spent the day in the studio cataloging Will's paintings as well as his watercolors and sketches. Finding more drawings of Cia, Patrick promised to send them to New York along with the unfinished portrait.

That night at dinner he touched his glass to hers. "Thank you for staying, and more importantly, for being part of Will's life."

"And you as well, Patrick. He couldn't have asked for a better friend."

He handed her an envelope. "When you return to New York, I want you to take this letter to Steve at the gallery."

"Can you tell me what it is?"

He smiled. "It's for you, Cia. I told you when Will stayed with me the night before he left for Scotland, he brought me some papers, instructions in case anything happened to him."

"What are you saying?"

"I'm sure he wasn't thinking anything dire would happen, not at that point. But he was a bit anxious about what he would find at Callanish. When I looked at them later, I realized they had more to do with you."

"I don't understand."

"His solicitor has already sent Steve a letter. It states that all proceeds from the sale of his paintings in New York, less the gallery percentage, will go to you. As I said, he had anticipated more shows, so it wasn't just those paintings he was concerned with."

"To me? Why?"

"Will wasn't a wealthy man, and yet he lived well off his art. Particularly the portraits. He wanted to leave you something. Since he never wore jewelry other than the ring, this was his way. Although," he said, taking a small box out of his pocket, "he did want you to have these, his mother's engagement and wedding rings."

She stared at him. "This is too much."

"Not at all. He truly loved you. He was planning to give them to you when he returned to New York. Along with the, um, other ring with the sapphire."

She took the rings and tried them on. They were small, but the wedding ring fit her pinky finger. "Thank you," she whispered, reaching for an ever-present tissue.

"When we go back to the flat, I think we should listen to the tape. That is, if you feel up to it."

She stared back at him. "It's not just the tape, is it?"

Later that night, unable to stop the otherworldly images churning through her mind, she lay awake holding Will's pillow. Patrick's account of McKenna coming up with the idea of killing the entity and the four of them actually going to the inn to confront it had been a revelation that combined wide-eyed astonishment with even a few nervous giggles.

When Patrick frowned at her, she had shaken her head. "Sorry. I couldn't help picturing the four of you trudging up that path to that scary house."

"It was only scary at the beginning, Cia. After that, it was terrifying. There was no chance to think, just to act. It was only later, when we got McKenna to the hospital, that we began to grasp not only the horror of it but that we might have actually accomplished what we came for."

"I wish I had known."

"No, Cia," he said, his voice solemn. "You don't."

With a sigh, she'd looked at the tape recorder. "Turn it on, Patrick. I think it's time to hear the rest of it."

Even after Patrick's somewhat graphic description of the supposed demise of the entity, the tape with Will's description of his visions at Mangersta came as a shock. Cia felt tears as some instinctive recognition shook her to her very core. She knew she'd have to listen to it again, probably several times, before even beginning to make sense of it.

Patrick, in stunned disbelief, had smoked over half a pack of cigarettes while polishing off half a bottle of scotch. Stumbling up to bed, he'd repeatedly mumbled, "This stuff just isn't possible."

After tucking the tape and Will's mother's rings safely in her bag, Cia took a last walk through the oddly hushed studio. She had loved the light as well as the pervasive scent of oil paint and turpentine. Now the deeply shadowed corners—where she'd convinced herself the whispers were coming from — seemed far less threatening. Thinking she heard a soft sigh, or perhaps a final whisper of the now silent voices, she turned towards her portrait. Seeing light flicker across it, she felt her heart pick up a beat. "Will? Are you here? I feel your energy enfolding me. Please, my love, if you can, give me a sign." When all remained silent, she reached out to the painting. "Do you know that Patrick explained how you killed the demon? Not just for you, but for us? I listened to the tape. I'm happy you found your answers. And yet did you go too far, search too deeply? And how do I now cope with this hidden knowledge, these ancient secrets? It all seems an impossible fantasy, all but your death. Was it truly you and I in that ancient stone circle with the sapphires? McKenna says it was our beginning. How many times have we been together throughout the centuries? And when will we meet again?" Drying her eyes, she whispered, "What's most important, my love, is how do I live without you?"

With silence surrounding her, she touched the unfinished image of Will's face before taking one last look around, knowing the next time she would visit London the studio would be gone, the flat sold.

Returning to Will's room, she curled up on the bed, her mind beginning to clear from the overwhelming grief that had enveloped her for the last week. She touched his pillow, remembering the last time they had made love. It had been in New York, the night before his return to London. He had whispered that her pleasure was his own, that her response enhanced his own desire. With his mouth kissing her breasts, his fingers had caressed and created magic, all the while guiding them both to the moment when they had become one.

What had added to the sensuality that night was his voice. For some unknown reason he had spoken in an odd cadence — an inflection such as one might hear in an old movie. Or perhaps it had been more of a rhythm of speech that evoked another life in another time when they had lain together in the act of love.

She wished she had been allowed to know more about their past lives; in what forms they had possessed the sapphires and what the fates, or perhaps the spirits, had held in store for them. And where had they lived? In some exotic place? Certainly as aristocracy, never serfs. She smiled at her own fantasies. And yet, after listening to the tape, she now believed they were on a timeless journey to meet, love, and lose one another in some other place, in some other season, in some other century. And always too soon. She wondered, as McKenna had said, if there would now be a moment in time when they would achieve the grace to love and live out their lives together, perhaps with children. But then, as he had also said, it might signal the end of their journey together.

Either way, it came down to one simple fact: she would never know.

Chapter 18

October 1976

Over a year passed. Despite that everyone in the office had gone out of their way to be solicitous, Cia still had not come to terms with Will's death. To avoid thinking, she threw herself into her work. And yet all too often she glanced at the phone as if expecting his call.

In March, Patrick had written that he'd returned to London to finish up with Will's solicitor and that all of Will's paintings and artwork had been moved to the gallery. Sales, not surprisingly, were brisk. Will had provided for a portion of his estate to go to his brother and his family, the remainder he bequeathed to various artists' organizations. The flat had been put up for sale and, as the residence of a famous artist, he expected to have a buyer soon. He also said he was planning a retrospective of Will's work the following spring and asked if she would come. She wrote back that she wouldn't miss it.

Sarah and Mike continually coaxed her out of her apartment, practically having to drag her to movies, concerts, and dinners. Whenever Sarah suggested that someone join them, Cia refused, saying she wasn't ready.

Sid invited her to accompany him to several charity balls, and she had gone, albeit with reluctance. At each one she had met men who later asked her out. Once, she saw Mark across the room but avoided his eyes. When Sarah asked why she hadn't spoken to him, she responded, "I feel like I'm being unfaithful to Will."

"That's crazy. Mark always asks about you. Will would want you to go on with your life. What are you waiting for? A sign? I don't think it works that way, Cia."

Then there had been the confrontation with Coralie. One morning, almost without thinking, Cia had gone to her office. When Coralie jumped up to hug her, she backed away. "You knew, didn't you? Somehow those cards told you what was going to happen."

"No, Cia. The cards don't predict the future."

"There were cards you avoided. You didn't even mention the one with the swords until I asked about it. You said it was black and white, no greys. Something about being final and irrevocable. That's death, isn't it?"

"The cards are about interpretation. It's true I was afraid that something might happen, but I couldn't have known what. There was no way I could have told you of his death. I'm sorry, and I feel for you. You have to know that."

She took a breath. "You're right, Coralie. I'm sorry. I didn't mean to put you on the spot."

"It's all right. I understand your grief."

Returning to her desk, she sat down with a sigh. As much as she wanted to believe Coralie, she couldn't stop wondering about the cards.

On a Friday in late October, she drove to the cottage. She hadn't been there in weeks. The house now felt empty, reminding her too much of Will. She was just as glad it was late and Sonny's store was closed. Whenever she stopped by, Sonny hugged her in sympathy. She tried to avoid hugs. Hugs made her cry. She was well aware that she had to get through her deep sadness, and yet no matter how anyone tried to help she seemed ever more mired in misery. That night, as many, she wondered if the ghost would come. In the back of her mind she almost wished for it. She and Cecily now had something in common: they were both longing for a ring.

She woke the next morning to bright sunlight, grateful for a rare night of dreamless sleep. After making coffee, she went outside to a day that promised the last warmth of autumn. At the pond, she sat on the log where she had watched Will sketching. The ducks that had populated the pond all summer had gone, replaced by honking Canadian geese. When they flew off, she went for a walk in the woods. The leaves were already past peak. What had been vibrant reds and oranges were fading, shriveling to dull brown husks that rained down to carpet the path. They, like the cicadas and the fireflies before them, would soon be gone, leaving only skeletal branches to survive the dark, silent winter to follow.

It was after nine when she looked in the fridge. Little seemed to interest her, particularly food. Picking up a book, she barely glanced at it before putting it down again. Instead, she grabbed her jacket, thinking a walk might take the edge off. A quarter moon, low on the horizon, shimmered through the trees. Stopping along the driveway, she breathed in the crisp tang of the changing season while trying not to dwell on things she had no power to change. Still, she was unable to escape the poignant memory of her and Will standing on this very spot. With his arm around her and her head on his shoulder, they had been caressed by warm breezes as swaying trees became silhouetted against a darkening summer sky. She smiled, recalling fireflies by the hundreds, maybe thousands, illuminating two moonless nights. She had been happy, believing her problems were in the past; that their love would carry them through a lifetime. For one sweet moment, she had been a truly sentient being—at one with the night, her lover, and the silent universe.

About to go back inside, she was surprised to see a tiny flickering light. Fireflies were long gone by late July; she had never seen one this late in the year. As it flew closer, she put out her hand, albeit with more caution than Will had shown. Watching it hover just beyond her outstretched fingers, its light flashing in the darkness, she was reminded of the tape McKenna had given her and Will's mention of glittering insects at the Callanish stones. Closing her eyes, she tried to imagine the scent of such a summer night, one that whispered of ancient memories in faraway lands. "Did you send me this gift, Will?" she asked, wiping away a tear. "Is this our last firefly?"

When it flew off toward the road, some instinct compelled her to follow. As it disappeared into the trees, she became aware of an unexpected, yet all-too-familiar sound underlying the murmur of the breeze; a sound she hadn't heard for over a year and never expected to hear again. After Will passed, she was sure the voices, along with their magic, had perished as well.

With a growing sense of unease, she began to turn back. Suddenly the wind picked up, sending withered leaves scuttling into small piles at her feet. Forgetting her fear, she stamped through them with childish delight, hearing the satisfying crunch beneath her boots. When she looked up, she was in front of her friends' house, the house where the light shone through low bushes, now bare of their summer flowers. The breeze eddied, creating a cascade of sere leaves that swirled around her while oak trees bowed graceful, feathered branches above her head.

Delight dissolved to apprehension as a more powerful gust pushed her further towards the light that brightened before fading to a soft, hazy glow. The wind stirred the trees with a sigh and then a whisper, *Don't be afraid. Come closer.* Not believing what she'd heard, her first instinct was to run, but an unknown voice told her to wait. With curiosity outweighing fear, she was about to take one more step when the light sputtered and died, shrouding her in darkness. Even the pale moonlight had vanished, succumbing to low clouds. On the edge of panic, she stood frozen, listening in disbelief to what sounded like the indistinct murmur of chants. As lightning split the night, the light flickered on, and through falling leaves she glimpsed a faint, shimmering image. Again, she heard the whisper, *Don't be afraid.*

With her heart beating in her throat, she reached out a shaking hand. "Will?"

The wind sighed, *Cia.*

Afraid she would faint, she began to step back, but the wind held her as though in an embrace.

Cia. Come closer.

She took a tentative step toward the mirage that wavered just beyond her fingers. "Oh, god. Will. Is that really you?'

Cia. You have to end your grief.

Holding back tears, she whispered. "I…I can't. I miss you too much. I only want to be with you."

You will, my love. Now you must go to the one who loves you.

She shook her head. "No one loves me. No one but you. Nothing matters anymore."

It all matters. Live your life. I will find you again. Suddenly the wind died, leaving only the singsong of the voices.

"Will? Please. Don't go."

I must, Cia. I love you. I have always loved you.

"I don't have the ring. How will you find me?"

Live your life. When it is through, I will be waiting. Our fate is already written. We will have our time again. With my love, I promise you.

Unable to stop weeping, she stepped back just as the light flared again. As leaves began tumbling around her, she heard a sound as if something, perhaps an acorn, had dropped in front of her. Looking down, she saw an object glittering at her feet. Falling to her knees, she brushed away a loose pile of leaves. With a sharp intake of breath, she saw a gold ring with a dark stone at the center. As she touched it, the stone erupted with a spark of blue fire. Unafraid, she scooped it up.

"Will," she whispered, holding it out toward the light. "You were right. Our lives may end, but our love will transcend death." The breeze swirled gently around her, caressing her face as with a kiss.

Sliding the ring on her finger, she walked toward the cottage, once more hearing the soft voice of the wind. *Our fate is already written. We will have our time again.*

"Yes, my love," she whispered through her tears. "I believe we will."

Other than the distant shriek of an owl, the night returned to silence.

Epilogue

Milton Keynes, Buckinghamshire, in Southern England
June, 2055

The door slid silently open. The room—in truth not much more than a high-tech cell, albeit a luxurious one—was pristine. In a rush that morning, she had left it a mess. Now it had not only been refreshed, but the walls had morphed from a cool morning blue to a soft, relaxing evening sand, and the temperature had been calibrated specifically for her arrival. There was even a scent; subtle, pleasant, yet unidentifiable, one that was purported to adjust according to the pheromones of the room's occupant.

After tossing her bag and tablet on the bed, Maia removed her pendant, carefully placing it on a narrow shelf. It was only then that she kicked off her heels, at the same time fondly recalling her mother doing the same after a long day at work. She still wondered why, after sending a bunch of astronauts to cultivate fruit trees on Mars, some engineer couldn't come up with comfortable high heels.

Slipping out of her mini dress, she tossed it over the single chair. Minis were making a comeback for, what, the tenth time? It seemed that every decade over the last hundred years had seen a resurgence of the fashion. But then, she mused, wasn't all fashion cyclical? Still, despite making kneeling down on the floor to examine stacked and often dusty artworks a tad dicey, minis were fine with her.

She waved at a sensor before stepping into the shower, the warm water magically washing away the stress of the day. She was due at a friend's flat in just over an hour, which would give her at least a brief respite. Wrapping herself in a warmed drying robe, she touched one of several lights on her pendant, watching as it woke

359

her tablet, transferring any verbal discussions as well as her notes from the rather unique afternoon.

She had come to Milton Keynes to meet with several art collectors who had fled the chaotic clutter, mega-crowding, and all-too-frequent floods that continually ravaged London, as well as other coastal cities, in recent years. She was a member of a small team putting together a show for the opening of the new Tate Contemporary currently under construction on a man-made mountain just outside the city. While it was designed to house art of the twenty-first century and beyond, the curators had decided to launch it with an exhibition of iconic works from the late twentieth century.

Of the three prominent collectors she'd met that day, Sir Stanley had been the most fascinating. An aging industrialist recently knighted by the newly crowned King George, he had been amenable, even anxious, to show off his collection. Following him to a tightly secured, climate-controlled vault where perhaps fifty twentieth-century paintings, all framed with provenances attached, were stacked in bins along thick, grey concrete walls, she had marveled at his extensive collection of works by David Hockney, Lucian Freud, Richard Hamilton, and Jenny Saville. To his obvious delight, she had chosen three; two Hockneys and a Hamilton. As they were about to leave the room, she noticed a few more canvases in a darkened corner. "What are those?"

Giving them a brief glance, he shook his head. "I don't think they're quite what you're looking for. If you'd like, however, I'll be glad to show you."

When she nodded, he pulled out the first painting. She stepped back with a look of surprise. "It's quite beautiful, evocative, even. Almost impressionistic, isn't it? Who's the artist?"

"William Jamieson," he answered, placing it against a wall where the light was better. "It's an interesting painting, unfinished as you can see. If you look carefully, you can make out a ghosted image behind the young woman, which I believe was intended to be a self-portrait of the artist. I had it up in the salon for several years. People are always fascinated by it. But it required some restoration. Now I'm giving it a rest."

"I don't think I know of that artist. When was it painted?"

"Mid-seventies. Jamieson was quite well-established; a popular painter from the '50s through the '70s. Like court painters of past centuries, he painted portraits, very flattering ones of the aristocracy. As you can imagine, he was in constant demand." He looked at her and winked. "Not only for his painting, if you get my drift."

"I expect he was carrying on quite a long tradition in that regard."

"Indeed. As the story goes, he met and fell in love with a woman, an American. The painting is of her. They were planning to marry when he was killed in a car crash outside Edinburgh."

"How tragic."

He nodded before glancing back at the painting. "It was returned, along with a landscape, to England after her death. In 2008, I believe it was."

"Returned? Do you know to whom?"

"Interestingly enough, I do. There was a gallery in Yorkshire run by his closest friend. He had quite a collection; a couple of Francis Bacons, Hockneys, Graham Sutherlands, and the like. He also had several paintings along with quite a few drawings of Jamiesons. While he never achieved the popularity of the others, his portraits grace aristocratic houses all over Great Britain. They are, as one would expect, handed down from one generation to the next. Anyway, after this fellow Patrick passed, an auction was held. I did purchase a nice Hockney that day, and later, when I saw this portrait, I knew I had to have it."

"And the woman? Do you know anything about her?"

"Not much. I know she did eventually marry. A prominent publisher, I believe. There were no children." He brushed a bit of imperceptible dust off the frame. "Otherwise, I doubt I'd have this painting. After Jamieson's death, she wrote several books on quite mystical subjects. One or two, I believe, became best sellers. Actually, I have a slim volume she wrote about Jamieson. Would you like to see it?"

"I haven't much time. But, sure. Why not?" As he was about to put the portrait away, she took one last glance, this time noticing an unusual ring on the woman's right hand. Although unfinished, it looked oddly similar to one she was wearing. Without thinking much about it, she followed him upstairs.

The book was on a table, already open to a photo of the same painting. "Look here," he said, turning a few pages. "This is the only photograph of the two of them. It was taken at Jamieson's exhibition in New York in the '70s." The photo showed a handsome, dark-haired man with the woman from the painting, both holding flutes of champagne. He was looking out at the camera while she regarded him with adoring eyes. Through the crowd behind them, Maia could see a large portrait of twin boys.

"Let me show you one more," he said, turning a few more pages to a watercolor sketch of a duck pond. "This is from one of his trips to the States."

"It's lovely, isn't it? Although I'm not sure his work is right for this exhibit, I will keep him in mind."

The pendant chimed, alerting a dozing Maia that it was time to get ready for the dinner party. She reapplied her makeup before putting on a new pink mini made of a supple new fabric that promised to adapt to a comfortable body temperature, no matter whether the surrounding air was cool or warm. With a quick glance in the mirror, she shook her head. Pressing a sensor in the sleeve, she watched the pink transform to a far more agreeable soft ivory. Satisfied, she picked up her pendant, saw no new messages, and placed the delicate gold chain around her neck. Although it appeared to be a small, decorative gold disk, it was, in fact, not only a communication device but contained practically all the information she was likely to ever need.

On the way out, she clicked off the telly, the picture dissolving into the wall and quickly replaced by the image of Renoir's *Luncheon of the Boating Party*. Far more pleasant, she thought, than the intrusive black rectangles she had grown up with. Picking up a tissue-wrapped orchid plant, she walked to the waiting elevator. The concierge had told her as soon as she opened the door to her room the elevator would be alerted. He appeared to be proud of the hotel's latest technology.

The warm midsummer afternoon was rapidly turning to dusk. She exited the building just as the hourly police drone whirred by, followed, as always, by two news drones, one barely avoiding a large heli-drone carrying deliveries from the Chinese restaurant down the street. In front were several Motos; while most seated two or four, others accommodated up to twelve. She chose a red two-seater. Touching her thumb to the ignition, she waited for the androgynous voice to request her destination. After she offered it, the same voice informed her it would be precisely twelve minutes to arrival. The sleek vehicle rose on a silent puff of air and began moving seamlessly into the street where it picked up momentum until it matched the pace of the rest of the synchronized traffic.

Motos ran at controlled speeds on grids that were smooth and safe. Over the past decades, they had not only eliminated disastrous accidents and endless traffic jams but effectively reduced the noxious fogs that plagued the increasingly congested cities. The early driverless cars of the twenties had only exacerbated the situation and it had taken the total elimination of vehicles within the burgeoning metropolises to solve the problems. Despite ongoing threats of violence, even the most powerful trucking companies had eventually been forced to yield to the ban. Trucks now parked well outside cities, their wares transported by specially designed Motos and low-flying heli-drones in the middle of the night.

By the late thirties, every major European and American city had adopted the grid system, with the exception of Los Angeles, where the residents had united to protest and even rage against it. Over the last decade, they'd maintained their resolve to drive their precious electric and fossil-fueled vehicles in spite of the ever-intensifying traffic and poisonous smog.

The Moto came to a gentle stop in front of a tall, newly constructed block of glass-walled flats. When Maia touched her thumb to the payment screen, the voice thanked her and the door slid open.

A liveried doorman asked politely whom she was visiting. She was pleased to see a human; more often than not these days, a somewhat tatty robot would approach to request the information.

On the fifty-fourth floor, she entered a short hallway. There were only two flats, and she touched the light next to Ariel's door. Sam, her husband, answered, pulling her into a crushing bear hug. "Maia. Welcome. It's been ages. I was hoping you would come."

A sprightly Ariel rushed to extract her from Sam's grasp and give her pecks on each cheek. When Maia handed her the orchid plant, she looked delighted. "Thank you. You know I adore orchids, especially the peach color. There are so many engineered flowers today that these seem almost exotic, even vintage. Come in. I believe you know everyone here. Most are from the university."

Sam grinned. "Have a drink. Scotch? I have some from the twenties. It's grand stuff."

She nodded. "With a splash of water, please. The flat is lovely. I love the floating sofas."

"Brilliant, aren't they? It's all done with opposing magnets. We have a chair on order, as well." Handing her a well-filled glass, he glanced around, "I think we're only missing Ari. He flew in today from Sri Lanka."

Not having any idea who Ari was, Maia thanked him and went to say hello to several former classmates as well as friends she had worked with before moving to London. She was in deep conversation with Madame Stahl, her graduate arts professor, when she heard Sam effusively greeting their last guest. With a quick glance back, she saw a man, quite tall, with dark hair just beginning to grey at the temples. Thinking there was something familiar about him, but not wanting to interrupt the conversation, she continued listening to Madame while trying to recall where she could have possibly met him. Eventually, Sam brought him around, introducing him first to a suddenly smiling and unexpectedly flirtatious Madame Stahl, a generally dour woman well into her sixties. When he turned to Maia, his eyes flickered for just a second. "Have we met before, Miss . . . ?"

"Simmons, Maia Simmons. And no, I don't think so." As he reached to shake her hand, she felt a tingle of electricity pass between them. When she looked up, it was into emerald-green eyes.

"Nice to meet you, Maia. Did you know the origin of your name is from Greek mythology? Maia was the most beautiful of the Pleiades, a daughter of Atlas and mother of Hermes by Zeus."

She laughed. "And if you've ever read Tolkien, the Maia were spirits, although far lesser ones, I'm afraid. And yet they helped to shape Middle-earth at the beginning of time."

When he smiled, she picked up a decidedly Asian cast to his handsome face. He was wearing a soft, cream-colored linen jacket over tan pants as though he'd just come from the tropics. "Which would you prefer?"

"Actually, I like them both. Perhaps the spirits take precedence."

"I tend to agree," he said, turning to the expansive floor-to-ceiling windows in front of them. The sun had just set, and the lights of the city were beginning to glitter around them. "I see you were admiring the view."

She nodded. "It's beginning to look like Hong Kong here. All the tall, narrow buildings."

"Did you know this city, Milton Keynes, is less than one hundred years old? It was founded as a so-called 'new city' in the mid-twentieth century. The 1960s, I believe."

"Yes. I went to university here. They still have one of the best fine arts programs in the country. The city has grown massively in the last years."

"Watch this," he said, picking up a gadget on the table next to him. As he pressed a button, the windows morphed into a painting of Monet's garden at Giverny.

She laughed and turned to him. "What is that?"

"New technology."

She shook her head. "There's new technology every hour it seems."

"True enough. Now one never has to look at the same boring view, or even darkness." He touched it again, and suddenly colorful fish were swimming in luminous turquoise water.

Maia clapped her hands. "This is amazing. It's like being in an aquarium. How do you know about it?"

He offered a slight bow. "I'm one of the designers. We used this apartment block as a test. I've come for a meeting this week on the latest building technology. Do you live here?"

"Not any more. I'm working on a project for the new Tate Contemporary. The Tate Modern has become outdated, and a new museum is being constructed to house twenty-first-century art. I'm only here for a couple of weeks to help assemble a show of late-twentieth-century paintings for the opening exhibition. The curators expect it to provide a dramatic introduction for the new collections."

"Why here?"

"Several prominent collectors have recently moved to this city. My job is to convince them to allow us to exhibit one or two of the works from their collections. The exhibition is slated to begin in the States and then travel to Geneva before the grand opening in the new building, which," she crossed her fingers, "we hope will be finished on time."

"I will make sure it is, Maia. If only for you."

She laughed. "And how, may I ask, will you accomplish that?"

"It just happens to be another of my company's projects," he answered with a grin. "Perhaps we should have dinner tomorrow to discuss it."

Trying to avoid him seeing her blush, she turned back to the fish still swimming along the window. "Will you show me how to change the image? I love the fish. What else is there?"

As he handed her the remote, she noticed the ring on his right hand. "What is it?"

"Your ring," she said, holding out her hand. "It appears to be similar to mine."

"Let me see," he said, taking her hand. She wanted to ask if he felt the faint current moving between them but held back, unsure how he might react.

"You're right. They are quite similar, although yours is thinner and gold. Where did you get it?"

"At a flea market in Edinburgh. It was a few years ago. I had some time between meetings and went for a walk. A funny little man with a stoop popped out of his stall saying he had something to show me. There were lots of people around and I asked him why me. 'Because you are special,' he answered."

"Did you go inside?"

She shook her head. "It looked too dicey. He brought out a tray of rings and bracelets. I picked up a bracelet of silver links, probably from the 1960s or '70s, but he shook his head and pointed to this ring. While it did look unique, I asked why he thought I should buy it. 'Because,' he said, 'it is a magical ring inhabited by spirits, and you are surrounded by those very same spirits.' I thought he was a bit daft."

Ari nodded. "And?"

"I was about to walk away when I heard him say 'Maia.' When I asked how he could possibly know my name, he just stared at me and held out the ring which, out of nowhere, seemed to flash. It was a bright day, and I thought it had just caught the sun. 'Please,' he said. 'You must try it on. If it doesn't fit. I'll bother you no more.'"

"Obviously, it fit."

"Yes, perfectly. When I tried it on, it felt quite warm, and the stone, which he insisted was an ancient sapphire, still glowed. I asked him how much he wanted for it, but he just shook his head. 'For you, there is no price. Take it with my blessings. It will bring you a life of endless love and success.' I thought it was nonsense, but when I tried to take the ring off, it almost felt like it was resisting. 'Wear it,' he said. 'If you don't want it, come back Saturday. I'll be here.' Since I wasn't leaving till Sunday, I said I would."

Ari cut in. "And when you went back, he wasn't there."

"Nor did anyone recall seeing such a man. How did you know?"

"My mother is British and my father is from Malaysia. I grew up in Hong Kong. When I was in my early twenties, I went to one of those techy jewelry stores in Kowloon to buy my mother a pendant. She was still wearing one of those dreadful watches, and whenever she wanted to talk to anyone she had to hold it up to her face. Silly invention. The new pendants, series 3X, I believe, had just come out, and I wanted to surprise her for her birthday. While the clerk was wrapping it, he indicated an old man with a beard talking with the proprietor of the shop. He said the man had brought some interesting antique jewelry from England, and why didn't I have a look. So, why not, I thought and glanced at the rather threadbare piece of velvet on which he had placed a few rings and other items."

Suddenly, they were interrupted by Sam shouting that dinner was ready.

Ari looked up. "Sam. Give us a minute."

"And that ring was there?"

He nodded. "It was, Maia. And when I touched it, it sent out a spark. I was obviously startled and jumped back. The old man picked it up, insisting I try it on. Although I was intrigued, I told him I was sure it was too expensive. 'Try it anyway,' he said."

She smiled. "And you did."

"When I put it on, it sparked again. You can imagine that I, as any young man, would want such an exotic ring. When I asked what it was made of, he looked me straight in the eye. 'The stone is a sapphire created in the conflagration when the earth was born. The ring is of gold and a metal still unknown. Although the hieroglyphs are ancient Celtic, no human hand fashioned that ring.'"

"It sounded not only profound but very mysterious. After that, I couldn't possibly have taken it off. 'How much?' I asked. Rather crassly, as I recall."

Maia looked up at him. "And he told you there was no price."

"Yes. He then asked my name. When I told him, he nodded as if he already knew it and took my hand. 'Take care, my son. This ring brings the promise of success beyond dreams. With it, you must live a life of fairness and honesty. It will also bring immortal love. But you must find the one.'

"I was taken aback. It sounded too crazy. Fairness and honesty, I understood. But 'the one?' I thought he was joking. When I asked how I would possibly know such a thing, he simply answered that I would. With that, he folded up his ratty velvet fabric and shook my hand. At the door he looked back, his eyes boring into mine. 'Take what I have offered and use the gifts it brings with wisdom. As time goes on, you will have questions that have no answers. Let them be and seek no more than your own success. Trust my words, and you will have a long and fruitful life.'"

Maia whispered, "I wasn't given that message."

He shrugged. "Whether I believed it or not, I was still curious. A couple of weeks later I returned to the store. When I asked the clerk about the old man, he looked blank, and when I showed him the ring, he just shrugged. Frustrated, I demanded to speak to the proprietor. The clerk flinched, saying he was in Switzerland; that he'd been traveling for weeks and wouldn't return until next month."

"How mysterious. Are you still looking for answers?"

"Not at all," he said. "To be honest, it really doesn't matter. The man not only told me I'd have a long, fruitful life, but I'd find immortal love." With a warm smile, he looked into her eyes. "What more can a man ask for?"

Unable to avoid another blush, she said, "I don't know what to say, except that this is quite the coincidence."

"I really don't believe in coincidence. Perhaps after dinner we should go out and chat some more."

"I don't want to impose. You're here on business. You must have plans."

"I can change them."

"I don't know. I have . . ."

He interrupted her. "Tomorrow then."

"I may be busy . . ."

He wrote down an address on a card that he took from a pocket in his jacket. "Meet me at The Feathers. It's only a few streets from here. At seven." It wasn't a question.

Before she could answer, he kissed her lightly on the lips.

"Hey, you two," Sam shouted. "Stop staring at one another. Come on. Dinner is waiting."

Maia looked up at Ari and touched her lips, still tingling with the same current she had felt at his touch.

"Life means all that it ever meant. It is the same as it ever was. There is absolute and unbroken continuity. What is this death but a negligible accident? Why should I be out of mind because I am out of sight? I am but waiting for you, for an interval, somewhere very near, just round the corner. All is well. Nothing is hurt; nothing is lost. One brief moment and all will be as it was before. How we shall laugh at the trouble of parting when we meet again!"
— Henry Scott Holland, *Death Is Nothing at All*

January 25, 2019

Acknowledgments

With heartfelt thanks to Lou Aronica, my extraordinary editor and publisher. I will be ever grateful for his encouragement to keep going and dig ever deeper, as well as his patience and guidance in making all the aspects of this story come together.

And to my dear friends Maureen Baker and Ruth Reinhold who read and re-read the work-in-progress through several drafts, with great appreciation for their time, perseverance and feedback. Special thanks as well to Eugenie Sills as advisor, critic and social media guru extraordinaire.

Thanks to Ariel Guidri and Robin Mansfield of *Goddess in Eden* who discussed guides and spirits with me and read Cia's cards. Also to Allison Maretti for her assistance and patience with the copy editing.

And my love and gratitude to James, my ever-patient husband, for once again putting up with me, my various characters and even the occasional demon for these last five years.